空间统计学理论——概述（英文）

Theory of Spatial Statistics—A Concise Introduction

●［荷］M. N. M. 范·利舒特（M. N. M. van Lieshout）著

HITP
哈爾濱工業大學出版社
HARBIN INSTITUTE OF TECHNOLOGY PRESS

黑版贸登字 08-2021-063 号

Theory of Spatial Statistics: A Concise Introduction/by M. N. M. van Lieshout/ISBN:978-0-367-14642-9

图书在版编目(CIP)数据

空间统计学理论:概述=Theory of Spatial Statistics: A Concise Introduction:英文/(荷)M. N. M. 范 · 利舒特(M. N. M. van Lieshout)著. —哈尔滨:哈尔滨工业大学出版社,2024. 3

ISBN 978-7-5767-1285-8

Ⅰ. ①空… Ⅱ. ①M … Ⅲ. ①空间-统计学-英文 Ⅳ. ①C8

中国国家版本馆 CIP 数据核字(2024)第 050746 号

KONGJIAN TONGJIXUE LILUN: GAISHU

策划编辑 刘培杰 杜莹雪
责任编辑 刘立娟 李兰静
封面设计 孙茵艾
出版发行 哈尔滨工业大学出版社
社　　址 哈尔滨市南岗区复华四道街 10 号 邮编 150006
传　　真 0451-86414749
网　　址 http://hitpress. hit. edu. cn
印　　刷 哈尔滨市颉升高印刷有限公司
开　　本 787 mm×1 092 mm 1/16 印张 12.25 字数 163 千字
版　　次 2024 年 3 月第 1 版 2024 年 3 月第 1 次印刷
书　　号 ISBN 978-7-5767-1285-8
定　　价 68.00 元

To Catharina Johanna Schoenmakers.

Contents

Preface

Today, much information reaches us in graphical form. From a mathematical point of view, such data may be divided into various classes, each having its own salient characteristics. For instance, in classical geostatistics, some spatially varying variable is observed at a given number of fixed locations and one is interested in its value at locations where it was not observed. One might think of the prediction of ore content in the soil based on measurements at some conveniently placed boreholes or the construction of air pollution maps based on gauge data. In other cases, due to technical constraints or for privacy reasons, data is collected in aggregated form as region counts or as a discrete image. Typical examples include satellite imagery, tomographic scans, disease maps or yields in agricultural field trials. In this case, the objective is often spatial smoothing or sharpening rather than prediction. Finally, data may consist of a set of objects or phenomena tied to random spatial locations and the prime interest is in the geometrical arrangement of the set, for instance in the study of earthquakes or of cellular patterns seen under a microscope.

The statistical analysis of spatial data merits treatment as a separate topic, as it is different from 'classical' statistical data in a number of aspects. Typically, only a single observation is available, so that artificial replication in the form of an appropriate stationarity assumption is called for. Also the size of images, or the number of objects in a spatial pattern, is typically large and, moreover, there may be interactions at various scales. Hence a conditional or hierarchical specification is useful, often in combination with Monte Carlo methods.

This book will describe the mathematical foundations for each of the data classes mentioned above, present some models and discuss statistical inference. Each chapter first presents the theory which is then applied to illustrative examples using an open source R-package, lists some exercises and concludes with pointers to the literature. The prerequisites consist of maturity in probability and statistics at the level expected of a graduate student in mathematics, engineering or statistics.

Indeed, the contents grew out of lectures in the Dutch graduate school 'Mastermath' and are suitable for a semester long introduction. Those wishing to learn more are referred to the excellent monographs by Cressie (Wiley, 2015), by Banerjee, Carlin and Gelfand (CRC, 2004) and by Gaetan and Guyon (Springer, 2010) or to the exhaustive *Handbook of Spatial Statistics* (CRC, 2010).

In closing, I would like to express my gratitude to the students who attended my 'Mastermath' courses for useful feedback, to the staff at Taylor and Francis, especially to Rob Calver, for their support, to three anonymous reviewers for constructive suggestions and to Christoph Hofer–Temmel for a careful reading of the manuscript.

Marie-Colette van Lieshout
Amsterdam, September 2018

Author

M.N.M. van Lieshout is a senior researcher at the Centre for Mathematics and Computer Science (CWI) in Amsterdam, The Netherlands, and holds a chair in spatial stochastics at the University of Twente.

CHAPTER 1

Introduction

The topic of these lecture notes is modelling and inference for spatial data. Such data, by definition, involve measurements at some spatial locations, but can take many forms depending on the stochastic mechanism that generated the data, on the type of measurement and on the choice of the spatial locations.

Ideally, the feature of interest is measured at every location in some appropriate region, usually a bounded subset of the plane. From a mathematical point of view, such a situation can be described by a random field indexed by the region. In practice, however, it is not possible to consider infinitely many locations. Additionally, there may be physical, administrative, social or economic reasons for limiting the number of sampling locations or for storing measurements in aggregated form over areal units. The locations may even be random, so that, in mathematical terms, they constitute a point process.

In the next three sections, we will present some typical examples to motivate the more mathematical treatment in subsequent chapters. Suggestions for statistical inference will also be given, but note that these should be taken as an indication. Indeed, any pertinent analysis should take into account the data collection process, the specific context and the scientific question or goal that prompted data collection in the first place.

1.1 GRIDDED DATA

Figure 1.1 shows 208 coal ash core samples collected on a grid in the Robena Mine in Greene County, Pennsylvania. The diameters of the discs are proportional to the percentage of coal ash at the sampled locations. The data can be found in a report by Gomez and Hazen [1] and

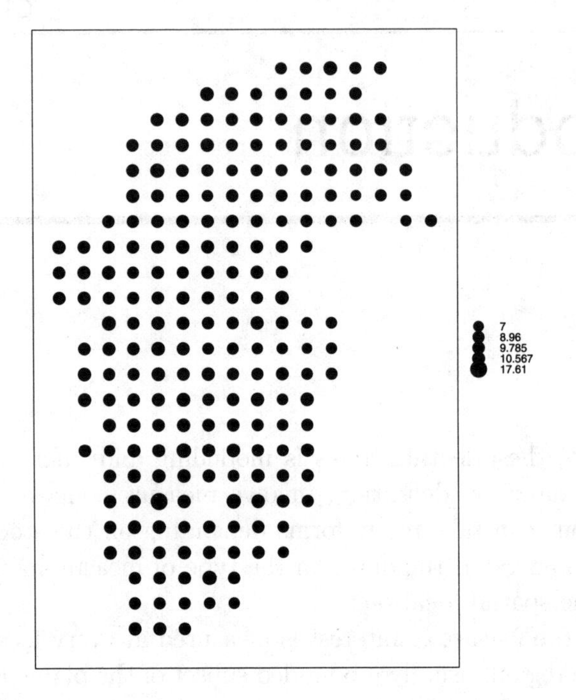

Figure 1.1 Percentage of coal ash sampled on a grid in the Robena Mine in Greene County, Pennsylvania.

were prepared for R by E. Pebesma using a digital version at a website maintained by D. Zimmerman.

A mining engineer might be interested in knowing basic summary statistics, including the first and second moments of the sample. Next, with model building in mind, he could ask himself whether the data could have come from a normal distribution, possibly after discarding some outliers, and if not, whether they are multi-modal or skewed. Such questions could be addressed by elementary tools including histograms, quantiles, boxplots and Q-Q plots.

On a higher conceptual level, the mining company could also be interested in local outliers, measured percentages that are markedly different from those around them, or in trends that could indicate good places to concentrate future mining efforts. Indications of these can be found by applying the elementary statistics across rows or columns. For instance, consideration of the mean across columns suggests that there is a decreasing trend in the percentage of coal ash from left to right. It would be of interest to quantify how strongly correlated measurements at adjacent sampling locations are too.

Another striking feature of Figure 1.1 is that there are holes in the sampling grid, for example in the seventh row from above and in the sixth one from below. Therefore, when the mining engineer has found and validated a reasonable model that accounts for both the global trends and the local dependencies in the data, he could proceed to try and fill in the gaps, in other words, to estimate the percentage of coal ash at missing grid points based on the sampled percentages. Such a spatial interpolation procedure is called kriging in honour of the South-African statistician and mining engineer D.G. Krige, one of the pioneers of what is now known as geostatistics.

1.2 AREAL UNIT DATA

The top-most panel of Figure 1.2 shows a graphical representation of the total number of deaths from Sudden Infant Death Syndrome (SIDS) in 1974 for each of the 100 counties in North Carolina. These data were collected by the state's public health statistics branch and analysed in [2]. More precisely, the counts were binned in five colour-coded intervals, where darker colours correspond to higher counts.

From the picture it is clear that the centroids of the counties do not lie on a regular grid. The sizes and shapes of the counties vary and can be quite irregular. Moreover, the recorded counts are not tied to a precise location but tallied up county-wise. This kind of accumulation over administrative units is usual for privacy-sensitive data in, for instance, the crime or public health domains.

A public health official could be interested in spatial patterns. Indeed, the original research question in [2] was whether or not there are clusters of counties with a high incidence of SIDS. However, death counts by themselves are quite meaningless without an indication of the population at risk. For this purpose, Symons, Grimson and Yuan [3] asked the North Carolina public health statistics branch for the counts of live births in each county during the same year 1974. These are shown in the lower panel of Figure 1.2.

Presented with the two pictures, our public health official might look for areas where the SIDS counts are higher than what would be expected based on the number of live births in the area. Such areas would be prime targets for an information campaign or a quest for factors specific to those areas that could explain the outlier. For the data at hand, when comparing counties at the north-east and the north-west with similar

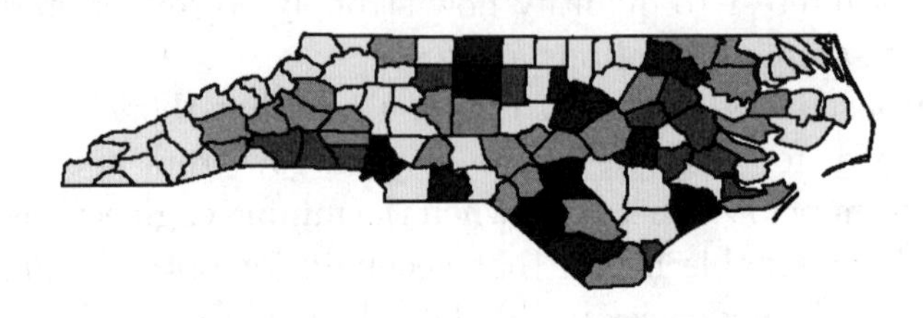

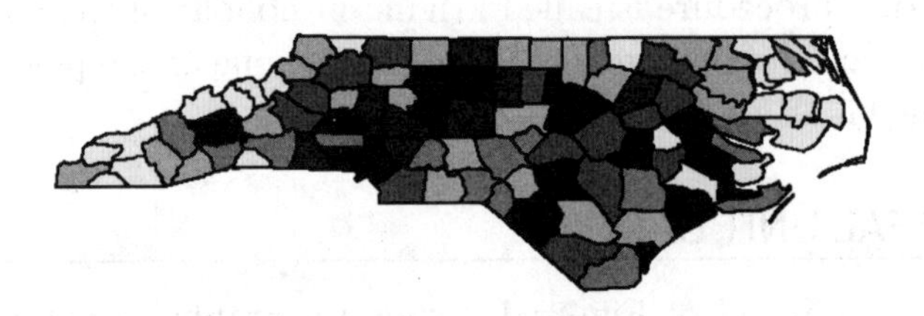

Figure 1.2 Numbers of cases of Sudden Infant Death Syndrome (top) and live births (bottom) during 1974 accumulated per county in North Carolina. The death counts are binned in five classes with breaks at $5, 10, 15$ and 20, the live birth counts in six classes with breaks at 1000, 2000, 3000, 4000 and 5000. Darker colours correspond to higher counts.

birth numbers, it is clear that there is a higher SIDS rate in the north-east. Note that there are also counties in the centre of the state with a high number of births but a rather low SIDS incidence. Other outliers can be identified using classic boxplots and quantile techniques on the rates of SIDS compared to live births.

Such an analysis, however, ignores the fact that the county borders are purely administrative and disease patterns are unlikely to follow. Moreover, rates in counties with many births are likely to be more stable than those with few. On a higher conceptual level, the public health authority may therefore wish for a model that explicitly accounts for large scale variations in expected rates and their associated variances as well as for local dependencies between adjacent counties.

1.3 MAPPED POINT PATTERN DATA

Figure 1.3 shows a mapped pattern consisting of $3,605$ Beilschmiedia trees in a rectangular stand of tropical rain forest at Barro Colorado

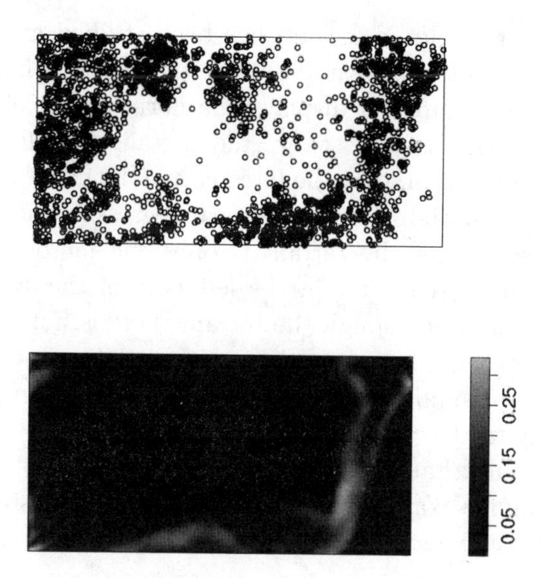

Figure 1.3 Top: positions of Beilschmiedia trees in a 1,000 by 500 metre stand in Barro Colorado Island, Panama. Bottom: norm of elevation (in metres) gradient in the stand.

Island, Panama. These data were prepared for R by R. Waagepetersen and taken from a larger data set described in [4].

We will only be interested in maps where the mechanism that generated the points is of interest. For instance, since the map of centroids of the North Carolina counties discussed in the previous section is purely artificial and has no bearing on the abundance of SIDS cases, there is no point in studying it. For genuine mapped point pattern data, research questions tend to focus on the arrangement of the points, in particular, on trends and interactions.

Returning to Figure 1.3, it is clear at first glance that the trees are not distributed over the plot in a uniform way. Rather, they seem to be concentrated in specific regions. Possible explanations could include local differences in soil quality or the availability of nutrients, differences in the terrain, or traces of a planting scheme. To quantify and test non-homogeneity, the forester may use quadrats, that is, a partition of the stand in disjoint spatial bins, and apply classical statistical dispersion tests to the quadrat counts. It might also be of interest to test whether the counts follow a Poisson distribution.

Since Barro Colorado island has been studied extensively over the past century, a lot is known about the terrain. The image in the lowermost panel of Figure 1.3 displays the norm of the elevation gradient. Visually, it seems that a steep gradient aligns well with a high tree intensity, a correlation that the forester may be interested in quantifying by means of a spatial generalised linear regression model.

The steepness of the terrain is only one factor in explaining the mapped pattern. A cluster in the left part of the stand, for example, is rich in trees, even though the terrain there is not steep at all. Additionally, there could be interaction between the trees due to competition for nutrients or sunlight or because of seed dispersion patterns that the forester may try to capture in a model.

Finally note that additional measurements might be taken at each tree location, for example the number of stems, the size of the crown or the diameter at breast height, but we will not pursue this topic further.

1.4 PLAN OF THE BOOK

Chapter 2 is devoted to gridded data such as the coal ash measurements displayed in Figure 1.1. The mathematical definition of a random field is given before specialising to Gaussian random fields. Such random fields are convenient to work with since their distribution is fully described by the mean and covariance functions. Next, various types of stationarity are discussed and shown to be equivalent for Gaussian random fields. The celebrated Bochner theorem provides a spectral representation for continuous covariance functions.

The second part of the chapter is dedicated to spatial interpolation. First, the semi-variogram and its empirical counterpart are introduced to quantify the local interaction structure in the data. A simple kriging procedure is developed that is appropriate when both the mean and the semi-variogram are known explicitly. It is shown that this procedure reduces to a Bayes estimator when the random field is Gaussian. In the last sections of the chapter, the strong assumptions on mean and semi-variogram are relaxed. More precisely, ordinary kriging is the name given to spatial interpolation when the mean is constant but unknown. Universal kriging is apt when explanatory variables are available to define a spatial regression for the mean.

Chapter 3 is concerned with areal unit data such as the infant death counts shown in Figure 1.2. Special attention is given to autoregression models, including Gaussian and logistic ones. It is shown that, provided a positivity condition holds, the distribution of such models is fully described by their local characteristics, that is, by the family of the conditional distributions of the measurement at each areal unit given those at other units. When these local characteristics are truly local in the sense that they depend only on the neighbours of the areal unit of interest, the random field is said to be Markov. Using the theory of Gibbs states, it is proved that the joint probability density of a Markov random field can be factorised in interaction functions on sets of mutual neighbours.

The second part of the chapter is devoted to statistical inference, in particular estimation of the model parameters. First, the maximum likelihood equations are derived for a Gaussian autoregression model. For most other models, the likelihood is available only up to a parameter dependent normalisation constant. Several techniques are discussed, including maximum pseudo-likelihood and Monte Carlo maximum likelihood estimation. The chapter closes with two examples of hierarchical modelling and inference, image segmentation and disease mapping.

The last chapter, Chapter 4, features mapped point pattern data such as the map of trees in Figure 1.3. The formal definition of a point process is given before specialising to Poisson processes. These processes are convenient to work with because of the lack of interaction between their points, and the fact that their distribution is fully described by the intensity function. Next, the moment measures and associated product densities are defined for general point processes, together with their empirical counterparts. Various concepts of stationarity are also discussed.

The remainder of the chapter is restricted to finite point processes. Following similar lines as those laid out in Chapter 3, a family of conditional distributions is defined on which a Markov property can be based and a factorisation of the joint probability density in terms of interaction functions defined on sets of mutual neighbours is seen to hold. A maximum likelihood theory is developed for Poisson processes, whilst the maximum pseudo-likelihood and Monte Carlo maximum likelihood methods apply more generally. Minimum contrast techniques can be used for point processes, including Cox and cluster processes, for which the likelihood is intractable. An application to cluster centre detection concludes the chapter.

Each chapter also contains worked examples and exercises to illustrate, complement and bring the theory into practice. In order to make the book suitable for self-study, solutions to selected exercises are collected in an appendix. The chapters close with pointers to the original sources of the results, in so far as it was possible to trace them, and to more specialised and elaborate textbooks for further study.

The calculations in this book were done using the **R**-language, a free, open source implementation of the **S** programming language created by J.M. Chambers [5]. **R** was created in the 1990s by R. Ihaka and R. Gentleman and is being developed by the **R** Development Core Team currently consisting of some twenty people. For an introduction, we refer to [6]. An attractive feature of the **R**-project is that it comes with a great many state of the art packages contributed by prominent researchers. The current list of packages is available at the site `cran.r-project.org`. A bit of a warning, though. Packages come with absolutely no warranty! Of course, it is also possible to write one's own functions and to load **C**-code.

REFERENCES

[1] M. Gomez and K. Hazen (1970). Evaluating sulfur and ash distribution in coal seams by statistical response surface regression analysis. U.S. Bureau of Mines Report RI 7377.

[2] D. Atkinson (1978). Epidemiology of sudden infant death in North Carolina: Do cases tend to cluster? North Carolina Department of Human Resources, Division of Health Services Public Health Statistics Branch Study 16.

[3] M.J. Symons, R.C. Grimson and Y.C. Yuan (1983). Clustering of rare events. *Biometrics* 39(1):193–205.

[4] S.P. Hubbell and R.B. Foster (1983). Diversity of canopy trees in neotropical forest and implications for conservation. In: *Tropical Rain Forest: Ecology and Management*. Edited by S. Sutton, T. Whitmore and A. Chadwick. Oxford: Blackwell.

[5] R.A. Becker, J.M. Chambers and A.R. Wilks (1988). *The New S Language*. Pacific Grove, California: Wadsworth & Brooks/Cole.

[6] P. Dalgaard (2008). *Introductory Statistics with R (2nd edition)*. New York: Springer-Verlag.

CHAPTER 2

Random field modelling and interpolation

2.1 RANDOM FIELDS

Climate or environmental data are often presented in the form of a map, for example the maximum temperatures on a given day in a country, the concentrations of some pollutant in a city or the mineral content in soil. In mathematical terms, such maps can be described as realisations from a random field, that is, an ensemble of random quantities indexed by points in a region of interest.

Definition 2.1 *A* random field *is a family $X = (X_t)_{t \in T}$ of random variables X_t that are defined on the same probability space and indexed by t in a subset T of $\mathbb{R}^d$.*

Let us consider a finite set $t_1, \ldots, t_n \in T$ of index values. Then the random vector $(X_{t_1}, \ldots, X_{t_n})'$ has a well-defined probability distribution that is completely determined by its joint cumulative distribution function

$$F_{t_1,\ldots,t_n}(x_1, \ldots, x_n) = \mathbb{P}(X_{t_1} \leq x_1; \cdots ; X_{t_n} \leq x_n),$$

where $x_i \in \mathbb{R}$ for $i = 1, \ldots, n$. The ensemble of all such joint cumulative distribution functions with n ranging through the natural numbers and $t_1, \ldots, t_n$ through T constitute the *finite dimensional distributions* or fidi's of X. Together, they uniquely define the probability distribution of X.

The proof relies on Kolmogorov's consistency theorem which states the following. Suppose that for every finite collection $t_1, \ldots, t_n$, we have a probability measure $\mu_{t_1,\ldots,t_n}$ on $\mathbb{R}^n$ with joint cumulative distribution function $F_{t_1,\ldots,t_n}$. If this family of fidi's is symmetric in the sense that

$$F_{t_{\pi(1)},\ldots,t_{\pi(n)}}(x_{\pi(1)},\ldots,x_{\pi(n)}) = F_{t_1,\ldots,t_n}(x_1,\ldots,x_n)$$

for all $n \in \mathbb{N}$, all $x_1,\ldots,x_n \in \mathbb{R}$, all $t_1,\ldots,t_n \in T$ and all permutations π of $(1,\ldots,n)$, and consistent in the sense that

$$\lim_{x_n \to \infty} F_{t_1,\ldots,t_n}(x_1,\ldots,x_n) = F_{t_1,\ldots,t_{n-1}}(x_1,\ldots,x_{n-1}),$$

for all $n \in \mathbb{N}$, all $x_1,\ldots,x_{n-1} \in \mathbb{R}$ and all $t_1,\ldots,t_n \in T$, then there exists a random field X whose fidi's coincide with those in F.

In summary, in order to define a random field model, one must specify the joint distribution of $(X_{t_1},\ldots,X_{t_n})'$ for all choices of n and $t_1,\ldots,t_n$ in a consistent way. In the next section, we will assume that these joint distributions are normal, and show that in that case it suffices to specify a mean and covariance function. For this reason, Gaussian models are widely used in practice. Alternative modelling strategies may be based on transformations, linear models, series expansions or deterministic or stochastic partitions of T, of which we present a few simple examples below.

Example 2.1 *Fix $n \in \mathbb{N}$ and consider a partition $A_1,\ldots,A_n$ of T. More precisely, the A_i are non-empty, disjoint sets whose union is equal to T. Let $(Z_1,\ldots,Z_n)'$ be a random n-vector and write*

$$X_t = \sum_{i=1}^{n} Z_i 1\{t \in A_i\}$$

for all $t \in T$. In other words, the random surface defined by X is flat on each partition element A_i. The value set of the Z_i may be finite, countable or a subset of $\mathbb{R}$. In all cases, X_t is a linear combination of random variables and therefore a random variable itself.

Example 2.2 *Fix $n \in \mathbb{N}$ and let $f_i : T \to \mathbb{R}$, $i = 1,\ldots,n$, be a set of functions. Let $(Z_1,\ldots,Z_n)'$ be a real-valued random n-vector and write*

$$X_t = \sum_{i=1}^{n} Z_i f_i(t), \quad t \in T.$$

Then X_t is a well-defined random variable. The f_i may, for example, be harmonic or polynomial base functions, or express some spatial characteristic of interest.

One may also apply transformations to a random field to obtain new ones.

Example 2.3 *Let* $X = (X_t)_{t \in T}$ *be a random field and* $\phi : \mathbb{R} \to \mathbb{R}$ *a measurable function. Then* $\phi(X) = (\phi(X_t))_{t \in T}$ *is also a random field. Note that the supports of the random variables* X_t *and* $\phi(X_t)$ *may differ. The transformation* $\phi : x \to \exp(x)$*, for instance, ensures that* $\phi(X_t)$ *takes positive values.*

2.2 GAUSSIAN RANDOM FIELDS

Recall that a random variable is normally or Gaussian distributed if it has probability density function

$$f(x) = \frac{1}{\sigma(2\pi)^{1/2}} \exp\left[-\frac{(x-\mu)^2}{2\sigma^2}\right], \quad x \in \mathbb{R},$$

with $\sigma^2 > 0$ or if it takes the value μ with probability one, in which case $\sigma^2 = 0$. The constant $\mu \in \mathbb{R}$ is the mean, σ^2 the variance.

Similarly, a random vector $X = (X_1, \ldots, X_n)'$ has a multivariate normal distribution with mean vector $m = (\mathbb{E}X_1, \ldots, \mathbb{E}X_n)' \in \mathbb{R}^n$ and $n \times n$ covariance matrix Σ with entries $\Sigma_{ij} = \mathrm{Cov}(X_i, X_j)$ if any linear combination $a'X = \sum_{i=1}^n a_i X_i$, $a \in \mathbb{R}^n$, is normally distributed.

The normal distribution plays a central role in classical statistics. In a spatial context, we need the following analogue.

Definition 2.2 *The family* $X = (X_t)_{t \in T}$ *indexed by* $T \subseteq \mathbb{R}^d$ *is a* Gaussian random field *if for any finite set* $t_1, \ldots, t_n$ *of indices the random vector* $(X_{t_1}, \ldots, X_{t_n})'$ *has a multivariate normal distribution.*

By the definition of multivariate normality, an equivalent characterisation is that any finite linear combination $\sum_{i=1}^n a_i X_{t_i}$ is normally distributed.

The finite dimensional distributions involve two parameters, the mean vector and the covariance matrix. The entries of the latter are $\mathrm{Cov}(X_{t_i}, X_{t_j})$, $i, j = 1, \ldots, n$. Define the functions

$$m : T \to \mathbb{R}; \quad m(t) = \mathbb{E}X_t$$

and

$$\rho : T \times T \to \mathbb{R}; \quad \rho(s,t) = \mathrm{Cov}(X_s, X_t).$$

They are called the *mean* and *covariance function* of X. If we know m and ρ, we know the distributions of all $(X_{t_1}, \ldots, X_{t_n})'$, $t_1, \ldots, t_n \in T$. However, not every function from $T \times T$ to $\mathbb{R}$ is a proper covariance function.

Example 2.4 *Examples of proper covariance functions include the following.*

1. *The choices* $T = \mathbb{R}^+ = [0, \infty)$, $m \equiv 0$ *and*

$$\rho(s,t) = \min(s,t)$$

   define a Brownian motion.

2. *For* $m \equiv 0$, $\beta > 0$, *and*

$$\rho(s,t) = \frac{1}{2\beta} \exp\left(-\beta ||t - s||\right), \quad s,t \in \mathbb{R}^d,$$

   we obtain an Ornstein–Uhlenbeck *process. The function* ρ *is alternatively known as an* exponential *covariance function.*

3. *For* $\beta, \sigma^2 > 0$, *the function*

$$\rho(s,t) = \sigma^2 \exp\left(-\beta ||t - s||^2\right), \quad s,t \in \mathbb{R}^d,$$

   is the Gaussian *covariance function.*

4. *Periodicities are taken into account by the covariance function*

$$\rho(s,t) = \sigma^2 \mathrm{sinc}(\beta ||\mathrm{t} - \mathrm{s}||), \quad \mathrm{s}, \mathrm{t} \in \mathbb{R}^{\mathrm{d}},$$

   for $\beta, \sigma^2 > 0$ *defined in terms of the sine cardinal function* $\mathrm{sinc(x)} = \mathrm{sin(x)/x}$ *for* $x \neq 0$ *and* 1 *otherwise. Note that the correlations are alternately positive and negative, and that their absolute value decreases in the spatial lag* $||t - s||$.

Proposition 2.1 *The function* $\rho : T \times T \to \mathbb{R}$, $T \subseteq \mathbb{R}^d$, *is the covariance function of a Gaussian random field if and only if* ρ *is non-negative definite, that is, for any* $t_1, \ldots, t_n$, $n \in \mathbb{N}$, *the matrix* $(\rho(t_i, t_j))_{i,j=1}^n$ *is non-negative definite.*

In other words, for any finite set $t_1, \ldots, t_n$, the matrix $(\rho(t_i, t_j))_{i,j=1}^n$ should be symmetric and satisfy the following property: for any $a \in \mathbb{R}^n$,

$$\sum_{i=1}^{n} \sum_{j=1}^{n} a_i \rho(t_i, t_j) a_j \geq 0.$$

Proof: "$\Rightarrow$" Since $(\rho(t_i, t_j))_{i,j=1}^n$ is the covariance matrix of $(X_{t_1}, \ldots, X_{t_n})'$, it is non-negative definite.

"$\Leftarrow$" Apply Kolmogorov's consistency theorem. To do so, we need to check the consistency of the fidi's. Define $\mu_{t_1,\ldots,t_n}$ to be a multivariate normal with covariance matrix $\Sigma(t_1, \ldots, t_n)$ having entries $\rho(t_i, t_j)$. By assumption, $\Sigma(t_1, \ldots, t_n)$ is non-negative definite so that $\mu_{t_1,\ldots,t_n}$ is well-defined. The $\mu_{t_1,\ldots,t_n}$ are also consistent since they are symmetric and the marginals of normals are normal with the marginal covariance matrix. □

Example 2.5 *For $T = \mathbb{R}^d$, set $\rho(s,t) = 1\{s = t\}$. Then ρ is a proper covariance function as, for any $t_1, \ldots, t_n \in T$, $n \in \mathbb{N}$, and all $a_1, \ldots, a_n \in \mathbb{R}$,*

$$\sum_{i=1}^{n} \sum_{j=1}^{n} a_i \rho(t_i, t_j) a_j = \sum_{i=1}^{n} a_i^2 \geq 0.$$

More can be said for Gaussian random fields under appropriate stationarity conditions, as will be discussed in the next two sections.

2.3 STATIONARITY CONCEPTS

Throughout this section, the index set will be $T = \mathbb{R}^d$.

Definition 2.3 *A random field $X = (X_t)_{t \in \mathbb{R}^d}$ is* strictly stationary *if for all finite sets $t_1, \ldots, t_n \in \mathbb{R}^d$, $n \in \mathbb{N}$, all $k_1, \ldots, k_n \in \mathbb{R}$ and all $s \in \mathbb{R}^d$,*

$$\mathbb{P}(X_{t_1+s} \leq k_1; \cdots; X_{t_n+s} \leq k_n) = \mathbb{P}(X_{t_1} \leq k_1; \cdots; X_{t_n} \leq k_n).$$

Let X be strictly stationary with finite second moments $\mathbb{E}X_t^2 < \infty$ for all $t \in \mathbb{R}^d$. Then

$$\mathbb{P}(X_t \leq k) = \mathbb{P}(X_{t+s} \leq k)$$

for all k so that X_t and X_{t+s} are identical in distribution. In particular, $\mathbb{E}X_t = \mathbb{E}X_{t+s}$. We conclude that the mean function must be constant.

Similarly,

$$\mathbb{P}(X_{t_1} \leq k_1; X_{t_2} \leq k_2) = \mathbb{P}(X_{t_1+s} \leq k_1; X_{t_2+s} \leq k_2)$$

for all k_1, k_2 so that the distributions of $(X_{t_1}, X_{t_2})'$ and $(X_{t_1+s}, X_{t_2+s})'$ are equal. Hence $\text{Cov}(X_{t_1}, X_{t_2}) = \text{Cov}(X_{t_1+s}, X_{t_2+s})$. In particular, for $s = -t_1$, we get that

$$\rho(t_1, t_2) = \rho(t_1 + s, t_2 + s) = \rho(0, t_2 - t_1)$$

is a function of $t_2 - t_1$. These properties are captured by the following definition.

Definition 2.4 *A random field $X = (X_t)_{t \in \mathbb{R}^d}$ is* weakly stationary *if*

- $\mathbb{E}X_t^2 < \infty$ *for all* $t \in \mathbb{R}^d$*;*
- $\mathbb{E}X_t \equiv m$ *is constant;*
- $\text{Cov}(X_{t_1}, X_{t_2}) = \rho(t_2 - t_1)$ *for some* $\rho : \mathbb{R}^d \to \mathbb{R}$.

Since a Gaussian random field is defined by its mean and covariance functions, in this case the reverse implication (weak stationarity implies strict stationarity) also holds. To see this, consider the random vector $(X_{t_1}, \ldots, X_{t_n})'$. Its law is a multivariate normal with mean vector $(m, \ldots, m)'$ and covariance matrix $\Sigma(t_1, \ldots, t_n)$ with ij-th entry $\rho(t_j - t_i)$. The shifted random vector $(X_{t_1+s}, \ldots, X_{t_n+s})'$ also follows a multivariate normal distribution with mean vector $(m, \ldots, m)'$ and covariance matrix $\Sigma(t_1 + s, \ldots, t_n + s)$ whose ij-th entry is $\rho(t_j + s - (t_i + s)) = \rho(t_j - t_i)$ regardless of s. We conclude that X is strictly stationary.

Defintion 2.4 can easily be extended to random fields that are defined on a subset T of $\mathbb{R}^d$.

Example 2.6 *Let $(X_t)_{t \in \mathbb{R}^d}$ be defined by*

$$X_t = \sum_{j=1}^{d} (A_j \cos t_j + B_j \sin(t_j)), \quad t = (t_1, \ldots, t_d) \in \mathbb{R}^d,$$

where A_j and B_j, $j = 1, \ldots, d$, are independent random variables that are uniformly distributed on $[-1, 1]$. Then X_t is not strictly stationary.

Indeed, for example the supports of $X_{(0,\dots,0)} = \sum_j A_j$ *and* $X_{(\pi/4,\dots,\pi/4)} = \sum_j (A_j + B_j)/\sqrt{2}$ *differ. However, the mean* $\mathbb{E}X_t = 0$ *is constant and*

$$\mathbb{E}(X_s X_t) = \sum_{j=1}^{d} \left\{ \mathbb{E}A_j^2 \cos t_j \cos s_j + \mathbb{E}B_j^2 \sin t_j \sin s_j \right\} = \mathbb{E}A_1^2 \sum_{j=1}^{d} \cos(t_j - s_j)$$

depends only on the difference $t - s$*. Hence* X_t *is weakly stationary.*

Proposition 2.2 *If* $\rho : \mathbb{R}^d \to \mathbb{R}$ *is the covariance function of a weakly stationary (Gaussian) random field, the following hold:*

- $\rho(0) \geq 0$;
- $\rho(t) = \rho(-t)$ *for all* $t \in \mathbb{R}^d$;
- $|\rho(t)| \leq \rho(0)$ *for all* $t \in \mathbb{R}^d$.

Proof: Note that $\rho(0) = \mathrm{Cov}(X_0, X_0) = \mathrm{Var}(X_0) \geq 0$. This proves the first assertion. For the second claim, write

$$\rho(t) = \mathrm{Cov}(X_0, X_t) = \mathrm{Cov}(X_t, X_0) = \rho(-t).$$

Finally, the Cauchy–Schwarz inequality implies

$$|\rho(t)|^2 = |\mathbb{E}\left[(X_t - m)(X_0 - m)\right]|^2 \leq \mathbb{E}\left[(X_t - m)^2\right]\mathbb{E}\left[(X_0 - m)^2\right] = \rho(0)^2.$$

Taking the square root on both sides completes the proof. □

Of course, defining a covariance function as it does, ρ is also non-negative definite.

To define an even weaker form of stationarity, let X be a weakly stationary random field and consider the increment $X_{t_2} - X_{t_1}$ for $t_1, t_2 \in T$. Since the second order moments exist by assumption, the variance of the increment is finite and can be written as

$$\mathrm{Var}(X_{t_2} - X_{t_1}) = \mathrm{Var}(X_{t_2}) + \mathrm{Var}(X_{t_1}) - 2\mathrm{Cov}(X_{t_2}, X_{t_1}) = 2\rho(0) - 2\rho(t_2 - t_1).$$

Hence, the variance of the increments depends only on the spatial lag $t_2 - t_1$.

Definition 2.5 *A random field* $X = (X_t)_{t \in \mathbb{R}^d}$ *is* intrinsically stationary *if*

- $\mathbb{E}X_t^2 < \infty$ *for all* $t \in \mathbb{R}^d$;
- $\mathbb{E}X_t \equiv m$ *is constant;*
- $\mathrm{Var}(X_{t_2} - X_{t_1}) = f(t_2 - t_1)$ *for some* $f : \mathbb{R}^d \to \mathbb{R}$.

As for weak stationarity, the definition of intrinsic stationarity remains valid for random fields defined on subsets T of $\mathbb{R}^d$.

Example 2.7 *The one-dimensional Brownian motion on the positive half-line (cf. Example 2.4) is not weakly stationary. However, since by definition the increment* $X_{t+s} - X_s$, $s, t > 0$, *is normally distributed with mean zero and variance* t, *this Brownian motion is intrinsically stationary. More generally, in any dimension, the fractional Brownian surface with mean function zero and covariance function*

$$\rho(s,t) = \frac{1}{2}(||s||^{2H} + ||t||^{2H} - ||t-s||^{2H}), \quad 0 < H < 1,$$

is intrinsically but not weakly stationary. The constant H *is called the Hurst index and governs the smoothness of realisations from the model.*

2.4 CONSTRUCTION OF COVARIANCE FUNCTIONS

This section presents several examples of techniques for the construction of covariance functions.

Example 2.8 *Let* $H : \mathbb{R}^d \to \mathbb{R}^k$, $k \in \mathbb{N}$, *be a function and set*

$$\rho(s,t) = \sum_{j=1}^{k} H(s)_j H(t)_j, \quad s, t \in \mathbb{R}^d.$$

Then for any $t_1, \dots, t_n \in \mathbb{R}^d$, $n \in \mathbb{N}$, *the matrix* $(\rho(t_i, t_j))_{i,j=1}^n$ *is symmetric. Furthermore, for all* $a \in \mathbb{R}^n$,

$$\sum_{i=1}^{n}\sum_{j=1}^{n} a_i \rho(t_i, t_j) a_j = \left\| \sum_{i=1}^{n} a_i H(t_i) \right\|^2 \geq 0.$$

Hence, by Proposition 2.1, ρ *is a covariance function.*

Example 2.9 *Let $\rho_m : \mathbb{R}^d \times \mathbb{R}^d \to \mathbb{R}$ be a sequence of covariance functions and suppose that the pointwise limits*

$$\rho(s,t) = \lim_{m\to\infty} \rho_m(s,t)$$

exist for all $s, t \in \mathbb{R}^d$. Then, for all $t_1, \ldots, t_n \in \mathbb{R}^d$, $n \in \mathbb{N}$, the matrix $(\rho(t_i,t_j))_{i,j=1}^n$ is non-negative definite. To see this, note that

$$\rho(s,t) = \lim_{m\to\infty} \rho_m(s,t) = \lim_{m\to\infty} \rho_m(t,s) = \rho(t,s)$$

as each ρ_m is symmetric. Furthermore, for all $a_1, \ldots, a_n \in \mathbb{R}$, $n \in \mathbb{N}$,

$$\begin{aligned} \sum_{i=1}^n \sum_{j=1}^n a_i \rho(t_i,t_j) a_j &= \sum_{i=1}^n \sum_{j=1}^n a_i \lim_{m\to\infty} \rho_m(t_i,t_j) a_j \\ &= \lim_{m\to\infty} \sum_{i=1}^n \sum_{j=1}^n a_i \rho_m(t_i,t_j) a_j \geq 0. \end{aligned}$$

The order of sum and limit may be reversed as $\lim_{m\to\infty} \rho_m(t_i,t_j)$ exists for all t_i and t_j.

Example 2.10 *Let μ be a finite, symmetric Borel measure on $\mathbb{R}^d$, that is, $\mu(A) = \mu(-A)$ for all Borel sets $A \subseteq \mathbb{R}^d$. Set*

$$\rho(t) = \int_{\mathbb{R}^d} e^{i<w,t>} d\mu(w), \quad t \in \mathbb{R}^d,$$

where $< w, t >$ denotes the inner product on $\mathbb{R}^d$. Since μ is symmetric, ρ takes real values and is an even function. Moreover, ρ defines a strictly stationary Gaussian random field. To see this, note that for all $a_1, \ldots, a_n \in \mathbb{R}$, $n \in \mathbb{N}$,

$$\begin{aligned} \sum_{k=1}^n \sum_{j=1}^n a_k a_j \rho(t_j - t_k) &= \int_{\mathbb{R}^d} \sum_{k=1}^n \sum_{j=1}^n a_k a_j e^{i<w,t_j-t_k>} d\mu(w) \\ &= \int_{\mathbb{R}^d} \sum_{k=1}^n \sum_{j=1}^n a_k e^{-i<w,t_k>} a_j e^{i<w,t_j>} d\mu(w) \\ &= \int_{\mathbb{R}^d} \left| \sum_{k=1}^n a_k e^{-i<w,t_k>} \right|^2 d\mu(w) \geq 0 \end{aligned}$$

and use Proposition 2.1. In particular, if μ admits an even density $f : \mathbb{R}^d \to \mathbb{R}^+$, then

$$\rho(t) = \int_{\mathbb{R}^d} e^{i<w,t>} f(w)\, dw = \int_{\mathbb{R}^d} f(w) \cos(< w, t >)\, dw.$$

By the inverse Fourier formula,

$$f(w) = \left(\frac{1}{2\pi}\right)^d \int_{\mathbb{R}^d} e^{-i<w,t>} \rho(t)\, dt.$$

In fact, by Bochner's theorem, *any* continuous covariance function of a strictly stationary Gaussian random field can be written in this form.

Theorem 2.1 *Suppose $\rho : \mathbb{R}^d \to \mathbb{R}$ is a continuous function. Then ρ is the covariance function of some strictly stationary Gaussian random field if and only if*

$$\rho(t) = \int_{\mathbb{R}^d} e^{i<w,t>} d\mu(w)$$

for some finite (non-negative) symmetric Borel measure μ on $\mathbb{R}^d$.

The measure μ is called the *spectral measure* of the random field.

The proof of Bochner's theorem is quite technical. For completeness' sake it will be given in Section 2.5. The reader may wish to skip the proof, though, and prefer to proceed directly to some examples and applications.

Example 2.11 *For every $\nu > 0$, the Whittle–Matérn spectral density is defined as*

$$f(w) \propto \left(1 + ||w||^2\right)^{-\nu - d/2}, \quad w \in \mathbb{R}^d.$$

In the special case $\nu = 1/2$, the spectral density $f(w)$ corresponds to an exponential covariance function with $\beta = 1$ as introduced in Example 2.4.

Example 2.12 *For the Gaussian covariance function $\rho(t) = \sigma^2 \exp[-\beta ||t||^2]$, $\beta, \sigma^2 > 0$, $t \in \mathbb{R}^d$, that we encountered in Example 2.4, the candidate spectral density is*

$$f(w) = \sigma^2 \left(\frac{1}{2\pi}\right)^d \int_{\mathbb{R}^d} e^{-i<w,t>} e^{-\beta||t||^2} dt.$$

The integral factorises in d one-dimensional terms of the form

$$\int_{-\infty}^{\infty} e^{-iwt} e^{-\beta t^2} dt = e^{-w^2/(4\beta)} \int_{-\infty}^{\infty} e^{-\beta(t + iw/(2\beta))^2} dt = e^{-w^2/(4\beta)} (\pi/\beta)^{1/2}$$

for $w \in \mathbb{R}$. Collecting the d terms and the scalar multiplier, one obtains

$$f(w) = \sigma^2 2^{-d} (\beta\pi)^{-d/2} \exp\left[-||w||^2/(4\beta) \right], \quad w \in \mathbb{R}^d.$$

In other words, the spectral density is another Gaussian function. One speaks of self-duality *in such cases.*

Without proof[1] we note that if X is a strictly stationary Gaussian random field with spectral measure μ such that

$$\int_{\mathbb{R}^d} ||w||^{\epsilon} d\mu(w) < \infty$$

for some $\epsilon \in (0,1)$, then X admits a continuous version. In particular this is true for the Gaussian covariance function in the example above.

From a practical point of view, the spectral representation of Bochner's theorem can be used to generate realisations of a Gaussian random field.

Proposition 2.3 *Let μ be a finite symmetric Borel measure on $\mathbb{R}^d$ and set*

$$\rho(t) = \int_{\mathbb{R}^d} e^{i<w,t>} d\mu(w) = \int_{\mathbb{R}^d} \cos(<w,t>)\, d\mu(w).$$

Suppose that R_j, $j = 1, \ldots, n$, $n \in \mathbb{N}$, are independent and identically distributed random d-vectors with distribution $\mu(\cdot)/\mu(\mathbb{R}^d)$. Also, let Φ_j, $j = 1, \ldots, n$, $n \in \mathbb{N}$, be independent and identically distributed random variables that are uniformly distributed on $[0, 2\pi)$ independently of the R_j. Then

$$Z_t = \sqrt{\frac{2\mu(\mathbb{R}^d)}{n}} \sum_{j=1}^{n} \cos(<R_j, t> + \Phi_j), \quad t \in \mathbb{R}^d,$$

converges in distribution to a zero mean Gaussian random field with covariance function ρ as $n \to \infty$.

Proof: Let R be distributed according to $\mu(\cdot)/\mu(\mathbb{R}^d)$ and, independently, let Φ follow a uniform distribution on $[0, 2\pi)$. Fix $t \in \mathbb{R}^d$. Then the random variable $Y_t = \cos(<R, t> + \Phi)$ has expectation

$$\mathbb{E}Y_t = \frac{1}{2\pi\mu(\mathbb{R}^d)} \int_0^{2\pi} \int_{\mathbb{R}^d} \cos(<r, t> + \phi) d\mu(r) d\phi.$$

[1] Adler (1981). The Geometry of Random Fields.

By the goniometric equation

$$\cos(< r,t > +\phi) = \cos(< r,t >)\cos\phi - \sin(< r,t >)\sin\phi \qquad (2.1)$$

and Fubini's theorem, it follows that $\mathbb{E}Y_t = 0$.

Next, fix $s, t \in \mathbb{R}^d$ and consider the random variables $Y_t = \cos(< R, t > +\Phi)$ and $Y_s = \cos(< R, s > +\Phi)$. Since their means are equal to zero, the covariance reads

$$\mathbb{E}[Y_t Y_s] = \frac{1}{2\pi\mu(\mathbb{R}^d)} \int_0^{2\pi} \int_{\mathbb{R}^d} \cos(< r,t > +\phi)\cos(< r,s > +\phi)\, d\mu(r)\, d\phi.$$

Using (2.1) and the fact that

$$\int_0^{2\pi} \sin\phi\cos\phi d\phi = 0,$$

the integral can be written as the sum of

$$\int_0^{2\pi} \int_{\mathbb{R}^d} [\cos(< r,t >)\cos(< r,s >)]\cos^2\phi\, d\mu(r)\, d\phi$$

and

$$\int_0^{2\pi} \int_{\mathbb{R}^d} [\sin(< r,t >)\sin(< r,s >)]\sin^2\phi\, d\mu(r)\, d\phi.$$

Hence, as $\int \sin^2\phi d\phi = \int \cos^2\phi d\phi = \pi$,

$$\mathbb{E}[Y_t Y_s] = \frac{1}{2\mu(\mathbb{R}^d)} \int_{\mathbb{R}^d} \cos(< r, t - s >)\, d\mu(r).$$

The claim follows by an application of the multivariate central limit theorem. □

2.5 PROOF OF BOCHNER'S THEOREM

In this section, we give a proof of Theorem 2.1. It requires a higher level of maturity and may be skipped.

Proof: (Bochner's theorem) We already saw that any ρ of the given form is non-negative definite. For the reverse implication, suppose ρ is non-negative definite and continuous. We are looking for a measure μ that is the inverse Fourier transform of ρ. Since we have information on *finite* sums only, we will approximate μ by a finite sum and use the continuity to take limits.

Let $K, n > 0$ be large integers and set $\delta = 1/n$. Then by assumption, for all $w \in \mathbb{R}^d$,

$$h_{K,n}(w) := \sum \sum_{(l,m) \in S_{K,n}} e^{i<w,\delta l>} \rho(\delta m - \delta l) e^{-i<w,\delta m>} \geq 0, \qquad (2.2)$$

upon recalling that ρ, being a covariance function, is symmetric, so that $h_{K,n}$ takes real values. Here the indices run through the set

$$S_{K,n} = \{(l,m) \in \mathbb{Z}^d \times \mathbb{Z}^d : \max_{j=1,\dots,d} |l_j| \leq Kn, \ \max_{j=1,\dots,d} |m_j| \leq Kn\}.$$

Note that the box of size $(2K)^d$ contains $(2Kn+1)^d$ index points, so each point represents a volume of $(2K)^d/(2Kn+1)^d$. Multiplying (2.2) by cell size and using the continuity and boundedness of ρ yields

$$\begin{aligned} h_K(w) &= \lim_{n\to\infty} \frac{(2K)^{2d}}{(2Kn+1)^{2d}} h_{K,n}(w) \\ &= \int_{||x||_\infty \leq K} \int_{||y||_\infty \leq K} \rho(y-x) e^{-i<w,y-x>} dy dx. \qquad (2.3) \end{aligned}$$

For fixed $v = y - x$, the j-th coordinate of x ranges through $[-K - v_j, K - v_j] \cap [-K, K]$, which has size $2K - |v_j|$. Hence a change of parameters implies that the integral in the right hand side of (2.3) is equal to

$$\int_{||v||_\infty \leq 2K} \prod_{j=1}^{d} (2K - |v_j|) \rho(v) e^{-i<w,v>} dv \geq 0$$

as limit of real non-negative numbers. Up to a factor $(2\pi)^{-d}$, it is the Fourier transform of $\rho(v) \prod_{j=1}^d (2K - |v_j|)$. Hence

$$\begin{aligned} (2\pi)^{-d}(2K)^{-d} h_K(w) &= (2\pi)^{-d} \int_{||v||_\infty \leq 2K} \prod_{j=1}^{d} \left(1 - \frac{|v_j|}{2K}\right) \rho(v) e^{-i<w,v>} dv \\ &= (2\pi)^{-d} \int_{\mathbb{R}^d} \prod_{j=1}^{d} \theta\left(\frac{v_j}{2K}\right) \rho(v) e^{-i<w,v>} dv = g_K(w) \end{aligned}$$

for

$$\theta(t) = \begin{cases} 1 - |t| & \text{if } |t| \leq 1; \\ 0 & \text{otherwise.} \end{cases}$$

We would like to define a symmetric measure on $\mathbb{R}^d$ by its density $g_K(w)$ with respect to Lebesgue measure. Thus, we must show that g_K is non-negative, symmetric and integrable. The first two properties are inherited from $h_{K,n}$. To show that g_K is integrable, multiply componentwise by $\theta(\cdot/(2M))$ for some large M and integrate. Then

$$\begin{aligned}
&\int_{\mathbb{R}^d} \prod_{j=1}^d \theta\left(\frac{w_j}{2M}\right) g_K(w)dw \\
&= (2\pi)^{-d} \int_{\mathbb{R}^d} \int_{\mathbb{R}^d} \prod_{j=1}^d \theta\left(\frac{v_j}{2K}\right) \rho(v) \prod_{j=1}^d \theta\left(\frac{w_j}{2M}\right) e^{-i<w,v>} dvdw \\
&= (2\pi)^{-d} \int_{\mathbb{R}^d} \left\{ \int_{\mathbb{R}^d} \prod_{j=1}^d \theta\left(\frac{w_j}{2M}\right) e^{-i<w,v>} dw \right\} \prod_{j=1}^d \theta\left(\frac{v_j}{2K}\right) \rho(v)dv.
\end{aligned}$$

The order of integration may be changed as the domains of integration are compact.

Since

$$\int_{-\infty}^{\infty} \theta(t)e^{-i\xi t}dt = \left(\frac{\sin(\xi/2)}{\xi/2}\right)^2,$$

which can be seen by computing the Fourier transform of the box function $t \mapsto 1\{|t| \leq 1/2\}$ and noting that θ is equal to the convolution of the box function with itself, the integral $\int_{\mathbb{R}^d} \prod_{j=1}^d \theta\left(\frac{w_j}{2M}\right) g_K(w)dw$ equals

$$\left(\frac{M}{\pi}\right)^d \int_{\mathbb{R}^d} \rho(v) \prod_{j=1}^d \theta\left(\frac{v_j}{2K}\right) \prod_{j=1}^d \left(\frac{\sin(Mv_j)}{Mv_j}\right)^2 dv.$$

Hence, since the integral is non-negative, $|\theta(\cdot)| \leq 1$ and $|\rho(\cdot)| \leq \rho(0)$,

$$\begin{aligned}
\int_{\mathbb{R}^d} \prod_{j=1}^d \theta\left(\frac{w_j}{2M}\right) g_K(w)dw &\leq \left(\frac{M}{\pi}\right)^d \rho(0) \int_{\mathbb{R}^d} \prod_{j=1}^d \left(\frac{\sin(Mv_j)}{Mv_j}\right)^2 dv \\
&= \frac{\rho(0)}{\pi^d} \int_{\mathbb{R}^d} \prod_{j=1}^d \left(\frac{\sin t_j}{t_j}\right)^2 dt = \rho(0).
\end{aligned}$$

The bound does not depend on M. The integrand in the left hand side increases in M. Hence the monotone convergence theorem implies that

$$\begin{aligned}
\lim_{M\to\infty} \int_{\mathbb{R}^d} \prod_{j=1}^d \theta\left(\frac{w_j}{2M}\right) g_K(w)dw &= \int_{\mathbb{R}^d} \lim_{M\to\infty} \prod_{j=1}^d \theta\left(\frac{w_j}{2M}\right) g_K(w)dw \\
&= \int_{\mathbb{R}^d} g_K(w)dw \leq \rho(0)
\end{aligned}$$

and g_K is integrable.

To recap, we have a well-defined symmetric density g_K on $\mathbb{R}^d$ such that

$$g_K(w) = \left(\frac{1}{2\pi}\right)^d \int_{\mathbb{R}^d} \rho(v) \prod_{j=1}^{d} \theta\left(\frac{v_j}{2K}\right) e^{-i<w,v>} dv.$$

By the inverse Fourier formula,

$$\rho(v) \prod_{j=1}^{d} \theta\left(\frac{v_j}{2K}\right) = \int_{\mathbb{R}^d} g_K(w) e^{i<w,v>} dw.$$

Taking $v = 0$, we get $\int g_K(w)dw = \rho(0)$, so $g_K(w)/\rho(0)$ is a probability density with characteristic function

$$\frac{\rho(v)}{\rho(0)} \prod_{j=1}^{d} \theta\left(\frac{v_j}{2K}\right).$$

For $K \to \infty$, this characteristic function tends to $\rho(v)/\rho(0)$. By assumption, ρ is continuous at zero, so the Lévy–Cramér continuity theorem states that $\rho(v)/\rho(0)$ is the characteristic function of some random variable, X say. In other words,

$$\frac{\rho(v)}{\rho(0)} = \mathbb{E}_X e^{i<v,X>}$$

or $\rho(v) = \rho(0)\mathbb{E}_X e^{i<v,X>}$. The probability distribution of X scaled by $\rho(0)$ finally gives us the sought-after measure μ. □

2.6 THE SEMI-VARIOGRAM

In geostatistics, one often prefers the semi-variogram to the covariance function.

Definition 2.6 *Let* $X = (X_t)_{t\in\mathbb{R}^d}$ *be intrinsically stationary. Then the* semi-variogram $\gamma : \mathbb{R}^d \to \mathbb{R}$ *is defined by*

$$\gamma(t) = \frac{1}{2}\mathrm{Var}(X_t - X_0), \quad t \in \mathbb{R}^d.$$

Note that

$$\gamma(t) = \rho(0) - \rho(t)$$

for weakly stationary random fields. In particular, $\gamma(0) = \rho(0) - \rho(0) = 0$. The definition of a semi-variogram, however, requires only the weaker assumption of intrinsic stationarity.

Example 2.13 *The semi-variogram of the fractional Brownian surface introduced in Example 2.7 is given by*

$$\gamma(t) = \frac{1}{2}||t||^{2H}$$

and coincides with that of the Brownian motion for $H = 1/2$.

Example 2.14 *Below, we list the semi-variograms corresponding to some of the covariance functions presented in Examples 2.4 and 2.10.*

1. *For the exponential covariance function $\rho(t) = \sigma^2 \exp[-\beta||t||]$,*

$$\gamma(t) = \sigma^2 (1 - \exp[-\beta||t||]) .$$

2. *For the Gaussian covariance function $\rho(t) = \sigma^2 \exp\left[-\beta||t||^2\right]$,*

$$\gamma(t) = \sigma^2 \left(1 - \exp\left[-\beta||t||^2\right]\right) .$$

3. *If $\rho(t) = \int e^{i<w,t>} f(w)dw$ for some even integrable function $f : \mathbb{R}^d \to \mathbb{R}^+$,*

$$\gamma(t) = \int (1 - e^{i<w,t>}) f(w)dw.$$

In practice, there is often additional measurement error. To be specific, suppose that the observations are realisations from the linear model

$$Y_i = X_{t_i} + E_i, \quad i = 1, \ldots, n,$$

for independent, identically distributed zero mean error terms E_i that are independent of the intrinsically stationary random field X and have variance σ_E^2. Then

$$\frac{1}{2}\text{Var}(Y_j - Y_i) = \gamma_X(t_j - t_i) + \frac{1}{2}\text{Var}(E_j - E_i) = \gamma_X(t_j - t_i) + \sigma_E^2 1\{i \neq j\}$$

so that

$$\gamma_Y(t) = \begin{cases} \gamma_X(t) + \sigma_E^2 & t \neq 0 \\ \gamma_X(t) & t = 0 \end{cases} \tag{2.4}$$

is discontinuous in $t = 0$. This phenomenon is known as the *nugget effect*.

It is natural to assume that the dependence between sampled values fades out as the distance between them increases, that is,

$\lim_{||t||\to\infty} \rho(t) = 0$, provided it exists. In this case, the limit $\lim_{||t||\to\infty} \gamma(t)$ is called the *sill*. Taking into account the nugget effect, the *partial sill* is defined as $\lim_{||t||\to\infty} \gamma(t) - \lim_{||t||\to 0} \gamma(t)$.

In many applications, there is only a single finite sample $X_{t_1}, \ldots, X_{t_n}$, $n \in \mathbb{N}$, available of the random field X. In order to be able to carry out statistical inference, one must obtain an artificial replication by assuming at least intrinsic stationarity. The idea is then, at lag t, to consider all pairs of observations that are 'approximately' t apart and to average. Doing so, one obtains the smoothed *Matheron estimator*

$$\hat{\gamma}(t) = \frac{1}{2|N(t)|} \sum_{(t_i,t_j)\in N(t)} (X_{t_j} - X_{t_i})^2, \tag{2.5}$$

where the t-neighbourhood $N(t)$ is defined by

$$N(t) = \{(t_i, t_j) : t_j - t_i \in B(t, \epsilon)\},$$

$B(t, \epsilon)$ is the closed ball of radius ϵ centred at t and $|\cdot|$ denotes cardinality.

The choice of ϵ is an art. It must be small enough to have $\gamma(t_j - t_i) \approx \gamma(t)$ for $t_j - t_i$ in the ϵ-ball around t and, on the other hand, large enough to have a reasonable number of points in $N(t)$ for the averaging to be stable. In other words, there is a trade-off between bias and variance.

The estimator (2.5) is approximately unbiased whenever $N(t)$ is not empty. Indeed, still assuming that X is intrinsically stationary,

$$2|N(t)|\mathbb{E}\hat{\gamma}(t) = \sum_{(t_i,t_j)\in N(t)} \mathbb{E}\left[(X_{t_j} - X_{t_i})^2\right] = 2 \sum_{(t_i,t_j)\in N(t)} \gamma(t_j - t_i).$$

In other words, $\mathbb{E}\hat{\gamma}(t)$ is the average value of $\gamma(t_j - t_i)$ over $N(t)$.

Note that although the Matheron estimator is non-parametric, a specific family γ_θ may be fitted by minimising the contrast

$$\sum_j w_j \left(\hat{\gamma}(h_j) - \gamma_\theta(h_j)\right)^2$$

with, for example, $w_j = |N(h_j)|$ or $w_j = |N(h_j)|/\gamma_\theta(h_j)^2$ and the sum ranging over a finite family of lags h_j. For the second choice, the smaller the value of the theoretical semi-variogram, the larger the weight given to a pair of observations at approximately that lag to compensate for their expected rare occurrence.

2.7 SIMPLE KRIGING

Suppose one observes values $X_{t_1} = x_{t_1}, \ldots, X_{t_n} = x_{t_n}$ of a random field $X = (X_t)_{t \in \mathbb{R}^d}$ at n locations $t_i \in \mathbb{R}^d$, $i = 1, \ldots, n$. Based on these observations, the goal is to predict the value at some location t_0 of interest at which no measurement has been made. We shall need the mean function m and the covariance function ρ of X.

Let us restrict ourselves to *linear predictors* of the form

$$\hat{X}_{t_0} = c(t_0) + \sum_{i=1}^{n} c_i X_{t_i}.$$

Then

$$\mathbb{E}\hat{X}_{t_0} = c(t_0) + \sum_{i=1}^{n} c_i m(t_i)$$

so $\hat{X}_{t_0}$ is *unbiased* in the sense that $\mathbb{E}\hat{X}_{t_0} = m(t_0)$ if and only if

$$c(t_0) = m(t_0) - \sum_{i=1}^{n} c_i m(t_i). \tag{2.6}$$

The *mean squared error* (mse) of $\hat{X}_{t_0}$ is given by

$$\mathbb{E}\left[(\hat{X}_{t_0} - X_{t_0})^2\right] = \text{Var}(\hat{X}_{t_0} - X_{t_0}) + \left(\mathbb{E}\left[\hat{X}_{t_0} - X_{t_0}\right]\right)^2, \tag{2.7}$$

which can by seen by sandwiching in the term $\mathbb{E}(\hat{X}_{t_0} - X_{t_0})$. In other words, the mean squared error is a sum of two terms, one capturing the variance, the other the bias. For unbiased predictors

$$\text{mse}(\hat{X}_{t_0}) = \text{Var}(\hat{X}_{t_0} - X_{t_0}). \tag{2.8}$$

To optimise (2.8), write

$$\hat{X}_{t_0} - X_{t_0} = c(t_0) + \sum_{i=1}^{n} c_i X_{t_i} - X_{t_0}.$$

Abbreviate the sum by $c'Z$ for $c' = (c_1, \ldots, c_n)$ and $Z' = (X_{t_1}, \ldots, X_{t_n})$. Then

$$\text{Var}(\hat{X}_{t_0} - X_{t_0}) = \text{Var}(c'Z - X_{t_0}) = c'\Sigma c - 2c'K + \rho(t_0, t_0)$$

where Σ is an $n \times n$ matrix with entries $\rho(t_i, t_j)$ and K an $n \times 1$ vector with entries $\rho(t_i, t_0)$. The gradient with respect to c is $2\Sigma c - 2K$, which is equal to zero whenever $c = \Sigma^{-1}K$ provided Σ is invertible. As an aside, even if Σ were singular, since K is in the column space of Σ, there would always be a solution.

To verify that the null solution of the gradient is indeed the minimiser of the mean squared error, let $\tilde{c}$ be any solution of $\Sigma\tilde{c} = K$. Any linear combination $c'Z$ can be written as $(\tilde{c} + (c - \tilde{c}))'Z$. Now, with $a = c - \tilde{c}$,

$$\begin{aligned}\text{Var}((\tilde{c} + a)'Z - X_{t_0}) &= \tilde{c}'\Sigma\tilde{c} + a'\Sigma a + 2\tilde{c}'\Sigma a - 2\tilde{c}'K - 2a'K + \rho(t_0, t_0) \\ &= \tilde{c}'\Sigma\tilde{c} - 2\tilde{c}'K + a'\Sigma a + \rho(t_0, t_0) \\ &= \rho(t_0, t_0) - \tilde{c}'K + a'\Sigma a\end{aligned}$$

where we use that $\Sigma\tilde{c} = K$. The addition of a to $\tilde{c}$ leads to an extra term $a'\Sigma a$ which is non-negative since Σ, being a covariance matrix, is non-negative definite. We already saw that adding a scalar constant only affects the bias.

We have proved the following theorem.

Theorem 2.2 *Let $X_{t_1}, \dots, X_{t_n}$ be sampled from a random field $(X_t)_{t \in \mathbb{R}^d}$ at n locations $t_i \in \mathbb{R}^d$, $i = 1, \dots, n$, and collect them in the n-vector Z. Write Σ for the covariance matrix of Z and assume Σ exists and is non-singular. Additionally let $K = (K_i)_{i=1}^n$ be the $n \times 1$ vector with entries $K_i = \rho(t_i, t_0)$. Then*

$$\hat{X}_{t_0} = m(t_0) + K'\Sigma^{-1}(Z - \mathbb{E}Z) \tag{2.9}$$

is the best linear predictor of X_{t_0}, $t_0 \in \mathbb{R}^d$, in terms of mean squared error. The mean squared prediction error is given by

$$\rho(t_0, t_0) - K'\Sigma^{-1}K. \tag{2.10}$$

It is worth noticing that (2.10) is smaller than $\rho(t_0, t_0)$, the variance of X_{t_0}. The reduction in variance is due to the fact that information from locations around t_0 is taken into account explicitly in the estimator $\hat{X}_{t_0}$.

Mean squared error based prediction was named 'kriging' by Matheron in honour of D.G. Krige, a South-African mining engineer and pioneer in geostatistics. Under the model assumptions of Theorem 2.2, we refer to (2.9) as the *simple kriging* estimator of X_{t_0}.

2.8 BAYES ESTIMATOR

In a loss function terminology, the mean squared error (2.7) of a predictor $\hat{X}_{t_0}$ is often referred to as the *Bayes loss*. The *Bayes estimator* optimises the Bayes loss over *all* estimators that are functions of the sample $Z = (X_{t_1}, \ldots, X_{t_n})'$, linear or otherwise.

Theorem 2.3 *Let $X_{t_1}, \ldots, X_{t_n}$ be sampled from a random field $(X_t)_{t \in \mathbb{R}^d}$ at n locations $t_i \in \mathbb{R}^d$, $i = 1, \ldots, n$, and collect them in the n-vector Z. Then the Bayes estimator of X_{t_0}, $t_0 \in \mathbb{R}^d$, is given by*

$$\hat{X}_{t_0} = \mathbb{E}\left[X_{t_0} \mid Z\right]. \tag{2.11}$$

Proof: Let $\tilde{X}_{t_0} = f(Z)$ be some estimator based on the sample Z and write $M = \mathbb{E}\left[X_{t_0} \mid Z\right]$. Then

$$\begin{aligned}\mathbb{E}\left[(\tilde{X}_{t_0} - X_{t_0})^2\right] &= \mathbb{E}\left[(\tilde{X}_{t_0} - M + M - X_{t_0})^2\right] \\ &= \mathbb{E}\left[(\tilde{X}_{t_0} - M)^2\right] + \mathbb{E}\left[(M - X_{t_0})^2\right] + 2\mathbb{E}\left[(\tilde{X}_{t_0} - M)(M - X_{t_0})\right].\end{aligned}$$

Since both M and $\tilde{X}_{t_0}$ are functions of Z,

$$\begin{aligned}\mathbb{E}\left[(\tilde{X}_{t_0} - M)(M - X_{t_0})\right] &= \mathbb{E}\left(\mathbb{E}\left[(\tilde{X}_{t_0} - M)(M - X_{t_0}) \mid Z\right]\right) \\ &= \mathbb{E}\left[(\tilde{X}_{t_0} - M)(M - \mathbb{E}(X_{t_0} \mid Z))\right] = 0.\end{aligned}$$

Consequently

$$\mathbb{E}\left[(\tilde{X}_{t_0} - X_{t_0})^2\right] = \mathbb{E}\left[(\tilde{X}_{t_0} - M)^2\right] + \mathbb{E}\left[(M - X_{t_0})^2\right] \geq \mathbb{E}\left[(M - X_{t_0})^2\right]$$

with equality if and only if $\mathbb{E}\left[(\tilde{X}_{t_0} - M)^2\right] = 0$. □

So far, we did not use any information about the distribution of the random field X. For multivariate normally distributed random vectors, it is well known that the Bayes estimator of a component given the other ones is linear in Z and given by $m(t_0) + K'\Sigma^{-1}(Z - \mathbb{E}Z)$. The conditional variance is $\rho(t_0, t_0) - K'\Sigma^{-1}K$ (in the notation of Theorem 2.2) and depends on Z only through the covariances. Hence, under the assumption of normality, the Bayes estimator coincides in distribution with the best linear predictor. Finally, note that the unconditional mean of the Bayes estimator is given by $m(t_0)$ and, by the variance decomposition formula

$$\mathrm{Var}(X_{t_0}) = \mathbb{E}\mathrm{Var}(X_{t_0} | Z) + \mathrm{Var}(\mathbb{E}(X_{t_0} | Z)),$$

its variance equals $\rho(t_0, t_0) - (\rho(t_0, t_0) - K'\Sigma^{-1}K) = K'\Sigma^{-1}K$.

Example 2.15 *As a simple example where the Bayes estimator is not linear, return to the framework of Example 2.1. Let A be a set in $\mathbb{R}^d$, $Y = (Y_1, Y_2)'$ a random vector with known mean and covariance matrix, and set*

$$X_t = Y_0 1\{t \notin A\} + Y_1 1\{t \in A\}, \quad t \in \mathbb{R}^d.$$

Then, for $t_0 \in A$ and $t_1 \notin A$, the Bayes estimator

$$\mathbb{E}\left[Y_1 | Y_0\right]$$

is not necessarily linear in Y_0, for instance when $Y_1 = Y_0^2$.

2.9 ORDINARY KRIGING

Consider the model

$$X_t = \mu + E_t, \quad t \in \mathbb{R}^d,$$

where $\mu \in \mathbb{R}$ is the unknown global mean and E_t is a zero mean random field with covariance function $\mathrm{Cov}(E_t, E_s) = \rho(t, s)$.

Based on samples of X at $t_1, \dots, t_n$, $n \in \mathbb{N}$, we look for a linear unbiased predictor

$$\hat{X}_{t_0} = c(t_0) + \sum_{i=1}^{n} c_i X_{t_i}$$

at some other location $t_0 \in \mathbb{R}^d$ that optimises the mean squared error. As in Theorem 2.2, let Z be the n-vector of the X_{t_i}, $i = 1, \dots, n$. Write Σ for the covariance matrix of Z and let $K = (K_i)_{i=1}^n$ be the $n \times 1$ vector with entries $K_i = \rho(t_i, t_0)$. The simple kriging estimator would be

$$\hat{X}_{t_0} = \mu + K'\Sigma^{-1}(Z - \mathbb{E}_\mu Z),$$

but we *cannot* compute it as μ is unknown.

Instead, we proceed as follows. First, consider unbiasedness

$$\mu = \mathbb{E}_\mu \hat{X}_{t_0} = c(t_0) + \mu \sum_{i=1}^{n} c_i$$

for *all* μ. The special case $\mu = 0$ implies that $c(t_0) = 0$ and therefore

$$\sum_{i=1}^{n} c_i = 1.$$

Turning to the variance term, with $c' = (c_1, \dots, c_n)$, one wishes to optimise

$$\mathrm{Var}_\mu(c'Z - X_{t_0})$$

under the scale constraint on the c_i by the Euler–Lagrange method. Note that

$$
\begin{aligned}
(\hat{X}_{t_0} - X_{t_0})^2 &= \left(\sum_{i=1}^{n} c_i (X_{t_i} - \mu) - (X_{t_0} - \mu) \right)^2 \\
&= E_{t_0}^2 + \left(\sum_{i=1}^{n} c_i E_{t_i} \right)^2 - 2 E_{t_0} \sum_{i=1}^{n} c_i E_{t_i}.
\end{aligned}
$$

Hence

$$
\mathbb{E}\left[(\hat{X}_{t_0} - X_{t_0})^2 \right] = \rho(t_0, t_0) + \sum_{i=1}^{n} \sum_{j=1}^{n} c_i c_j \rho(t_i, t_j) - 2 \sum_{i=1}^{n} c_i \rho(t_0, t_i).
$$

For ease of notation, write $\mathbf{1}' = (1, \ldots, 1)$. Then we must optimise

$$
\rho(t_0, t_0) + c' \Sigma c - 2c' K + \lambda (c' \mathbf{1} - 1).
$$

The score equations are

$$
\begin{cases}
0 &= 2\Sigma c - 2K + \lambda \mathbf{1}; \\
1 &= c' \mathbf{1}.
\end{cases}
$$

From now on, assume that Σ is non-singular. Multiply the first equation by $\mathbf{1}' \Sigma^{-1}$ to obtain

$$
\begin{cases}
0 &= 2\mathbf{1}' c - 2\mathbf{1}' \Sigma^{-1} K + \lambda \mathbf{1}' \Sigma^{-1} \mathbf{1}; \\
1 &= c' \mathbf{1}.
\end{cases}
$$

Consequently the Lagrange multiplier equals

$$
\lambda = 2 \frac{\mathbf{1}' \Sigma^{-1} K - \mathbf{1}' c}{\mathbf{1}' \Sigma^{-1} \mathbf{1}} = 2 \frac{\mathbf{1}' \Sigma^{-1} K - 1}{\mathbf{1}' \Sigma^{-1} \mathbf{1}}.
$$

Substitution into the first score equation yields

$$
c = \Sigma^{-1} K - \frac{\lambda}{2} \Sigma^{-1} \mathbf{1} = \Sigma^{-1} K + \frac{1 - \mathbf{1}' \Sigma^{-1} K}{\mathbf{1}' \Sigma^{-1} \mathbf{1}} \Sigma^{-1} \mathbf{1}.
$$

The corresponding mean squared error is

$$
\rho(t_0, t_0) + c' \Sigma c - 2c' K = \rho(t_0, t_0) - K' \Sigma^{-1} K + \frac{(1 - \mathbf{1}' \Sigma^{-1} K)^2}{\mathbf{1}' \Sigma^{-1} \mathbf{1}}.
$$

As one would expect, the mean squared error is larger than that for simple kriging.

To see that, indeed, the mean squared error is optimised, write any unbiased linear predictor as $(c+a)'Z$, where c is the solution of the score equations and $(c+a)'\mathbf{1} = 1$, i.e. $a'\mathbf{1} = 0$. Its mean squared error is

$$\rho(t_0, t_0) + c'\Sigma c - 2c'K + a'\Sigma a + 2c'\Sigma a - 2a'K.$$

Now, $a'\Sigma c = a'K$ using the unbiasedness and the expression for c. Hence, the mean squared error is indeed optimal for $a = 0$.

We have proved the following.

Theorem 2.4 *Let $X_{t_1}, \dots, X_{t_n}$ be sampled from a random field $(X_t)_{t\in\mathbb{R}^d}$ with unknown constant mean at n locations $t_i \in \mathbb{R}^d$, $i = 1, \dots, n$, and collect them in the n-vector Z. Write Σ for the covariance matrix of Z and assume Σ exists and is non-singular. Additionally let $K = (K_i)_{i=1}^n$ be the $n \times 1$ vector with entries $K_i = \rho(t_i, t_0)$. Then*

$$\hat{X}_{t_0} = K'\Sigma^{-1}Z + \frac{1 - \mathbf{1}'\Sigma^{-1}K}{\mathbf{1}'\Sigma^{-1}\mathbf{1}}\mathbf{1}'\Sigma^{-1}Z \qquad (2.12)$$

is the best linear predictor in terms of mean squared error. The mean squared prediction error is given by

$$\rho(t_0, t_0) - K'\Sigma^{-1}K + \frac{(1 - \mathbf{1}'\Sigma^{-1}K)^2}{\mathbf{1}'\Sigma^{-1}\mathbf{1}}. \qquad (2.13)$$

The additional variance contribution $(1-\mathbf{1}'\Sigma^{-1}K)^2/\mathbf{1}'\Sigma^{-1}\mathbf{1}$ in (2.13) compared to (2.10) in Theorem 2.2 is due to the uncertainty regarding the mean.

In the remainder of this section, let us specialise to the case where Z is sampled from a Gaussian random field $(X_t)_{t\in\mathbb{R}^d}$. In other words, Z is multivariate normally distributed with unknown constant mean μ and known non-singular covariance matrix Σ. The log likelihood evaluated at Z, up to constants that do not depend on μ, is given by

$$-\frac{1}{2}(Z - \mu\mathbf{1})'\Sigma^{-1}(Z - \mu\mathbf{1}) = -\frac{1}{2}\sum_i\sum_j (X_{t_i} - \mu)\Sigma^{-1}_{ij}(X_{t_j} - \mu).$$

The derivative with respect to μ equals

$$-\frac{1}{2}\sum_i\sum_j \left[-\Sigma^{-1}_{ij}(X_{t_i} - \mu) - \Sigma^{-1}_{ij}(X_{t_j} - \mu)\right] = \mathbf{1}'\Sigma^{-1}(Z - \mu\mathbf{1})$$

and is equal to zero if and only if $\mathbf{1}'\Sigma^{-1}Z = \mu\mathbf{1}'\Sigma^{-1}\mathbf{1}$. Hence

$$\hat{\mu} = \frac{\mathbf{1}'\Sigma^{-1}Z}{\mathbf{1}'\Sigma^{-1}\mathbf{1}}.$$

Note that since Σ is non-negative definite, the second order derivative $-\mathbf{1}'\Sigma^{-1}\mathbf{1}$ is non-positive, which implies that $\hat{\mu}$ is the unique maximiser of the log likelihood. Upon substitution of $\hat{\mu}$ in the simple kriging estimator (2.9), one obtains

$$\hat{X}_{t_0} = \hat{\mu} + K'\Sigma^{-1}(Z - \hat{\mu}\mathbf{1}),$$

which is equal to the ordinary kriging predictor (2.12).

2.10 UNIVERSAL KRIGING

Universal kriging relaxes the constant mean assumption of ordinary kriging to the more general assumption that

$$\mathbb{E}X_t = m(t)'\beta$$

for some known function $m : \mathbb{R}^d \to \mathbb{R}^p$ and unknown parameter vector $\beta \in \mathbb{R}^p$. Such a model would be appropriate in a spatial regression context where the sampled values are deemed to depend linearly on p explanatory variables $m(t)_i$, $i = 1, \ldots, p$.

A linear estimator $\hat{X}_{t_0} = c(t_0) + \sum_{i=1}^n c_i X_{t_i}$ is unbiased whenever

$$m(t_0)'\beta = c(t_0) + \sum_{i=1}^n c_i m(t_i)'\beta$$

for all β. Note that both sides are polynomial in β. Therefore, all coefficients must be equal. In other words, $c(t_0) = 0$ and

$$m(t_0) = \sum_{i=1}^n c_i m(t_i). \tag{2.14}$$

Universal kriging optimises the mean squared error

$$\mathbb{E}\left[\left(\sum_{i=1}^n c_i X_{t_i} - X_{t_0}\right)^2\right]$$

under the constraint (2.14). Provided $M'\Sigma^{-1}M$ is non-singular for the $n \times p$ matrix M whose rows are given by $m(t_i)'$, it can be shown that the optimal vector of linear coefficients is

$$c = \Sigma^{-1}\left[K + M(M'\Sigma^{-1}M)^{-1}(m(t_0) - M'\Sigma^{-1}K)\right]. \qquad (2.15)$$

The corresponding mean squared prediction error is

$$\rho(t_0, t_0) - K'\Sigma^{-1}K + (m(t_0) - M'\Sigma^{-1}K)'(M'\Sigma^{-1}M)^{-1}(m(t_0) - M'\Sigma^{-1}K).$$

Note that we have been working under *minimal model assumptions* based on *a single sample*. This implies that we are forced to violate the golden standard in statistics that parameters are estimated from one sample, whereas prediction or validation is carried out on another. Moreover, to calculate (2.15), the covariance matrix Σ needs to be known. To make matters worse, it cannot even be estimated from the empirical semi-variogram, as the random field $(X_t)_{t\in\mathbb{R}^d}$ is neither weakly nor intrinsically stationary (its mean is not constant). It would be natural to focus on the residual process $(E_t)_{t\in\mathbb{R}^d}$ instead. However, this would require knowledge of β, estimation of which depends on knowing the law of the random field, in other words, on knowing Σ.

A pragmatic solution is to estimate β in a least squares sense. Write

$$Z = M\beta + E,$$

where, as before, the vector Z collects the sample X_{t_i}, the rows of M consist of the $m(t_i)'$ and E denotes the vector of residuals. Pretending that $\mathrm{Var}(E) = \sigma^2 I$, I being the $n \times n$ identity matrix, minimise

$$\sum_{i=1}^{n}(X_{t_i} - m(t_i)'\beta)^2 = (Z - M\beta)'(Z - M\beta)$$

over β. The gradient is $-2M'(Z - M\beta)$, so

$$\hat{\beta} = (M'M)^{-1}M'Z,$$

provided $M'M$ is non-singular. The vector $Z - M\hat{\beta}$ has a constant mean equal to zero when the residuals have mean zero, and one might estimate its covariance function by using the empirical semi-variogram of $Z - M\hat{\beta}$. Indeed, this is the procedure implemented in standard statistical software. Bear in mind, though, that the approach is based on an approximation and may incur a bias.

As always, if one would be prepared to make more detailed model assumptions, maximum likelihood ideas would apply.

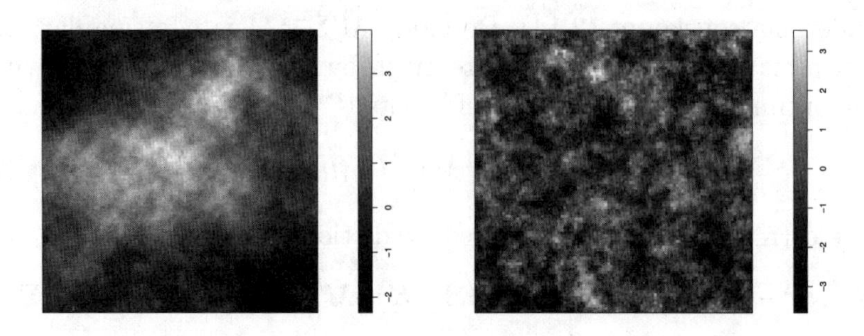

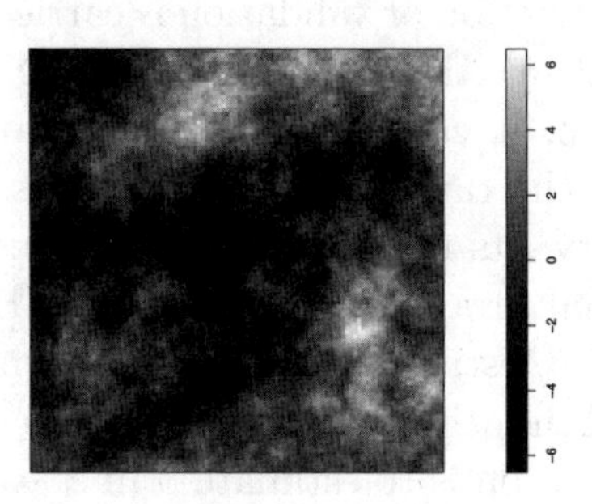

Figure 2.1 Realisations of a Gaussian random field on $[0,5]^2$ with mean zero and exponential covariance function $\rho(s,t) = \sigma^2 \exp(-\beta||t-s||)$. Top row: $\sigma^2 = 1$, $\beta = 1/2$ (left) and $\sigma^2 = 1$, $\beta = 5$ (right). Bottom: $\sigma^2 = 10$, $\beta = 1/2$.

2.11 WORKED EXAMPLES WITH R

Samples from a Gaussian random field may be obtained using the package *RandomFields: Simulation and analysis of random fields.* We used version 3.1.50 to obtain the pictures shown in this section. The package is maintained by M. Schlather. An up-to-date list of contributors and a reference manual can be found on

`https://CRAN.R-project.org/package=RandomFields.`

As an illustration, consider the covariance function

$$\rho(s,t) = \sigma^2 e^{-\beta||t-s||}, \quad t,s \in \mathbb{R}^2.$$

The script

```
model <- RMexp(var, scale)
RFsimulate(model, x=seq(0,5,0.05), y=seq(0,5,0.05))
```

defines the model and generates a realisation with $\sigma^2 =$ `var` and $\beta = 1/$ `scale`. The arguments `x` and `y` define a planar grid in $[0,5]^2$ with square cells of side length 0.05. A few samples are shown in Figure 2.1. Note that increasing σ^2 results in a wider spread in values as can be seen from the ribbons displayed alongside the samples. Increasing β means that the correlation decays faster, resulting in rougher realisations with more fluctuations.

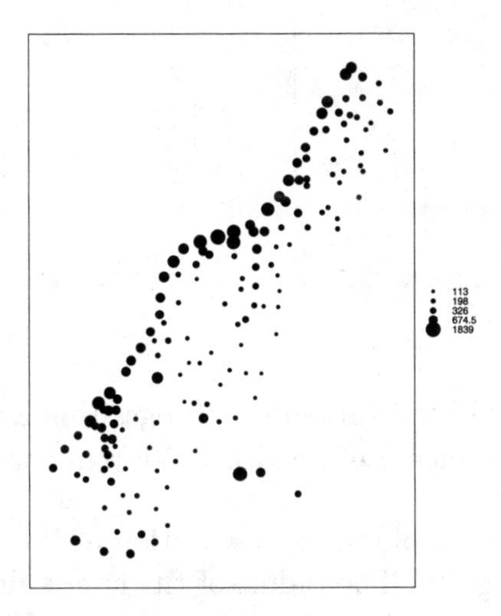

Figure 2.2 Concentrations of zinc (mg/kg) in the top soil measured at 155 locations in a flood plain of the Meuse river near Stein.

We illustrate the basic kriging ideas by means of the package *Gstat: Spatial and spatio-temporal geostatistical modelling, prediction and simulation* maintained by E. Pebesma in collaboration with B. Graeler. Further details can be found on

`https://CRAN.R-project.org/package=gstat`

including a reference manual. The results here were obtained using version 1.1-5.

The package imports the data set 'Meuse' from the package *sp*. The data were collected by M.G.J. Rikken and R.P.G. van Rijn for their 1993 thesis 'Soil pollution with heavy metals - an inquiry into spatial variation, cost of mapping and the risk evaluation of copper, cadmium, lead and zinc in the floodplains of the Meuse west of Stein, the Netherlands' at Utrecht University and compiled for R by E. Pebesma. The description was extended by D. Rossiter. The data include topsoil heavy metal concentrations for 155 locations in a flood plain of the Meuse river in the southern-most province of the Netherlands close to the village of Stein. The metal concentrations were computed from composite samples of an area of about $15m \times 15m$. Additionally, a number of soil and landscape variables are available, including the distance to the river bed.

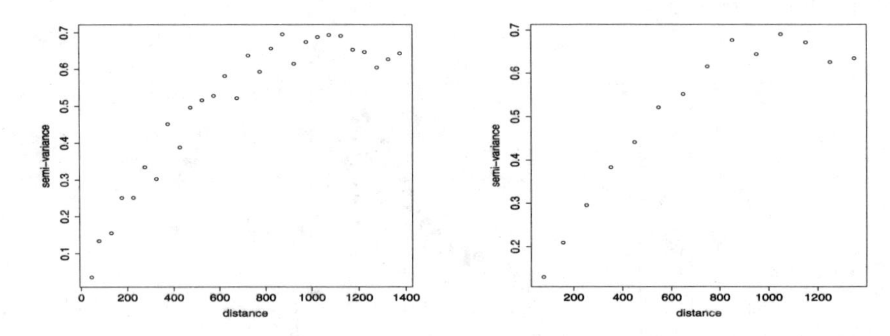

Figure 2.3 Estimated semi-variogram of logarithmic zinc concentrations as a function of distance. Left: width = 50; right: width = 100.

In Figure 2.2, a graphical representation of the zinc concentrations (in mg/kg soil) is given. The radius of the circles drawn at the sample locations are proportional to the concentrations. The window is about three by four kilometers. It may be seen that the larger concentrations follow the curve of the river bed.

We begin our analysis by fitting a semi-variogram. Since the zinc concentrations are heavily skewed to the right, we use a logarithmic transformation and calculate the Matheron estimator using the script

```
coordinates(meuse) = ~x+y
v <- variogram(log(zinc)~1, meuse, cutoff=1400, width=w)
```

The cutoff value is set to about half the minimum side length of the observation window. To select an appropriate width, one may start at the minimum interpoint distance of 43.9 metres between sampling locations and gradually increase the value until the plotted semi-variogram

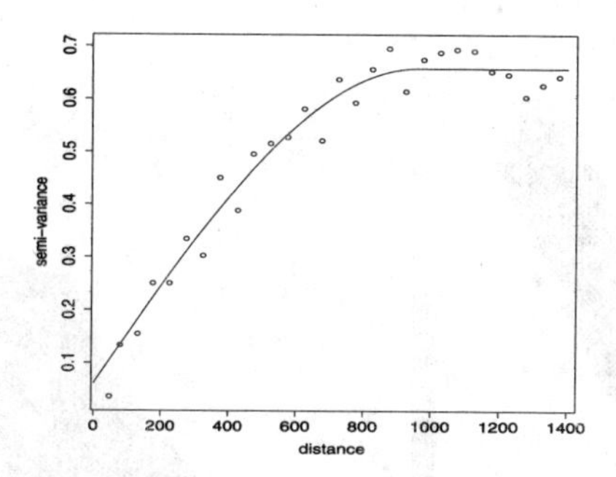

Figure 2.4 Estimated semi-variogram (width = 50) of logarithmic zinc concentrations as a function of distance (dots) and fitted spherical semi-variogram model (line).

is deemed smooth enough. Figure 2.3 shows the results for $w = 50$ and $w = 100$.

To fit a parametric function γ to the estimated semi-variogram $\hat{\gamma}$, numerical optimisation may be used to minimise the contrast

$$\sum_j w_j \left(\hat{\gamma}(h_j) - \gamma_\theta(h_j) \right)^2 ,$$

where j ranges over a finite number of range bins. This procedure is implemented in the function `fit.variogram`. If the parameter `fit.method` is set to 1, the weights read $w_j = N(h_j)$; a parameter value of 2 uses $w_j = N(h_j)/\gamma_\theta(h_j)^2$. Since Figure 2.3 suggests that the semi-variogram increases almost linearly up to about 900 metres and then levels off, we use the so-called spherical semi-variogram

$$\gamma(t) = \begin{cases} 0 & t = 0 \\ \alpha + \beta \left[\frac{3||t||}{2R} - \frac{||t||^3}{2R^3} \right] & 0 < ||t|| < R \qquad t \in \mathbb{R}^2 \\ \alpha + \beta & ||t|| \geq R \end{cases}$$

for nugget $\alpha > 0$, scale parameter $\beta > 0$ and range parameter $R > 0$. Fitting this model to the empirical semi-variogram shown in the left-most panel of Figure 2.3 results in $\hat{\alpha} = 0.06$, $\beta = 0.6$, and $R = 958.7$. The graph of the fitted model $\hat{\gamma}$ is plotted in Figure 2.4.

Having fitted a plausible model, one may proceed to calculate the ordinary kriging predictor $\widehat{X}_t$ for t in a grid over the region of interest. For our example, the data frame `meuse.grid` supplies such a grid. Writing `m` for the fitted semi-variogram model, the script

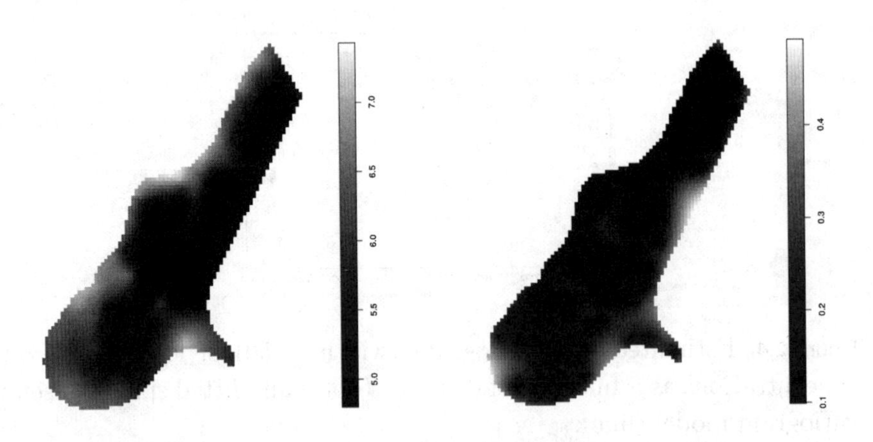

Figure 2.5 Left: logarithmic zinc concentrations in the top soil interpolated by ordinary kriging from measured values at 155 locations in a flood plain of the Meuse river near Stein using the semi-variogram plotted in Figure 2.4. Right: estimated mean squared prediction errors.

```
gridded(meuse.grid) = ~x+y
Xhat <- krige(log(zinc)~1, meuse, meuse.grid, model=m)
```

carries out the calculations. The formula `log(zinc)`$\sim$`1` demands a constant mean in accordance with the ordinary kriging assumptions. The resulting kriging predictor and estimated mean squared prediction error are shown in Figure 2.5. It can be seen that larger concentrations tend to occur near the river bed. The variance tends to be higher in regions where there are few observations.

The assumption of a constant mean inherent in the ordinary kriging framework does not seem realistic (cf. Figure 2.2). In particular, zinc concentrations seem to be correlated with the distance to the river bed. In the `meuse` data set, these distances are discretised in a grid and rescaled so that they take values in the interval $[0, 1]$. To find a proper functional form for the correlation, in Figure 2.6 the logarithmic zinc concentration is plotted against the normalised distance to the river bed (left-most panel) as well as against its square root. Note that the square root transformation improves the linear approximation.

Based on the above observations, we apply universal kriging with the square root of the discretised and normalised distance, denoted by

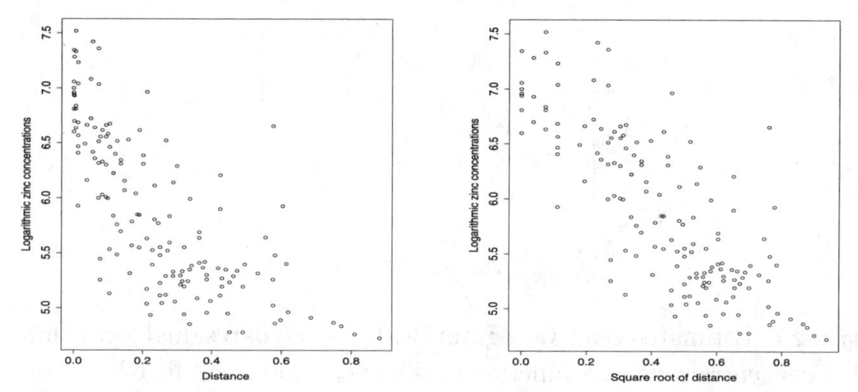

Figure 2.6 Logarithmic zinc concentrations in the top soil at 155 locations in a flood plain of the Meuse river near Stein plotted against the normalised distance to the river bed (left) and the square root of the normalised distance to the river bed (right).

$d(t)$, as a covariate. Thus, the log zinc concentrations follow the linear regression model

$$X_t = \beta_0 + \beta_1 d(t) + E_t,$$

where E_t is a zero mean random field. The parameters β_0 and β_1 are assumed to be unknown.

To compute an empirical semi-variogram of the random field $(E_t)_t$, one must first estimate $\beta = (\beta_0, \beta_1)'$. The least squares estimator is

$$\hat{\beta} = (M'M)^{-1}M'Z,$$

where Z is the observation vector and M a 155×2 matrix whose first column contains entries that are all equal to 1. The i-th entry of the second column of M is the square root of the normalised distance from the grid cell of sampling location i to the river bed. Next, the semi-variogram of $(E_t)_t$ can be estimated as before for the residuals $X_t - \hat{\beta}_0 - \hat{\beta}_1 d(t)$. The following script carries out these two tasks:

```
vdist <- variogram(log(zinc)~sqrt(dist), meuse, cutoff=1300,
width=50)
```

Figure 2.7 shows the residuals and the fitted spherical semi-variogram

```
mdist <- fit.variogram(vdist, vgm(0, "Sph", 100, 0),
fit.method=1).
```

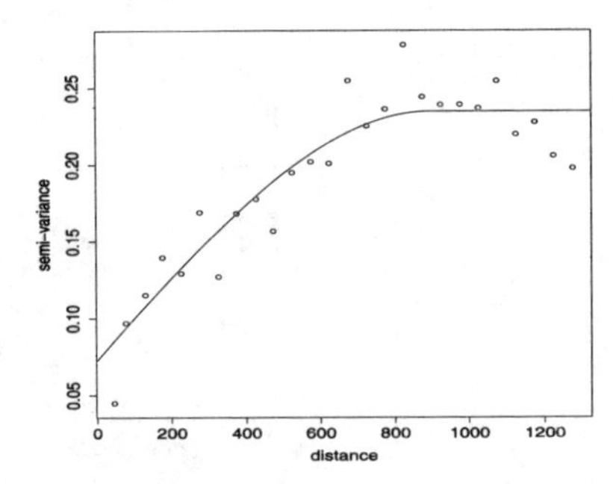

Figure 2.7 Estimated semi-variogram (width = 50) of residual logarithmic zinc concentrations as a function of distance (dots) and fitted spherical semi-variogram model (line). The residuals are obtained from a linear regression against the square root of the normalised distance to the river bed.

Having fitted a plausible model incorporating the covariate information, we calculate the universal kriging predictor $\hat{X}_t$ for t in the grid supplied with the data. Writing `mdist` for the fitted semi-variogram model, the command

```
krige(log(zinc)~sqrt(dist), meuse, meuse.grid, model=mdist)
```

carries out the calculations. Note that the formula now involves the covariate `dist` in the the `meuse` data frame. The resulting kriging predictor and estimated mean squared prediction error are shown in Figure 2.8. Upon comparison with Figure 2.5, it can be seen that taking the distance to the river into account leads to a smoother predictor and a smaller estimated mean squared prediction error.

To validate the final model, appropriate residuals are needed. Since data are available only at the measurement locations, we predict the logarithmic zinc concentration in the top soil at a selected measurement location based on the concentrations at all other measurement locations using the model and subtract the result from the actual measurement. Repeating this procedure for all 155 locations yields the set of so-called cross-validation residuals. The script

```
krige.cv(log(zinc)~sqrt(dist), meuse, meuse.grid,
model=mdist)
```

carries out the computations. A graphical representation of the cross-validation procedure is shown in Figure 2.9. Since the mean value -0.003 of the residuals is close to zero and there does not appear to be any spatial pattern, we conclude that the model seems adequate.

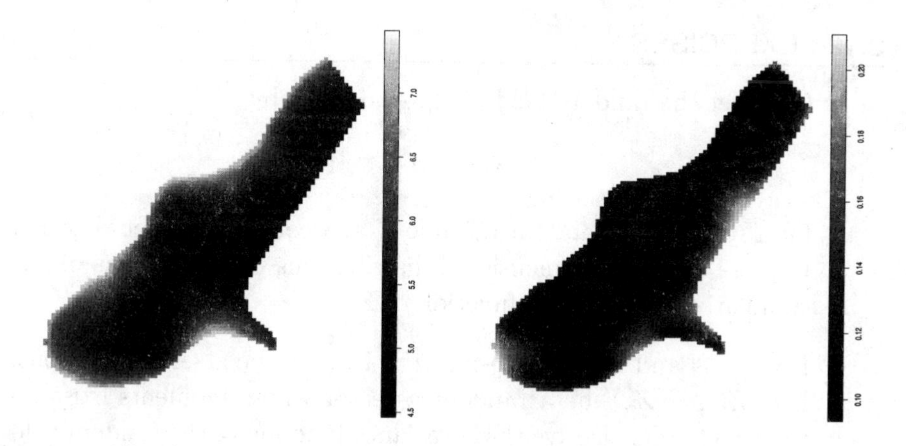

Figure 2.8 Left: logarithmic zinc concentrations in the top soil interpolated by universal kriging from measured values at 155 locations in a flood plain of the Meuse river near Stein using the semi-variogram plotted in Figure 2.7. Right: estimated mean squared prediction errors.

For further details, we refer to the vignettes of *RandomFields* and *gstat* that are available on the CRAN website

`https://cran.r-project.org`.

Figure 2.9 Residuals of logarithmic zinc concentrations in the top soil interpolated by cross-validated universal kriging from measured values at 155 locations in a flood plain of the Meuse river near Stein using the semi-variogram plotted in Figure 2.7.

2.12 EXERCISES

1. Consider the random field $(X_t)_{t\in\mathbb{R}^d}$ defined by

$$X_t = Z1\{t \in A\}$$

for a real-valued random variable Z and compact subset A of $\mathbb{R}^d$. Express the finite dimensional distributions of X in terms of the cumulative distribution function of Z.

2. Fix $n \in \mathbb{N}$ and let $f_i : \mathbb{R}^d \to \mathbb{R}$, $i = 1, \dots, n$, be a set of functions. Let $(Z_1, \dots, Z_n)'$ be a random n-vector whose moments exist up to second order. Derive the covariance function of the random field

$$X_t = \sum_{i=1}^{n} Z_i f_i(t), \quad t \in \mathbb{R}^d.$$

3. Let $X = (X_t)_{t\in\mathbb{R}^d}$ be a Gaussian random field with mean function m and covariance function ρ. Set $Y_t = X_t^2$. Show that the mean function m_Y and covariance function ρ_Y of the random field $(Y_t)_{t\in\mathbb{R}^d}$ are given by

$$\begin{aligned} m_Y(t) &= m(t)^2 + \rho(t,t) \\ \rho_Y(s,t) &= 2\rho(s,t)\left\{\rho(s,t) + 2m(s)m(t)\right\} \end{aligned}$$

for $s, t \in \mathbb{R}^d$.
Hint: You may use the Isserlis theorem stating that if $(Z_1, \dots, Z_4)'$ is a zero mean multivariate normally distributed random vector, then

$$\begin{aligned} \mathbb{E}\left[Z_1 Z_2 Z_3 Z_4\right] = {} & \mathbb{E}\left[Z_1 Z_2\right]\mathbb{E}\left[Z_3 Z_4\right] + \mathbb{E}\left[Z_1 Z_3\right]\mathbb{E}\left[Z_2 Z_4\right] \\ & + \mathbb{E}\left[Z_1 Z_4\right]\mathbb{E}\left[Z_2 Z_3\right]. \end{aligned}$$

4. Show that if $\rho_1, \rho_2 : \mathbb{R}^d \times \mathbb{R}^d \to \mathbb{R}$ are non-negative definite, then so are $\alpha\rho_1 + \beta\rho_2$ $(\alpha, \beta \geq 0)$ and $\rho_1\rho_2$.

5. Consider the function

$$\rho(t_1, t_2) = \min(t_1, t_2), \quad t_1, t_2 \in (0, \infty).$$

Show that ρ is non-negative definite.
Hint: Use the Sylvester criterion.

6. Compute the spectral measure of the 1-dimensional Ornstein–Uhlenbeck process with covariance function $\rho(t) = \exp(-\beta|t|)/(2\beta)$, $t \in \mathbb{R}$, $\beta > 0$. Does this process admit a version with continuous sample paths?

7. Let $\theta(t) = (1 - |t|)^+$ for $t \in \mathbb{R}$. Show that, for all $\xi \in \mathbb{R}$,
$$\int_{-\infty}^{\infty} \theta(t) e^{-i\xi t} dt = \left(\frac{\sin(\xi/2)}{\xi/2} \right)^2$$
by computing the Fourier transform of $\phi(t) = 1\{-1/2 \le t \le 1/2\}$, $t \in \mathbb{R}$, and relating ϕ to the triangle function θ.

8. Consider the function
$$\rho(\theta) = \sum_{j=0}^{\infty} \sigma_j^2 \cos(j\theta), \quad \theta \in [-\pi, \pi],$$
for $\sigma_j^2 = (\alpha + \beta j^{2p})^{-1}$ and $\alpha, \beta > 0$ (the generalised p-order model of Hobolth, Pedersen and Jensen). For which p is ρ the covariance function of a Gaussian random field X? For which p does X admit a continuous version?

9. Consider the spherical semi-variogram
$$\gamma(t) = \begin{cases} 0 & t = 0 \\ \alpha + \beta \left[\frac{3|t|}{2} - \frac{|t|^3}{2} \right] & 0 < |t| < 1 \\ \alpha + \beta & |t| \ge 1 \end{cases} \qquad t \in \mathbb{R}$$
for $\alpha, \beta > 0$. What are the nugget, sill and partial sill? Sketch the graph.

10. Let X be a zero mean random field from which two observations are available at $t_1 \neq t_2$. Moreover, suppose that
$$\begin{aligned} \mathrm{Cov}(X_{t_1}, X_{t_2}) &= \rho\sigma^2 \\ \mathrm{Cov}(X_{t_i}, X_{t_i}) &= \sigma^2, \quad i \in \{1, 2\}, \end{aligned}$$
for some known $\rho \in (-1, 1)$ and $\sigma^2 > 0$.

    - Give the general expression for the best linear predictor (kriging estimator) at $t_0 \notin \{t_1, t_2\}$.

- Specialise to the case where $\rho \neq 0$, $\text{Cov}(X_{t_0}, X_{t_1}) \neq 0$ and $\text{Cov}(X_{t_0}, X_{t_2}) = 0$.
- Specialise to the case where $\rho \neq 0$, $\text{Cov}(X_{t_0}, X_{t_1}) = 0$ and $\text{Cov}(X_{t_0}, X_{t_2}) = 0$.
- What does your estimator look like when $\rho = 0$?
- Calculate the mean squared prediction error for the above special cases.

11. Consider the linear model

$$X_t = m(t)'\beta + E_t, \quad t \in \mathbb{R}^d,$$

for some function $m : \mathbb{R}^d \to \mathbb{R}^p$, $\beta \in \mathbb{R}^p$ and zero mean Gaussian random field $(E_t)_{t \in \mathbb{R}^d}$.

- Propose a kriging estimator $\hat{X}_{t_0}$ based on observations $X_{t_1}, \ldots, X_{t_n}$ when m and β are known. What assumptions do you make regarding $(E_t)_t$?
- If β were unknown, how would you proceed?

12. Let X be a random field from which two observations are available at $t_1 \neq t_2$. Assume that

$$\mathbb{E}X_{t_1} = \mathbb{E}X_{t_2} = \mathbb{E}X_{t_0} = m$$

for some unknown $m \in \mathbb{R}$ and write

$$\begin{aligned} \text{Cov}(X_{t_1}, X_{t_2}) &= \rho\sigma^2 \\ \text{Cov}(X_{t_i}, X_{t_i}) &= \sigma^2, \quad i \in \{1, 2\}, \end{aligned}$$

for known $\rho \in (-1, 1)$ and $\sigma^2 > 0$.

- Give the general expression for the best linear predictor (kriging estimator) at $t_0 \notin \{t_1, t_2\}$.
- Specialise to the case where $\rho \neq 0$, $\text{Cov}(X_{t_0}, X_{t_1}) \neq 0$ and $\text{Cov}(X_{t_0}, X_{t_2}) = 0$.
- Specialise to the case where $\rho \neq 0$, $\text{Cov}(X_{t_0}, X_{t_1}) = 0$ and $\text{Cov}(X_{t_0}, X_{t_2}) = 0$.
- What does your estimator look like when $\rho = 0$?
- Calculate the mean squared prediction error and compare to that of simple kriging (cf. Exercise 10).

13. Let $X_{t_1}, \ldots, X_{t_n}$ be sampled from a zero mean random field $(X_t)_{t \in \mathbb{R}^d}$ at n locations $t_i \in \mathbb{R}^d$, $i = 1, \ldots, n$, and collected in the n-vector Z. Write $\Sigma = \text{Cov}(Z)$ and let $K = (K_i)_{i=1}^n$ be the $n \times 1$ vector with entries $K_i = \rho(t_i, t_0)$. If some eigenvalue of Σ is zero, show that K lies in the column space of Σ.

14. Consider the linear model

$$X_t = m(t)'\beta + E_t, \quad t \in \mathbb{R}^d,$$

for some given function $m : \mathbb{R}^d \to \mathbb{R}^p$, unknown parameter $\beta \in \mathbb{R}^p$ and zero mean random field $(E_t)_{t \in \mathbb{R}^d}$. Carry out the Euler–Lagrange optimisation to verify that the universal kriging predictor $\hat{X}_{t_0}$ of X_{t_0} based on observation of X_t at $t_1, \ldots, t_n$ has the form (2.15).

15. The `gstat` package contains a data set `coalash`. Fit a semi-variogram model to these data and carry out an appropriate kriging analysis with particular attention to trends in the east-west direction.

2.13 POINTERS TO THE LITERATURE

The mathematical theory of probability distributions defined as measures, that is, satisfying a set of axioms, dates back to the famous 1933 monograph by A.N. Kolmogoroff, which also contains the consistency theorem [1, Section III.4]. The first textbook on stochastic processes was published by J.L. Doob in 1953 [2]. We refer specifically to Chapter II.3 for a definition of Gaussian random fields and a proof of Proposition 2.1, and to Chapter II.8 for various concepts of stationarity. A current textbook is that by P. Billingsley [3]. In Chapter 7, he proves the consistency theorem and applies it to the finite dimensional distributions of a random field. Part I of the book by Adler and Taylor [4] may be consulted for a comprehensive overview of the theory of Gaussian random fields.

The Brownian motion, named in honour of the botanist R. Brown who studied the movements of particles in a fluid, seems to have been modelled mathematically by T.N. Thiele [5] and, independently, by L.J.-B.A. Bachelier [6]. The Ornstein–Uhlenbeck covariance function was introduced in [7], whilst Mandelbrot and Van Ness [8] introduced the fractional Brownian surface. The latter is an example of the wider class of intrinsic random functions [9].

Covariance functions are at the heart of geostatistics. For a survey of the state of the art one may consult, for example, Chapter 2 by M. Schlather in [10] or M.L. Stein's book [11]. In particular, Section 2.3 in [11] collects elementary properties of covariance functions, including Proposition 2.2. The Whittle–Matérn function is named after the pioneers B. Matérn (see [12], section 2.4) and P. Whittle [13]. Theorem 2.1 is due to S. Bochner and can be found in Section 8 of his 1933 paper [14]. The proof given here is due to H. Cramér [15]. For the relations between the spectral density and sample path properties, one may consult the early monograph by Cramér and Leadbetter [16], or the more recent textbooks by R.J. Adler [17], Adler and Taylor [4] or Rogers and Williams [18], for example. Proposition 2.3 is a spectral version of G. Matheron's turning bands method (Section 4 in [9]). On a practical note, the R-package `RandomFields` may be used to generate realisations.

The origins of kriging are traced in a survey paper [19] by N. Cressie who argues that L.S. Gandin [20] and G. Matheron [21, 22] independently discovered ordinary and simple kriging during the early 1960s. The Matheron estimator of the semi-variogram can be found in [21]. Universal kriging is also due to G. Matheron [23]. There are many other variations on kriging. For further details, including discussions on the merits and drawbacks, we refer the reader to the textbooks by Journel and Huijbregts [24], Diggle and Ribeiro [25], Chilès and Delfiner [26] or to the relevant parts of Cressie [28], Bivand, Pebesma and Gómez–Rubio [29] and the *Handbook of Spatial Statistics* [27]. Implementations of kriging methods are available in the R-packages `gstat`, `geoR`, `RandomFields` and `spatial`. Finally, the Bayes estimator is well known in statistical decision theory; see for example Chapter 4 in Lehmann and Casella's textbook in statistics [30].

REFERENCES

[1] A.N. Kolmogoroff (1933). Grundbegriffe der Wahrscheinlichkeitsrechnung. Reprinted in 1973 by Springer-Verlag.

[2] J.L. Doob (1953). *Stochastic Processes.* New York: John Wiley & Sons.

[3] P. Billingsley (2012). *Probability and Measure (anniversary edition).* Hoboken, New Jersey: John Wiley & Sons.

[4] R.J. Adler and J.E. Taylor (2007). *Random Fields and Geometry.* New York: Springer-Verlag.

[5] T.N. Thiele (1880). Sur la compensation de quelques erreurs quasi-systématiques par la méthode des moindres carrés. Reitzel.

[6] L.J.-B.A. Bachelier (1900). Théorie de la spéculation. PhD thesis, University of Paris.

[7] G.E. Uhlenbeck and L.S. Ornstein (1930). On the theory of Brownian motion. *Physical Review* 36(5):823–841.

[8] B. Mandelbrot and J.W. van Ness (1968). Fractional Brownian motions, fractional noises and applications. *SIAM Review* 10(4):422–437.

[9] G. Matheron (1973). The intrinsic random functions and their applications. *Advances in Applied Probability* 5(3):439–468.

[10] M. Schlather (2012). Construction of covariance functions and unconditional simulation of random fields. Chapter 2 in: Advances and challenges in space-time modelling of natural events. Springer Lecture Notes in Statistics 207.

[11] M.L. Stein (1999). *Interpolation of Spatial Data. Some Theory for Kriging.* New York: Springer-Verlag.

[12] B. Matérn (1986). *Spatial Variation (2nd edition).* Berlin: Springer-Verlag.

[13] P. Whittle (1962). Topographic correlation, power-law covariance functions, and diffusion. *Biometrika* 49(3/4):305–314.

[14] S. Bochner (1933). Monotone Funktionen, Stieltjessche Integrale und harmonische Analyse. *Mathematische Annalen* 108(1):378–410.

[15] H. Cramér (1939). On the representation of a function by certain Fourier integrals. *Transactions of the American Mathematical Society* 46(2):191–201.

[16] H. Cramér and M.R. Leadbetter (1967). *Stationary and Related Stochastic Processes. Sample Function Properties and Their Applications.* New York: John Wiley & Sons.

[17] R.J. Adler (1981). *The Geometry of Random Fields.* New York: John Wiley & Sons.

[18] L.C.G. Rogers and D. Williams (1994). *Diffusions, Markov Processes and Martingales. Volume 1: Foundations (2nd edition).* Chichester: John Wiley & Sons.

[19] N. Cressie (1990). The origins of kriging. *Mathematical Geology* 22(3):239–252.

[20] L.S. Gandin (1963). *Objective Analysis of Meteorological Fields.* Translated by Israel Program for Scientific Translations, 1965.

[21] G. Matheron (1962). Traité de geostatistique appliquée, Volume I. Memoires du Bureau de Recherches Géologiques et Miniéres no 14. Editions Technip.

[22] G. Matheron (1963). Traité de geostatistique appliquée, Volume II. Memoires du Bureau de Recherches Géologiques et Miniéres no 24. Editions Technip.

[23] G. Matheron (1969). Le krigeage universel. Cahiers du Centre de Morphologie Mathematique no 1.

[24] A.G. Journel and C.J. Huijbregts (1978). *Mining Geostatistics.* London: Academic Press.

[25] P.J. Diggle and P.J. Ribeiro Jr (2008). *Model-Based Geostatistics.* New York: Springer-Verlag.

[26] J.-P. Chilès and P. Delfiner (2012). *Geostatistics: Modeling Spatial Uncertainty (2nd edition).* Hoboken, New Jersey: John Wiley & Sons.

[27] A.E. Gelfand, P.J. Diggle, M. Fuentes and P. Guttorp, editors (2010). *Handbook of Spatial Statistics.* Boca Raton, Florida: Chapman & Hall/CRC.

[28] N.A.C. Cressie (2015). *Statistics for Spatial Data (revised edition).* New York: John Wiley & Sons.

[29] R.S. Bivand, E. Pebesma and V. Gómez–Rubio (2013). *Applied Spatial Data Analysis with R (2nd edition).* New York: Springer-Verlag.

[30] E.L. Lehmann and G. Casella (1998). *Theory of Point Estimation (2nd edition).* New York: Springer-Verlag.

CHAPTER 3

Models and inference for areal unit data

3.1 DISCRETE RANDOM FIELDS

In this chapter, we will study random field models with a discrete index set. Such models are useful when observations are collected over areal units such as pixels, census districts or tomographic bins. In contrast to the previous chapter, the aims are noise removal and smoothing rather than interpolation.

Mathematically speaking, the index set T of the random field X is finite. In statistical physics, T may be a collection of atoms and genuinely finite; more often, X_i represents an integral or average of the phenomenon of interest over some region represented by $i \in T$. Often, there is a natural adjacency relation or neighbourhood structure.

Definition 3.1 *Let $T \neq \emptyset$ be a finite collection of 'sites'. A* random field *X on T with values in L is a random vector $(X_i)_{i \in T}$ having L–valued components. If L is finite or countably infinite, the distribution of X is specified by the probability mass function*

$$\pi_X(x) = \mathbb{P}(X = x) = \mathbb{P}(X_i = x_i, i \in T), \quad x \in L^T.$$

Otherwise, we assume that $L \subseteq \mathbb{R}$ and that X is absolutely continuous with a joint probability density π_X.

An example with a finite label set L is the following.

Example 3.1 *Presence/absence data record 1 if a phenomenon of interest is observed in the region represented by $i \in T$ and 0 otherwise.*

Hence $L = \{0, 1\}$. *Write* $i \sim j$ *if the regions corresponding to* i *and* j *are adjacent. Then the* Ising *model is defined by the probability mass function*

$$\pi_X(x) \propto \exp\left[\alpha \sum_{i \in T} x_i + \beta \sum_{\{i,j\}: i \sim j} x_i x_j\right], \quad x \in L^T,$$

for constants $\alpha, \beta \in \mathbb{R}$. *The parameter* α *influences the prevalence. Indeed, if* $\beta = 0$, *in each region, the phenomenon of interest is observed with probability* $e^\alpha/(1 + e^\alpha)$ *independently of other regions. For* $\beta > 0$, *presence in a given region encourages presence in neighbouring regions, whereas for* $\beta < 0$ *such presence is discouraged. As an aside, the Ising model is also used in statistical physics to describe magnetisation, usually with the label set* $L = \{-1, +1\}$.

In the next example, the label set L is equal to $\mathbb{R}$.

Example 3.2 Conditional autoregression *(CAR) models can be defined by requiring the random field* X *to be multivariate normally distributed with mean zero and covariance matrix* $(I - B)^{-1}K$, *where* $K = diag(\kappa_i)$ *is a diagonal matrix with* $\kappa_i > 0$, $I - B$ *is non-singular and* $(I - B)^{-1}K$ *is symmetric and positive definite. The scale is fixed by assuming that the diagonal elements of* B *are zero.*

Usually the matrix B *is sparse; for instance* $B = \phi N$ *could be proportional to the* neighbourhood matrix N *defined by* $N_{ij} = 1\{i \sim j\}$ *for some symmetric neighbourhood relation* $\sim$ *on* T. *To ensure that* $b_{ii} = 0$, *the relation should be non-reflexive, that is* $i \not\sim i$ *for all* $i \in T$. *In the literature,* N *is also known as the* adjacency *or* contiguity *matrix.*

To verify that a matrix is positive definite, the Gershgorin disc theorem *is useful. It states that, for a symmetric matrix* A, *the conditions* $a_{ii} > 0$ *and* $a_{ii} > \sum_{j \neq i} |a_{ij}|$ *imply that* A *is positive definite. Applied to* $I - \phi N$, *a sufficient condition is that for each site,* $|\phi|$ *is smaller than the reciprocal of the number of neighbours of that site.*

Write X_A for the restriction of X to sites in the set $A \subset T$. In the case of finite L, conditional probabilities of the type

$$\pi_A(x_A \mid x_{T \setminus A}) = \mathbb{P}(X_A = x_A \mid X_{T \setminus A} = x_{T \setminus A})$$

are of interest. In the absolutely continuous case, π_A is defined as the conditional probability density, provided it exists.

An important special case is $A = \{i\}$, yielding the following definition. To improve readability, write $T \setminus i$ for the set $T \setminus \{i\}$.

Definition 3.2 *Let $T \neq \emptyset$ be a finite collection of sites. The local characteristics of a random field X on T with values in L are*

$$\pi_i(x_i \mid x_{T\setminus i}), \quad i \in T, x \in L^T,$$

whenever well-defined.

Example 3.3 *For the Ising model introduced in Example 3.1,*

$$\log \left[\frac{\pi_i(1 \mid x_{T\setminus i})}{\pi_i(0 \mid x_{T\setminus i})} \right] = \alpha + \beta \sum_{j \sim i} x_j.$$

Therefore, the Ising model is also known as (first-order) auto-logistic regression *and*

$$\pi_i(1 \mid x_{T\setminus i}) = \frac{\exp\left[\alpha + \beta \sum_{j\sim i} x_j\right]}{1 + \exp\left[\alpha + \beta \sum_{j\sim i} x_j\right]}.$$

It is interesting to note that $\pi_i(\cdot \mid x_{T\setminus i})$ depends only on values x_j for regions indexed by neighbours of i.

Example 3.4 *For the CAR model of Example 3.2, the local characteristics are Gaussian distributions with*

$$\begin{cases} \mathbb{E}(X_i \mid X_j, j \neq i) & = & \sum_{j\neq i} b_{ij} X_j \\ \mathrm{Var}(X_i \mid X_j, j \neq i) & = & \kappa_i \end{cases} \tag{3.1}$$

These expressions justify the name 'conditional autoregression'. In particular, if $b_{ij} = \phi N_{ij}$, (3.1) involves only the neighbours of site i. The result can be proved by basic but tedious matrix algebra. We will give a more elegant proof below.

For strictly positive distributions, the local characteristics determine the entire distribution. The proof relies on the following theorem.

Theorem 3.1 (Besag's factorisation theorem – Brook's lemma) *Let X be an L-valued random field on $T = \{1, \ldots, N\}$, $N \in \mathbb{N}$, such that $\pi_X(x) > 0$ for all $x \in L^T$. Then, for all $x, y \in L^T$,*

$$\frac{\pi_X(x)}{\pi_X(y)} = \prod_{i=1}^{N} \frac{\pi_i(x_i \mid x_1, \ldots, x_{i-1}, y_{i+1}, \ldots, y_N)}{\pi_i(y_i \mid x_1, \ldots, x_{i-1}, y_{i+1}, \ldots, y_N)}. \tag{3.2}$$

Proof: Due to the positivity assumption, one never divides by zero. Now,

$$\pi_X(x) = \frac{\pi_N(x_N \mid x_1, \dots, x_{N-1})}{\pi_N(y_N \mid x_1, \dots, x_{N-1})} \pi_X(x_1, \dots, x_{N-1}, y_N).$$

Similarly, $\pi_X(x_1, \dots, x_{N-1}, y_N)$ factorises as

$$\frac{\pi_{N-1}(x_{N-1} \mid x_1, \dots, x_{N-2}, y_N)}{\pi_{N-1}(y_{N-1} \mid x_1, \dots, x_{N-2}, y_N)} \pi_X(x_1, \dots, x_{N-2}, y_{N-1}, y_N).$$

The claim is seen to hold by iterating the above argument. □

On a cautionary note, the converse does not hold in the sense that it is not always possible to construct a joint distribution from arbitrarily chosen $\pi_i(\cdot|\cdot)$.

Corollary 3.1 *Let X be an L-valued random field on a finite collection $T \neq \emptyset$ of sites such that $\pi_X(x) > 0$ for all $x \in L^T$. Then the local characteristics determine the whole distribution, that is, if Y is a random field having the same local characteristics as X, necessarily $\pi_Y \equiv \pi_X$.*

Proof: Choose any element $a \in L$. Then, by Besag's factorisation theorem, $\pi_X(x)/\ \pi_X(a, \dots, a)$ is determined by the local characteristics. The distribution is obtained by normalisation. □

3.2 GAUSSIAN AUTOREGRESSION MODELS

Recall the following definition (cf. Example 3.2).

Definition 3.3 *Let $K = diag(\kappa_i)$ be a diagonal $N \times N$ matrix with $\kappa_i > 0$ and B an $N \times N$ matrix whose diagonal elements b_{ii} are zero. Then, provided $I - B$ is invertible and $(I-B)^{-1}K$ is positive definite, a random field X that is normally distributed with mean zero and covariance matrix $(I-B)^{-1}K$ is said to follow a* conditional autoregression *(CAR) model.*

The name is justified by the fact that if one specifies local characteristics as in (3.1), then relative to $(y_i)_{i=1,\dots,N} = 0$,

$$\frac{\pi_i(x_i|x_1, \dots, x_{i-1}, y_{i+1}, \dots, y_N)}{\pi_i(y_i|x_1, \dots, x_{i-1}, y_{i+1}, \dots, y_N)} = \frac{\exp\left[-\frac{1}{2\kappa_i}(x_i - \sum_{j<i} b_{ij}x_j)^2\right]}{\exp\left[-\frac{1}{2\kappa_i}(\sum_{j<i} b_{ij}x_j)^2\right]}$$

$$= \exp\left[-\frac{1}{2\kappa_i}(x_i^2 - 2x_i \sum_{j<i} b_{ij}x_j)\right],$$

cf. Besag's factorisation theorem, so the joint relative density

$$\frac{\pi_X(x)}{\pi_X(0)} = \exp\left[-\frac{1}{2}\sum_i \frac{x_i^2}{\kappa_i} + \sum_i \sum_{j<i} \frac{b_{ij}x_i x_j}{\kappa_i}\right]$$
$$= \exp\left[-\frac{1}{2}x'K^{-1}x + \frac{1}{2}x'K^{-1}Bx\right]$$

is well-defined and proportional to the density of a zero-mean normal distribution with covariance matrix $(I-B)^{-1}K$.

In matrix notation, define $E = (I-B)X$. Then E is normally distributed with mean zero and covariance matrix

$$(I-B)(I-B)^{-1}K(I-B)' = K(I-B)'.$$

Consequently,

$$X = BX + E$$

is an autoregression formula. Note, though, that the 'noise' field E may be spatially correlated.

It may feel more natural to assume independent noise, that is, to let E be normally distributed with diagonal covariance matrix $L = \text{diag}(\lambda_i) = (\lambda_i)_i$ with $\lambda_i > 0$ for $i = 1, \ldots, N$. In this case, the covariance matrix of $X = (I-B)^{-1}E$ is given by

$$(I-B)^{-1}L(I-B')^{-1}.$$

The resulting random field X is known as a *simultaneous autoregression* (SAR). Although both CAR and SAR are expressed in terms of an autoregression equation, and by Proposition 3.1 below any simultaneous autoregression model may be reformulated as a conditional autoregression, it is important to bear in mind that the interpretation of the b_{ij} in the two models is different!

Proposition 3.1 *Any SAR model can be written as a CAR model.*

Proof: Let L be an $N \times N$ positive definite diagonal matrix, B an $N \times N$ matrix such that $I - B$ is non-singular and $b_{ii} = 0$. Then

$(I-B)^{-1}L(I-B')^{-1}$ is well-defined, symmetric and positive definite. One needs to solve

$$(I-B)^{-1}L(I-B')^{-1} = (I-C)^{-1}K$$

for C and $K = \text{diag}(\kappa_i)$, or, equivalently,

$$(I-B')L^{-1}(I-B) = K^{-1}(I-C).$$

Setting $c_{ii} = 0$, it remains to solve for the scale factors κ_i. Indeed, writing λ_i for the i-th element on the diagonal of L, for all $i \in \{1, \dots, N\}$,

$$\frac{1}{\lambda_i} + \sum_{j=1}^{N} \frac{b_{ji}^2}{\lambda_j} = \frac{1}{\kappa_i},$$

and therefore $\kappa_i > 0$. □

There is a price to pay for the uncorrelated noise in SAR models. To see this, note that for a CAR model

$$\text{Cov}(E, X) = \mathbb{E}(EX') = \text{Cov}((I-B)X, X) = (I-B)(I-B)^{-1}K = K.$$

Consequently X_i and E_j are independent for $i \neq j$. For SAR models, such a remark does not necessarily hold. Indeed,

$$\text{Cov}(X, E) = \text{Cov}((I-B)^{-1}E, E) = (I-B)^{-1}L$$

may be non-diagonal.

To conclude this section, it is worth noticing that one would often like to define

$$\begin{cases} \mathbb{E}(X_i \mid X_j, j \neq i) & = \dfrac{\sum_{j \neq i} N_{ij} X_j}{\sum_{j \neq i} N_{ij}} \\ \text{Var}(X_i \mid X_j, j \neq i) & = \kappa_i \end{cases} \tag{3.3}$$

for N_{ij} as in Example 3.2. In other words, $b_{ij} = N_{ij} / \sum_{k \neq i} N_{ik}$. However, for such models $I - B$ may no longer be invertible due to the row sums being zero. Nevertheless, *intrinsic autoregression* models 'defined' by (3.3) are often used as 'prior distribution' in a hierarchical Bayesian model.

3.3 GIBBS STATES

The log probability mass function of the Ising model can be interpreted as a sum of contributions from single sites and pairs of sites. Breaking up a high-dimensional joint probability mass function in lower dimensional components in this way is often useful, both from a computational point of view and conceptually, for example in defining new models or in formalising the notion of interaction.

Definition 3.4 *Let $T \neq \emptyset$ be a finite collection of sites, L a subset of $\mathbb{R}$. An* interaction potential *is a collection $\{V_A : A \subseteq T\}$ of functions $V_A : L^T \to \mathbb{R}$ such that $V_\emptyset(\cdot) \equiv 0$ and $V_A(x)$ depends only on the restriction x_A of $x \in L^T$ to sites in A.*

The interaction potential V is said to be normalised with respect to *$a \in L$ if the property that $x_i = a$ for some $i \in A$ implies that $V_A(x) = 0$.*

A random field whose distribution is defined in terms of interaction potentials is known as a Gibbs state.

Definition 3.5 *Let X be an L-valued random field on a finite collection $T \neq \emptyset$ of sites and V an interaction potential. Then X is a* Gibbs state *with interaction potentials $V = \{V_A : A \subseteq T\}$, $V_A : L^T \to \mathbb{R}$, if*

$$\pi_X(x) = \frac{1}{Z} \exp\left[\sum_{A \subseteq T} V_A(x_A)\right], \quad x \in L^T. \tag{3.4}$$

The constant Z in (3.4) is called the *partition function* and is usually intractable, both analytically and numerically.

Example 3.5 *The auto-logistic regression model introduced in Example 3.1 is a Gibbs state with interaction potentials*

$$\begin{aligned} V_{\{i\}}(x) &= \alpha x_i \\ V_{\{i,j\}}(x) &= \begin{cases} \beta x_i x_j & \text{if } i \sim j \\ 0 & \text{else} \end{cases} \end{aligned}$$

and $V_A(x) = 0$ for sets A of cardinality larger than two.

Example 3.6 *Let X be multivariate normally distributed with mean vector μ and positive definite covariance matrix Σ and write $Q = \Sigma^{-1}$ for the precision matrix. Then, since*

$$\pi_X(x) \propto \exp\left[-\frac{1}{2}\sum_i\sum_j(x_i - \mu_i)Q_{ij}(x_j - \mu_j)\right],$$

X is a Gibbs state with interaction potentials

$$\begin{aligned} V_{\{i\}}(x) &= -Q_{ii}(x_i - \mu_i)^2/2 \\ V_{\{i,j\}}(x) &= -Q_{ij}(x_i - \mu_i)(x_j - \mu_j) \end{aligned} \tag{3.5}$$

upon recalling that Q, being a precision matrix, is symmetric. For sets A of cardinality larger than two, $V_A(x) = 0$.

In fact, any random field X such that $\pi_X(x) > 0$ for all x is a Gibbs state.

Theorem 3.2 *Let X be an L-valued random field on a finite collection $T \neq \emptyset$ of sites such that $\pi_X(x) > 0$ for all $x \in L^T$. Then X is a Gibbs state with respect to the canonical potential*

$$V_A(x) = \sum_{B\subseteq A}(-1)^{|A\setminus B|}\log \pi_X(x^B), \quad x \in L^T,$$

where $x_i^B = x_i$ for $i \in B$ and a prefixed value $a \in L$ otherwise. This is the unique normalised potential with respect to a. Moreover, for any element $i \in A$,

$$V_A(x) = \sum_{B\subseteq A}(-1)^{|A\setminus B|}\log \pi_i(x_i^B \mid x_{T\setminus i}^B), \quad x \in L^T. \tag{3.6}$$

The proof relies on the following combinatorial identity.

Theorem 3.3 (Möbius inversion formula) *If T is a finite set and $f, g : P(T) \to \mathbb{R}$ are two functions defined on the power set $P(T)$ of T, then*

$$f(A) = \sum_{B\subseteq A} g(B) \text{ for all } A \subseteq T \tag{3.7}$$

if and only if

$$g(A) = \sum_{B\subseteq A}(-1)^{|A\setminus B|}f(B) \text{ for all } A \subseteq T. \tag{3.8}$$

In particular, there is only one way to represent a given function f in the form (3.7).

Proof: First suppose g is fixed and define $f(A) = \sum_{B\subseteq A} g(B)$ for $A \subseteq T$. Then

$$\begin{aligned}\sum_{B\subseteq A}(-1)^{|A\setminus B|}f(B) &= \sum_{B\subseteq A}(-1)^{|A\setminus B|}\left[\sum_{C\subseteq B} g(C)\right]\\ &= \sum_{B\subseteq A}\left[\sum_{C\subseteq B}(-1)^{|A\setminus C|}(-1)^{-|B\setminus C|}g(C)\right]\\ &= \sum_{C\subseteq A}\left[\sum_{B:C\subseteq B\subseteq A}(-1)^{|B\setminus C|}\right](-1)^{|A\setminus C|}g(C) = g(A).\end{aligned}$$

For the last equality, note that the inner sum

$$\sum_{k=0}^{|A\setminus C|}\binom{|A\setminus C|}{k}(-1)^k$$

equals 0, unless $A = C$.

Conversely, if f is fixed and $g(A) = \sum_{B\subseteq A}(-1)^{|A\setminus B|}f(B)$, then

$$\begin{aligned}\sum_{B\subseteq A} g(B) &= \sum_{B\subseteq A}\left[\sum_{C\subseteq B}(-1)^{|B\setminus C|}f(C)\right]\\ &= \sum_{C\subseteq A}\left[\sum_{B:C\subseteq B\subseteq A}(-1)^{|B\setminus C|}\right]f(C) = f(A)\end{aligned}$$

by similar arguments. □

We are now ready to give the proof of Theorem 3.2.

Proof: Fix $x \in L^T$. Since $\pi_X(x) > 0$ we can set, for $A \subseteq T$, $f_x(A) = \log \pi_X(x^A)$. Define the interaction potential $V_A : L^T \to \mathbb{R}$ by

$$V_A(x) = \sum_{B\subseteq A}(-1)^{|A\setminus B|}f_x(B), \quad x \in L^T.$$

By the Möbius inversion formula

$$f_x(T) = \sum_{A\subseteq T} V_A(x)$$

or, equivalently,

$$\pi_X(x) = \exp[f_x(T)] = \exp\left[\sum_{A\subseteq T} V_A(x)\right].$$

Now letting x vary, this identity shows that π_X is a Gibbs state with interaction potential $\{V_A : A \subseteq T\}$ upon incorporating $V_\emptyset$ into the partition function if necessary.

To prove that the interaction potential is normalised, choose any $i \in A$. Then

$$\begin{aligned} V_A(x) &= \sum_{i \notin B \subseteq A} (-1)^{|A \setminus B|} \log \pi_X(x^B) + \sum_{i \in B \subseteq A} (-1)^{|A \setminus B|} \log \pi_X(x^B) \\ &= \sum_{B \subseteq A \setminus \{i\}} (-1)^{|A \setminus B|} \log \pi_X(x^B) - \sum_{B \subseteq A \setminus \{i\}} (-1)^{|A \setminus B|} \log \pi_X(x^{B \cup \{i\}}) \\ &= \sum_{B \subseteq A \setminus \{i\}} (-1)^{|A \setminus B|} \left[\log \pi_X(x^B) - \log \pi_X(x^{B \cup \{i\}}) \right]. \end{aligned}$$

If $x_i = a$, then $x^B = x^{B \cup \{i\}}$ for all $B \subseteq A \setminus \{i\}$ and therefore $V_A(x) = 0$. We conclude that the interaction potential is normalised with respect to a. Moreover $x^B_{T \setminus i} = x^{B \cup \{i\}}_{T \setminus i}$ for all $B \subseteq A \setminus \{i\}$. Therefore

$$\frac{\pi_X(x^B)}{\pi_X(x^{B \cup \{i\}})} = \frac{\pi_i(x_i^B \mid x^B_{T \setminus i})}{\pi_i(x_i^{B \cup \{i\}} \mid x^{B \cup \{i\}}_{T \setminus i})}$$

and the expression in terms of the local characteristics follows.

Next suppose π_X is a Gibbs state with respect to normalised potentials U_A. We will show that $U_A \equiv V_A$. Write a_T for the realisation with only a–labels and fix $x \in L^T$. Define the set function $h_x(A)$ by

$$h_x(A) = \log \frac{\pi_X(x^A)}{\pi_X(a_T)} = \sum_{B \subseteq A} [U_B(x) - U_B(a_T)] = \sum_{B \subseteq A} U_B(x).$$

The last equation uses the assumption that the interaction potential U is normalised. By Theorem 3.3, for all $A \neq \emptyset$,

$$U_A(x) = \sum_{B \subseteq A} (-1)^{|A \setminus B|} h_x(B) = V_A(x) - \log \pi_X(a_T) \sum_{B \subseteq A} (-1)^{|A \setminus B|} = V_A(x).$$

Finally, since $V_A(x) = U_A(x) = 0$ by assumption when $A = \emptyset$, the proof is complete. □

Example 3.7 *Consider a multivariate normally distributed random field X with precision matrix Q as in Example 3.6. If the mean vector is constant, that is, $\mu_i \equiv \mu_0$ for all $i \in T$, the natural potential (3.5)* *is clearly normalised with respect to* μ_0. *For inhomogeneous models, one may normalise with respect to zero. Then for* $x \in \mathbb{R}^T$, *using the notation of Theorem 3.2, by definition* $V_\emptyset(x) = 0$,

$$V_{\{i\}}(x) = \log \pi_X(x^{\{i\}}) - \log \pi_X(0) = -\frac{1}{2}x_i^2 Q_{ii} + x_i \sum_{j \in T} \mu_j Q_{ij}$$

and, for $i \neq j$,

$$V_{\{i,j\}}(x) = \log \pi_X(x^{\{i,j\}}) - \log \pi_X(x^{\{i\}}) - \log \pi_X(x^{\{j\}}) + \log \pi_X(0)$$
$$= -x_i x_j Q_{ij}.$$

Note that $V_{\{i,j\}}$ *is equal to zero when* Q_{ij} *is.*

3.4 MARKOV RANDOM FIELDS

Suppose that the set of sites T is equipped with a symmetric relation $\sim$. If the interaction potentials $V_A(x)$ vanish except when A is a singleton or consists of a pair $\{i, j\}$ of $\sim$-related sites, as in Example 3.5, the local characteristics $\pi_i(\cdot \mid x_{T \setminus i})$ depend only on the values x_j at sites $j \in T \setminus i$ that are $\sim$-neighbours of i. More generally, one may formulate the following definition.

Definition 3.6 *Let* $\sim$ *be a symmetric relation on the finite set* $T \neq \emptyset$ *and define the boundary of* $A \subseteq T$ *by* $\partial A = \{s \in T \setminus A : s \sim t$ *for some* $t \in A\}$. *A random field* X *on* T *is a* Markov random field *with respect to* $\sim$ *if*

$$\pi_i(x_i \mid x_{T \setminus i}) = \pi_X(X_i = x_i \mid X_{\partial i} = x_{\partial i})$$

whenever $\pi_X(x_{T \setminus i}) > 0$, *where* π_X *denotes the probability mass function of* X *if* X *takes values in a finite or countable set* L *and a probability density if* X *is absolutely continuous on* $L \subseteq \mathbb{R}$.

In other words, for a Markov random field, the conditional distribution of the label at some site i given those at all other sites depends only on the labels at neighbours of site i.

Definition 3.7 *Let* $T \neq \emptyset$ *be a finite collection of sites. Let* $\sim$ *be a symmetric relation on* T. *A* clique, *with respect to* $\sim$, *is a subset* $C \subset T$ *for which* $s \sim t$ *for all* $s \neq t \in C$. *The family of all cliques is denoted by* $\mathcal{C}$.

Note that, by default, singletons and the empty set are cliques.

Theorem 3.4 (Hammersley–Clifford) *Let X be an L-valued random field on a finite collection $T \neq \emptyset$ of sites such that $\pi_X(x) > 0$ for all $x \in L^T$. Let $\sim$ be a symmetric relation on T. Then X is a Markov random field with respect to $\sim$ if and only if*

$$\pi_X(x) = \prod_{C \in \mathcal{C}} \varphi_C(x_C) \tag{3.9}$$

for some interaction functions $\varphi_C : L^C \to \mathbb{R}^+$ defined on cliques $C \in \mathcal{C}$.

In other words, the distribution of any Markov random field such that π_X is positive can be expressed in terms of interactions between neighbours. Moreover, by the positivity condition, equation (3.9) can be rewritten as

$$\pi_X(x) = \exp\left[\sum_{C \in \mathcal{C}} \log \varphi_C(x_C)\right],$$

so X is a Gibbs state with non-zero interaction potentials $\log \varphi_C$ restricted to cliques.

Proof: First we show that any distribution of the form (3.9) has the Markov property. Suppose that L is countable and write $T_i^a x$ for the configuration in which x_i is replaced by a. Then

$$\pi_i(x_i \mid x_{T\setminus i}) = \frac{\prod_{C \ni i} \varphi_C(x_C)}{\sum_{a \in L} \left[\prod_{C \ni i} \varphi_C(T_i^a x_C)\right]}$$

and the right-hand side depends only on x_i and $x_{\partial i}$. In the absolutely continuous case, replace the sum over L by an integral.

Conversely suppose that X is a Markov random field with $\pi_X > 0$. By Theorem 3.2, X is a Gibbs state with canonical potential (3.6). We claim that $V_A(x) = 0$ for all $A \notin \mathcal{C}$. Indeed, if $A \subseteq T$ is *not* a clique, there are two distinct sites $s, t \in A$ with $s \not\sim t$. Then

$$V_A(x) = \sum_{B \subseteq A} (-1)^{|A \setminus B|} \log \pi_s(x_s^B \mid x_{T\setminus s}^B),$$

which can be written as the sum of four terms:

$$\sum_{B \subseteq A \setminus \{s,t\}} (-1)^{|A \setminus B|} \log \pi_s(x_s^B \mid x_{T\setminus s}^B)$$
$$+ \sum_{B \subseteq A \setminus \{s,t\}} (-1)^{|A \setminus (B \cup \{s\})|} \log \pi_s(x_s^{B \cup \{s\}} \mid x_{T\setminus s}^{B \cup \{s\}})$$

$$+ \sum_{B \subseteq A \setminus \{s,t\}} (-1)^{|A \setminus (B \cup \{t\})|} \log \pi_s(x_s^{B \cup \{t\}} \mid x_{T \setminus s}^{B \cup \{t\}})$$
$$+ \sum_{B \subseteq A \setminus \{s,t\}} (-1)^{|A \setminus (B \cup \{s,t\})|} \log \pi_s(x_s^{B \cup \{s,t\}} \mid x_{T \setminus s}^{B \cup \{s,t\}}).$$

Rearranging terms, it follows that

$$V_A(x) = \sum_{B \subseteq A \setminus \{s,t\}} (-1)^{|A \setminus B|} \log \left[\frac{\pi_s(x_s^B \mid x_{T \setminus s}^B) \pi_s(x_s^{B \cup \{s,t\}} \mid x_{T \setminus s}^{B \cup \{s,t\}})}{\pi_s(x_s^{B \cup \{t\}} \mid x_{T \setminus s}^{B \cup \{t\}}) \pi_s(x_s^{B \cup \{s\}} \mid x_{T \setminus s}^{B \cup \{s\}})} \right].$$

Since $s \not\sim t$, $\pi_s(x_s^B \mid x_{T \setminus s}^B) = \pi_s(x_s^{B \cup \{t\}} \mid x_{T \setminus s}^{B \cup \{t\}})$ and $\pi_s(x_s^{B \cup \{s\}} \mid x_{T \setminus s}^{B \cup \{s\}}) = \pi_s(x_s^{B \cup \{s,t\}} \mid x_{T \setminus s}^{B \cup \{s,t\}})$ and hence $V_A(x) = 0$. Thus the only nonzero interaction potentials are for cliques and (3.9) holds. □

Example 3.8 *For the auto-logistic regression model, the interaction functions are*

$$\begin{aligned} \varphi_\emptyset &= 1/Z \\ \varphi_{\{i\}}(x_i) &= \exp(\alpha x_i) \\ \varphi_{\{i,j\}}(x_{\{i,j\}}) &= \begin{cases} \exp(\beta x_i x_j) & \text{if } i \sim j \\ 1 & \text{else} \end{cases} \end{aligned}$$

All higher order interaction functions take the constant value 1.

The positivity condition is needed, as demonstrated by the following example.

Example 3.9 *Let T be a 2×2 grid equipped with the relation $\sim$ under which horizontally or vertically adjacent sites are related. Order the sites in row major order. Set $L = \{0, 1\}$ and let X be an L-valued random field on T such that*

$$\pi_X(0,0,0,0) = \pi_X(0,1,0,0) = \pi_X(0,1,0,1) = \pi_X(0,1,1,1)$$

$$= \pi_X(1,1,1,1) = \pi_X(1,0,1,1) = \pi_X(1,0,1,0) = \pi_X(1,0,0,0) = 1/8$$

and zero otherwise. Then X is Markov, since, for example,

$$\pi_1(1 \mid 0,1,0) = 1 = \pi_1(1 \mid 0,1,1) = \mathbb{P}(X_1 = 1 \mid X_2 = 0, X_3 = 1)$$

or

$$\pi_1(1 \mid 0,0,0) = 1/2 = \mathbb{P}(X_1 = 1 \mid X_2 = 0, X_3 = 0).$$

It is left to the reader to verify the remaining cases. The probability mass function π_X cannot be factorised over cliques. To see this, suppose that it is. Then, as $\pi_X(0,1,1,0) = 0$, the product

$$\varphi_\emptyset \varphi_{\{1\}}(0)\varphi_{\{2\}}(1)\varphi_{\{3\}}(1)\varphi_{\{4\}}(0)\varphi_{\{1,2\}}(0,1)\varphi_{\{1,3\}}(0,1)\varphi_{\{2,4\}}(1,0)\varphi_{\{3,4\}}(1,0)$$

must also be zero. However, all terms are positive, occurring as they do in the factorisation of some $x \in L^T$ for which $\pi_X(x) > 0$, and one arrives at a contradiction.

Corollary 3.2 *Let X be an L-valued random field on a finite collection $T \neq \emptyset$ of sites such that $\pi_X(x) > 0$ for all $x \in L^T$. Then the* spatial Markov property

$$\pi(X_A = x_A \mid X_{T\setminus A} = x_{T\setminus A}) = \pi(X_A = x_A \mid X_{\partial A} = x_{\partial A})$$

holds for all nonempty sets $A \subseteq T$.

Proof: Write $T_A^y x$ for the configuration in which x_A is replaced by y ($x_A, y \in L^A$) on the set $A \subseteq T$. By the Hammersley-Clifford theorem,

$$\pi(X_A = x_A \mid X_{T\setminus A} = x_{T\setminus A}) = \frac{\prod_{A\cap C\neq\emptyset} \varphi_C(x_C)}{\sum_{y\in L^A} \prod_{A\cap C\neq\emptyset} \varphi_C((T_A^y x)_C)}$$

depends only on $x_{\partial A}$. □

3.5 INFERENCE FOR AREAL UNIT MODELS

Suppose that some spatial variable of interest is observed in a finite set of areal units and that the dependence of the variable on covariates is expressed through a design matrix X and parameter vector $\beta \in \mathbb{R}^p$.

In an autoregression context, for example in a SAR model, this idea is formalised as follows. Write $Y = (Y_1, \ldots, Y_n)'$ for the random field. If $\mathbb{E}Y = X\beta$ for the $n \times p$ design matrix X and $\beta \in \mathbb{R}^p$, the simultaneous auto-regression equation for $Y - X\beta$ reads

$$Y = BY + (I - B)X\beta + E$$

where B is a known $n \times n$ matrix with $b_{ii} = 0$, for example proportional to the neighbourhood matrix, and E is n-variate Gaussian noise. For simplicity, assume that $\text{Cov}(E) = \sigma^2 I$. As before, we assume that $(I - B)$ is non-singular, in which case the covariance matrix of Y is $\sigma^2(I - B)^{-1}(I - B')^{-1}$.

Inference regarding the parameters β and σ^2 can be based on the log likelihood $L(\beta, \sigma^2; Y)$, which reads

$$-\frac{1}{2\sigma^2}(Y - X\beta)'(I - B)'(I - B)(Y - X\beta) + \log \det(\sigma^2(I - B)^{-1}(I - B')^{-1})^{-1/2}.$$

Since the determinant is equal to $\sigma^{2n} \det(I - B)^{-2}$, upon deletion of terms that do not depend on the parameters σ^2 and β, the log likelihood reduces to

$$L(\beta, \sigma^2; Y) = -\frac{1}{2\sigma^2}(Y - X\beta)'(I - B)'(I - B)(Y - X\beta) - n \log \sigma.$$

Therefore, the score equations are

$$\begin{aligned} 0 &= \frac{-n}{\sigma} + \frac{1}{\sigma^3}(Y - X\beta)'(I - B)'(I - B)(Y - X\beta); \\ 0 &= X'(I - B)'(I - B)(Y - X\beta), \end{aligned}$$

which can be solved explicitly. Indeed

$$\hat{\sigma}^2 = \frac{1}{n}(Y - X\hat{\beta})'(I - B)'(I - B)(Y - X\hat{\beta})$$

is the usual population variance and

$$\hat{\beta} = (X'(I - B)'(I - B)X)^{-1}X'(I - B)'(I - B)Y,$$

provided $X'(I - B)'(I - B)X$ is non-singular. Since Y is Gaussian, so is $\hat{\beta}$. Moreover,

$$\begin{aligned} \mathbb{E}\hat{\beta} &= \beta; \\ \text{Cov}(\hat{\beta}) &= \sigma^2(X'(I - B)'(I - B)X)^{-1}. \end{aligned}$$

As for $n\hat{\sigma}^2$, it is of quadratic form $U'U = \sum_{j=1}^n U_j^2$. The random vector $U = (I - B)(Y - X\hat{\beta})$ is normally distributed with mean vector zero. In general, however, the U_j are not independent.

As a second example, consider the auto-logistic regression model

$$\pi_Y(y) = \frac{1}{Z(\alpha, \theta)} \exp\left[\sum_{i=1}^{n} \alpha_i y_i + \theta \sum_{i \sim j; i<j} y_i y_j\right]$$

for $\theta \in \mathbb{R}$, $\alpha = X\beta$, $\beta \in \mathbb{R}^p$ and $y = (y_1, \dots, y_n) \in L^T$. The log likelihood for the parameters β and θ evaluated at y is

$$L(\beta, \theta; y) = -\log Z(X\beta, \theta) + \sum_{i=1}^{n} \alpha_i y_i + \theta \sum_{i \sim j; i<j} y_i y_j.$$

Since the computational effort to calculate

$$Z(X\beta, \theta) = \sum_{y \in L^T} \exp\left[\sum_{i=1}^{n} (X\beta)_i y_i + \theta \sum_{i \sim j; i<j} y_i y_j\right]$$

becomes prohibitive as the cardinality, n, of T gets large, alternative methods have been proposed to estimate β and θ. Perhaps the simplest one is to consider the *log pseudo-likelihood* function

$$PL(\beta, \theta; y) = \sum_{i=1}^{n} \log \pi_i(y_i \mid y_{T \setminus i})$$

and optimise it over β and θ. For the auto-logistic regression model,

$$\log \frac{\pi_i(1 \mid y_{T \setminus i})}{1 - \pi_i(1 \mid y_{T \setminus i})} = \alpha_i + \theta \sum_{j \sim i} y_j, \quad y \in L^T,$$

so the log pseudo-likelihood is given by

$$PL(\beta, \theta; y) = \sum_{i=1}^{n} y_i(\alpha_i + \theta \sum_{j \sim i} y_j) - \sum_{i=1}^{n} \log\left[1 + \exp(\alpha_i + \theta \sum_{j \sim i} y_j)\right].$$

It does not depend on the normalising constant $Z(X\beta, \theta)$ and can be optimised numerically.

Another approach is to consider, for $y \in L^T$, the ratio

$$\frac{\pi_Y(y; \beta, \theta)}{\pi_Y(y; \beta_0, \theta_0)} = \frac{Z(\beta_0, \theta_0)}{Z(\beta, \theta)} \frac{\exp\left[\sum_{i=1}^{n} y_i (X\beta)_i + \theta \sum_{i \sim j; i<j} y_i y_j\right]}{\exp\left[\sum_{i=1}^{n} y_i (X\beta_0)_i + \theta_0 \sum_{i \sim j; i<j} y_i y_j\right]}$$

with respect to some fixed reference parameter values β_0 and θ_0. A crucial observation is that the ratio of partition functions can be written as

$$\frac{Z(\beta,\theta)}{Z(\beta_0,\theta_0)} = \mathbb{E}_{\beta_0,\theta_0}\left[\frac{\exp\left[\sum_{i=1}^n Y_i(X\beta)_i + \theta\sum_{i\sim j;i<j} Y_iY_j\right]}{\exp\left[\sum_{i=1}^n Y_i(X\beta_0)_i + \theta_0\sum_{i\sim j;i<j} Y_iY_j\right]}\right],$$

where $\mathbb{E}_{\beta_0,\theta_0}$ denotes the expectation of the random field Y having probability distribution π_Y with parameters β_0 and θ_0. Therefore, the ratio of normalising constants can be approximated by an empirical average over a sample from the auto-logistic regression model under the reference parameters β_0 and θ_0. We shall discuss in Section 3.6 how to generate such a sample.

The auto-logistic regression model is an exponential family. For such models, under mild conditions, maximum likelihood estimators exist.

Theorem 3.5 *Let Y be an L-valued random field on a finite collection $T \neq \emptyset$ of sites whose probability mass function or joint probability density is of the form*

$$\pi_Y(y) = \frac{1}{Z(\theta)}\exp\left[\theta' S(y)\right], \quad y \in L^T,$$

for some function $S : L^T \to \mathbb{R}^p$, the sufficient statistic, and parameter $\theta \in \mathbb{R}^p$. Provided the moments of the random variable $S(Y)$ exist up to second order, the log likelihood function $L(\theta; y)$ is twice differentiable with gradient

$$S(y) - \mathbb{E}_\theta S(Y)$$

and non-positive definite Hessian $-\mathrm{Cov}_\theta S(Y)$.

Proof: For the realisation $y \in L^T$ the log likelihood function

$$L(\theta; y) = -\log Z(\theta) + \theta' S(y)$$

is differentiable with gradient

$$\nabla L(\theta; y) = S(y) - \frac{1}{Z(\theta)}\nabla Z(\theta).$$

Since $Z(\theta) = \sum_{y\in L^T}\exp\left[\theta' S(y)\right]$, its gradient can be written as

$$\nabla Z(\theta) = \sum_{y\in L^T} S(y)\exp\left[\theta' S(y)\right],$$

from which the expression for the gradient follows. In the absolutely continous case, the sum is replaced by an integral and the dominated convergence theorem is invoked to change the order of integration and differentiation.

To calculate the Hessian, note that

$$\nabla^2 Z(\theta) = \sum_{y \in L^T} S(y) S(y)' \exp\left[\theta' S(y)\right],$$

so

$$\nabla^2 L(\theta; y) = -\frac{1}{Z(\theta)} \nabla^2 Z(\theta) + \frac{1}{Z(\theta)^2} \nabla Z(\theta)(\nabla Z(\theta))' = -\mathrm{Cov}_\theta S(Y),$$

the negative of a covariance matrix and therefore non-positive definite. □

The expectation $\mathbb{E}_\theta S(Y)$ and covariance matrix $\mathrm{Cov}_\theta S(Y)$ can be estimated by their Monte Carlo approximations. For the log pseudo-likelihood function, Theorem 3.5 applies site-wise because the local characteristics of an exponential family are exponential families themselves.

Little is known about the precision of maximum likelihood estimators and their approximations. One would like to have a central limit theorem to form the basis of asymptotic confidence intervals. A complication is that when T grows to, say, $\mathbb{Z}^d$, there may not be a unique limiting random field defined on $\mathbb{Z}^d$ whose conditional specification on T coincides with π_Y. Similarly, there may not exist a scaling function so that the rescaled maximum likelihood estimator tends to a normal distribution. Furthermore, in Monte Carlo maximum likelihood estimation, the approximation error must be taken into account, but this error can be controlled by the user and is usually negligable. For the pseudo-likelihood method, under rather mild conditions, large deviation techniques may be used to prove a central limit theorem. In general, though, the asymptotic variance is intractable and must be estimated, for instance using parametric bootstrap ideas.

The maximum likelihood estimator, or its Monte Carlo approximation, may be used to test whether the observations depend significantly on some covariate. Indeed, the likelihood ratio test statistic for covariate i is defined as

$$\Lambda(Y_1, \ldots, Y_n) = \frac{\sup\{\pi_Y(Y_1, \ldots, Y_n; \beta, \theta) : \beta_i = 0\}}{\pi_Y(Y_1, \ldots, Y_n; \hat{\beta}, \hat{\theta})}.$$

Under the null hypothesis of no influence of the i-th covariate, i.e. $\beta_i = 0$, the transformed likelihood ratio test statistic $-2 \log \Lambda(Y_1, \ldots, Y_n)$ is approximately χ^2-distributed with one degree of freedom.

3.6 MARKOV CHAIN MONTE CARLO SIMULATION

The Monte Carlo maximum likelihood estimation method requires samples from the model of interest. In this section, we shall describe how such samples may be obtained. The idea is to run a Markov chain with the model of interest as its limit distribution. If the chain is run for a sufficiently long time and sub-sampled, we obtain an approximate sample from the model of interest. There are many ways to define such a Markov chain. Here, we will describe a flexible strategy that is widely used and give sufficient conditions for convergence.

Recall that a sequence $M_0, M_1, \ldots$ of random variables is a *Markov chain* with transition kernel $p(\cdot, \cdot)$ if

$$\mathbb{P}(M_t \in A_t; M_{t-1} \in A_{t-1}; \ldots; M_1 \in A_1 \mid M_0 = m_0) =$$

$$\int_{A_1} \cdots \int_{A_{t-1}} \int_{A_t} p(m_0, m_1) \cdots p(m_{t-2}, m_{t-1}) p(m_{t-1}, m_t) dm_1 \cdots dm_{t-1} dm_t$$

for all $t \in \mathbb{N}$ and all measurable $A_i \subseteq \Omega$, $i = 1, \ldots, t$. Note that the fixed starting state m_0 may be replaced by any probability distribution on Ω. For countable state spaces, the integral is replaced by a sum.

For random fields X, the joint distribution π_X may be difficult to handle but the local characteristics $\pi_i(x_i \mid x_{T \setminus i})$ are easy to work with. It therefore makes sense to define transitions by changing the components X_i one at a time. This idea is implemented by the *Metropolis–Hastings algorithm* that runs as follows. Suppose that the current state is $M_t = x \in L^T$. Then

- sample a site $i \in T$ and a new label $l \in L$ to yield state

$$y = (y_j)_{j \in T} = \begin{cases} y_j = l, & j = i; \\ y_j = x_j, & j \neq i, \end{cases}$$

  according to some probability density or mass function $q(x, y)$;

- accept the proposal with probability

$$A(x, y) = \begin{cases} 1 & \text{if } \pi_X(y) q(y, x) \geq \pi_X(x) q(x, y); \\ \frac{\pi_X(y) q(y, x)}{\pi_X(x) q(x, y)} & \text{otherwise.} \end{cases}$$

Note that the acceptance probabilities $A(x, y)$ depend on the ratio

$$\frac{\pi_X(y)}{\pi_X(x)} = \frac{\pi_i(l \mid x_{T\setminus i})}{\pi_i(x_i \mid x_{T\setminus i})}$$

only. In particular, any normalising constants cancel out. The transition kernel is obtained by combining the proposal and acceptance probabilities. In particular, $p(x, y) = q(x, y)A(x, y)$ for $x \neq y$.

Proposition 3.2 *Let X be an L-valued random field on a finite collection $T \neq \emptyset$ of sites. Then the Metropolis–Hastings algorithm satisfies the following properties:*

- *'detailed balance'*

$$\pi_X(x)p(x, y) = \pi_X(y)p(y, x);$$

- *π_X is an* invariant measure, *that is, for all measurable $A \subseteq L^T$,*

$$\begin{aligned}\pi_X(X \in A) &= \int \mathbb{P}(M_1 \in A \mid M_0 = x)\pi_X(x)dx \quad (L = \mathbb{R}); \\ &= \sum_x \mathbb{P}(M_1 \in A \mid M_0 = x)\pi_X(x) \quad (L \textit{ countable}).\end{aligned}$$

Proof: Without loss of generality, assume that $x \neq y$ and $\pi_X(x)q(x, y) < \pi_X(y)q(y, x)$. Then

$$\begin{aligned}\pi_X(x)p(x, y) &= \pi_X(x)q(x, y) \times 1 \\ &= \frac{\pi_X(x)q(x, y)}{\pi_X(y)q(y, x)}\pi_X(y)q(y, x) \\ &= A(y, x)\pi_X(y)q(y, x) = \pi_X(y)p(y, x).\end{aligned}$$

Invariance is a consequence of detailed balance. Indeed, for example in the absolutely continuous case,

$$\int \mathbb{P}(M_1 \in A \mid M_0 = x)\pi_X(x)dx = \int \left(\int_A p(x, y)\pi_X(x)dy \right) dx =$$

$$\int \left(\int_A p(y, x)\pi_X(y)dy \right) dx = \int_A \pi_X(y) \left(\int p(y, x)dx \right) dy = \int_A \pi_X(y)dy.$$

□

To study the convergence of the Metropolis–Hastings algorithm, recall the following key definitions from Markov chain theory.

Definition 3.8 *A Markov chain $(M_t)_{t \in \mathbb{N}_0}$ on a countable state space Ω is* irreducible *if for all $x, y \in \Omega$ there exists some $t \in \mathbb{N}$ such that $\mathbb{P}(M_t = y \mid M_0 = x) > 0$.*

*A Markov chain $(M_t)_{t \in \mathbb{N}_0}$ with state space $\Omega = \mathbb{R}^T$ is π_X-*irreducible *if for all $x \in \Omega$ and all Borel sets $A \subset \mathbb{R}^T$ for which $\pi_X(A) > 0$ there exists some $t \in \mathbb{N}$ such that $\mathbb{P}(M_t \in A \mid M_0 = x) > 0$.*

The restriction to sets with positive probability is needed in the case that $\Omega = \mathbb{R}^T$, since in general the probability of returning to a single state will be zero. For π_X-irreducible Markov chains, it is also possible to define a concept of periodicity.

Definition 3.9 *A π_X-irreducible Markov chain $(M_t)_{t \in \mathbb{N}_0}$ is* aperiodic *if there is no partition into non-empty measurable sets $B_0, \ldots, B_{r-1}$, $r \geq 2$, such that for all $t \in \mathbb{N}$, $\mathbb{P}(M_t \in B_{t \bmod r} \mid M_0 = x \in B_0) = 1$ and the union of $B_0, \ldots, B_{r-1}$ has π_X-mass one.*

We then have the following result.

Theorem 3.6 *(***Fundamental convergence theorem***) If π_X is an invariant probability measure for a Markov chain $(M_t)_{t \in \mathbb{N}_0}$ that is π_X-irreducible and aperiodic, then M_t converges to π_X in total variation from π_X-almost all initial states, that is,*

$$\lim_{t \to \infty} \sup_A |\mathbb{P}(M_t \in A \mid M_0 = x) - \pi_X(A)| = 0$$

for π_X-almost all x. The supremum is taken over all measurable sets.

Aperiodicity and irreducibility for the Metropolis–Hastings chain are inherited from those of the proposal distribution in the following sense.

Theorem 3.7 *Let X be an L-valued random field on a finite collection $T \neq \emptyset$ of sites and $(M_t)_{t \in \mathbb{N}_0}$ a Metropolis–Hastings chain on $D_\pi = \{x \in L^T : \pi_X(x) > 0\}$. If the Markov chain governed by q is π_X-irreducible and $q(x, y) = 0 \Leftrightarrow q(y, x) = 0$, then $(M_t)_{t \in \mathbb{N}_0}$ is π_X-irreducible.*

Proof: The condition that $q(x, y)$ is zero precisely when $q(y, x)$ is implies that the acceptance probabilities are strictly positive on D_π.

Now, let $(Q_t)_{t \in \mathbb{N}_0}$ denote the Markov chain governed by the $q(x, y)$ and denote its t-step transition kernel by q^t. In other words, all proposed transitions are accepted. We shall show by induction that $q^t(x, y) > 0$ implies $p^t(x, y) > 0$, where p^t is the t-step transition kernel of M_t.

To do so, let $t = 1$ and suppose that $q(x, y) > 0$ for $x, y \in D_\pi$. Then, since $A(x, y) > 0$, also $p(x, y) \geq q(x, y)A(x, y) > 0$. For the step from t to $t+1$, suppose that $q^{t+1}(x, z) > 0$ for some x and z in D_π. Additionally, write $S_p^t(x)$ for the support of $p^t(x, \cdot)$, $S_q^t(x)$ for that of $q^t(x, \cdot)$, and assume that $S_q^t(x) \subseteq S_p^t(x)$. Since $z \in S_q^{t+1}(x)$ by assumption,

$$\int_{S_p^t(x)} q^t(x, y)q(y, z)dy \geq \int_{S_q^t(x)} q^t(x, y)q(y, z)dy > 0.$$

If z would not be an element of $S_p^{t+1}(x)$, then the support of the function $y \mapsto p^t(x, y)q(y, z)$ would be a null-set. By the induction assumption, the support of $q^t(x, \cdot)q(\cdot, z)$ would also have measure zero in contradiction with the above inequality.

Finally, for any A having positive π_X-mass, since q is π_X-irreducible, one may find a $t \geq 1$ such that

$$\mathbb{P}(Q_t \in A \mid Q_0 = x) = \int_A q^t(x, y)dy > 0.$$

By the induction result, also $\mathbb{P}(M_t \in A \mid M_0 = x) > 0$. □

As a corollary, suppose that M_t is π_X-irreducible. Clearly, if there are self-transitions, $\mathbb{P}(M_t = M_{t-1}) > 0$ for some $t \in \mathbb{N}$, then M_t is aperiodic. Otherwise, if q is aperiodic, proposals do not cycle. The same is then true for accepted proposals, implying the Metropolis–Hastings chain inherits aperiodicity from q.

Example 3.10 *In the context of Example 3.1, choose site and label uniformly. More formally,* $q(x, y) = \frac{1}{2|T|}$ *for those* $x, y \in \{0, 1\}^T$ *that differ in at most one site. Then the proposal chain, and hence the Metropolis–Hastings sampler based on it, are irreducible and aperiodic.*

3.7 HIERARCHICAL MODELLING

The goal of this section is to introduce the modern hierarchical modelling approach by means of two concrete examples: image segmentation and disease mapping.

3.7.1 Image segmentation

Suppose that one is not interested in all details of an image, but only wishes to partition it into certain areas. For example, a cartographer might want to classify the pixels in a satellite image according to its land use. In another context, an oncologist may wish to distinguish between healthy tissue and malignancies in a CT-scan of a patient.

Let x denote the target labelled image and y the vector of observed signals. Each pixel value x_i, $i \in T$, belongs to a finite class L of labels, the signals y_i take values in some set S that is not necessarily identical to L, and the goal is to reconstruct x from y.

In many applications it is reasonable to assume that, given the labels, the signals are conditionally independent and the signal at site $i \in T$ follows a conditional probability density or mass function $g(y_i|x_i)$ that depends only on the label x_i at site i. Hence, for $x \in L^T$, the *forward model* becomes

$$f(y|x) = \prod_{i \in T} g(y_i|x_i), \quad y \in S^T.$$

The parameter of interest is the labelled image x. Its naive maximum likelihood estimate $\hat{x} = \hat{X}(y)$ based on the observed signal y is easy to calculate:

$$\hat{x}_i = \text{argmax}\ \{g(y_i|x_i) : x_i \in L\}, \quad i \in T.$$

However, such estimators do not yield nice and smooth labellings because they completely ignore the spatial context. In other words, $\hat{X} = (\hat{X}_i)_{i \in T}$ is sensitive to noise.

To obtain more robust estimators, a Bayesian approach may be taken. In addition to the forward model $f(y|x)$, a *prior* distribution $\pi_X(x)$ is used that assigns low probability to images x that are rough in the sense of having small connected components. By Bayes' rule, the posterior distribution of x given the data image $y \in S^T$ has probability mass function

$$f(x|y) \propto f(y|x)\pi_X(x) = \pi_X(x) \prod_{i \in T} g(y_i|x_i), \quad x \in L^T.$$

Then, the *maximum a posteriori estimator* (MAP) $\tilde{X}$ of X is chosen so as to maximise this posterior distribution. More specifically, if the observed signal image is y, $\tilde{x} = \tilde{X}(y)$ is given by

$$\tilde{x} = \text{argmax}\ \{f(y|x)\pi_X(x) : x \in L^T\}. \tag{3.10}$$

This approach is also known as *penalised maximum likelihood estimation*, as optimising (3.10) is equivalent to maximising

$$\log f(y|x) + \log \pi_X(x)$$

over all possible x. The first term $\log f(y|x)$ expresses the 'goodness of fit' of x to the data, the second term the smoothness. Moreover, $\tilde{X}$ is the Bayes estimator (cf. Section 2.8) for the $0 - 1$ loss function. To see this, note that for any function $X(\cdot)$ of the random field Y,

$$\mathbb{E}\left[1\{X(Y) \neq X\}\right] = \sum_{y \in S^T} \sum_{x \in L^T} 1\{X(y) \neq x\} f(x|y) \pi_Y(y),$$

assuming S is countable. Otherwise, simply replace the sum over y by an integral. Therefore, upon observing $Y = y$, the Bayes estimator minimises the posterior expectation

$$\sum_{x \in L^T} 1\{X(y) \neq x\} f(x|y)$$

and hence coincides with $\tilde{X}$.

The role of the prior distribution is to encourage spatial coherence. This can be achieved, for example, by a multi-label generalisation of the auto-logistic regression model of Example 3.1, which has probability mass function

$$\pi_X(x) \propto \exp\left[-\theta \sum_{i \sim j; i < j} 1\{x_i \neq x_j\}\right], \quad x \in L^T, \tag{3.11}$$

for $\theta > 0$. The model is known as the *Potts model* with label set L. Under the *white noise* assumption that the labels are observed subject to independent zero-mean Gaussian noise with variance σ^2, the posterior probability mass function given $y \in \mathbb{R}^T$ is equal to

$$f(x|y) \propto \exp\left(-\frac{1}{2\sigma^2} \sum_{i \in T} (y_i - x_i)^2 - \theta \sum_{i \sim j; i < j} 1\{x_i \neq x_j\}\right), \quad x \in L^T.$$

Direct computation of (3.10) is very difficult in general, but Monte Carlo ideas apply. Alternatively, and computationally faster, a local optimum can be found in a greedy fashion by iterative pointwise optimisation:

$$\tilde{x}_i = \operatorname{argmax} \{g(y_i|x_i) \pi_i(x_i|x_{T \setminus i}) : x_i \in L\},$$

where the pixels i are visited in a systematic fashion, for example in row major order. Since the computations are local, this method is very fast. However, the initial reconstruction may influence which local optimum

 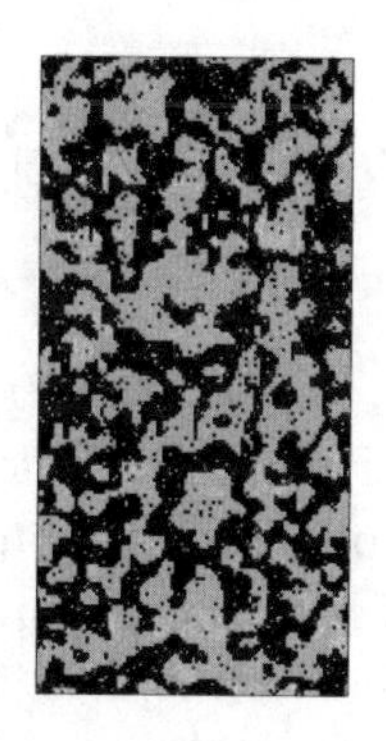 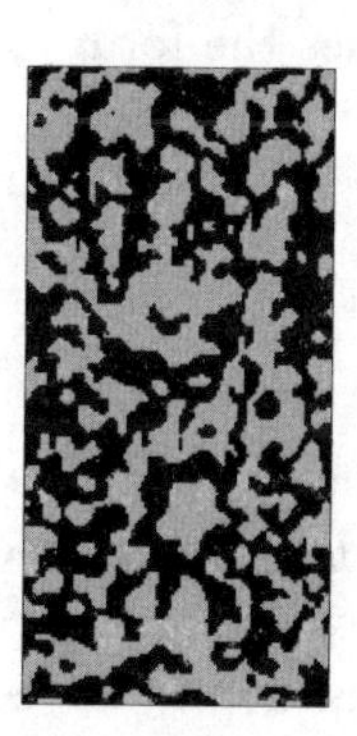

Figure 3.1 Segmentation of a noisy image of heather. From left to right: data image, MLE and MAP classifiers.

is reached so it is important to start well, for example in the maximum likelihood estimate $\hat{x}$.

As a simple illustration, the left-most panel of Figure 3.1 displays a pattern of heather in Jädraås, Sweden, digitised at 100×200 pixels with a resolution of 10 pixels to the metre. The data was corrupted by white noise with variance $\sigma^2 = 15$. The two right-most panels show greedy MAP-reconstructions for a Potts model with $\theta = 0$ (corresponding to the naive maximum likelihood estimator) and with $\theta = 25$. In this case, using a prior reduces the misclassification error from five to one percent.

3.7.2 Disease mapping

The second example concerns spatially correlated count data arising from small area sampling of some underlying process. For instance, a local public health authority may be interested in the reported cases of some disease. For privacy reasons, these are typically aggregated over areas that are large enough to ensure that the counts cannot be traced back to individuals. The goal of the analysis is to estimate the local disease risk, perhaps based on spatial covariates such as pollution levels or characteristics of the population.

For counts, it is natural to assume a Poisson distribution and define a model in the spirit of the auto-logistic regression model. Thus, writing Y for the vector of counts, the local characteristic at areal unit i

takes the form

$$\pi_i(y_i \mid y_{T\setminus i}) = \frac{e^{-\mu_i}\mu_i^{y_i}}{y_i!}, \quad y_i \in \mathbb{N}_0,$$

with

$$\log \mu_i = \alpha_i + \theta \sum\nolimits_{j\sim i, j\neq i}.$$

Since $L = \mathbb{N}_0$, we must verify that any putative joint distribution (3.2) is well-defined, which turns out to be true only when θ is non-positive. For negative values of θ, when the regions surrounding i have high disease counts, the expected number of incidences in i itself will be low. Such behaviour is unrealistic for most diseases. Another disadvantage is that the logarithmic transform does not readily scale with respect to the size of the areal units (the so-called 'modifiable area unit' or 'change of support' problem). In conclusion, Poisson auto-regression models are not suitable in the current context.

It is possible to model μ_i in terms of an integrated random field, but the technical details are beyond the scope of this book. An alternative is to consider a mixture model for the rates μ_i directly. As usual, covariate information is captured by a design matrix X and parameter vector $\beta \in \mathbb{R}^p$. Set, for $\alpha = X\beta$,

$$\mu_i = c_i \, e^{\alpha_i} \, \Lambda_{Z_i},$$

where c_i is a base rate of expected counts based on the population size of areal unit i and Λ_{Z_i} is the area-specific relative risk. In a mixture model, random allocation variables Z_i assign areal unit i to one of k mixture components $\lambda_1, \dots, \lambda_k \in \mathbb{R}^+$. Spatial coherence can be achieved by assuming that $(Z_i)_{i\in T}$ are distributed according to a Potts model (3.11). Provided that the covariates do not fluctuate too wildly, μ_i scales appropriately with size.

The goal of a statistical analysis is to infer Z, or, equivalently, Λ_Z, the spatial distribution of the relative risks, as well as the model parameters β, θ and $\lambda_1, \dots, \lambda_k$. In the nomenclature of the previous section, the forward model is

$$f(y|z; \beta, \lambda_1, \dots, \lambda_k) = \prod_{i\in T} g(y_i|(X\beta)_i, \lambda_{z_i}), \quad y \in \mathbb{N}_0^T,$$

with $g(\cdot|\alpha_i, \lambda_{z_i})$ the probability mass function of a Poisson distribution with mean $\mu_i = c_i e^{\alpha_i}\lambda_{z_i}$. The posterior probability mass function of the allocations conditional on the observed disease counts is

$$f(z|y; \beta, \theta, \lambda_1, \dots, \lambda_k) \propto f(y|z; \beta, \lambda_1, \dots, \lambda_k)\pi_Z(z; \theta), \quad z \in \{1, \dots, k\}^T,$$

for a proportionality constant that depends on the parameters. In a fully Bayesian framework, additional prior distributions may be placed on θ, the parameter of the Potts distribution $\pi_Z(\cdot;\theta)$, on β, on the mixture components λ_j, $j = 1, \ldots, k$, and even on k, leading to a joint distribution of the form

$$f(y|z;\beta,\lambda_1,\ldots,\lambda_k)\pi_Z(z;\theta,k)p(\lambda_1,\ldots,\lambda_k|k)p(\beta)p(\theta)p(k).$$

In any case, the posterior distribution can be approximated by Monte Carlo sampling and optimised numerically.

3.7.3 Synthesis

The two examples discussed in, respectively, Sections 3.7.1 and 3.7.2, share a common structure that can be found throughout spatial statistics. In both cases, a spatial process of interest – the pixel classification in Section 3.7.1, the relative risks in Section 3.7.2 – cannot be observed directly, but only through other random variables (the noisy pixel values in Section 3.7.1, the counts in Section 3.7.2). Moreover, there may be unknown parameters. Thus, the joint distribution is of the form

> forward model[data | process, parameters] × prior[process | parameters],

optionally complemented by a hyper prior distribution on the model parameters. This framework is extremely flexible and may be adapted to many different contexts.

Inference is usually based on the posterior distribution of the process and/or the parameters conditional on the observations, which can be approximated by Monte Carlo methods. Sometimes a reconstruction of the process is required, as in the segmentation example. However, since the full posterior distribution is available, histograms of any marginal distribution of interest can be plotted, e.g. the posterior distribution of the number of mixture components and allocation probabilities in the disease mapping example. Further examples will be presented in Chapter 3. In the meantime, we refer to Section 3.10 for pointers to modern textbooks in this area.

3.8 WORKED EXAMPLES WITH R

The package *spdep: Spatial dependence: Weighting schemes, statistics and models* can be used to find neighbourhood matrices and for estimating the parameters of Gaussian spatial autoregression schemes. The package is maintained by R. Bivand. An up-to-date list of contributors and a reference manual can be found on

`https://CRAN.R-project.org/package=spdep.`

The results shown below were obtained using version 0.7-4.

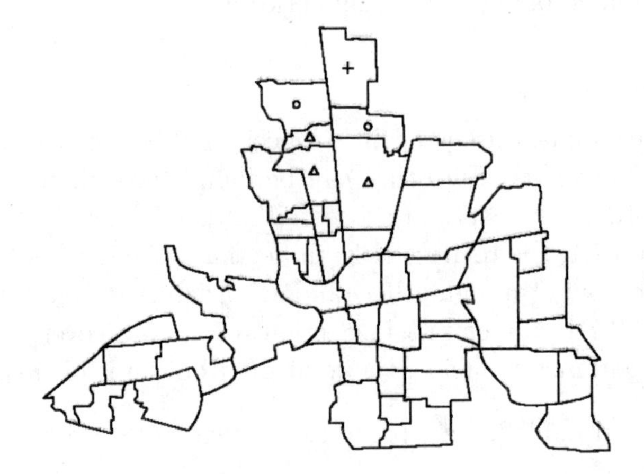

Figure 3.2 Map of 49 districts in Columbus. The first district is indicated by '+'.

The package contains a shape file 'columbus.shp' which includes a polygonal approximation of the borders of 49 neighbourhoods in the city of Columbus, Ohio, in the United States of America as well as the coordinates of their centroids in arbitrary digitising units. All source data files were prepared by L. Anselin as described in his 1988 textbook *Spatial Econometrics: Methods and Models.* From now on, we assume that the polygons have been extracted and stored in a data frame, say `columbus.poly`.

We are interested in the first of the Columbus neighbourhoods, which is indicated by a cross in Figure 3.2. Be warned, though, that the labels in the data frame are "0" up to "48"! The following script extracts the centroids of the neighbourhoods and places a cross to indicate the neighbourhood of interest.

```
plot(columbus.poly)
columbus.centre <- coordinates(columbus.poly)
```

```
points(columbus.centre[1,1], columbus.centre[1,2], pch=3)
```

First, consider the contiguity relation, in which two polygonal regions are neighbours if and only if they share a common border. The following script can be used to find the neighbours of the region whose centroid is indicated by '+' in Figure 3.2. It appears that there are two contiguous polygons, the centroids of which are indicated by a circle in Figure 3.2.

```
columbus.nb <- poly2nb(columbus.poly)
columbus.id <- attr(columbus.nb, "region.id")
columbus.id[columbus.nb[[match("0", columbus.id)]]]
[1] "1" "2"
```

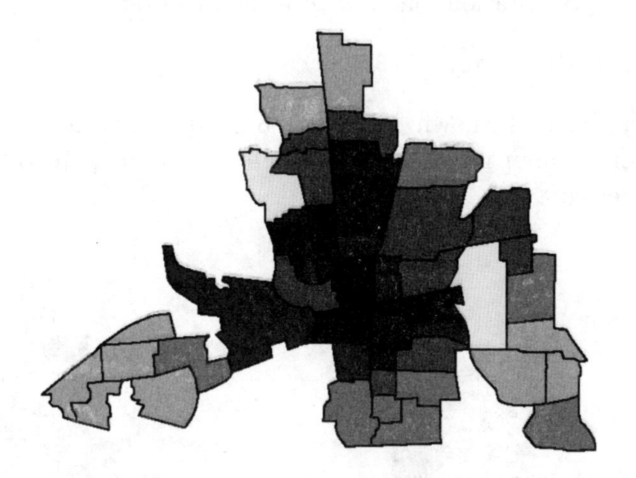

Figure 3.3 Map of 49 districts in Columbus. The colours indicate the rate of property crime (number per thousand households) in 1980. The rates are binned in $[0, 10)$, $[10, 20)$, $\ldots$, $[50, 60)$ and $[60, 70]$. Light colours correspond to low numbers.

Next, we consider the relation that declares two polygonal regions to be neighbours if and only if the distance between their centroids does not exceed some upper bound. The following scripts find the neighbours for upper bounds of, respectively, 0.62 and 1.24 units.

```
columbus.dnb <- dnearneigh(columbus.centre, 0, 0.62)
columbus.id[columbus.dnb[[match("0", columbus.id)]]]
[1] "1" "2"
```

```
columbus.dnb <- dnearneigh(columbus.centre, 0, 2*0.62)
columbus.id[columbus.dnb[[match("0", columbus.id)]]]
[1] "1" "2" "3" "4" "7"
```

It turns out that for the smaller of the upper bounds, the region whose centroid is indicated by '+' in Figure 3.2 has the same neighbours as it has with respect to the contiguity relation. Increasing the upper bound results in three additional neighbouring regions, whose centroids are indicated by a triangle in Figure 3.2.

The data frame `columbus.poly` contains a column `CRIME` which lists the number of residential burglaries and vehicle thefts that occurred in 1980 per thousand households for each of the 49 neighbourhoods. For a graphical representation, one may use the function

```
spplot(columbus.poly, "CRIME")
```

to obtain the plot shown in Figure 3.3; for convenience, we used a monochrome colour map. Note that higher crime rates tend to be found in the inner city.

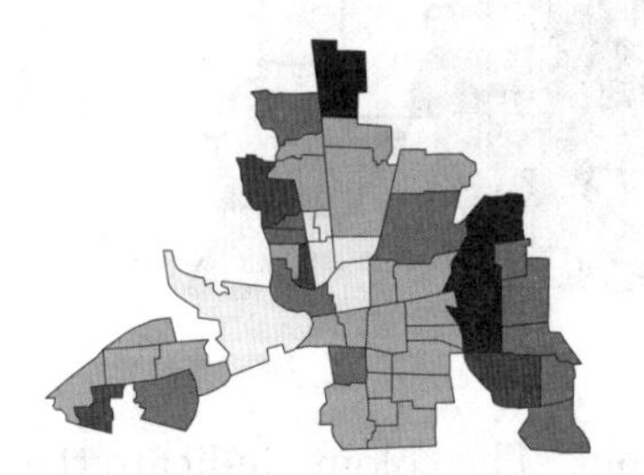
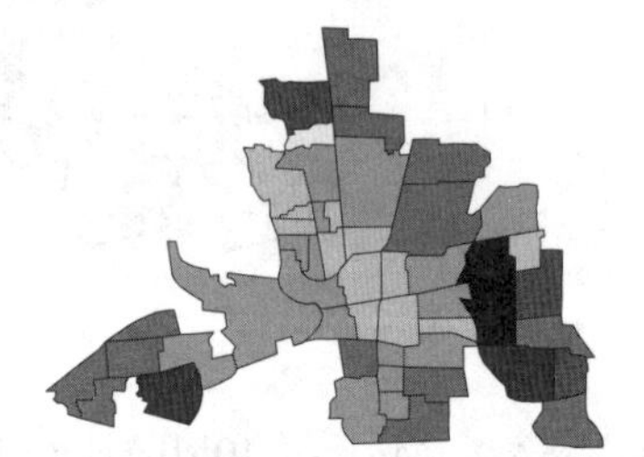

Figure 3.4 Map of 49 districts in Columbus. The colours indicate the values of explanatory variables. Left: mean property values (in k$) binned in $[0, 20)$, $[20, 40)$, $[40, 60)$, $[60, 80)$ and $[80, 100]$. Right: mean household income (in k$) binned in $[0, 5)$, $[5, 10)$, $[10, 15)$, $[15, 20)$, $[20, 25)$, $[25, 30)$ and $[30, 35]$. Light colours correspond to low numbers.

Some explanatory variables are available. Here we select two: mean property value and mean household income (in thousand dollars). As can be seen from Figure 3.4, low values of both tend to be found predominantly in inner city neighbourhoods. Including an offset value, we may formulate a conditional autoregression model

$$Y = X\beta + B(Y - X\beta) + E$$

where $Y = (Y_1, \ldots, Y_{49})'$ denotes the random field of crime rates, X is the 49×3 design matrix, $B = \phi N$ is proportional to the neighbourhood matrix N and the 3×1 vector β contains parameters to be estimated. Specifically, all entries of the first column of X are 1, the second column lists the mean property values, the third the average household incomes. Finally, E is spatially correlated noise with mean zero and covariance matrix $\sigma^2(I - B)$.

The following script fits the model by estimating its five parameters using the contiguity neighbourhood relation: the components of β, ϕ and σ^2.

```
columbus.listw <- nb2listw(columbus.nb, style="B")
car.out <- spautolm(formula= CRIME ~ HOVAL + INC,
   data=columbus.poly, listw=columbus.listw, family="CAR")
columbus.poly$fitted.car <- fitted(car.out)
```

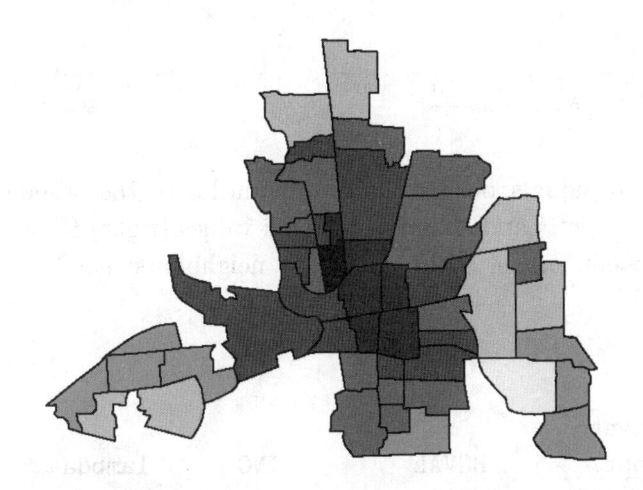

Figure 3.5 Map of 49 districts in Columbus. The colours indicate the fitted rate of property crime (number per thousand households) in 1980 for a conditional autoregression model with contiguous neighbours. The rates are binned in $[0, 10), [10, 20), \ldots, [50, 60)$ and $[60, 70]$. Light colours correspond to low numbers.

The estimated values of the parameters can be read off from the output of the print function:

```
> print(car.out)

Call:
spautolm(formula = CRIME ~ HOVAL + INC, data = columbus.poly,
    listw = columbus.listw, family = "CAR")
```

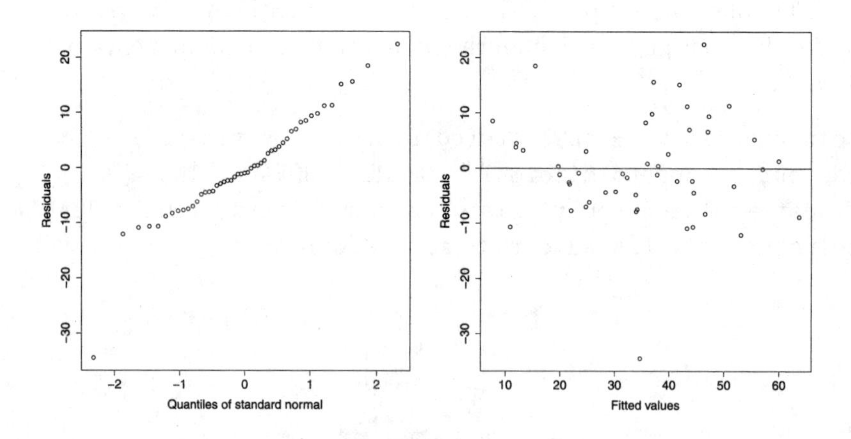

Figure 3.6 Residuals plotted against quantiles of the standard normal distribution (left) and against the fitted values (right) for a conditional autoregression model with contiguous neighbours fitted by maximum likelihood.

```
Coefficients:
(Intercept)        HOVAL          INC       lambda
 54.3139189   -0.2821969   -0.9882862    0.1589004

Log likelihood: -182.2198
```

and

```
>  car.out$fit$s2
[1] 87.65356
```

In other words, $\hat{\phi} = 0.16$, $\hat{\sigma} = 9.36$ and $\hat{\beta} = (54.31, -0.28, -0.99)'$. We conclude that the model predicts less crime in affluent districts. The fitted model is displayed graphically in Figure 3.5. Note that it is smoother than the data due to the spatial averaging explicit in the model formulation.

To validate the model, consider the residuals $Y - X\hat{\beta} - \hat{\phi}N(Y - X\hat{\beta})$. If the model were correct, the residuals would be normally distributed. The QQ-plot

```
qqnorm(residuals(car.out))
```

indicates a deviation from normality due to a single negative outlier corresponding to neighbourhood "6". This conclusion is confirmed by plotting the residuals against the fitted values, cf. Figure 3.6. The outlier is clearly visible, but otherwise the plot shows no apparent trend.

Neighbourhood "6" is the neighbourhood just west of the polygons whose centroids are marked by a triangle in Figure 3.2. This particular neighbourhood enjoys a crime rate that is markedly smaller than that of the surrounding neighbourhoods. Although property values there are rather high, the household incomes are not and after taking into account the weighted averages over the surrounding neighbourhoods, the predicted crime rate is higher than the actual one.

As an aside, note that realisations from the fitted model may easily be obtained by adding multivariate normally distributed noise (with covariance matrix $\hat{\sigma}^2(I - \hat{\phi}N)$) to the fitted values.

The script for fitting a SAR model is similar to that for fitting a CAR model. Indeed,

```
sar.out <- spautolm(formula= CRIME ~ HOVAL + INC,
   data=columbus.poly, listw=columbus.listw, family="SAR")
columbus.poly$fitted.sar <- fitted(sar.out)
```

results in

```
> print(sar.out)

Call:
spautolm(formula = CRIME ~ HOVAL + INC, data = columbus.poly,
    listw = columbus.listw, family = "SAR")
```

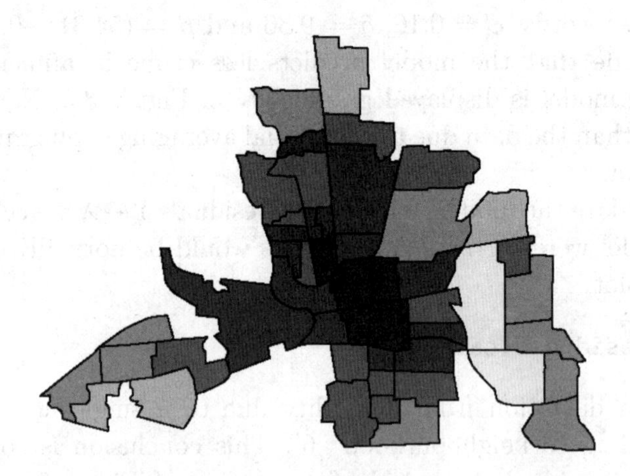

Figure 3.7 Map of 49 districts in Columbus. The colours indicate the fitted rate of property crime (number per thousand households) in 1980 for a simultaneous autoregression model with contiguous neighbours. The rates are binned in [0, 10), [10, 20), ..., [50, 60) and [60, 70]. Light colours correspond to low numbers.

```
Coefficients:
(Intercept)        HOVAL         INC       lambda
 56.3315730   -0.2998181  -0.9515649    0.1211682

Log likelihood: -182.5554
```

and

```
> sar.out$fit$s2
[1] 91.43706
```

In other words, $\hat{\phi} = 0.12$, $\hat{\sigma} = 9.56$ and $\hat{\beta} = (56.33, -0.30, -0.95)'$. A comparison of Figures 3.5 and 3.7 shows that the two models handle sharp discontinuities in the data somewhat differently; in such cases the fitted crime rates under the conditional autoregression seem a little smoother. The diagnostic plots shown in Figure 3.8 suggest the fit is slightly worse for a simultaneous autoregression but still adequate, except for neighbourhood "6".

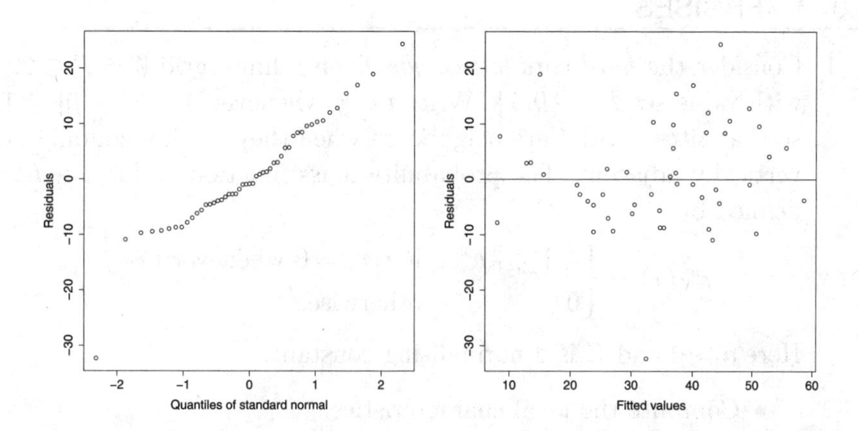

Figure 3.8 Residuals plotted against quantiles of the standard normal distribution (left) and against the fitted values (right) for a simultaneous autoregression model with contiguous neighbours fitted by maximum likelihood.

3.9 EXERCISES

1. Consider the *hard core lattice gas* X on a finite grid $\emptyset \neq T \subset \mathbb{Z}^2$ with value set $L = \{0, 1\}$. Write $i \sim j$ whenever $0 < ||i - j|| \leq 1$ so that sites i and j are neighbours when they are horizontally or vertically adjacent. The probability mass function is, for $x \in L^T$, defined by

$$\pi_X(x) = \begin{cases} \frac{1}{Z} \prod_{i \in T} a^{x_i} & \text{if } x_i x_j = 0 \text{ whenever } i \sim j; \\ 0 & \text{otherwise.} \end{cases}$$

Here $a > 0$ and Z is a normalising constant.

- Compute the local characteristics.
- Order the sites in T lexicographically. Show that there exist $x = (x_i)_{i \in T}$, $y = (y_i)_{i \in T}$ and $i \in T$ such that $\pi_i(y_i \mid x_{\{j:j<i\}}, y_{\{j:j>i\}})$ is zero but both $\pi_X(x)$ and $\pi_X(y)$ are positive.

2. In a conditional autoregression model, show that $b_{ij} = 0$ implies that X_i and X_j are conditionally independent given $(X_t)_{t \in T \setminus \{i,j\}}$. Are X_i and X_j independent?
Hint: Recall that if A is a symmetric, non-singular block matrix

$$A = \begin{bmatrix} I & A_{12} \\ A_{21} = A_{12}' & A_{22} \end{bmatrix},$$

then its inverse is given by

$$\begin{bmatrix} I + A_{12}(A_{22} - A_{21}A_{12})^{-1}A_{21} & -A_{12}(A_{22} - A_{21}A_{12})^{-1} \\ -(A_{22} - A_{21}A_{12})^{-1}A_{21} & (A_{22} - A_{21}A_{12})^{-1} \end{bmatrix}.$$

3. Show that the local characteristics

$$\pi_1(x \mid y) = \pi_2(y \mid x) = \frac{1}{(2\pi)^{1/2}} \exp\left[-\frac{1}{2}(x - y)^2\right]$$

do not define a proper joint distribution on $\mathbb{R}^{\{1,2\}}$.

4. Suppose that T is a finite set equipped with a symmetric relation $\sim$ which contains at least two $\sim$-related elements. Show that the Poisson auto-regression model with putative local characteristics

$$\begin{cases} \pi_i(y_i \mid y_{T \setminus i}) & = & e^{-\mu_i} \mu_i^{y_i} / y_i! \\ \log \mu_i & = & \theta \sum_{j \sim i, j \neq i} y_j \end{cases}$$

for $y \in \mathbb{N}_0^T$ is well-defined if and only if $\theta \leq 0$.

5. Consider the conditional autoregression model on a finite family $T \neq \emptyset$ of sites defined by Gaussian local characteristics with $\text{Var}(X_t \mid X_{T\setminus t}) = 1$ and

$$\mathbb{E}(X_t \mid X_{T\setminus t}) = \mu + \sum_{s\neq t} b_{ts}(X_s - \mu), \quad t \in T,$$

for some unknown parameter $\mu \in \mathbb{R}$. Propose a two-sided test for the hypothesis that $\mu = 0$. What assumptions do you need to impose on the b_{ts}?

6. Show that the potential in Example 3.5 is normalised with respect to $a = 0$.

7. Suppose that T is a finite set that contains at least two elements and is equipped with a symmetric relation $\sim$. For the Poisson auto-regression model defined by

$$\begin{cases} \pi_i(y_i \mid y_{T\setminus i}) & = & e^{-\mu_i} \mu_i^{y_i} / y_i! \\ \log \mu_i & = & -\sum_{j\sim i, j\neq i} y_j \end{cases}$$

for $y \in \mathbb{N}_0^T$, $i \in T$, find the canonical potential with respect to $a = 0$.

8. Let $\emptyset \neq T \subset \mathbb{Z}^2$ be a finite grid. For $i \neq j \in T$, write $i \sim j$ if and only if $0 < ||i - j|| \leq 1$. Show that if X is a Markov random field on T with respect to $\sim$, then the 'x' sites in the following picture are conditionally independent given the 'o' sites:

x	o	x	o	x	o	x
o	x	o	x	o	x	o
x	o	x	o	x	o	x
o	x	o	x	o	x	o
x	o	x	o	x	o	x
o	x	o	x	o	x	o
x	o	x	o	x	o	x

9. Let $\sim$ be a symmetric relation on the finite set $\emptyset \neq T$ and consider a conditional autoregression model on $\mathbb{R}^T$ defined by a square non-singular matrix B whose diagonal entries are zero and a diagonal matrix K with positive entries κ_i on the diagonal such that $(I - B)^{-1}K$ is positive definite.

Suppose that the entries b_{ij} of the matrix B satisfy the property that $b_{ij} = 0$ if $i \not\sim j$, $i, j \in T$. Show that this model is a Markov random field with respect to $\sim$ and find an explicit expression for the interaction functions.

10. Consider the hard core lattice gas X on a finite grid $\emptyset \neq T \subset \mathbb{Z}^2$ with value set $L = \{0, 1\}$ and probability mass function

$$\pi_X(x) = \begin{cases} \frac{1}{Z(a)} \prod_{i \in T} a^{x_i} & \text{if } x_i x_j = 0 \text{ whenever } i \sim j \\ 0 & \text{otherwise} \end{cases}$$

for $a > 0$ and $x \in L^T$. Here $i \sim j$ whenever $0 < ||i - j|| \leq 1$. Design a suitable Monte Carlo method for approximating the maximum likelihood estimator of a. Prove its convergence.

11. Consider the model

$$Y = X\beta + B(Y - X\beta) + E$$

where X is an $n \times p$ design matrix, $\beta \in \mathbb{R}^p$ an unknown parameter, B an $n \times n$ symmetric positive definite matrix with zero elements on the diagonal and E normally distributed with mean zero and covariance matrix $\sigma^2(I - B)$ for unknown parameter $\sigma^2 > 0$. Compute the maximum pseudo-likelihood estimators for the parameters β and σ^2. Compare your answer to the maximum likelihood estimators $\hat{\beta}$ and $\hat{\sigma}^2$.

12. Suppose that the random field X on a finite index set $T \neq \emptyset$ is defined by the probability mass function

$$\pi_X(x) = \frac{e^{\theta S(x)}}{Z(\theta)}, \quad x \in \{0, 1\}^T,$$

for some function $S : \{0, 1\}^T \to \mathbb{R}$. Given a realisation $x \in \{0, 1\}^T$, show that the maximum pseudo-likelihood estimator $\hat{\theta}$ satisfies

$$\frac{1}{|T|} \sum_{i \in T} \mathbb{E}_{\hat{\theta}} \left[S(X) \mid X_j = x_j, j \neq i \right] = S(x).$$

13. Let $\pi_X > 0$ be a probability distribution on L^T for non-empty finite sets L and T. Consider the Metropolis–Hastings algorithm with proposal distribution

$$q(x, y) = \sum_{i \in T} \frac{1}{|T|} \pi_i(y_i \mid x_{T \setminus i}) 1\{y_{T \setminus i} = x_{T \setminus i}\}, \quad x, y \in L^T.$$

Show that all proposals for which $q(x, y) > 0$ are accepted with probability one.

14. Consider the greedy algorithm for the Gaussian–Potts model used to obtain Figure 3.1. Describe the updates for $\theta = 0$ and $\theta \to \infty$.

15. The `spdep` package contains a data set `nc.sids` which contains information on the number of births as well as the number of deaths from Sudden Infant Death Syndrome in counties in North Carolina. Fit an appropriate auto-binomial model.

3.10 POINTERS TO THE LITERATURE

The mathematical theory of Markov random fields was developed in the 1960s, although specific examples had been studied before. For instance, the Ising model originates from the 1924 graduate thesis of E. Ising [1] under supervision of W. Lenz [2]. An early paper on a Gaussian autoregression is [3] by P. Whittle (1954).

Besag's factorisation theorem occurs as (2.2) in [4] building on work by D. Brook [5]. Indeed, Brook appears to be the first author to study consistency conditions for conditional specifications. The name Markov random field was coined by P.L. Dobrushin for random fields defined on infinite lattices that satisfy a spatial Markov property with respect to a distance based relation [6]. Section 4 of [4] is concerned with spatial autoregression models including the auto-logistic regression of Example 3.1, and the Gaussian models of Section 3.2. Proposition 3.1 and likelihood based inference can be found in section 5.2 of B.D. Ripley's pioneering textbook in spatial statistics [7].

Gibbs states are named after J.W. Gibbs, the founder of modern statistical physics. The proof of Theorems 3.2 and 3.4 based on the Möbius inversion theorem of G.-C. Rota [8, Proposition 3.2] is due to G.R. Grimmett [9]. Alternative proofs can be found in the paper by J. Moussouris [10]. Example 3.9 is also taken from this paper. The Hammersley–Clifford theorem was named after J.M. Hammersley and P.E. Clifford [11] by J.E. Besag [4, Section 3], who also noted the equivalence of local and spatial Markov properties established in Corollary 3.2.

For more details on Markov random fields, we refer the reader to the textbooks by Kinderman and Snell [12] and Y.A. Rozanov [13], or the more recent one by X. Guyon [14]. For an introduction to the wider class of graphical models, one may consult S.L. Lauritzen's monograph [15].

Gaussian autoregression models are discussed in great detail in [16]. The `R`-package `spdep` can be used to fit such models to data. Alternatively, the `R-INLA` package maintained by H. Rue may be used.

For random field models with an intractable likelihood, J.E. Besag proposed to use maximum pseudo-likelihood estimation instead [17] and showed that for CAR models, the technique reduces to least squares estimation. The Monte Carlo maximum likelihood method in the form presented here is due to Geyer and Thompson [18] and Theorem 3.5 is taken from this paper.

The study of stochastic processes in which the future and the past are conditionally independent given the present was inspired by A.A.

Markov's 1913 study of the succession of vowels and consonants in the classic novel *Eugene Onegin* by Pushkin. An excellent introduction to the theory of such Markov chains on general state spaces is given in the textbook by Meyn and Tweedie [19]. Our definition in terms of transition probability kernels can be found in section 3.4 of the second edition. The concept of π_X-irreducibility dates back to W. Doeblin [20, 21] and is discussed in chapter 4 of [19]. Cycles were also considered by Doeblin [21]. The consideration of ergodic theorems for Markov chains with finite state space is already found in work by A.N. Kolmogoroff [22], who used contraction principles and differential equations. The proof for general state spaces may be based on techniques from E. Nummelin [23], a coherent account of which is given in [19, Section 13]. Theorem 3.7 is due to Roberts and Smith [24, Theorem 3].

From a computational point of view, the Metropolis–Hastings algorithm was introduced in the paper by Metropolis, the Rosenbluths and the Tellers [25] and is a special case of a class of methods proposed by W.K. Hastings [26], designed to satisfy the detailed balance equations in Proposition 3.2. For an exhaustive overview of these and other Markov chain Monte Carlo techniques and their applications, we refer the reader to the Handbook edited by Brooks, Gelman, Jones and Meng [27].

The modern hierarchical modelling approach to image analysis, and to spatial statistics in general, can be traced back to J.E. Besag's note [28] and seminal paper [29] and to the pioneering work by the Geman brothers [30]. Textbooks on this topic include G. Winkler's monograph [31] on Bayesian image analysis and the more general volume by Banerjee, Carlin and Gelfand [32]. In particular, the segmentation example is inspired by [29] which also contains the greedy iterative pointwise optimisation algorithm. The heather data that we used as an illustration was collected by P.J. Diggle [33] and is available in the `R`-package `spatstat`. The prior Potts model was introduced in R.B. Potts' doctoral thesis [34]. Finally, our account of disease mapping is inspired by a paper by Green and Richardson [35]. Further details and alternative modelling strategies can be found in chapter 14 of the *Handbook of Spatial Statistics* [36].

REFERENCES

[1] E. Ising (1924). Beitrag zur Theorie des Ferro- und Paramagnetismus. PhD thesis, University of Hamburg.

[2] W. Lenz (1920). Beiträge zum Verständnis der magnetischen Eigenschaften in festen Kőrpern. *Physikalische Zeitschrift* 21:613–615.

[3] P. Whittle (1954). On stationary processes in the plane. *Biometrika* 41(3/4):434–449.

[4] J.E. Besag (1974). Spatial interaction and the statistical analysis of lattice systems. *Journal of the Royal Statistical Society* B36(2):192–236.

[5] D. Brook (1964). On the distinction between the conditional probability and the joint probability approaches in the specification of nearest-neighbour systems. *Biometrika* 51(3/4):481–483.

[6] P.L. Dobrushin (1968). The description of a random field by means of conditional probabilities and conditions of its regularity. *Theory of Probability and its Applications*, 13(2):197–224.

[7] B.D. Ripley (1981). *Spatial Statistics.* New York: John Wiley & Sons.

[8] G.-C. Rota (1964). On the foundations of combinatorial theory I. Theory of Möbius functions. *Zeitschrift fűr Wahrscheinlichkeitstheorie und Verwandte Gebiete* 2(4):340–368.

[9] G.R. Grimmett (1973). A theorem about random fields. *Bulletin of the London Mathematical Society* 5(1):81–84.

[10] J. Moussouris (1974). Gibbs and Markov random systems with constraints. *Journal of Statistical Physics* 10(1):11–33.

[11] J.M. Hammersley and P.E. Clifford (1971). Markov fields on finite graphs and lattices. Unpublished manuscript.

[12] R. Kinderman and J.L. Snell (1980). *Markov Random Fields and Their Applications.* Providence, Rhode Island: American Mathematical Society.

[13] Y.A. Rozanov (1982). *Markov Random Fields.* New York: Springer-Verlag.

[14] X. Guyon (1995). *Random Fields on a Network: Modeling, Statistics, and Applications.* New York: Springer-Verlag.

[15] S.L. Lauritzen (1996). *Graphical Models.* Oxford: Oxford University Press.

[16] H. Rue and L. Held (2005). *Gaussian Markov Random Fields. Theory and Applications.* Boca Raton, Florida: Chapman & Hall/CRC.

[17] J. Besag (1975). Statistical analysis of non-lattice data. *Journal of the Royal Statistical Society* D24(3):179–195.

[18] C.J. Geyer and E.A. Thompson (1992). Constrained maximum likelihood for dependent data. *Journal of the Royal Statistical Society* B54(3):657–699.

[19] S. Meyn and R.L. Tweedie (2009). *Markov Chains and Stochastic Stability (2nd edition).* Cambridge: Cambridge University Press.

[20] W. Doeblin (1937). Sur les propriétés asymptotiques de mouvement régis par certain types de chaînes simples. *Bulletin Mathématique de la Société Roumaine des Sciences* 39(1):57–115; 39(2):3–61.

[21] W. Doeblin (1940). Eléments d'une théorie générale des chaînes simples constantes de Markoff. *Annales Scientifiques de l'École Normale Supérieure* 57(3):61–111.

[22] A. Kolmogoroff (1931). Über die analytischen Methoden in der Wahrscheinlichkeitsrechnung. *Mathematische Annalen* 104(1):415–458.

[23] E. Nummelin (1984). *General Irreducible Markov Chains and Non-negative Operators.* Cambridge: Cambridge University Press.

[24] G.O. Roberts and A.F.M. Smith (1994). Simple conditions for the convergence of the Gibbs sampler and Metropolis–Hastings algorithms. *Stochastic Processes and Their Applications* 49(2):207–216.

[25] N. Metropolis, A.W. Rosenbluth, M.N. Rosenbluth, A.H. Teller and E. Teller (1953). Equation of state calculations by fast computing machines. *Journal of Chemical Physics* 21(6):1087–1092.

[26] W.K. Hastings (1970). Monte Carlo sampling methods using Markov chains and their application. *Biometrika* 57(1):97–109.

[27] S. Brooks, A. Gelman, G.L. Jones and X.-L. Meng, editors (2011). *Handbook of Markov Chain Monte Carlo.* Boca Raton, Florida: Chapman & Hall/CRC.

[28] J.E. Besag (1983). Discussion of paper by P. Switzer. *Bulletin of the International Statistical Institute* 50(3):422–425.

[29] J.E. Besag (1986). On the statistical analysis of dirty pictures (with discussion). *Journal of the Royal Statistical Society* B48(3):259–302.

[30] S. Geman and D. Geman (1984). Stochastic relaxation, Gibbs distributions, and the Bayesian restoration of images. *IEEE Transactions on Pattern Analysis and Machine Intelligence* 6(6):721–741.

[31] G. Winkler (2003). *Image Analysis, Random Fields and Markov Chain Monte Carlo Methods. A Mathematical Introduction (2nd edition).* Berlin: Springer-Verlag.

[32] S. Banerjee, B.P. Carlin and A.E. Gelfand (2015). *Hierarchical Modeling and Analysis for Spatial Data (2nd edition).* Boca Raton, Florida: Chapman & Hall/CRC.

[33] P.J. Diggle (1981). Binary mosaics and the spatial pattern of heather. *Biometrics* 37(3):531–539.

[34] R.B. Potts (1951). The mathematical investigation of some cooperative phenomena. D.Phil. thesis, University of Oxford.

[35] P.J. Green and S. Richardson (2002). Hidden Markov models and disease mapping. *Journal of the American Statistical Association* 97(460):1055–1070.

[36] A.E. Gelfand, P.J. Diggle, M. Fuentes and P. Guttorp, editors (2010). *Handbook of Spatial Statistics*. Boca Raton, Florida: Chapman & Hall/CRC.

CHAPTER 4

Spatial point processes

4.1 POINT PROCESSES ON EUCLIDEAN SPACES

Up to now, data were collected at fixed locations or regions. Sometimes, however, the locations at which events occur are random. Typical examples include the epicentres of earthquakes or the outbreaks of forest fires. Such random configurations of locations are said to form a *point process*.

To exclude pathological cases, the following definition will be needed.

Definition 4.1 *The family* $N^{\mathrm{lf}}(\mathbb{R}^d)$ *of* locally finite *point configurations in* $\mathbb{R}^d$ *consists of all subsets* $\mathbf{x} \subset \mathbb{R}^d$ *that place finitely many points in every bounded Borel set* $A \subset \mathbb{R}^d$.

In particular, locally finite configurations are at most countably infinite and do not contain accumulation points. It is possible to find two points at exactly the same location, though.

Definition 4.2 *A* point process $X \in N^{\mathrm{lf}}(\mathbb{R}^d)$ *on* $\mathbb{R}^d$ *is a random locally finite configuration of points such that for all bounded Borel sets* $A \subset \mathbb{R}^d$ *the number of points of* X *that fall in* A *is a finite random variable which we shall denote by* $N_X(A)$.

Example 4.1 *Let* W *be a bounded Borel set in* $\mathbb{R}^d$ *having positive d-volume* $|W| > 0$*, and, for* $n \in \mathbb{N}$*, let* $X_1, \dots, X_n$ *be independent and uniformly distributed on* W*. Then,* $X = \{X_1, \dots, X_n\}$ *is the* binomial point process. *Indeed,*

$$N_X(A) = \sum_{i=1}^{n} 1\{X_i \in A\} \leq n$$

is a finite random variable for every Borel set $A \subseteq W$.

As for the random fields studied in Chapter 2, the distribution of a point process is completely specified by the *finite dimensional distributions* (fidi's)

$$\mathbb{P}(N_X(A_1) = n_1; \cdots ; N_X(A_m) = n_m).$$

Here, for $m \in \mathbb{N}$, $i = 1, \ldots, m$, the $A_i \subset \mathbb{R}^d$ are bounded Borel sets and $n_i \in \mathbb{N}_0$.

Example 4.2 *Consider the binomial point process of Example 4.1. Let* A, B *be two Borel subsets of* W. *Note that* A *and* B *partition* W *in four disjoint subsets,* $A \cap B$, $A \setminus B$, $B \setminus A$ *and the complement of* $A \cup B$. *The uniform distribution of the* X_i *implies that the probability of falling in* $A \cap B$ *is* $|A \cap B|/|W|$, *with similar expressions for the hitting probabilities of the other three sets. Therefore,*

$$\mathbb{P}(N_X(A \setminus B) = n_1; N_X(B \setminus A) = n_2; N_X(A \cap B) = n_3)$$

$$= \frac{n!}{n_1!n_2!n_3!(n - \sum_i n_i)!} \left(\frac{|A \setminus B|}{|W|}\right)^{n_1} \left(\frac{|B \setminus A|}{|W|}\right)^{n_2} \left(\frac{|A \cap B|}{|W|}\right)^{n_3} \times$$

$$\times \left(1 - \frac{|A \cup B|}{|W|}\right)^{n - \sum_i n_i}.$$

Summation over appropriate values of n_1, n_2, n_3 *yields an explicit expression for* $\mathbb{P}(N_X(A) = n_A;\ N_X(B) = n_B)$.

The fidi's are not very tractable, even for the binomial point process considered above. However, if one assumes that the point process X is *simple* in the sense that its realisations almost surely do not contain multiple points at exactly the same location, it suffices to consider only the one-dimensional fidi's.

Theorem 4.1 *The distribution of a simple point process* X *on* $\mathbb{R}^d$ *is completely determined by the* void probabilities

$$v(A) = \mathbb{P}(N_X(A) = 0)$$

of bounded Borel sets $A \subset \mathbb{R}^d$.

Proof: Define a family of difference operators $S_k(\cdot; A_1, \ldots, A_k)$ indexed by bounded Borel sets $A_1, \ldots, A_k$, $k \in \mathbb{N}$, inductively as follows:

$$S_1(B; A_1) = v(B) - v(A_1 \cup B)$$

and

$$S_k(B; A_1, \ldots, A_k) = S_{k-1}(B; A_1, \ldots, A_{k-1}) - S_{k-1}(B \cup A_k; A_1, \ldots, A_{k-1}),$$

where $B \subset \mathbb{R}^d$ is a bounded Borel set. Note that

$$S_k(B; A_1, \ldots, A_k) = \mathbb{P}(N_X(A_i) > 0, i = 1, \ldots, k; N_X(B) = 0)$$

depends only on events that record presence or absence of points and hence is completely determined by the void probabilities.

By the topological properties of the Euclidean space $\mathbb{R}^d$, there exists a series of nested partitions $T_{n,i}$, $i = 0, \ldots, k_n$, such that for large n distinct points $x, y \in \mathbb{R}^d$ lie in different members of $(T_{n,i})_i$. Here n is the level in the nesting and i ranges through the members of the partition at level n. For any bounded Borel set $A \subset \mathbb{R}^d$, intersection with the members of the partition results in a nested partition of A that separates the points, so the limit

$$\lim_{n \to \infty} \sum_i 1\{N_X(A \cap T_{ni}) > 0\} = N_X(A)$$

exists almost surely. Here we use the fact that X is simple!

The joint distribution of the random variables $1\{N_X(A \cap T_{n,i})\}$, $i = 0, \ldots, k_n$, can be expressed in terms of the difference operators. Indeed, since indicator variables take binary values only, for $i_j \in \{0, 1\}$,

$$\mathbb{P}(1\{N_X(A \cap T_{n,0}) > 0\} = i_0; \cdots ; 1\{N_X(A \cap T_{n,k_n}) > 0\} = i_{k_n})$$
$$= S_l(\cup_{j:i_j=0}(A \cap T_{n,j}); A \cap T_{n,j}, i_j = 1)$$

where $l = \sum_j 1\{i_j = 1\}$. Hence, writing $H_n(A) = \sum_i 1\{N_X(A \cap T_{n,i}) > 0\}$, the probability that $H_n(A)$ takes the value l is equal to

$$\sum \mathbb{P}(1\{N_X(A \cap T_{n,0}) > 0\} = i_0; \cdots ; 1\{N_X(A \cap T_{n,k_n}) > 0\} = i_{k_n}),$$

where the sum is taken over all combinations of i_js that sum to $l \in \mathbb{N}_0$. Thus, $\mathbb{P}(H_n(A) = l)$ can be expressed solely in terms of the difference operators and hence in terms of the void probabilities. A similar reasoning applies to the joint distribution of $(H_n(A_1), \ldots, H_n(A_k))$ for any $k \in \mathbb{N}$. Letting n increase to infinity completes the proof. □

Example 4.3 *Let W be a bounded Borel set in $\mathbb{R}^d$ having positive d-volume $|W| > 0$. For the binomial process on W (cf. Example 4.1), the void probability of a bounded Borel set $A \subset \mathbb{R}^d$ is*

$$v(A) = (1 - |A \cap W|/|W|)^n.$$

To conclude this section, we present a constructive way to define *finite* point patterns, namely to specify

- a discrete probability distribution $(p_n)_{n\in\mathbb{N}_0}$ for the total number of points;
- a family of symmetric joint probability densities $j_n(x_1, \dots, x_n)$, $n \in \mathbb{N}$, on $(\mathbb{R}^d)^n$ for the locations of the points given that there are n of them.

Example 4.4 *For the binomial process of Example 4.1, $p_n = 1$ and $p_m = 0$ for $m \neq n$. Moreover, $j_n \equiv |W|^{-n}$ is symmetric.*

4.2 THE POISSON PROCESS

Recall that the Poisson distribution arises as the limit of binomial distributions with ever more trials having ever smaller success probabilities. The same idea applies to binomial point processes.

To be specific, fix $k \in \mathbb{N}_0$ and let $B_n \subset \mathbb{R}^d$ be a series of growing balls centred at the origin such that $n/|B_n| \equiv \lambda$ is constant $(0 < \lambda < \infty)$. Then any bounded Borel set A is covered by B_n for $n \geq k$ sufficiently large, and, in this case,

$$\mathbb{P}^{(n)}(N(A) = k) = \binom{n}{k} \left(\frac{|A|}{|B_n|}\right)^k \left(1 - \frac{|A|}{|B_n|}\right)^{n-k},$$

where the notation $\mathbb{P}^{(n)}$ is used for the distribution of the binomial point process of n points in B_n. Under the assumptions on n and B_n,

$$\mathbb{P}^{(n)}(N(A) = k) \to e^{-\lambda|A|} \frac{(\lambda|A|)^k}{k!}$$

as $n \to \infty$. Similarly, for disjoint bounded Borel sets A and B and $k, l \in \mathbb{N}_0$,

$$\mathbb{P}^{(n)}(N(A) = k; N(B) = l) = \binom{n}{k} \left(\frac{|A|}{|B_n|}\right)^k \binom{n-k}{l} \left(\frac{|B|}{|B_n|}\right)^l \times \left(1 - \frac{|A \cup B|}{|B_n|}\right)^{n-k-l}$$

for $n \geq k + l$ large enough for B_n to cover $A \cup B$. As $n \to \infty$, the limit

$$\lim_{n\to\infty} \mathbb{P}^{(n)}(N(A) = k; N(B) = l) = e^{-\lambda|A|}\frac{(\lambda|A|)^k}{k!}e^{-\lambda|B|}\frac{(\lambda|B|)^l}{l!}$$

is a product of Poisson probabilities with parameters $\lambda|A|$ and $\lambda|B|$, respectively.

The above calculations suggest the following definition.

Definition 4.3 *A point process X on $\mathbb{R}^d$ is a* homogeneous Poisson process *with* intensity $\lambda > 0$ *if*

- *$N_X(A)$ is Poisson distributed with mean $\lambda|A|$ for every bounded Borel set $A \subset \mathbb{R}^d$;*
- *for any k disjoint bounded Borel sets $A_1, \ldots, A_k$, $k \in \mathbb{N}$, the random variables $N_X(A_1), \ldots, N_X(A_k)$ are independent.*

The void probabilities of a Poisson process are given by

$$v(A) = \exp\left[-\lambda|A|\right].$$

At this point, it should be mentioned that the second property in the definition above is crucial and implies that the restrictions of X to disjoint sets behave independently. The first property may be relaxed in the sense that $\lambda|A|$ may be replaced by

$$\int_A \lambda(x)dx \tag{4.1}$$

for some function $\lambda : \mathbb{R}^d \to \mathbb{R}^+$ that is integrable on bounded sets but not necessarily constant. The resulting point process is an *inhomogeneous Poisson process.*

Theorem 4.2 *Let X be a homogeneous Poisson process on $\mathbb{R}^d$ with intensity $\lambda > 0$ and $A \subset \mathbb{R}^d$ a bounded Borel set with $|A| > 0$. Then, conditional on the event $\{N_X(A) = n\}$, $n \in \mathbb{N}$, the restriction of X to A is a binomial point process of n points.*

Proof: Let $B \subset A$ be a bounded Borel set. Its conditional void probability is given by

$$\mathbb{P}(N_X(B) = 0|N_X(A) = n) = \frac{\mathbb{P}(N_X(B) = 0; N_X(A) = n)}{\mathbb{P}(N_X(A) = n)}$$

$$= \frac{\mathbb{P}(N_X(B) = 0; N_X(A \setminus B) = n)}{\mathbb{P}(N_X(A) = n)} = \frac{e^{-\lambda|B|}e^{-\lambda|A \setminus B|}(\lambda|A \setminus B|)^n/n!}{e^{-\lambda|A|}(\lambda|A|)^n/n!}$$

$$= \left(\frac{|A \setminus B|}{|A|}\right)^n,$$

since $N_X(B)$ and $N_X(A \setminus B)$ are independent and Poisson distributed with rates $\lambda|B|$ and $\lambda|A \setminus B|$, respectively. Note that the conditional void probability of B is equal to the corresponding void probability of the binomial point process (cf. Example 4.3). Therefore, an appeal to Theorem 4.1 concludes the proof. □

As a corollary, observe that the joint probability densities j_n of a Poisson process on a bounded window A coincide with those of the binomial point process.

4.3 MOMENT MEASURES

The moments, especially the first two, are important descriptors of random variables, as are the mean and covariance functions of random fields. For point processes, their analogues are the *moment measures.*

Definition 4.4 *Let X be a point process on $\mathbb{R}^d$. Define, for Borel sets $A, B \subseteq \mathbb{R}^d$,*

$$\begin{aligned} \alpha^{(1)}(A) &= \mathbb{E}N_X(A); \\ \mu^{(2)}(A \times B) &= \mathbb{E}\left[N_X(A)N_X(B)\right]; \\ \alpha^{(2)}(A \times B) &= \mathbb{E}\left[\sum_{x \in X}\sum_{y \in X}^{\neq} 1\{x \in A; y \in B\}\right]. \end{aligned}$$

Here, the notation $\sum^{\neq}$ is used to indicate that the sum is taken over all $(x, y) \in X^2$ for which $x \neq y$.

The set functions introduced in Definition 4.4 are not necessarily finite, even for finite point processes. To see this, let, for example, the number of points be governed by the probability density $(p_n)_n$ with $p_n = 1/(n(n-1))$ for $n \geq 2$ and zero otherwise. Then the p_n sum to one, but the expected total number of points is infinite. For finite point processes, a sufficient condition for $\mu^{(2)}$ and, a fortiori, $\alpha^{(1)}$ and $\alpha^{(2)}$ to take finite values is that $\mathbb{E}\left[N_X(\mathbb{R}^d)^2\right] < \infty$. More generally, provided that they take finite values on bounded Borel sets, classic results from measure theory imply that these set functions can be extended to unique (σ-finite) Borel measures which are necessarily symmetric.

Definition 4.5 *Suppose that the set functions defined in Definition 4.4 are finite for bounded Borel sets. Then they can be uniquely extended to symmetric Borel measures. The resulting measures $\alpha^{(k)}$, $k = 1, 2$, are the k-th order* factorial moment measures *of X, whereas the extension of $\mu^{(2)}$ will be referred to as the* second order moment measure.

In fact, for every $\alpha^{(k)}$-integrable function $f : (\mathbb{R}^d)^k \to \mathbb{R}$,

$$\mathbb{E}\left[\sum_{(x_1,\ldots,x_k)\in X^k}^{\neq} f(x_1,\ldots,x_k)\right] = \int\cdots\int f(x_1,\ldots,x_k)d\alpha^{(k)}(x_1,\ldots,x_k). \tag{4.2}$$

Example 4.5 *Let X be a Poisson process on $\mathbb{R}^d$ with intensity function λ. Then, by definition, $N_X(A)$ is Poisson distributed with expectation $\Lambda(A) = \int_A \lambda(x)dx < \infty$ for every bounded Borel set A. Hence, $\alpha^{(1)}(A) = \Lambda(A)$.*

To compute the second order moment measure, use the fact that the counts in disjoint sets are independent to write, for bounded Borel sets $A, B \subset \mathbb{R}^d$,

$$\begin{aligned}
\mu^{(2)}(A \times B) &= \mathbb{E}\left[N(A)\{N(A\cap B) + N(B\setminus A)\}\right] \\
&= \mathbb{E}\left[\{N(A\cap B) + N(A\setminus B)\}N(A\cap B)\right] + \Lambda(A)\Lambda(B\setminus A) \\
&= \Lambda(A\cap B) + \Lambda(A\cap B)^2 + \Lambda(A\setminus B)\Lambda(A\cap B) + \Lambda(A)\Lambda(B\setminus A) \\
&= \Lambda(A\cap B) + \Lambda(A\cap B)\left[\Lambda(A\cap B) + \Lambda(A\setminus B)\right] + \Lambda(A)\Lambda(B\setminus A) \\
&= \int_A\int_B \lambda(x)\lambda(y)dxdy + \int_{A\cap B}\lambda(x)dx.
\end{aligned}$$

Since

$$\mu^{(2)}(A\times B) = \alpha^{(2)}(A\times B) + \alpha^{(1)}(A\cap B),$$

the second order factorial moment measure is

$$\alpha^{(2)}(A\times B) = \int_A\int_B \lambda(x)\lambda(y)dxdy.$$

In the current context, the covariance is defined in terms of the first two moments as follows:

$$\mathrm{Cov}(N_X(A), N_X(B)) = \mu^{(2)}(A\times B) - \alpha^{(1)}(A)\alpha^{(1)}(B).$$

Definition 4.6 *Let X be a point process on $\mathbb{R}^d$. If the factorial moment measure $\alpha^{(k)}$ exists and admits a density in the sense that*

$$\alpha^{(k)}(A_1 \times \cdots \times A_k) = \int_{A_1} \cdots \int_{A_k} \rho^{(k)}(x_1, \ldots, x_k) dx_1 \cdots dx_k$$

for all Borel sets $A_1, \ldots, A_k$, then $\rho^{(k)}$ is the k-th order product density, $k = 1, 2$.

Intuitively speaking, $\rho^{(k)}(x_1, \ldots, x_k)dx_1 \cdots dx_k$ is the infinitesimal probability of finding points of X at regions $dx_1, \ldots, dx_k$ around $x_1, \ldots, x_k$.

Example 4.6 *Let X be a Poisson process on $\mathbb{R}^d$ with intensity function λ. Then, for $x, y \in \mathbb{R}^d$, $\rho^{(1)}(x) = \lambda(x)$ and $\rho^{(2)}(x, y) = \lambda(x)\lambda(y)$. When well-defined, the* pair correlation function $g(x, y) = \rho^{(2)}(x, y)/(\rho^{(1)}(x)\rho^{(1)}(y)) \equiv 1$, *reflecting the lack of correlation between points of X.*

4.4 STATIONARITY CONCEPTS AND PRODUCT DENSITIES

In this section, we consider estimation of the product densities of a spatial point process. In order to do so, some stationarity concepts will be needed.

Definition 4.7 *A point process X on $\mathbb{R}^d$ is* stationary *if for all bounded Borel sets $A_1, \ldots, A_k$ in $\mathbb{R}^d$, all $n_1, \ldots, n_k$ in $\mathbb{N}_0$ and all $s \in \mathbb{R}^d$,*

$$\mathbb{P}(N_X(s + A_1) \leq n_1; \ldots; N_X(s + A_k) \leq n_k) = \mathbb{P}(N_X(A_1) \leq n_1; \ldots; N_X(A_k) \leq n_k).$$

In other words, the distribution of X is invariant under translations. A fortiori, the same is true for the moment measures of X provided that they exist. A weaker property that allows some spatial variation is the following.

Definition 4.8 *Let X be a point process on $\mathbb{R}^d$ for which the first and second order factorial moment measures exist and admit a product density $\rho^{(k)}$, $k = 1, 2$. Then X is said to be* second order intensity-reweighted moment stationary *if*

$$\rho^{(1)}(x) \geq \rho_{\min} > 0$$

is bounded away from zero and, for all $s \in \mathbb{R}^d$, *the* pair correlation function

$$g(x,y) = \frac{\rho^{(2)}(x,y)}{\rho^{(1)}(x)\rho^{(1)}(y)}$$

satisfies the property that $g(x,y) = g(x+s, y+s)$ *for almost all* $x, y \in \mathbb{R}^d$.

In other words, for a second order intensity-reweighted moment stationary point process, the pair correlation function $g(x,y)$ is well-defined and a function of $y-x$ in analogy to the same property of the covariance function of a weakly stationary random field (cf. Definition 2.4). This definition may be extended to point processes defined on a subset of $\mathbb{R}^d$.

Example 4.7 *The homogeneous Poisson process is stationary since its fidi's are defined in terms of d-dimensional volumes that are invariant under translations.*

In Example 4.6, we saw that the pair correlation function of a Poisson process is identically one, whenever well-defined. Consequently, an inhomogeneous Poisson process whose intensity function is bounded away from zero is second order intensity-reweighted moment stationary.

Next, let us turn to estimation and suppose that a realisation $\mathbf{x} = \{x_1, \dots, x_n\}$ of a stationary point process X is observed within a bounded Borel set W of positive volume $|W|$. By definition, if the first order moment measure of X exists, then it is invariant under translations and therefore of the form

$$\mathbb{E}\left[N_X(A)\right] = \lambda|A|$$

for all Borel subsets A of $\mathbb{R}^d$. The scalar multiplier λ is the *intensity* of X. It can be estimated by

$$\hat{\lambda} = \frac{N_X(W)}{|W|}. \tag{4.3}$$

Proposition 4.1 *Let* X *be a stationary point process with intensity* $\lambda > 0$ *whose factorial moment measures exist up to second order and admit product densities. Then (4.3) is an unbiased estimator of* λ. *Its variance is given by*

$$\frac{\lambda}{|W|} + \frac{\lambda^2}{|W|^2}\int_W \int_W (g(x,y) - 1)dxdy,$$

where g *is the pair correlation function of* X.

Proof: The second moment of (4.3) can be written as

$$\begin{aligned}\mathbb{E}\left[\left(\frac{N_X(W)}{|W|}\right)^2\right] &= \frac{1}{|W|^2}\mathbb{E}\left[\sum_{x\in X}\sum_{y\in X} 1\{x\in W; y\in W\}\right]\\ &= \frac{1}{|W|^2}\int_W\int_W \rho^{(2)}(x,y)dxdy + \frac{\lambda}{|W|}\end{aligned}$$

by (4.2) upon splitting the double sum into tuples of different and identical points. Hence the variance of $\hat{\lambda}$ is given by

$$\frac{1}{|W|^2}\int_W\int_W \rho^{(2)}(x,y)dxdy + \frac{\lambda}{|W|} - \lambda^2$$

in accordance with the claim. □

Example 4.8 *Let X be a homogeneous Poisson process with intensity $\lambda > 0$ observed in some bounded Borel set W of positive volume $|W|$. Then the variance of (4.3) is given by $\lambda/|W|$. As one would expect, the variance is a decreasing function of the volume $|W|$.*

By Proposition 4.1, the intensity estimator has a larger variance for point processes for which $g(x,y) > 1$ $(x, y \in W)$, that is, for which the presence of a point at x increases the probability of finding a point at y relative to a Poisson process with the same intensity. Such point processes may be called clustered.

Point processes with pair correlation functions $g < 1$ are called regular *and their intensity estimator has a smaller variance than that of a Poisson process with the same intensity.*

To estimate the product density $\rho^{(2)}$ or the pair correlation function g, ideas similar to those that underlie the Matheron estimator (2.5) may be used. To obtain artificial replication, we assume stationarity and, at lag t, consider all pairs of points in the observed point pattern $\mathbf{x}$ that are 'approximately' t apart:

$$\widehat{\rho^{(2)}(t)} = \frac{1}{|B(t,\epsilon)|}\sum_{x\in X\cap W}\sum_{y\in X\cap W}^{\neq}\frac{1\{y-x\in B(t,\epsilon)\}}{|W\cap W_{y-x}|}. \tag{4.4}$$

Here $B(t,\epsilon)$ is the closed ball of radius ϵ centered at $t\in\mathbb{R}^d$ and $W_a = \{w+a : w\in W\}$ is the set W translated over the vector $a\in\mathbb{R}^d$. Not all lags t can be chosen, as $W \cap W_{y-x}$ will be empty when the distance between x and y gets large.

Regarding the choice of the bandwidth ϵ, similar considerations as for (2.5) apply: ϵ should be small enough for $\rho^{(2)}$ not to fluctuate too much in ϵ-balls but large enough to contain a reasonable number of points. The term $1/|W \cap W_{y-x}|$ is an edge correction to compensate for the fact that large lags $y - x \approx t$ will not be observed frequently in the bounded window W.

For t small enough, the estimator (4.4) is approximately unbiased. Indeed, under the stationarity assumption, by (4.2),

$$\begin{aligned}\mathbb{E}\widehat{\rho^{(2)}(t)} &= \frac{1}{|B(t,\epsilon)|}\int_W\int_W \frac{1\{y-x \in B(t,\epsilon)\}}{|W \cap W_{y-x}|}\rho^{(2)}(x,y)dxdy \\ &= \frac{1}{|B(t,\epsilon)|}\int_W\left[\int_{W-x}\frac{1\{z \in B(t,\epsilon)\}}{|W \cap W_z|}\rho^{(2)}(0,z)dz\right]dx.\end{aligned}$$

Change the order of integration to obtain

$$\frac{1}{|B(t,\epsilon)|}\int_{\mathbb{R}^d}\left[\int_{W\cap W_{-z}}\frac{1}{|W \cap W_z|}dx\right]1\{z \in B(t,\epsilon)\}\rho^{(2)}(0,z)dz$$

$$= \frac{1}{|B(t,\epsilon)|}\int_{B(t,\epsilon)}\rho^{(2)}(0,z)dz.$$

In summary, for small t and provided that $\rho^{(2)}$ does not fluctuate too wildly in $B(t,\epsilon)$,

$$\mathbb{E}\widehat{\rho^{(2)}(t)} = \frac{1}{|B(t,\epsilon)|}\int_{B(t,\epsilon)}\rho^{(2)}(0,z)dz \approx \rho^{(2)}(0,t).$$

To conclude this section, a few remarks are in order. Firstly, (4.4) is by no means the only estimator in common use; there exist many variations on the themes of edge correction and neighbourhood selection. Secondly, for second order intensity-reweighted moment stationary point processes, instead of estimating ρ^2, one may consider the pair correlation function. To do so, the first order product density $\rho^{(1)}$ must be estimated, for instance by

$$\widehat{\rho^{(1)}(t)} = \sum_{x \in X\cap W}\frac{1\{x \in B(t,\epsilon)\}}{|B(x,\epsilon)\cap W|}, \quad t \in W. \tag{4.5}$$

If, for example, W is open, the volume $|B(x,\epsilon) \cap W|$ is positive for all $x \in X \cap W$ and (4.5) is well-defined. However, as there is no replication –

artificial or otherwise – such estimators should be interpreted carefully. In particular, based on a single pattern it is not possible to distinguish between inhomogeneity and clustering. Anyway, the combination of (4.4) and (4.5) yields the estimator

$$\widehat{g(t)} = \frac{1}{|B(t,\epsilon)|} \sum_{x \in X \cap W} \sum_{y \in X \cap W}^{\neq} \frac{1\{y - x \in B(t,\epsilon)\}}{|W \cap W_{y-x}| \widehat{\rho^{(1)}(x)} \widehat{\rho^{(1)}(y)}} \tag{4.6}$$

for the pair correlation function at lag t. Bear in mind, though, that this function is sensitive to errors in $\widehat{\rho^{(1)}}$.

Finally, both (4.4) and (4.5) suffer from discretisation effects. Therefore, kernel smoothing ideas are often applied. For example, ignoring edge effects, an alternative to (4.5) would be the estimator

$$\frac{1}{\epsilon^d} \sum_{x \in X \cap W} \kappa \left(\frac{t - x}{\epsilon} \right)$$

where $\kappa : \mathbb{R}^d \to \mathbb{R}^+$ is a d-dimensional symmetric probability density function. Of course, kernel smoothing may be combined with edge correction.

4.5 FINITE POINT PROCESSES

In this section, consider a finite point process X on a bounded Borel set $W \subset \mathbb{R}^d$ that is defined by means of a probability distribution for the total number of points in combination with a family of conditional probability densities for the locations of the points given their number.

More formally, write p_n, $n \in \mathbb{N}_0$, for the probability that X consists of n points and j_n for the joint conditional probability density governing the locations of these points. In fact, one may combine the p_n and j_n in a single function

$$f(\{x_1, \ldots, x_n\}) = e^{|W|} n! p_n j_n(x_1, \ldots, x_n), \quad x_1, \ldots, x_n \in W, \tag{4.7}$$

the probability density of X with respect to the distribution of a unit rate Poisson process on W. The factor $n!$ in the right-hand side occurs because f is a function of *unordered sets*, whereas j_n has *ordered vectors* as its argument. The constant $e^{|W|}$ is simply a normalisation.

Clearly, f is defined uniquely in terms of p_n and j_n. The reverse is also true. Indeed, $p_0 = \exp(-|W|) f(\emptyset)$ and, for $n \in \mathbb{N}$, integration of both sides of equation (4.7) yields

$$p_n = \frac{e^{-|W|}}{n!} \int_W \cdots \int_W f(\{u_1, \ldots, u_n\}) du_1 \cdots du_n.$$

Also, if $p_n > 0$,

$$j_n(x_1,\ldots,x_n) = \frac{f(\{x_1,\ldots,x_n\})}{\int_W \cdots \int_W f(\{u_1,\ldots,u_n\})du_1\cdots du_n}, \qquad x_1,\ldots,x_n \in W.$$

If $p_n = 0$, j_n may be chosen arbitrarily.

Example 4.9 *Let X be a homogeneous Poisson process with intensity λ on a bounded Borel set W of positive volume. Then the number of points is Poisson distributed with mean $\lambda|W|$ and, conditionally on the number, the points are scattered independently and uniformly according to Theorem 4.2. Hence*

$$p_n = e^{-\lambda|W|}\frac{(\lambda|W|)^n}{n!}$$

and $j_n \equiv 1/|W|^n$, so (4.7) reads

$$f(\{x_1,\ldots,x_n\}) = \lambda^n \exp\left[(1-\lambda)|W|\right]$$

for $n \in \mathbb{N}_0$ and $x_i \in W$, $i = 1,\ldots,n$. Similarly, for inhomogeneous Poisson processes with intensity function $\lambda : W \to \mathbb{R}^+$,

$$f(\{x_1,\ldots,x_n\}) = \exp\left[\int_W (1-\lambda(u))du\right]\prod_{i=1}^n \lambda(x_i). \tag{4.8}$$

It is also possible to specify the probability density f directly, as in the following definition.

Definition 4.9 *Let $W \subset \mathbb{R}^d$ be a bounded Borel set. A* pairwise interaction process *X on W is a point process whose probability density is of the form*

$$f(\mathbf{x}) \propto \prod_{x\in\mathbf{x}} \beta(x) \prod_{\{u,v\}\subseteq\mathbf{x}} \gamma(u,v), \quad \mathbf{x} \in N^{\mathrm{lf}}(W),$$

with respect to the distribution of a unit rate Poisson process on W for some measurable function $\beta : W \to \mathbb{R}^+$ and some symmetric, measurable function $\gamma : W \times W \to \mathbb{R}^+$.

Example 4.10 *A pairwise interaction process with*

$$\gamma(u,v) = \begin{cases} \gamma_0 & \text{if } ||u-v|| \le R \\ 1 & \text{if } ||u-v|| > R \end{cases}$$

for $\gamma_0 \in [0,1]$ *is called a* Strauss process. *Setting* $\gamma_0 = 0$, *one obtains the* hard core process *in which no point is allowed to fall within distance* R *of another point. For* $\gamma_0 = 1$, f *reduces to the probability density of a Poisson process. For intermediate values of* γ_0, *points tend to avoid lying closer than* R *together, the tendency being stronger for smaller values of* γ_0.

Example 4.11 *The* Lennard–Jones interaction function *is defined as*

$$\gamma(u,v) = \exp\left[\alpha\left(\frac{1}{||u-v||}\right)^6 - \beta\left(\frac{1}{||u-v||}\right)^{12}\right]$$

for $\alpha, \beta > 0$. *In this model for interacting particles in a liquid or dense gas, the particles avoid coming very close to one another but cluster at larger scales.*

It is important to realise that not all choices of β and γ in Definition 4.9 give rise to a function f that can be normalised to a probability density, that is, for which

$$\sum_{n=0}^{\infty} \frac{e^{-|W|}}{n!} \int_W \cdots \int_W \prod_{i=1}^{n} \beta(x_i) \prod_{i<j} \gamma(x_i, x_j) dx_1 \cdots dx_n < \infty.$$

A sufficient condition is stated in the next definition.

Definition 4.10 *A function* $f : N^{\mathrm{lf}}(\mathbb{R}^d) \to \mathbb{R}^+$ *is said to be* locally stable *if there exists some* $\beta > 0$ *such that*

$$f(\{x_1, \ldots, x_n, x_{n+1}\}) \le \beta f(\{x_1, \ldots, x_n\})$$

for all $\{x_1, \ldots, x_n\} \subset \mathbb{R}^d$, $n \in \mathbb{N}_0$, *and all* $x_{n+1} \in \mathbb{R}^d$.

Proposition 4.2 *Suppose that the function* $f : N^{\mathrm{lf}}(\mathbb{R}^d) \to \mathbb{R}^+$ *is locally stable. Then* f *is hereditary in the sense that* $f(\mathbf{x}) > 0$ *implies that* $f(\mathbf{y}) > 0$ *for all* $\mathbf{y} \subseteq \mathbf{x}$. *If* $f(\emptyset) \neq 0$, f *can be normalised into a probability density on bounded Borel sets* $W \subset \mathbb{R}^d$.

Proof: Suppose that $f(\mathbf{x}) > 0$ and that $\mathbf{y}$ is a strict subset of $\mathbf{x}$. Let $\{z_1, \ldots, z_m\}$ be the collection of points in $\mathbf{x}$ that do not belong to $\mathbf{y}$ and write $\beta > 0$ for the local stability constant. If $f(\mathbf{y})$ would be equal to zero, also

$$f(\mathbf{y} \cup \{z_1\}) \le \beta f(\mathbf{y}) = 0.$$

Similarly, $f(\mathbf{y} \cup \{z_1, z_2\}) \leq \beta f(\mathbf{y} \cup \{z_1\}) = 0$ and, proceeding in this fashion, $f(\mathbf{x}) = 0$ in contradiction with the assumption. Consequently $f(\mathbf{y}) > 0$ so f is hereditary.

To show that f may be normalised, we claim that

$$\int_W \cdots \int_W f(x_1, \ldots, x_n) dx_1 \cdots dx_n \leq (\beta |W|)^n f(\emptyset).$$

Then

$$\sum_{n=0}^{\infty} \frac{e^{-|W|}}{n!} \int_W \cdots \int_W f(\{x_1, \ldots, x_n\}) dx_1 \cdots dx_n$$

$$\leq f(\emptyset) \sum_{n=0}^{\infty} \frac{e^{-|W|}}{n!} \beta^n |W|^n = f(\emptyset) \exp\left[(\beta - 1)|W|\right],$$

which can be scaled to one provided $f(\emptyset) \neq 0$.

The claim can be proved by induction. Obviously $f(\emptyset) \leq \beta^0 |W|^0 f(\emptyset)$. Assume that the claim is true for point patterns having at most $n \geq 0$ points. Then local stability implies that

$$\int_{W^{n+1}} f(x_1, \ldots, x_n, x_{n+1}) dx_1 \cdots dx_n dx_{n+1}$$
$$\leq \int_{W^{n+1}} \beta f(x_1, \ldots, x_n) dx_1 \cdots dx_n dx_{n+1},$$

which, by the induction assumption, is bounded from above by

$$\int_W \beta \beta^n |W|^n f(\emptyset) dx_{n+1} = \beta^{n+1} |W|^{n+1} f(\emptyset).$$

Therefore, the claim holds for patterns with at most $n+1$ points too, and the proof is complete. □

Example 4.12 *The Strauss process introduced in Example 4.10 is locally stable whenever $\beta(\cdot) \leq B$ is bounded. To see this, let $n \in \mathbb{N}_0$ and $\{x_1, \ldots, x_n\} \subset W$. First, suppose that $\beta(x_i) > 0$ for $i = 1, \ldots, n$ and that $\gamma_0 \in (0, 1]$. Then $f(\{x_1, \ldots, x_n\}) > 0$ and*

$$\frac{f(\{x_1, \ldots, x_n, x_{n+1}\})}{f(\{x_1, \ldots, x_n\})} = \beta(x_{n+1}) \gamma_0^{S_R(x_{n+1} | \{x_1, \ldots, x_n\})} \leq \beta(x_{n+1}) \leq B \tag{4.9}$$

where $S_R(x_{n+1}|\{x_1,\ldots,x_n\}) = \sum_{i=1}^n 1\{||x_i - x_{n+1}|| \leq R\}$. *Secondly, suppose that* $\beta(x_i) > 0$ *for* $i = 1,\ldots,n$ *and* $\gamma_0 = 0$. *If* $f(\{x_1,\ldots,x_n\}) = 0$, *there is a pair of points, say* x_i *and* x_j, *that violate the hard core condition. Since these points belong to the set* $\{x_1,\ldots,x_{n+1}\}$ *too,* $f(\{x_1,\ldots,x_{n+1}\}) = 0$ *as well. If* $f(\{x_1,\ldots,x_n\}) > 0$, *(4.9) applies. Finally, if* $\beta(x_i) = 0$ *for some* $i = 1,\ldots,n$, *then*

$$0 = f(\{x_1,\ldots,x_n,x_{n+1}\}) \leq Bf(\{x_1,\ldots,x_n\}) = 0.$$

4.6 THE PAPANGELOU CONDITIONAL INTENSITY

The purpose of this section is to prove an analogue of Besag's factorisation theorem for point processes. To do so, we need to describe the conditional intensity of finding a point of the process at some fixed location given the pattern around it.

Definition 4.11 *Let* X *be a finite point process on a bounded Borel set* $W \subset \mathbb{R}^d$ *whose distribution is defined by a probability density* f *with respect to the distribution of a unit rate Poisson process and let* $\mathbf{x} \subset W$ *be a finite point pattern. Then the* Papangelou conditional intensity *at* $u \in W$ *given* $\mathbf{x}$ *is defined as*

$$\lambda(u|\mathbf{x}) = \frac{f(\mathbf{x} \cup \{u\})}{f(\mathbf{x})}$$

for $u \notin \mathbf{x}$ *provided* $f(\mathbf{x}) \neq 0$. *Set* $\lambda(u|\mathbf{x}) = 0$ *otherwise.*

If the probability density of X is locally stable, then the Papangelou conditional intensity is bounded.

Example 4.13 *For an inhomogeneous Poisson process with density (4.8),*

$$\lambda(u|\mathbf{x}) = \lambda(u)$$

whenever $u \notin \mathbf{x}$, *regardless of* $\mathbf{x}$. *The Papangelou conditional intensity of the Strauss process considered in Examples 4.10 and 4.12 is given by*

$$\lambda(u|\mathbf{x}) = \beta(u)\gamma_0^{S_R(u|\mathbf{x})}, \quad u \notin \mathbf{x},$$

and depends only on points in $\mathbf{x}$ *that are at most a distance* R *removed from* u.

We are now ready to state the analogue of Theorem 3.1. As a corollary, the probability density of a hereditary point process that is absolutely continuous with respect to the distribution of a unit rate Poisson process is uniquely determined by the Papangelou conditional intensity.

Theorem 4.3 *Let X be a finite hereditary point process on a bounded Borel set W with probability density f with respect to the distribution of a unit rate Poisson process on W. Then*

$$f(\{x_1,\dots,x_n\}) = f(\emptyset)\prod_{i=1}^{n}\lambda(x_i|\{x_1,\dots,x_{i-1}\})$$

and the product does not depend on the labelling of the points $x_1,\dots,x_n \in W$, $n \in \mathbb{N}_0$.

Proof: Consider a point pattern $\mathbf{x} = \{x_1,\dots,x_n\}$ of points and fix a labelling of the points arbitrarily. If $f(\{x_1,\dots,x_n\}) > 0$, the assumption that X is hereditary implies that $f(\{x_1,\dots,x_i\}) > 0$ for all $i < n$ and therefore

$$f(\emptyset)\prod_{i=1}^{n}\lambda(x_i|\{x_1,\dots,x_{i-1}\}) = f(\emptyset)\prod_{i=1}^{n}\frac{f(\{x_1,\dots,x_i\})}{f(\{x_1,\dots,x_{i-1}\})}$$
$$= f(\{x_1,\dots,x_n\}).$$

If $f(\{x_1,\dots,x_n\}) = 0$, order the points according to the labelling and let i_n be the largest $i < n$ such that $f(\{x_1,\dots,x_i\}) > 0$. By definition, $\lambda(x_{i_n+1}|\{x_1,\dots,x_{i_n}\}) = 0$ and the claimed equality holds. □

The condition that f is hereditary is needed as demonstrated by the following example.

Example 4.14 *Let W be a bounded Borel set with positive volume $|W|$ and consider the binomial point process $X = \{X_1\}$ introduced in Example 4.1, where X_1 is uniformly distributed on W. Clearly X is not hereditary. Now,*

$$f(\emptyset)\prod_{i=1}^{n}\lambda(x_i|\{x_1,\dots,x_{i-1}\}) \equiv 0$$

for all finite point configurations as $f(\emptyset) = 0$. On the other hand, for any $x \in W$, $f(\{x\}) = e^{|W|}/|W| > 0$.

4.7 MARKOV POINT PROCESSES

As we saw in the previous section, the Papangelou conditional intensity (cf. Definition 4.11) plays a similar role to the local characteristics for random fields. This observation suggests that the Papangelou conditional intensity may be used to define a notion of Markovianity in full analogy to Definition 3.6.

Definition 4.12 *Let $\sim$ be a symmetric reflexive relation on $\mathbb{R}^d$ and define the boundary of $A \subseteq \mathbb{R}^d$ by $\partial(A) = \{s \in \mathbb{R}^d \setminus A : s \sim a$ for some $a \in A\}$. A point process defined by a probability density f with respect to the distribution of a unit rate Poisson process on a bounded Borel set $W \subset \mathbb{R}^d$ is a* Markov point process *with respect to $\sim$ if for all finite configurations $\mathbf{x}$ in W such that $f(\mathbf{x}) > 0$,*

(a) *$f(\mathbf{y}) > 0$ for all $\mathbf{y} \subseteq \mathbf{x}$;*

(b) *for all $u \in W$, $u \notin \mathbf{x}$, $\lambda(u|\mathbf{x})$ depends only on u and $\partial(\{u\}) \cap \mathbf{x}$.*

Two points $x, y \in W$ that are related, $x \sim y$, will be called neighbours.

Recalling that a clique is a set whose elements are pairwise neighbours, the analogue of Theorem 3.4 in the current context reads as follows.

Theorem 4.4 (Hammersley–Clifford) *Let X be a finite point process on a bounded Borel set $W \subset \mathbb{R}^d$ whose distribution is defined by a probability density f with respect to the distribution of a unit rate Poisson process. Let $\sim$ be a symmetric reflexive relation on W. Then X is a Markov point process with respect to $\sim$ if and only if f can be written as a product over $\sim$-cliques, that is,*

$$f(\mathbf{x}) = \prod_{\text{cliques } \mathbf{y} \subseteq \mathbf{x}} \varphi(\mathbf{y})$$

for some measurable non-negative interaction function φ defined on finite point configurations.

Proof: Suppose that for all $\mathbf{x}$, $f(\mathbf{x})$ is defined by $f(\mathbf{x}) = \prod_{\text{cliques } \mathbf{y} \subseteq \mathbf{x}} \varphi(\mathbf{y})$ for some non-negative function φ and that f is a probability density, that is, integrates to unity. In order to show that f is Markov, we need to check conditions (a) and (b) of definition 4.12. To verify (a), suppose that $f(\mathbf{x}) \neq 0$. Then $\varphi(\mathbf{y}) \neq 0$ for all cliques $\mathbf{y} \subseteq \mathbf{x}$. If $\mathbf{z} \subseteq \mathbf{x}$, a fortiori $\varphi(\mathbf{y}) \neq 0$ for any clique $\mathbf{y} \subseteq \mathbf{z}$, and therefore

$$f(\mathbf{z}) = \prod_{\text{cliques } \mathbf{y} \subseteq \mathbf{z}} \varphi(\mathbf{y}) > 0.$$

As for (b), let $\mathbf{x}$ be a finite point configuration such that $f(\mathbf{x}) > 0$, and take $u \notin \mathbf{x}$. Then, upon extending φ by setting $\varphi(\mathbf{z}) = 1$ whenever $\mathbf{z}$ is no clique,

$$\begin{aligned} \frac{f(\mathbf{x} \cup \{u\})}{f(\mathbf{x})} &= \frac{\prod_{\text{cliques } \mathbf{y} \subseteq \mathbf{x}} \varphi(\mathbf{y}) \prod_{\text{cliques } \mathbf{y} \subseteq \mathbf{x}} \varphi(\mathbf{y} \cup \{u\})}{\prod_{\text{cliques } \mathbf{y} \subseteq \mathbf{x}} \varphi(\mathbf{y})} \\ &= \prod_{\text{cliques } \mathbf{y} \subseteq \mathbf{x}} \varphi(\mathbf{y} \cup \{u\}). \end{aligned}$$

Since $\varphi(\mathbf{y} \cup \{u\}) = 1$ whenever $\mathbf{y} \cup \{u\}$ is no clique, the conditional intensity $\lambda(u|\mathbf{x})$ depends only on u and its neighbours in $\mathbf{x}$.

Conversely, suppose f is a Markov density. Define an interaction function φ inductively by

$$\begin{aligned} \varphi(\emptyset) &= f(\emptyset) & \\ \varphi(\mathbf{x}) &= 1 & \text{if } \mathbf{x} \text{ is not a clique} \\ \varphi(\mathbf{x}) &= \frac{f(\mathbf{x})}{\prod_{\mathbf{y}:\mathbf{x} \neq \mathbf{y} \subset \mathbf{x}} \varphi(\mathbf{y})} & \text{if } \mathbf{x} \text{ is a clique} \end{aligned}$$

with the convention $0/0 = 0$. Note that if $\prod_{\mathbf{y}:\mathbf{x} \neq \mathbf{y} \subset \mathbf{x}} \varphi(\mathbf{y}) = 0$, necessarily $f(\mathbf{y}) = 0$ for some $\mathbf{y}$, and therefore $f(\mathbf{x}) = 0$. Hence φ is well-defined. To show that f has the required product form, we use induction on the number of points. By definition the factorisation holds for the empty set. Assume that the factorisation holds for configurations with up to $n-1$ points and consider a pattern $\mathbf{x}$ of cardinality $n \geq 1$. We will distinguish three cases.

First, suppose that $\mathbf{x}$ is no clique and that $f(\mathbf{x}) = 0$. Then there exist $v, w \in \mathbf{x}$ such that $v \not\sim w$. Furthermore, assume $\prod_{\mathbf{y}:\mathbf{x} \neq \mathbf{y} \subset \mathbf{x}} \varphi(\mathbf{y}) > 0$. By the induction hypothesis, $f(\mathbf{y}) > 0$ for all proper subsets $\mathbf{y}$ of $\mathbf{x}$; hence, with $\mathbf{z} = \mathbf{x} \setminus \{v, w\}$,

$$0 = \frac{f(\mathbf{x})}{f(\mathbf{z} \cup \{v\})} f(\mathbf{z} \cup \{v\}) = \frac{f(\mathbf{z} \cup \{w\})}{f(\mathbf{z})} f(\mathbf{z} \cup \{v\}) > 0$$

as $w \not\sim v$. The assumption $\prod_{\mathbf{y}:\mathbf{x} \neq \mathbf{y} \subset \mathbf{x}} \varphi(\mathbf{y}) > 0$ leads to a contradiction; hence we conclude that $\prod_{\mathbf{y}:\mathbf{x} \neq \mathbf{y} \subset \mathbf{x}} \varphi(\mathbf{y}) = 0 = f(\mathbf{x})$.

Next, let $\mathbf{x}$ be a clique for which $f(\mathbf{x}) = 0$. Then $\varphi(\mathbf{x}) = 0$ by definition and hence $f(\mathbf{x}) = \prod_{\mathbf{y} \subseteq \mathbf{x}} \varphi(\mathbf{y})$.

Finally, consider the case $f(\mathbf{x}) > 0$. If $\mathbf{x}$ is a clique, $f(\mathbf{x}) = \varphi(\mathbf{x}) \prod_{\mathbf{y}:\mathbf{x} \neq \mathbf{y} \subset \mathbf{x}} \varphi(\mathbf{y}) = \prod_{\mathbf{y} \subseteq \mathbf{x}} \varphi(\mathbf{y})$. If $\mathbf{x}$ is no clique, write $\mathbf{x} = \mathbf{z} \cup \{v, w\}$ for some $v \not\sim w$. Since f is a Markov density, $f(\mathbf{z}) > 0$, $f(\mathbf{z} \cup \{v\}) > 0$ and therefore

$$\begin{aligned} f(\mathbf{x}) &= \frac{f(\mathbf{z} \cup \{v, w\})}{f(\mathbf{z} \cup \{v\})} f(\mathbf{z} \cup \{v\}) = \frac{f(\mathbf{z} \cup \{w\})}{f(\mathbf{z})} f(\mathbf{z} \cup \{v\}) \\ &= \prod_{\mathbf{y} \subseteq \mathbf{z}} \varphi(\mathbf{y} \cup \{w\}) \prod_{\mathbf{y} \subseteq \mathbf{z} \cup \{v\}} \varphi(\mathbf{y}) = \prod_{\text{cliques } \mathbf{y} \subseteq \mathbf{x}} \varphi(\mathbf{y}), \end{aligned}$$

using the fact that the interaction function takes the value one for non-cliques. In particular, $\varphi(\mathbf{y}) = 1$ for any $\mathbf{y}$ containing both v and w. □

The Hammersley–Clifford theorem is useful for breaking up a high-dimensional joint distribution into manageable clique interaction functions. Some care is needed, though, as a particular choice of interaction functions must result in a density f that is integrable and may be normalised into a probability density. Proposition 4.2 provides one sufficient condition. Alternatively, imposing a hard core as in Example 4.10 also guarantees that the number of points is almost surely bounded.

Example 4.15 *The Strauss process of Example 4.10 is a Markov point process with respect to the fixed range relation*

$$u \sim v \Leftrightarrow ||u - v|| \leq R, \quad u, v \in \mathbb{R}^d.$$

Its interaction function is equal to

$$\begin{aligned} \varphi(\{u\}) &= \beta(u) \\ \varphi(\{u, v\}) &= \gamma_0 \quad \text{if } u \sim v \end{aligned}$$

For all other patterns $\mathbf{x}$ except the empty set, $\varphi(\mathbf{x}) = 1$. The value of $\varphi(\emptyset)$ serves to normalise the Strauss function into a probability density.

4.8 LIKELIHOOD INFERENCE FOR POISSON PROCESSES

Suppose that a realisation $\mathbf{x} = \{x_1, \ldots, x_n\}$ of a Poisson process X is observed in some bounded Borel set $W \subset \mathbb{R}^d$ and that the abundance of points depends on real-valued covariate functions $C_j : W \to \mathbb{R}$,

$j = 1, \ldots, p$, $p \in \mathbb{N}$. For specificity, assume that the intensity function satisfies a log-linear regression model

$$\lambda(u) = \lambda_\beta(u) = \exp\left[\beta_0 + \sum_{j=1}^{p} \beta_j C_j(u)\right], \quad u \in W.$$

Then the log likelihood function $L(\beta; \mathbf{x})$ reads

$$L(\beta; \mathbf{x}) = n\beta_0 + \sum_{j=1}^{p}\sum_{i=1}^{n} \beta_j C_j(x_i) - e^{\beta_0} \int_W \exp\left[\sum_{j=1}^{p} \beta_j C_j(u)\right] du.$$

The partial derivatives with respect to β yield the score equations

$$\int_W C_j(u)\lambda_\beta(u)du = \sum_{i=1}^{n} C_j(x_i) \tag{4.10}$$

for $j = 0, \ldots, p$ under the convention that $C_0 \equiv 1$. The Hessian matrix of second order partial derivatives is

$$H(\beta) = -\int_W C(u)C(u)'\lambda_\beta(u)du,$$

where $C(u) \in \mathbb{R}^{p+1}$ is the $(p+1)$-vector $(1, C_1(u), \ldots, C_p(u))'$. To be precise, its ij-th entry is equal to $-\int_W C_i(u)C_j(u)\lambda_\beta(u)du$. The Hessian matrix does not depend on the data pattern. Therefore the Fisher information can be written as

$$I(\beta) = -H(\beta) = \int_W C(u)C(u)'\lambda_\beta(u)du.$$

In conclusion: any $\hat{\beta}$ that solves the score equations (4.10) and for which $H(\hat{\beta})$ is negative definite is a local maximum of the log likelihood function $L(\beta; \mathbf{x})$. Little is known about the properties of $\hat{\beta}$. Under suitable regularity conditions[1], it can be shown that when W grows to $\mathbb{R}^d$, $\hat{\beta}$ tends to a multivariate normal distribution with mean β and covariance matrix $I(\beta)^{-1}$. For this reason, error estimates in statistical software packages are based on the estimated covariance matrix $(I(\hat{\beta}))^{-1} = (-H(\hat{\beta}))^{-1}$ with numerical approximation of the integral involved.

[1]Kutoyants (1998). Statistical Inference for Spatial Poisson Processes.

The maximum likelihood estimator may be used to test whether the observations depend significantly on some covariate. Writing f for the density function with respect to the distribution of a unit rate Poisson process, the likelihood ratio test statistic for covariate function C_j is defined by

$$\Lambda(X) = \frac{\sup\{f(X;\beta) : \beta_j = 0\}}{f(X;\hat{\beta})}.$$

Under the null hypothesis of no influence of the j-th covariate, i.e. $\beta_j = 0$, the transformed likelihood ratio test statistic $-2\log\Lambda(X)$ is approximately χ^2-distributed with one degree of freedom. Similarly, under the composite null hypothesis that X is a homogeneous Poisson process, or, in other words, that $\beta_j = 0$ for all $j = 1, \dots, p$, the likelihood ratio test statistic is

$$\Lambda(X) = \frac{\sup\{f(X;\beta) : \beta_1 = \dots = \beta_p = 0\}}{f(X;\hat{\beta})}$$

and $-2\log\Lambda(X)$ is approximately χ^2-distributed with p degrees of freedom.

4.9 INFERENCE FOR FINITE POINT PROCESSES

From an inference point of view, a Poisson process is very convenient to work with because its likelihood is available in closed form. For most other models, this is not the case.

As an illustration, consider the Strauss process X of Example 4.10. Suppose that a realisation $\mathbf{x} = \{x_1, \dots, x_n\}$ is observed in some bounded Borel set W and that the first order interaction function β depends on real-valued covariate functions $C_j : W \to \mathbb{R}$, $j = 1, \dots, p$, $p \in \mathbb{N}$, via a log-linear regression

$$\log\beta(u) = \beta_0 + \sum_{j=1}^{p} \beta_j C_j(u), \quad u \in W.$$

Write

$$S(\mathbf{x}) = \sum_{\{u,v\}\subseteq\mathbf{x}} 1\{0 < ||u - v|| \leq R\}$$

for the number of R-close pairs in $\mathbf{x}$. Then the log likelihood function is

$$L(\beta, \gamma_0; \mathbf{x}) = S(\mathbf{x})\log\gamma_0 - \log Z(\beta, \gamma_0) + \sum_{i=1}^{n}\left(\beta_0 + \sum_{j=1}^{p} \beta_j C_j(x_i)\right).$$

The normalising constant $Z(\beta, \gamma_0)$ depends on the parameter vector $\theta = (\beta, \gamma_0)$ with $\beta \in \mathbb{R}^{p+1}$ and $\gamma_0 \in [0, 1]$, and cannot be evaluated explicitly. Consequently, maximum likelihood estimation is not as straightforward as it was for Poisson models.

In full analogy to similar problems in the context of the areal unit models discussed in Chapter 3, one may proceed by a pseudo-likelihood or Monte Carlo approach. To start with the former, replace the intensity function in (4.8) with the Papangelou conditional intensity to obtain the log pseudo-likelihood function

$$PL(\theta; \mathbf{x}) = \sum_{i=1}^{n} \log \lambda_\theta(x_i|\mathbf{x} \setminus \{x_i\}) + \int_W (1 - \lambda_\theta(u|\mathbf{x}))\, du.$$

For the Strauss process, it reduces to

$$\sum_{i=1}^{n} \left(\beta_0 + \sum_{j=1}^{p} \beta_j C_j(x_i) + S_R(x_i|\mathbf{x} \setminus \{x_i\}) \log \gamma_0 \right) + \int_W \left(1 - \beta(u) \gamma_0^{S_R(u|\mathbf{x})}\right) du$$

where, as before, for $u \notin \mathbf{x}$,

$$S_R(u|\mathbf{x}) = \sum_{x_i \in \mathbf{x}} 1\{||u - x_i|| \leq R\}.$$

The log pseudo-likelihood function is optimised numerically over the parameter θ to obtain $\hat{\theta}$.

Alternatively, Monte Carlo ideas may be used. To do so, note that the Strauss density is of the general form

$$f(\mathbf{x}; \theta) = \frac{1}{Z(\theta)} g(\mathbf{x}; \theta)$$

where the unnormalised density

$$g(\mathbf{x}; \theta) = \gamma_0^{S(\mathbf{x})} \prod_{x_i \in \mathbf{x}} \beta(x_i)$$

is known explicitly and $Z(\theta)$ normalises g to integrate to unity. For such models, the likelihood ratio with respect to θ_0 can be written as

$$\frac{f(\mathbf{x}; \theta)}{f(\mathbf{x}; \theta_0)} = \frac{g(\mathbf{x}; \theta)}{g(\mathbf{x}; \theta_0)} \Big/ \frac{Z(\theta)}{Z(\theta_0)}.$$

Since

$$\frac{Z(\theta)}{Z(\theta_0)} = \mathbb{E}_{\theta_0} \left[\frac{g(X; \theta)}{g(X; \theta_0)} \right],$$

the log likelihood ratio can be approximated by the Monte Carlo log likelihood ratio

$$\log \left[\frac{g(\mathbf{x}; \theta)}{g(\mathbf{x}; \theta_0)} \right] - \log \left[\frac{1}{N} \sum_{j=1}^{N} \frac{g(X_j; \theta)}{g(X_j; \theta_0)} \right].$$

An analogue of Theorem 3.5 holds for the important special case that f is the unnormalised density of an exponential family.

With respect to the precision of maximum likelihood estimators and their approximations, similar remarks as in Chapter 3 apply. When the window W grows to $\mathbb{R}^d$, there may not be a unique limiting point process defined on $\mathbb{R}^d$ whose conditional specification on W coincides with the given one and asymptotic normality of estimators has been proved under strong ergodicity conditions only.

The Monte Carlo approach requires samples X_j from a Strauss process under the reference parameter vector θ_0. In principle, such samples could be obtained by a Metropolis–Hastings method. In the current context, however, the state space $N^{\text{lf}}(W)$ is the union of Euclidean spaces W^n of variable dimension. Therefore, the proposal distribution must be able to change the total number of points, perhaps in addition to changing the location of an existing point. This can be achieved by 'birth' and 'death' proposals as follows. In a birth proposal, add a new point u to the current pattern $\mathbf{x}$ uniformly on W; for deaths select one of the current points with equal probability and delete it. Then, the acceptance probability for, e.g., the birth transition from $\mathbf{x} = \{x_1, \ldots, x_n\}$ to $\mathbf{x} \cup \{u\}$ is

$$\min \left\{ 1, \lambda(u|\mathbf{x}) \frac{p_d |W|}{p_b (n+1)} \right\}$$

where $p_b, p_d \in (0,1)$ are the selection probabilities for, respectively, birth and death proposals.

Theorem 4.5 *Let X be a finite point process on a bounded Borel set $W \subset \mathbb{R}^d$ of positive volume whose distribution is defined by a probability density f with respect to the distribution of a unit rate Poisson process. If $p_b = 1 - p_d \in (0,1)$ and the probability density f of X is locally stable, the Metropolis–Hastings algorithm on the support $D_f = \{\mathbf{x} \in N^{\text{lf}} : f(\mathbf{x}) > 0\}$ is f-irreducible and f defines an invariant measure.*

Proof: First, write $A(\mathbf{x}, \mathbf{y})$ for the acceptance probability for a transition from $\mathbf{x}$ to $\mathbf{y}$ and consider the detailed balance equation

$$f(\mathbf{x}) \frac{p_b}{|W|} A(\mathbf{x}, \mathbf{x} \cup \{u\}) = f(\mathbf{x} \cup \{u\}) \frac{p_d}{n(\mathbf{x}) + 1} A(\mathbf{x} \cup \{u\}, \mathbf{x}), \quad \mathbf{x} \in D_f, u \in W.$$

If $\mathbf{x} \cup \{u\} \notin D_f$, then $A(\mathbf{x} \cup \{u\}, \mathbf{x}) = 0$. Otherwise,

$$\frac{A(\mathbf{x}, \mathbf{x} \cup \{u\})}{A(\mathbf{x} \cup \{u\}, \mathbf{x})} = \frac{\lambda(u|\mathbf{x}) p_d |W|}{p_b (n(\mathbf{x}) + 1)}.$$

Since the Metropolis–Hastings acceptance probabilities satisfy this equation, indeed f defines an invariant measure.

Next, we show that the Metropolis–Hastings chain is ϕ-irreducible for the probability measure ϕ that places all its mass on the empty pattern. To do so, note that the probability of accepting a death proposal from $\mathbf{x}$ is at least

$$\frac{p_b}{(1 - p_b)\beta |W|} > 0$$

where the local stability constant β is chosen large enough for the lower bound to be less than one. The death proposal probability is $1 - p_b$ so, if the current state $\mathbf{x}$ contains m points, the empty pattern can be reached in m steps with probability

$$P^m(\mathbf{x}, \{\emptyset\}) \geq (1 - p_b)^m \left(\frac{p_b}{(1 - p_b)\beta |W|} \right)^m = \left(\frac{p_b}{\beta |W|} \right)^m > 0.$$

Hence, the Metropolis–Hastings algorithm is ϕ-irreducible. Finally, recall from Markov chain theory that if a chain is ϕ-irreducible and π is invariant, then the chain is also π-irreducible[2]. □

Since self-transitions occur with positive probability, the Metropolis–Hastings chain is aperiodic. An appeal to Theorem 3.6 leads us to conclude that it converges in total variation to the distribution of X from almost all initial states in D_f.

4.10 COX PROCESSES

Not all point process distributions are conveniently expressed by their density with respect to the distribution of a unit rate Poisson process. For such models, moment methods may be used to estimate the parameters. In this section, we consider two specific models for clustered point patterns in more detail.

[2] Meyn and Tweedie (2009). Markov Chains and Stochastic Stability.

4.10.1 Cluster processes

A *cluster process* is defined in two steps. In the first step, sample a 'parent' point process. Secondly, conditionally on the parents, let each of them generate a new point process of 'daughters' and take the superposition of all daughters.

The special case in which the parents form a homogeneous Poisson process with intensity λ_p and in which a Poisson number of daughters (with mean λ_c) are scattered independently around their parent according to a probability density f is known as a *Neyman–Scott Cox process.*

Definition 4.13 *Let X be a homogeneous Poisson process on $\mathbb{R}^d$ with intensity $\lambda_p > 0$. For $x \in \mathbb{R}^d$, let Z_x be an inhomogeneous Poisson process with intensity function $\lambda_c f(\cdot - x)$ for some probability density f on $\mathbb{R}^d$ and $\lambda_c > 0$ such that*

$$\int_{\mathbb{R}^d} \left(1 - \exp\left[-\lambda_c \int_A f(y-x)dy\right]\right) dx < \infty$$

for every bounded Borel set $A \subset \mathbb{R}^d$. Then $\cup_{x \in X} Z_x$ is a Neyman–Scott Cox process.

Note that the integrand is the probability that a parent at x places at least one point in A. The condition is needed to ensure that the resulting process is locally finite. For example, if each parent were to place its daughters in some neighbourhood A of the origin, the result would be countably many points in A. As an aside, Definition 4.13 can be extended to allow parents to be distributed according to an inhomogeneous Poisson process.

Theorem 4.6 *The intensity of a Neyman–Scott Cox process is $\lambda_p \lambda_c$ and the pair correlation function is given by*

$$g(x,y) = 1 + \frac{1}{\lambda_p} \int_{\mathbb{R}^d} f(x-z)f(y-z)dz$$

for $x, y \in \mathbb{R}^d$.

Since $g(x,y) \geq 1$, a Neyman–Scott Cox process indeed models aggregation.

Proof: Conditionally on the parent process X, since the superposition of independent Poisson processes is a Poisson process, the total offspring form a Poisson process. Its intensity function is

$$\lambda(y) = \lambda_c \sum_{x \in X} f(y - x), \quad y \in \mathbb{R}^d.$$

Similarly, conditionally on X, the second order product density $\rho^{(2)}(y, z)$, $y, z \in \mathbb{R}^d$, is given by

$$\begin{aligned} \lambda(y)\lambda(z) &= \lambda_c^2 \sum_{x_1 \in X} \sum_{x_2 \in X} f(y - x_1) f(z - x_2) \\ &= \lambda_c^2 \sum_{x_1 \in X} \sum_{x_2 \in X}^{\neq} f(y - x_1) f(z - x_2) + \lambda_c^2 \sum_{x_1 \in X} f(y - x_1) f(z - x_1). \end{aligned}$$

To obtain the product densities, take the expectation with respect to the distribution of X aided by (4.2). Doing so, the intensity reads

$$\lambda_c \lambda_p \int_{\mathbb{R}^d} f(y - x) dx = \lambda_c \lambda_p.$$

Similarly, the second order product density is

$$\lambda_c^2 \lambda_p^2 \int_{\mathbb{R}^d} \int_{\mathbb{R}^d} f(y - x_1) f(z - x_2) dx_1 dx_2 + \lambda_c^2 \lambda_p \int_{\mathbb{R}^d} f(y - x_1) f(z - x_1) dx_1$$

which reduces to

$$\lambda_c^2 \left(\lambda_p^2 + \lambda_p \int_{\mathbb{R}^d} f(y - x_1) f(z - x_1) dx_1 \right).$$

Finally, the pair correlation function is as claimed. □

Example 4.16 *A planar* modified Thomas process *is a Neyman–Scott Cox process in which the daughters are located according to a normal distribution, that is,*

$$f(x) = \frac{1}{2\pi\sigma^2} \exp\left[-\frac{1}{2\sigma^2} ||x||^2 \right]$$

for $x \in \mathbb{R}^2$. Then,

$$\int_{\mathbb{R}^2} f(x-z) f(y-z) dz = \frac{1}{4\pi^2\sigma^4} \int_{\mathbb{R}^2} \exp\left[-\frac{1}{2\sigma^2} (||x - z||^2 + ||y - z||^2) \right] dz.$$

Now,

$$\int_{-\infty}^{\infty} \exp\left[-\frac{1}{2\sigma^2}((x_1-z)^2+(y_1-z)^2)\right] dz =$$

$$\exp\left[-\frac{1}{2\sigma^2}(x_1^2+y_1^2)+\frac{1}{4\sigma^2}(x_1+y_1)^2\right]\int_{-\infty}^{\infty} \exp\left[-\frac{1}{\sigma^2}\left(z-\frac{x_1+y_1}{2}\right)^2\right] dz.$$

The first term above is equal to $\exp\left[-\frac{1}{4\sigma^2}(x_1-y_1)^2\right]$*, the integral is* $(2\pi\sigma^2/2)^{1/2}$*. Hence, returning to two dimensions,*

$$\int f(x-z)f(y-z)dz = \frac{1}{4\pi^2\sigma^4}\pi\sigma^2 \exp\left[-\frac{1}{4\sigma^2}||x-y||^2\right]$$

and the pair correlation function satisfies

$$g(x,y) = 1 + \frac{1}{\lambda_p}\frac{1}{4\pi\sigma^2}\exp\left[-\frac{1}{4\sigma^2}||x-y||^2\right].$$

4.10.2 Log-Gaussian Cox processes

A *log-Gaussian Cox process*, like a cluster process, is defined in two steps. In the first step, specify a Gaussian random field $(X_t)_{t\in T}$ for some Borel set $T \subseteq \mathbb{R}^d$ as in Section 2.2 and define a random Borel measure Λ by

$$\Lambda(A) = \int_A \exp(X_t)dt$$

for $A \subseteq T$. In step two, conditional on X_t, generate an inhomogeneous Poisson process with intensity function $\exp(X_t)$. For the above definition to make sense, it is necessary that $\exp(X_t)$ is almost surely integrable on bounded Borel sets. It is sufficient to assume that $(X_t)_{t\in T}$ admits a continuous version, cf. Theorem 2.1 and the surrounding discussion.

Theorem 4.7 *For a log-Gaussian Cox process defined by the Gaussian random field* $(X_t)_{t\in\mathbb{R}^d}$ *with mean function* $m(\cdot)$ *and covariance function* $\rho(\cdot,\cdot)$,

$$\rho^{(1)}(t) = \exp\left[m(t)+\rho(t,t)/2\right], \quad t \in \mathbb{R}^d.$$

The pair correlation function is given by

$$g(t,s) = \exp\left[\rho(t,s)\right], \quad t,s \in \mathbb{R}^d.$$

Proof: Conditional on the random field, the first and second order product densities read, respectively, e^{X_t} and $e^{X_t}e^{X_s}$. Hence

$$\begin{aligned} \rho^{(1)}(t) &= \mathbb{E}\exp\left[X_t\right]; \\ \rho^{(2)}(t,s) &= \mathbb{E}\exp\left[X_t+X_s\right]. \end{aligned}$$

Recall that the moment generating function of a normally distributed random variable Z with mean μ and variance σ^2 is given by

$$\mathbb{E}e^{kZ} = \exp\left[k\mu + \frac{k^2}{2}\sigma^2\right], \quad k \in \mathbb{R}.$$

Therefore,

$$\mathbb{E}\exp\left[X_t\right] = \exp\left[m(t) + \frac{1}{2}\rho(t,t)\right].$$

Similarly, as $X_t + X_s$ is normally distributed with mean $m(t) + m(s)$ and variance $\rho(t,t) + \rho(s,s) + 2\rho(t,s)$,

$$\mathbb{E}\exp\left[X_t + X_s\right] = \exp\left[m(t) + m(s) + \frac{1}{2}(\rho(t,t) + \rho(s,s) + 2\rho(t,s))\right].$$

The proof is complete upon writing

$$g(t,s) = \frac{\rho^{(2)}(t,s)}{\rho^{(1)}(t)\rho^{(1)}(s)} = e^{\rho(t,s)}.$$

□

4.10.3 Minimum contrast estimation

For point processes that are not defined by means of a probability density, maximum likelihood estimation cannot be used. Likewise, the Papangelou conditional intensity, being defined as a ratio of probability densities, is not available in closed form in such cases, ruling out the pseudo-likelihood method.

On the other hand, for Cox models the product densities have a simple form and can be used for estimation purposes. More precisely, the idea is to look for parameters that minimise the difference between the theoretical pair correlation function, say, and an estimator of the same function based on the data.

Definition 4.14 *Let X be a second order intensity-reweighted moment stationary point process on $\mathbb{R}^d$ that is observed in the bounded Borel set $W \subset \mathbb{R}^d$. Suppose that the pair correlation function $g(\cdot;\theta) : (\mathbb{R}^d)^2 \to \mathbb{R}$ depends on a parameter θ and is rotation-invariant in the sense that $g(x,y;\theta) = g(||x-y||;\theta)$ is a function of the norm $||x-y||$.*

A minimum contrast estimator *of the model parameter vector* $\theta \in \mathbb{R}^p$ *minimises the integrated squared error*

$$\int_{t_0}^{t_1} |\hat{g}(r) - g(r;\theta)|^2 dr,$$

where $\hat{g}$ *is an estimator of* $g(r;\theta)$ *and* $0 < t_0 < t_1$.

Of course, the integrated squared error may be replaced by the integrated absolute error, by the maximal absolute error or by weighted versions thereof.

The selection of t_0 and t_1 is an art. As a general rule of thumb, t_0 may be chosen around the minimal distance between points. The choice of t_1 tends to be less critical as both $\hat{g}(r)$ and $g(r;\theta)$ will be close to one at large distances. Regarding $\hat{g}(r)$, since for rotation-invariant pair correlation functions g in the plane, with slight abuse of notation,

$$g(r) = \frac{1}{2\pi} \int_0^{2\pi} g(r\cos\phi, r\sin\phi) d\phi,$$

a rotational average of (4.6) would serve to estimate $g(r)$, $r > 0$.

Example 4.17 *Let* X *be a log-Gaussian Cox process defined by a Gaussian random field with Gaussian covariance function*

$$\rho(x,y) = \sigma^2 \exp\left[-\beta||x-y||^2\right], \quad x, y \in \mathbb{R}^d,$$

for $\sigma^2 > 0$ *and* $\beta > 0$. *Note that* ρ *is a function of* $||x-y||$. *By Theorem 4.7,* X *has rotation-invariant pair correlation function*

$$g(r) = \exp\left[\sigma^2 e^{-\beta r^2}\right], \quad r > 0,$$

so the minimum contrast estimator minimises

$$\int_{t_0}^{t_1} \left(\exp\left[\sigma^2 e^{-\beta r^2}\right] - \hat{g}(r)\right)^2 dr$$

numerically over $\beta > 0$ *and* $\sigma^2 > 0$. *It is worth noticing that* $g(r) \geq 1$; *that is,* X *is clustered. Furthermore, as a function of the interpoint distance* r, $g(\cdot)$ *is decreasing. In other words, as points lie further apart, they influence each other less.*

In closing, it should be emphasised that the minimum contrast idea applies equally to other summary statistics such as the *empty space function*

$$F(r) = \mathbb{P}(X \cap B(0,r) \neq \emptyset), \quad r \geq 0,$$

based on the void probability of closed balls $B(0,r)$ centred at the origin.

4.11 HIERARCHICAL MODELLING

In the previous section, we met Cox processes and discussed the minimum contrast method for estimating their parameters. However, from the perspective outlined in Section 3.7, one may also be interested in estimating the 'process', that is, the driving random intensity. For example for a Neyman–Scott Cox process, the random intensity takes the form

$$\lambda_c \sum_{x \in X} f(y - x), \quad y \in \mathbb{R}^d.$$

Here, X is the point process of parents, $\lambda_c > 0$ is the mean number of daughters per parent and $f(\cdot - x)$ is the probability density for the daughter locations relative to their parent at x. Hence, estimating the process amounts to estimating X.

In practice, there is sampling bias in that the offspring process is observed within some bounded window W. Also, there may be noise in the sense of points that cannot be regarded as offspring, for example because they are far away from the parents. We model the ensemble of noise points by means of a homogeneous Poisson process with intensity $\epsilon > 0$, independently of the cluster process. With these assumptions, given parents $X = \mathbf{x}$, the forward model is a Poisson process on W with intensity function

$$\lambda_{\mathbf{x}}(y) = \epsilon + \lambda_c \sum_{x \in \mathbf{x}} f(y - x) \tag{4.11}$$

for $y \in W$.

To complete a hierarchical model, specify a prior distribution $p_X(\mathbf{x})$ on the parent point process, for example a hard core or Strauss process to avoid 'over-fitting'. After observing $\mathbf{y} = \{y_1, \ldots, y_m\}$, inference is based on the posterior probability density

$$f(\mathbf{x}|\mathbf{y}) = c(\mathbf{y}) p_X(\mathbf{x}) \exp\left[\int_W (1 - \lambda_{\mathbf{x}}(y))dy\right] \prod_{j=1}^{m} \lambda_{\mathbf{x}}(y_j) \tag{4.12}$$

with respect to the distribution of a unit rate Poisson process on the parent space. Provided that $f(\mathbf{x}|\mathbf{y})$ is locally stable, realisations of the parent point process can be obtained by the Metropolis–Hastings method.

Proposition 4.3 *Consider the posterior probability density (4.12). If the prior p_X is hereditary, so is the posterior. If the scatter density $f(y - x)$ is uniformly bounded in both arguments x and y and p_X is locally stable, so is the posterior.*

Proof: To show that the posterior is hereditary, suppose that $f(\mathbf{x}|\mathbf{y}) > 0$ for some $\mathbf{x}$ and consider a subset $\mathbf{x}' \subseteq \mathbf{x}$. Since $\lambda_{\mathbf{x}'}(y_j) \geq \epsilon > 0$ for all $j = 1, \ldots, m$, $f(\mathbf{x}'|\mathbf{y})$ can only take the value zero if $p_X(\mathbf{x}') = 0$. But this would contradict the assumption that p_X is hereditary.

For local stability, note that the posterior Papangelou conditional intensity $f(\mathbf{x} \cup \{u\}|\mathbf{y})/f(\mathbf{x}|\mathbf{y})$ is given by

$$\frac{p_X(\mathbf{x} \cup \{u\})}{p_X(\mathbf{x})} \exp\left[-\lambda_c \int_W f(y-u)dy\right] \prod_{j=1}^m \left[1 + \frac{\lambda_c f(y_j - u)}{\lambda_{\mathbf{x}}(y_j)}\right]$$

for all $u \notin \mathbf{x}$ and $p_X(\mathbf{x}) > 0$. Now, since p_X is locally stable, there exists some $\beta > 0$ such that $p_X(\mathbf{x} \cup \{u\})/p_X(\mathbf{x}) \leq \beta$. Moreover, the exponential term $\exp[-\lambda_c \int f(\cdot - u)]$ is bounded by one and, since $f(y_j - u)$ is uniformly bounded by, say, F,

$$\prod_{j=1}^m \left[1 + \frac{\lambda_c f(y_j - u)}{\lambda_{\mathbf{x}}(y_j)}\right] \leq \left(1 + \frac{\lambda_c F}{\epsilon}\right)^m.$$

In summary, the posterior Papangelou conditional intensity is bounded. □

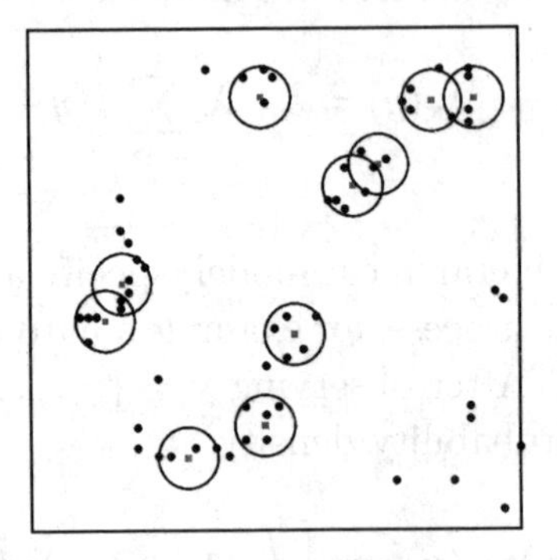

Figure 4.1 Cluster detection for a pattern of 62 redwood seedlings. Data (dots) and realisation from the posterior distribution of cluster centres (grey squares). The radius of the circles around the cluster centres is $R_c = 0.061$.

As an illustration, consider the mapped pattern consisting of 62 redwood seedlings in a rectangle with sides of approximately 23 metres renormalised to the unit square that is displayed in Figure 4.1. It is believed that the seedlings are clustered around the stumps of felled trees.

To reconstruct these stumps, let us adopt model (4.11) with a uniform scatter density f supported in a ball of radius R_c. This density is invariant under rotations with respect to the centre of the ball, and, by Theorem 4.6, the pair correlation function $g(x, y) = g(||y - x||)$ depends only on the distance $||y - x||$ between its arguments. The radius R_c may be estimated by the minimum contrast method. For the summary statistic $\log K(t)$, where

$$K(t) = 2\pi \int_0^t rg(r)dr$$

is the integrated pair correlation function g over a ball of radius $t > 0$, and the discrepancy measured by integrated absolute error, we obtain $R_c = 0.061$.

For the prior, we choose the hard core model of Example 4.10 with parameters $\beta \equiv 1$ and $R = 0.03$. The forward model parameters may be estimated by Monte Carlo maximum likelihood, resulting in $\hat{\epsilon} = 19.65$ and $\hat{\lambda}_c = 4.14$. Having all ingredients at hand, realisations from the posterior distribution (4.12) of the stumps can be generated. A typical one is shown in Figure 4.1.

We conclude this section with a few remarks on log-Gaussian Cox processes. Recall that such a Cox process is defined by a random Borel measure of the form

$$\Lambda(A) = \int_A \exp(X_t)dt$$

for some Gaussian random field $(X_t)_{t \in \mathbb{R}^d}$ for which the integral is well-defined. Based on an observation $\mathbf{y}$ of the Cox process in some bounded Borel set $W \subset \mathbb{R}^d$, it is possible to write down an expression for the posterior finite dimensional distributions. Indeed, given $\mathbf{y}$, Bayes' rule implies that the conditional joint probability density of $(X_{t_1}, \ldots, X_{t_n})$ at $(x_{t_1}, \ldots, x_{t_n})$ is proportional to

$$\mathbb{E}\left[\exp(-\Lambda(W)) \prod_{j=1}^{m} \Lambda(y_j) | X_{t_1} = x_{t_1}, \ldots, X_{t_n} = x_{t_n}\right] f(x_{t_1}, \ldots, x_{t_n}),$$

where $f(x_{t_1}, \ldots, x_{t_n})$ is a Gaussian probability density. However, the expression above is not tractable. A further complication is that $\Lambda(W)$ is an integral which must be discretised. Hence, advanced Monte Carlo methods are called for that fall beyond the scope of this book.

4.12 WORKED EXAMPLES WITH R

The package *spatstat: Spatial point pattern analysis, model-fitting, simulation, tests* provides a large toolbox for working with planar point patterns. The package is maintained by A. Baddeley. An up-to-date list of contributors and a reference manual can be found on
`https://CRAN.R-project.org/package=spatstat.`
The analyses reported here were carried out using version 1.54.0.

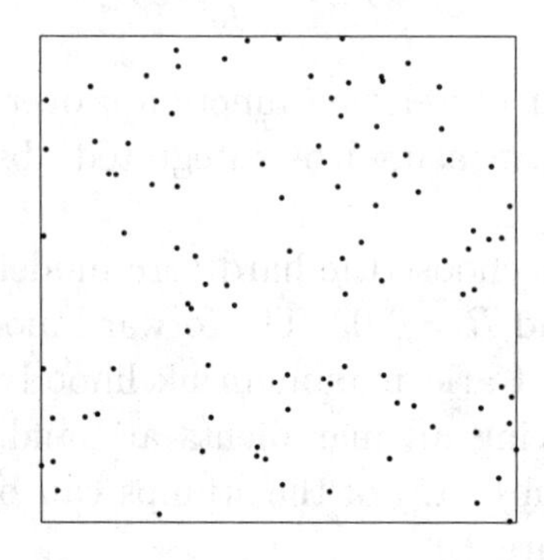

Figure 4.2 Realisation of a binomial point process with 100 points in the unit square $[0, 1]^2$.

A realisation from a binomial point process can be obtained by the script

```
X <- runifpoint(n=100)
plot(X, main="", pch=19)
```

A typical result is shown in Figure 4.2.

As we saw in Section 4.2, the distribution of a Poisson process is completely specified by its intensity function. For example,

$$\lambda(x, y) = 250x, \quad (x, y) \in [0, 1]^2,$$

models a trend in the horizontal direction,

$$\lambda(x, y) = 1000 \left(1/2 - \sqrt{(x - 1/2)^2 + (y - 1/2)^2} \right)$$

for $(x, y) \in \{(u, v) \in \mathbb{R}^2 : (u - 1/2)^2 + (v - 1/2)^2 \leq 1/4\}$, a drop in the expected number of points as the distance from $(1/2, 1/2)$ increases.

The functions may be implemented in R by

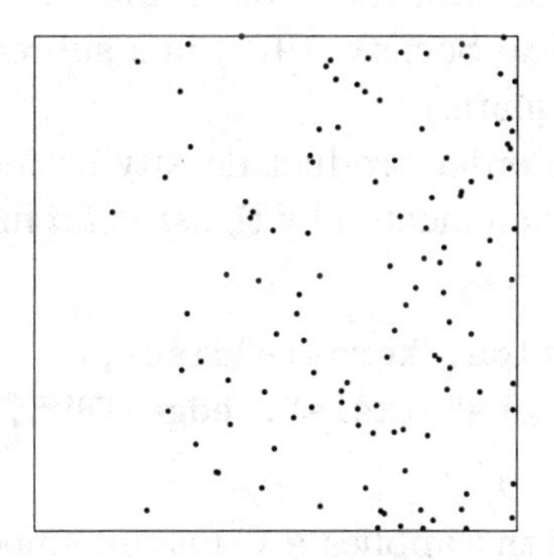

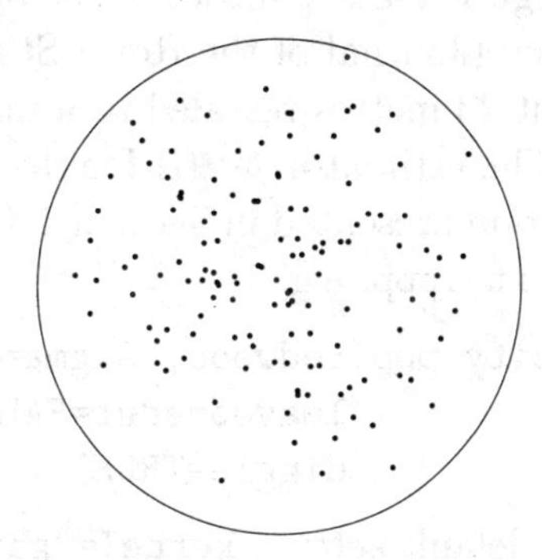

Figure 4.3 Realisations of a Poisson point process. Left: intensity function $\lambda(x, y) = 250x$ on the unit square. Right: intensity function $\lambda(x, y) = 1000\left(1/2 - \sqrt{(x - 1/2)^2 + (y - 1/2)^2}\right)$ on the ball of radius 1/2 centred at $(1/2, 1/2)$.

```
lambda1 <- function(x,y) {
   return( 250 * x )
}
```

for the linear trend model, and by

```
lambda2 <- function(x,y) {
  dist <- sqrt( ( x - 0.5 )^2 + ( y - 0.5 )^2 )
  return ( 1000 * ( 0.5 - dist ) )
}
```

for the radial decay function. To generate realisations of Poisson processes with the intensity functions defined above, type

```
X1 <- rpoispp(lambda=lambda1, lmax=250, win=owin(c(0,1),
c(0,1)))
X2 <- rpoispp(lambda=lambda2, lmax=500,
              win=disc(radius=1/2, centre=c(1/2, 1/2)))
```

The argument `lmax` for the maximal value of the intensity function is optional, but results in faster simulation.

The package includes the data set 'redwood' which lists the locations of 62 seedlings and saplings of California redwood trees. These data originate from a paper by D. Strauss (Biometrika, 1975). The pattern shown in Figure 4.4 is a subset of the original data that was extracted by B.D. Ripley (Journal of the Royal Statistical Society, 1977) in a subregion of about 23 metres rescaled to a unit square.

The estimator $\hat{\rho}^{(1)}(\cdot)$ for the first order product density or *intensity function* presented in Section 4.4 is implemented by the *spatstat* function `density.ppp`, e.g.

```
density.ppp(redwood, sigma=epsilon, kernel="disc",
            leaveoneout=FALSE, at="pixels", edge=TRUE,
            diggle=TRUE)
```

The default setting `kernel="gaussian"` applies a Gaussian smoothing kernel. A good initial value for its standard deviation σ can be found by applying formula (4.2) to the function $f(x) = 1/\rho^{(1)}(x)$. Indeed,

$$\mathbb{E}\left\{ \sum_{x \in X \cap W} \frac{1}{\rho^{(1)}(x)} \right\} = \int_W \frac{1}{\rho^{(1)}(x)} \rho^{(1)}(x)\, dx = |W|,$$

the area of W. Replacing $\rho^{(1)}$ by $\hat{\rho}^{(1)}$ and solving for σ often gives a plausible value (Cronie and Van Lieshout. Biometrika, 2018).

For the redwood data, the method described above leads to $\sigma = 0.14$. The resulting intensity function is displayed in the bottom right panel in Figure 4.4. For comparison, the top row shows the intensity function obtained with a Gaussian kernel for $\sigma = 0.07$ (left-most panel) and $\sigma = 0.28$ (right-most panel). Note that the mass is spread more evenly when σ is increased, whilst if one lowers the value of σ, the mass is more concentrated around the points in the pattern. The figure also shows the estimated intensity function using a disc kernel for the same choice of bandwidth (half radius $\epsilon = 0.14$). The discontinuities inherited from the indicator function are clearly visible. Furthermore, mass from different clumps tends to build up in the voids between the clumps.

Moving on to the second order moment characteristics, assume that the redwood tree pattern is a realisation from a stationary point process with intensity λ. The script

```
pcfr <- pcf.ppp(redwood, kernel="rectangular",
                bw=epsilon, correction="trans")
```

then estimates the pair correlation function. Commonly, Stoyan and Stoyan's rule of thumb (Wiley, 1994), which recommends use of an Epanechnikov kernel

$$\kappa_\epsilon(t) = \frac{3}{4\epsilon}\left(1 - \frac{t^2}{\epsilon^2}\right), \quad -\epsilon \le t \le \epsilon,$$

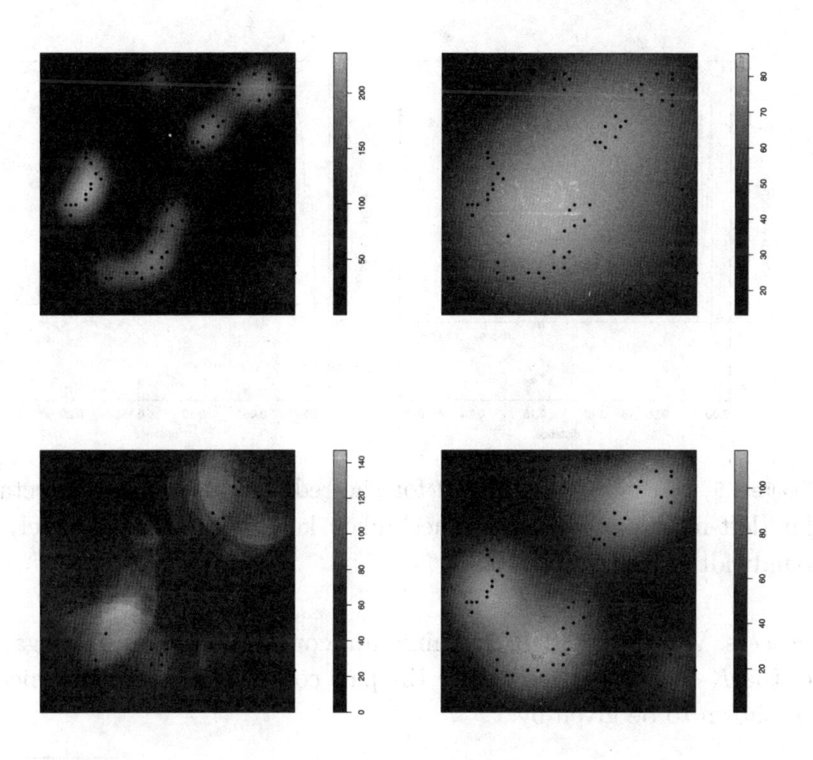

Figure 4.4 Kernel estimates $\hat{\rho}^{(1)}(\cdot)$ for the redwood data. Top row: Gaussian kernel with standard deviation $\sigma = 0.07$ (left) and 0.28 (right). In the bottom row, estimates for $\epsilon = \sigma = 0.14$ are displayed using a disc (left) and Gaussian kernel (right).

with bandwidth $0.15(5\hat{\lambda})^{-1/2}$, is followed and is also the default setting in *spatstat*. For the redwood data, $\epsilon \approx 0.0085$. The results for rectangular and Epanechnikov kernels are given in Figure 4.5. Both pictures suggest clustered behaviour up to range 0.15. As expected, the graph is rougher for the rectangular kernel. Do experiment with larger and smaller values for ϵ!

The empirical pair correlation function suggests clustering. Moreover, it seems plausible from a biological point of view that seedlings grow up around mature trees. Therefore, one might try to fit a cluster process. In Section 4.11, we assumed that seedlings were scattered around the stumps of mature trees uniformly in a ball of radius R_c. The corresponding Neyman-Scott Cox process is known as a Matérn cluster

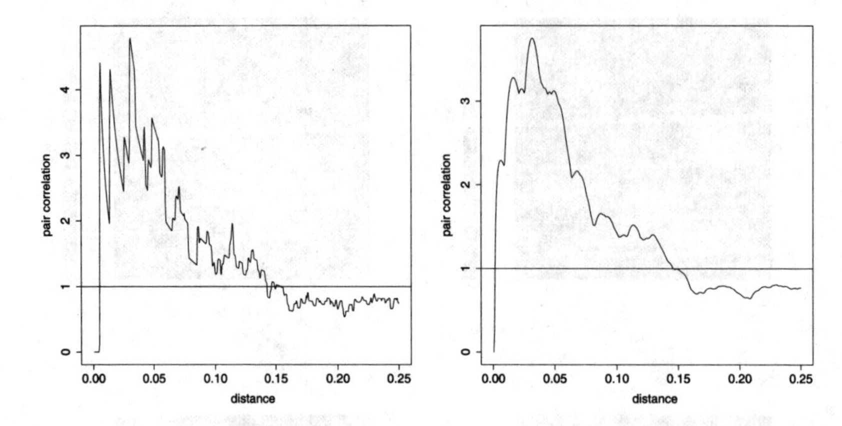

Figure 4.5 Kernel estimates $\hat{g}(\cdot)$ for the redwood data using a rectangular (left-most panel) and Epanechnikov kernel (right-most panel) with bandwidth $\epsilon = 0.0085$.

process. We estimated R_c by minimum contrast based on the logarithm of the K-function. Here we use the pair correlation function, which can be shown to be given by

$$g(r;\theta) = 1 + \frac{4}{\lambda_p \pi^2 r R_c} \left(\frac{r}{2R_c} \arccos\left(\frac{r}{2R_c}\right) - \frac{r^2}{4R_c^2} \sqrt{1 - \frac{r^2}{4R_c^2}} \right),$$
$$r \in [0, 2R_c],$$

to estimate the parameter vector $\theta = (\lambda_p, \lambda_c, R_c)$. The minimum contrast method requires the optimisation of the function

$$\int_{t_0}^{t_1} |\hat{g}(r) - g(r;\theta)|^2 dr$$

over θ. A complication is that $g(r;\theta)$ does not depend on λ_c. Nevertheless, since the intensity is equal to $\lambda_p \lambda_c$ and $|W| = 1$, we may set

$$\hat{\lambda}_c = \frac{N(W)}{\hat{\lambda}_p}.$$

The script

```
range(nndist(redwood))
[1] 0.02 0.12
fitMatern <- matclust.estpcf(redwood, q=1, rmin=0.02)
plot(fitMatern)
```

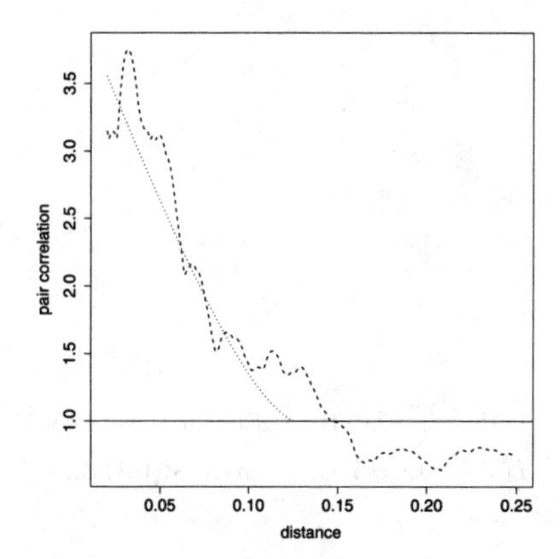

Figure 4.6 Kernel estimates $\hat{g}(\cdot)$ for the redwood data using an Epanechnikov kernel with bandwidth $\epsilon = 0.0085$ (broken line) and pair correlation function of the fitted Matérn cluster process with $\hat{\lambda}_p = 25.01$, $\hat{\lambda}_c = 2.48$ and $\hat{R}_c = 0.063$ (dotted line).

carries out this procedure. The parameter estimates are $\hat{\lambda}_p = 25.01$ and $\hat{R}_c = 0.063$ and therefore $\hat{\lambda}_c = 2.48$.

To validate the model, one may plot the fitted pair correlation function (or some other statistic) and compare it to the empirical one using the command `plot(fitMatern)` as in Figure 4.6. An alternative is to generate a few realisations of the fitted model,

```
rMatClust(kappa=fitMatern$par[1], scale=fitMatern$par[2],
          mu=redwood$n/fitMatern$par[1], win=redwood$window,
          nsim=3)
```

Three such realisations are displayed in Figure 4.7. Under the fitted model, on average 25 parents each generate an average of 2.48 children. Taking into account the size of mature redwood trees, the high parent number seems unrealistic. Indeed, the hierarchical model described in Section 4.11 uses a hard core distance for the parents to reduce their number and provides a more plausible fit.

Another data set provided in *spatstat* is 'bei', shown in Figure 4.8, which gives the positions of 3,605 Beilschmiedia trees in a 1,000 by 500 metre rectangular stand in a tropical rain forest at Barro Colorado Island, Panama. These data were supplied by R. Waagepetersen and taken from a larger data set described in the chapter by Hubbell and Foster in the 1983 textbook *Tropical Rain Forest: Ecology and Management*

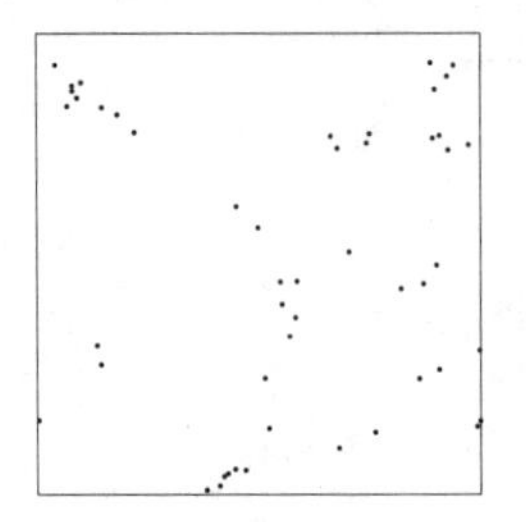  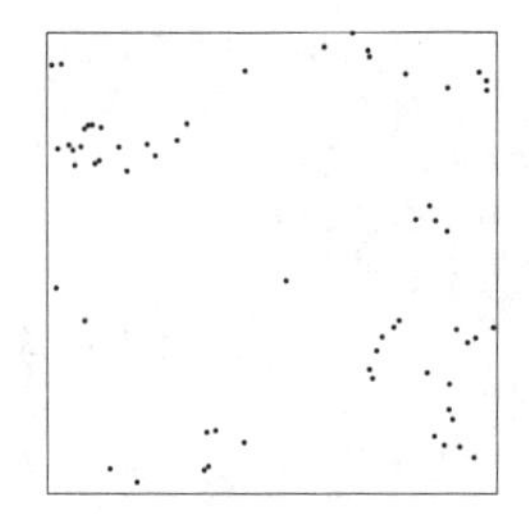

Figure 4.7 Realisations of a Matérn cluster process with parameters $\lambda_p = 25.01$, $\lambda_c = 2.48$ and $R_c = 0.063$ in a unit square.

edited by S. Sutton, T. Whitmore and A. Chadwick. The extended data may be accessed at

`https://dx.doi.org/10.5479/data.bci.20130603`

The research at Barro Colorado Island is financially supported by the U.S. National Science Foundation, the John D. and Catherine T. MacArthur Foundation and the Smithsonian Tropical Research Institute.

A visual inspection of the data suggests a lack of homogeneity. We therefore try to fit an inhomogeneous Poisson process with a polynomial approximation

$$\log \lambda(x,y) = \theta_0+\theta_1 x+\theta_2 y+\theta_3 x^2+\theta_4 xy+\theta_5 y^2+\theta_6 x^3+\theta_7 x^2 y+\theta_8 xy^2+\theta_9 y^3$$

$$+\theta_{10}x^4 + \theta_{11}x^3 y + \theta_{12}x^2 y^2 + \theta_{13}xy^3 + \theta_{14}y^4, \qquad (x,y) \in \mathbb{R}^2,$$

to the log intensity function by means of the commands

```
fitbeiXY <- ppm(bei~polynom(x,y,4))
plot(predict(fitbeiXY))
```

The `ppm` function calculates the parameter estimates, the function `predict` returns the corresponding intensity function. The result is shown in the left-most panel of Figure 4.9.

To validate the model, one may compare a kernel estimator of the intensity function to that of the fitted model. More formally, write $\mathbf{x}$ for the observed pattern in stand W. Then the smoothed residual at $x \in W$ is defined by

$$s(x) = \frac{1}{\epsilon^2}\sum_{y\in\mathbf{x}} \kappa\left(\frac{x-y}{\epsilon}\right) w_\epsilon(x,y)^{-1} - \frac{1}{\epsilon^2}\int_W \kappa\left(\frac{x-w}{\epsilon}\right) w_\epsilon(x,w)^{-1}\hat{\lambda}(w)dw,$$

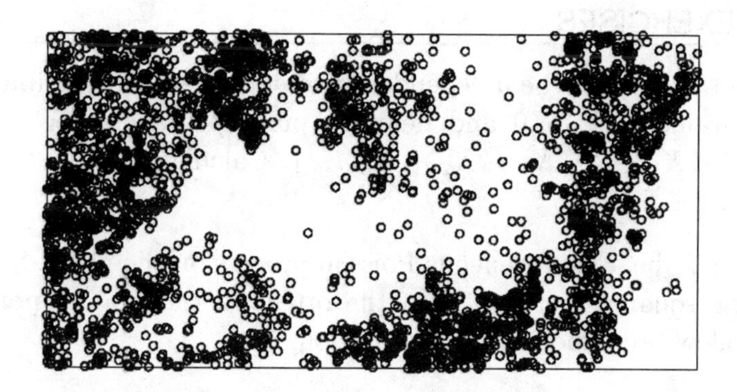

Figure 4.8 The positions of Beilschmiedia trees in a 1,000 by 500 metre stand in Barro Colorado Island, Panama.

where κ is a symmetric probability density function and w_ϵ an edge correction factor. These residuals may be calculated using the function

```
diagnose.ppm(fitbeiXY, which="smooth", sigma=100)
```

and are plotted in the right-most panel of Figure 4.9.

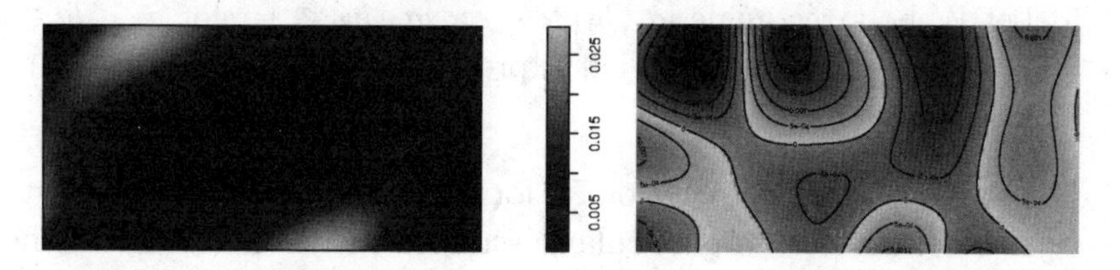

Figure 4.9 Left: fitted intensity function $\hat{\lambda}(x, y)$ for Beilschmiedia trees in Barro Colorado Island using a fourth order polynomial approximation to the log intensity function. Right: smoothed residual surface using a Gaussian kernel with $\sigma = 100$.

To test for homogeneity, apply the likelihood ratio test using the script

```
hombei <- ppm(bei~1)
anova(hombei, fitbeiXY, test = "LR")
```

and find that the null hypothesis is emphatically rejected.

For further details, we refer to the vignettes of *spatstat* that are available on the CRAN website

```
https://cran.r-project.org.
```

4.13 EXERCISES

1. Let $X_1, X_2, \ldots$ be independent and exponentially distributed with parameter $\lambda > 0$ and define a point process on $\mathbb{R}^+$ by $X = \{X_1, X_1 + X_2, X_1 + X_2 + X_3, \ldots\}$. Calculate $\mathbb{P}(N_X((0,t]) = 0)$ for $t \in \mathbb{R}^+$.

2. Let X be a homogeneous Poisson process on the plane. Show that the squared distance from the origin to the nearest point of X follows an exponential distribution.

3. Let X be a Poisson process on $\mathbb{R}^d$ with intensity function λ_X, Y a Poisson process with intensity function λ_Y. If X and Y are independent, show that the superposition $X \cup Y$ is a Poisson process.

4. Let X be a binomial point process of $n \in \mathbb{N}$ points on the unit square $[0,1]^2$. Calculate its factorial moment measures up to second order. Derive the covariance and pair correlation functions. Is X stationary and/or second order intensity-reweighted moment stationary?

5. Let W be a rectangle $[a_1, b_1] \times \cdots \times [a_d, b_d] \subset \mathbb{R}^d$ for $a_i < b_i \in \mathbb{R}$, $i = 1, \ldots, d$. Give an explicit expression for the volume of $W \cap W_x$ as a function of $x \in \mathbb{R}^d$.

6. Let X be a point process on $\mathbb{R}^d$ for which product densities exist up to second order. In particular, assume that the first order moment measure exists and is absolutely continuous with density $\lambda : \mathbb{R}^d \to \mathbb{R}^+$. Denote by $B(x, \epsilon)$ the closed ball centred at $x \in \mathbb{R}^d$ with radius $\epsilon > 0$ and write

$$\widehat{\lambda(x_0)} = \sum_{x \in X \cap W} \frac{1\{x \in B(x_0, \epsilon)\}}{|B(x, \epsilon) \cap W|}, \quad x_0 \in W,$$

for some open bounded Borel set W such that $|W| > 0$.

   - Compute the expectation and variance of $\widehat{\lambda(x_0)}$.
   - Suppose that n independent samples from the distribution of $X \cap W$ are available. How would you estimate $\lambda(x_0)$? What are the expectation and variance of your estimator?

7. Let X be a Poisson process on $[0,1]^2$ with intensity function $\lambda(x, y) = \beta e^{\alpha y}$ for $\alpha, \beta \geq 0$.

- Estimate the parameters α and β based on an observed pattern $\mathbf{x} = \{(x_i, y_i) : i = 1, \ldots, 10\}$ for which $\sum_i y_i = 5.82$.
- Test the composite null hypothesis that X is homogeneous.

8. Is the Lennard–Jones interaction function of Example 4.11 locally stable? Is it hereditary?

9. For any finite point pattern $\mathbf{x} \subset W$ in the bounded Borel set W, let

$$C_{\mathbf{x}}(w) = \sum_{x \in \mathbf{x}} 1\{w \in B(x, R)\}, \quad w \in W,$$

be the coverage function of $\mathbf{x}$. Here $B(x, R) = \{w \in W : ||x - w|| \leq R\}$. Additionally, let V be a potential, that is, a function $V : \mathbb{N} \to \mathbb{R}$ such that $V(0) = 0$. We would like to define a *shot noise-weighted* point process X on W by means of an unnormalised density of the form

$$f(\mathbf{x}) \propto \exp\left[-\int_W V(C_{\mathbf{x}}(w))dw\right]$$

with respect to the distribution of a unit rate Poisson process on W.

- Give a sufficient condition on the potential V for f to be integrable.
- Show that X is a Markov point process with respect to the relation $\sim$ defined by $x \sim y$ if and only if $||x - y|| \leq 2R$, $x, y \in W$. Find an explicit expression for the clique interaction functions.
  Hint: Proceed as in the proof of the Hammersley–Clifford theorem.

10. Let X be a hard core process on some bounded Borel set $W \subset \mathbb{R}^d$ with probability density

$$f(\mathbf{x} = \{x_1, \ldots, x_n\}) \propto \beta^n \prod_{\{u,v\} \in \mathbf{x}} 1\{||u - v|| \geq R\}$$

with respect to the distribution of a unit rate Poisson process. Estimate the interaction range $R \geq 0$ and the parameter $\beta \geq 0$.

11. Show that the pair correlation function of a planar Neyman–Scott process in which the daughters are located uniformly in a ball of

radius $R > 0$ around their parent depends only on the distance r between its arguments and is given by

$$g(r) = 1 + \frac{4}{\lambda_p \pi^2 r R}\left(\frac{r}{2R}\arccos\left(\frac{r}{2R}\right) - \frac{r^2}{4R^2}\sqrt{1 - \frac{r^2}{4R^2}}\right)$$

whenever $0 \leq r \leq 2R$. This model is known as the *Matérn cluster process.*

Hint: use that the intersection area $A(r, R)$ of two balls of radius R whose centres are r apart is given by

$$A(r, R) = 2R^2 \arccos(r/(2R)) - r(4R^2 - r^2)^{1/2}/2$$

for $r \in [0, 2R]$.

12. Let the random variable Λ be exponentially distributed with parameter $m > 0$. Let X be a Cox process on $\mathbb{R}^d$ driven by Λ; that is, given $\Lambda = \lambda$, X is a homogeneous Poisson process with intensity λ.
    - Give an explicit expression for the empty space function of X in terms of the parameter m.
    - How can you use your result to estimate m?
13. Let X be an inhomogeneous Poisson process on a bounded Borel set $A \subset \mathbb{R}^d$ defined by the intensity function $\lambda : A \to \mathbb{R}^+$. Assume that $\int_A \lambda(a)da > 0$. Prove that conditional on the number of points, they are independent and identically distributed according to the probability density function
$$\frac{\lambda(a)}{\int_A \lambda(a)da}$$
on A. Compare the result to Theorem 4.2 and specialise to (4.11).
14. Let the random variable Λ be exponentially distributed with parameter $m > 0$. Let Y be a Cox process on the bounded Borel set $W \subset \mathbb{R}^d$ driven by Λ; that is, given $\Lambda = \lambda$, Y is a homogeneous Poisson process on W with intensity λ. Compute the posterior distribution of Λ given a realisation $\mathbf{y}$ of Y and its mean $\mathbb{E}[\Lambda \mid \mathbf{y}]$.
15. The `spatstat` package contains a data set `bei` that contains tree locations in a tropical rain forest. Covariate information about the altitude and slope in the study region is available in the accompanying data set `bei.extra`. Investigate whether altitude and slope affect the abundance of trees.

4.14 POINTERS TO THE LITERATURE

It is difficult to point to the first documented use of the Poisson process. The name was probably coined in the late 1930s at the University of Stockholm and appears in the 1940 paper [1] by W. Feller who worked in Stockholm from 1934 until 1939. The phrase 'point process' is due to C. Palm [2]. This early work is mostly concerned with point processes on the real line. The foundations of a mathematically rigorous theory of point processes on general state spaces were laid in the early 1960s by J.E. Moyal [3] who used the now obsolete term 'stochastic population process' in his title. We refer to a paper by Guttorp and Thorarinsdottir [4] for a more detailed historical overview and to the two volumes by Daley and Vere–Jones [5] for an exhaustive account of the theory of point processes on Polish spaces.

The definition of a point process given in Section 4.1 can be found in [3]. In [6], A. Rényi proved that the void probabilities determine the distribution of a Poisson process with diffuse intensity function, a result that was generalised to all simple point processes by G. Mőnch [7]. The basic facts concerning a Poisson process are summarised in the monograph by J.F.C. Kingman [8]. For example, his section 2.4 is devoted to a more general version of Theorem 4.2. Perhaps confusingly, the name 'Bernoulli process' is used for the binomial point process, which is usually reserved for sequences of binary valued random variables. Moment measures are defined in Section 3 of [3]. Earlier work in the context of point processes on the real line includes that by A. Ramakrishnan [9], who advocated the use of product densities. The implications of various concepts of stationarity, including homogeneity of the moments, are discussed exhaustively in Chapter 12 of [5]. Definition 4.8 is adapted from a slightly more general one due to Baddeley, Møller and Waagepetersen [10].

The consideration of stability can be traced back to L. Onsager [11] who called a probability density function f stable if the energy of a configuration $\mathbf{x}$ satisfies a linear lower bound in the number of points, that is, $-\log(f(\mathbf{x})/f(\emptyset)) \geq -\beta n(\mathbf{x})$ for some $\beta > 0$. Additionally, Onsager showed that the so-called hard core condition, which states that no two points can occur within a given positive distance of one another, implies stability. We refer to the textbook by D. Ruelle [12] for a rigorous treatment of this and other notions of stability, their implications and mutual relations. The local stability condition, being defined in terms of the Papangelou conditional intensity [13], has become popular following Ripley and Kelly's introduction of Markov point processes [14] specified by their unnormalised densities. It implies the Onsager–Ruelle stability condition. As an aside, unnormalised densities of the form $\exp(-|W|)f$ with f given by (4.7) are known as Jánossy densities to honour pioneering work [15]. The Strauss model was proposed in [16], the Lennard–Jones interaction function in [17]. Further examples of pairwise interaction models can be found in the textbooks [5] or [18].

Markov point processes were introduced in the statistical literature by Ripley and Kelly [14], and our proof of Theorem 4.4 is taken from their paper. It should be noted, though, that the similar concept of a Gibbs point process was already known in statistical physics; see for example the textbooks by C. Preston [19] and by D. Ruelle [12]. More recent developments are reviewed in the monograph by M.N.M. van Lieshout [18].

Turning to statistics, the edge correction weight $1/|W \cap W_{y-x}|$, commonly known as the translation correction, in the kernel estimator (4.4) was proposed by Ohser and Stoyan [20]. For a fuller discussion of edge effects and ways to correct for them, we refer to Chapter 3 in the Adams prize winning essay [21] by B.D. Ripley. Kernel estimators for the first order product density were introduced by P.J. Diggle [22], although with a focus on point processes on the real line. The mass-preserving kernel estimator (4.5) was suggested by M.N.M. van Lieshout [23].

Inference for Poisson processes based on their likelihood is treated in great detail in the book by Y.A. Kutoyants [24]. For non-Poisson models, the Monte Carlo maximum likelihood method of C.J. Geyer and E.A. Thompson [25] may be used. This method is generally applicable when an unnormalised density function is explicitly available. The details for finite point patterns are spelled out in [26], including Theorem 4.5 and the Metropolis–Hastings sampler with birth and death proposals due to C.J. Geyer and J. Møller [27].

The idea to use maximum pseudo-likelihood for point processes can be traced back to J.E. Besag, who, in [28], considered the special case of the Strauss process. His approach is to approximate a spatial point process by a series of random fields on finer and finer grids [29], with labels in $L = \{0, 1\}$ to denote presence or absence of points, and apply pseudo-likelihood to the approximation. Our direct definition is taken from Jensen and Møller [30]. The method is implemented as the default parameter estimation technique in the `R`-package `spatstat`, the most complete `R`-package devoted to spatial point pattern analysis [31]. Its error estimates are based on a paper by Cœurjolly and Rubak [32]. The smoothed residuals implemented in the package are taken from an article by Baddeley, Turner, Møller and Hazelton [33], which generalises earlier ideas of Stoyan and Grabarnik [34]. Core functions are also implemented in the R-package `spatial` that comes with the default R implementation and in `splancs`.

A historical account on the introduction of Cox processes is given by Guttorp and Thorarinsdottir [4]. They trace the Neyman–Scott cluster process to [35] and note that the special case where the daughters are scattered according to a bivariate normal distribution (cf. Example 4.16) is called a modified Thomas process after work by M. Thomas [36] on a doubly stochastic model for the number of potato beetle larvae, even though their spatial location is not taken into account. The Matérn cluster process can be found in Section 3.6 of [37]. The product densities up to second order were calculated by D. Vere–Jones [38] using generating functional techniques. Although they are quite natural, log-Gaussian Cox processes seem to have been introduced as recently as 1991 by Coles and Jones [39], who derived the pair correlation function heuristically. The proof of Theorem 4.7 given here follows that in [40]. Parameter estimation for such models by means of a minimum contrast method was proposed by P.J. Diggle [41]. The estimate of R_c in the cluster detection example of Section 4.11 is taken from this paper; the hierarchical analysis with a hard core prior follows Van Lieshout and Baddeley [42].

In closing, we recommend the textbooks by Møller and Waagepetersen [43], Illian, Penttinen, Stoyan and Stoyan [44] and Diggle [45] or part IV in [46] for further reading.

REFERENCES

[1] W. Feller (1940). On the integro-differential equations of purely discontinuous Markoff processes. *Transactions of the American Mathematical Society* 48(3):488–515.

[2] C. Palm (1943). Intensitätsschwenkungen im Fernsprechverkehr. Ericsson Technics, Volume 44.

[3] J.E. Moyal (1962). The general theory of stochastic population processes. *Acta Mathematica* 108(1):1–31.

[4] P. Guttorp and T.L. Thorarinsdottir (2012). What happened to discrete chaos, the Quenouille process, and the sharp Markov property? Some history of stochastic point processes. *International Statistical Review* 80(2):253–268.

[5] D.J. Daley and D. Vere-Jones (2003, 2008). *An Introduction to the Theory of Point Processes (2nd edition).* New York: Springer-Verlag.

[6] A. Rényi (1967). Remarks on the Poisson process. *Studia Scientiarum Mathematicarum Hungarica* 2:119–123.

[7] G. Mőnch (1971). Verallgemeinerung eines Satzes von A. Rényi. *Studia Scientiarum Mathematicarum Hungarica* 6:81–90.

[8] J.F.C. Kingman (1993). *Poisson Processes.* Oxford: Clarendon Press.

[9] A. Ramakrishnan (1950). Stochastic processes relating to particles distributed in a continuous infinity of states. *Proceedings of the Cambridge Philosophical Society* 46(4):595–602.

[10] A.J. Baddeley, J. Møller and R. Waagepetersen (2000). Non- and semiparametric estimation of interaction in inhomogeneous point patterns. *Statistica Neerlandica* 54(3):329–350.

[11] L. Onsager (1939). Electrostatic interaction of molecules. *Journal of Physical Chemistry* 43(2):189–196.

[12] D. Ruelle (1969). *Statistical Mechanics. Rigorous Results.* New York: W.A. Benjamin.

[13] F. Papangelou (1974). The conditional intensity of general point processes and an application to line processes. *Zeitschrift für Wahrscheinlichkeitstheorie und verwandte Gebiete* 28(3):207–226.

[14] B.D. Ripley and F.P. Kelly (1977). Markov point processes. *Journal of the London Mathematical Society* 15(1):188–192.

[15] L. Jánossy (1950). On the absorption of a nucleon cascade. *Proceedings of the Royal Irish Academy* 53(A):181–188.

[16] D.J. Strauss (1975). A model for clustering. *Biometrika* 62(2):467–475.

[17] J.E. Lennard–Jones (1924). On the determination of molecular fields. *Proceedings of the Royal Society of London* A106(838):441–477.

[18] M.N.M. van Lieshout (2000). *Markov Point Processes and Their Applications.* London: Imperial College Press.

[19] C. Preston (1976). *Random Fields.* Berlin: Springer-Verlag.

[20] J. Ohser and D. Stoyan (1981). On the second-order and orientation analysis of planar stationary point processes. *Biometrical Journal* 23(6):523–533.

[21] B.D. Ripley (1988). *Statistical Inference for Spatial Processes.* Cambridge: Cambridge University Press.

[22] P.J. Diggle (1985). A kernel method for smoothing point process data. *Applied Statistics* 34(2):138–147.

[23] M.N.M. van Lieshout (2012). On estimation of the intensity function of a point process. *Methodology and Computing in Applied Probability* 14(3):567–578.

[24] Y.A. Kutoyants (1998). *Statistical Inference for Spatial Poisson Processes.* New York: Springer-Verlag.

[25] C.J. Geyer and E.A. Thompson (1992). Constrained Monte Carlo maximum likelihood for dependent data. *Journal of the Royal Statistical Society* B54(3):657–699.

[26] C.J. Geyer (1999). Likelihood inference for spatial point processes. In: *Stochastic Geometry. Likelihood and Computation.* Papers from the 3rd Séminaire Européen de Statistique on Stochastic Geometry, Theory and Applications, Toulouse, 1996. Edited by O.E. Barndorff-Nielsen, W.S. Kendall and M.N.M. van Lieshout. Boca Raton, Florida: Chapman & Hall/CRC.

[27] C.J. Geyer and J. Møller (1994). Simulation procedures and likelihood inference for spatial point processes. *Scandinavian Journal of Statistics* 21(4):359–373.

[28] J. Besag (1977). Some methods of statistical analysis for spatial data (with discussion). Proceedings of the 41st session of the ISI, New Delhi, 1977. *Bulletin of the International Statistical Institute* 47(2):77–91, 138–147.

[29] J. Besag, R. Milne and S. Zachary (1982). Point process limits of lattice processes. *Journal of Applied Probability* 19(1):210–216.

[30] J.L. Jensen and J. Møller (1991). Pseudolikelihood for exponential family models of spatial point processes. *The Annals of Applied Probability* 1(3):445–461.

[31] A. Baddeley, E. Rubak and R. Turner (2015). *Spatial Point Patterns: Methodology and Applications with R.* Boca Raton, Florida: Chapman & Hall/CRC.

[32] J.-F. Cœurjolly and E. Rubak (2013). Fast covariance estimation for innovations computed from a spatial Gibbs point process. *Scandinavian Journal of Statistics* 40(4):669–684.

[33] A. Baddeley, R. Turner, J. Møller and M. Hazelton (2005). Residual analysis for spatial point processes (with discussion). *Journal of the Royal Statistical Society* B67(5):617–666.

[34] D. Stoyan and P. Grabarnik (1991). Second-order characteristics for stochastic structures connected with Gibbs point processes. *Mathematische Nachrichten* 151(1):95–100.

[35] J. Neyman and E.L. Scott (1952). A theory of the spatial distribution of galaxies. *Astrophysical Journal* 116:144–163.

[36] M. Thomas (1949). A generalization of Poisson's binomial limit for use in ecology. *Biometrika* 36(1/2):18–25.

[37] B. Matérn (1986). *Spatial Variation (2nd edition).* Berlin: Springer-Verlag.

[38] D. Vere–Jones (1970). Stochastic models for earthquake occurrence. *Journal of the Royal Statistical Society* B32(1):1–62.

[39] P. Coles and B. Jones (1991). A lognormal model for the cosmological mass distribution. *Monthly Notices of the Royal Astronomical Society* 248(1):1–13.

[40] J. Møller, A.R. Syversveen and R.P. Waagepetersen (1998). Log Gaussian Cox processes. *Scandinavian Journal of Statistics* 25(3):451–482.

[41] P.J. Diggle (1978). On parameter estimation for spatial point processes. *Journal of the Royal Statistical Society* B40(2):178–181.

[42] M.N.M. van Lieshout and A.J. Baddeley (2002). Extrapolating and interpolating spatial patterns. In: *Spatial Cluster Modelling.* Edited by A.B. Lawson and D.G.T. Denison. Boca Raton, Florida: Chapman & Hall/CRC.

[43] J. Møller and R.P. Waagepetersen (2004). *Statistical Inference and Simulation for Spatial Point Processes.* Boca Raton, Florida: Chapman & Hall/CRC.

[44] J. Illian, A. Penttinen, H. Stoyan and D. Stoyan (2008). *Statistical Analysis and Modelling of Spatial Point Patterns.* Chichester: John Wiley & Sons.

[45] P.J. Diggle (2014). *Statistical Analysis of Spatial and Spatio-Temporal Point Patterns (3rd edition).* Boca Raton, Florida: Chapman & Hall/CRC.

[46] A.E. Gelfand, P.J. Diggle, M. Fuentes and P. Guttorp, editors (2010). *Handbook of Spatial Statistics.* Boca Raton, Florida: Chapman & Hall/CRC.

Appendix: Solutions to theoretical exercises

EXERCISES IN CHAPTER 2

1. For k and m in $\mathbb{N}$, without loss of generality suppose that $t_1, \ldots, t_k \in A$ and $t_{k+1}, \ldots, t_{k+m} \notin A$. Pick $x_1, \ldots, x_{k+m} \in \mathbb{R}$. Then

$$F_{t_1,\ldots,t_{k+m}}(x_1, \ldots, x_{k+m}) = \mathbb{P}(Z \leq \min\{x_1, \ldots, x_k\}; 0 \leq \min\{x_{k+1}, \ldots, x_{k+m}\}),$$

which in terms of the cumulative distribution function F_Z of Z reads

$$F_Z(\min\{x_1, \ldots, x_k\})$$

if $0 \leq \min\{x_{k+1}, \ldots, x_{k+m}\}$ and zero otherwise. If $m = 0$ and $k \in \mathbb{N}$, then $F_{t_1,\ldots,t_k}(x_1, \ldots, x_k) = F_Z(\min\{x_1, \ldots, x_k\})$. Finally, if $k = 0$ and $m \in \mathbb{N}$, then

$$F_{t_1,\ldots,t_m}(x_1, \ldots, x_m) = \begin{cases} 1 & \text{if } 0 \leq \min\{x_1, \ldots, x_m\}; \\ 0 & \text{otherwise.} \end{cases}$$

2. Since

$$\mathrm{Cov}(X_s, X_t) = \sum_{i=1}^{n} \sum_{j=1}^{n} \mathrm{Cov}(Z_i f_i(s), Z_j f_j(t)),$$

the covariance function ρ of X is given by

$$\rho(s,t) = \sum_{i=1}^{n} \sum_{j=1}^{n} f_i(s) f_j(t) \mathrm{Cov}(Z_i, Z_j).$$

3. First, note that $m_Y(t) = \mathbb{E}Y_t = \mathbb{E}X_t^2 = \rho(t,t) + m(t)^2$. Moreover

$$\rho_Y(s,t) = \mathbb{E}(X_s^2 X_t^2) - m_Y(s)m_Y(t).$$

It remains to calculate $\mathbb{E}(X_s^2 X_t^2)$. Now,

$$\begin{aligned}\mathbb{E}(X_s^2X_t^2) &= \mathbb{E}\left[(X_s - m(s) + m(s))^2(X_t - m(t) + m(t))^2\right] \\ &= \mathbb{E}\left[(X_s - m(s))^2(X_t - m(t))^2\right] \\ &+ \mathbb{E}\left[(X_s - m(s))^2 m(t)^2 + (X_t - m(t))^2 m(s)^2\right] \\ &+ \mathbb{E}\left[4m(s)m(t)(X_s - m(s))(X_t - m(t))\right] + m(s)^2m(t)^2\end{aligned}$$

since the odd central moments of a multivariate normal distribution are zero. Hence

$$\begin{aligned}\mathbb{E}(X_s^2X_t^2) = \mathbb{E}&\left[(X_s - m(s))^2(X_t - m(t))^2\right] + m(t)^2\rho(s,s) \\ &+ m(s)^2\rho(t,t) + m(s)^2m(t)^2 + 4m(s)m(t)\rho(s,t).\end{aligned}$$

By the hint, if $Z = (Z_s, Z_t)$ is bivariate normally distributed with mean zero,

$$\mathbb{E}(Z_s^2Z_t^2) = \rho_Z(s,s)\rho_Z(t,t) + 2\rho_Z(s,t)^2,$$

where ρ_Z is the covariance function of Z, so

$$\begin{aligned}\mathbb{E}(X_s^2X_t^2) &= \rho(s,s)\rho(t,t) + 2\rho(s,t)^2 + m(t)^2\rho(s,s) \\ &\quad + m(s)^2\rho(t,t) + m(s)^2m(t)^2 + 4m(s)m(t)\rho(s,t) \\ &= \rho(s,s)m_Y(t) + m(s)^2m_Y(t) + 2\rho(s,t)^2 \\ &\quad + 4m(s)m(t)\rho(s,t) \\ &= m_Y(s)m_Y(t) + 2\rho(s,t)^2 + 4m(s)m(t)\rho(s,t).\end{aligned}$$

In conclusion,

$$\rho_Y(s,t) = \mathbb{E}(X_s^2X_t^2) - m_Y(s)m_Y(t) = 2\rho(s,t)^2 + 4m(s)m(t)\rho(s,t).$$

4. Regarding the first claim note that, for $a_1, \dots, a_n \in \mathbb{R}$, $n \in \mathbb{N}$, the double sum

$$\sum_{i=1}^{n}\sum_{i=1}^{n} a_i a_j \left(\alpha\rho_1(t_i,t_j) + \beta\rho_2(t_i,t_j)\right)$$

$$= \alpha\sum_{i=1}^{n}\sum_{j=1}^{n} a_i a_j \rho_1(t_i,t_j) + \beta\sum_{i=1}^{n}\sum_{j=1}^{n} a_i a_j \rho_2(t_i,t_j)$$

is non-negative when α and β are non-negative.

To prove the second claim, let X and Y be independent zero mean Gaussian random fields with covariance functions ρ_1 and ρ_2 respectively (cf. Proposition 2.1). Then the covariance function of the random field Z defined by $Z_t = X_t Y_t$, $t \in \mathbb{R}^d$, is equal to

$$\mathrm{Cov}(Z(t_1), Z(t_2)) = \mathbb{E}\left[X(t_1)Y(t_1)X(t_2)Y(t_2)\right] = \rho_1(t_1,t_2)\rho_2(t_1,t_2)$$

by the assumed independence. In other words, the product $\rho_1\rho_2$ is the covariance function of Z and therefore non-negative definite.

5. For $n \in \mathbb{N}$ and $0 < t_1 < \cdots < t_n$, consider the $n \times n$ matrix Σ_n with entries $\rho(t_i, t_j)$, $i, j \in \{1, \ldots, n\}$:

$$\Sigma_n = \begin{pmatrix} t_1 & t_1 & \cdots & t_1 & t_1 \\ t_1 & t_2 & \cdots & t_2 & t_2 \\ \cdots & \cdots & \cdots & \cdots & \cdots \\ t_1 & t_2 & \cdots & t_{n-1} & t_{n-1} \\ t_1 & t_2 & \cdots & t_{n-1} & t_n \end{pmatrix}.$$

We proceed to show that Σ_n is non-negative definite. Using the Sylvester criterion, we shall show that the determinants of all upper-left sub-blocks are positive. Note that they take the same shape as the matrix Σ_n itself. Equivalently therefore, it suffices to show that the determinant of Σ_n is positive for all $n \in \mathbb{N}$.

For $n = 1$, the matrix (t_1) has determinant $t_1 > 0$. For $n = 2$, the matrix

$$\begin{pmatrix} t_1 & t_1 \\ t_1 & t_2 \end{pmatrix}$$

has determinant $t_1(t_2 - t_1) > 0$. We claim that the determinant of Σ_n is $t_1(t_2 - t_1) \cdots (t_n - t_{n-1}) > 0$ by the chronological ordering. The claim may be proven by induction and the fact that

$$\begin{aligned} \det\Sigma_n &= \det \begin{pmatrix} t_1 & t_1 & \cdots & t_1 & t_1 \\ 0 & t_2 - t_1 & \cdots & t_2 - t_1 & t_2 - t_1 \\ 0 & \cdots & \cdots & \cdots & \cdots \\ 0 & t_2 - t_1 & \cdots & t_{n-1} - t_1 & t_{n-1} - t_1 \\ 0 & t_2 - t_1 & \cdots & t_{n-1} - t_1 & t_n - t_1 \end{pmatrix} \\ &= t_1 \det \begin{pmatrix} t_2 - t_1 & \cdots & t_2 - t_1 & t_2 - t_1 \\ \cdots & \cdots & \cdots & \cdots \\ t_2 - t_1 & \cdots & t_{n-1} - t_1 & t_{n-1} - t_1 \\ t_2 - t_1 & \cdots & t_{n-1} - t_1 & t_n - t_1 \end{pmatrix}, \end{aligned}$$

which has the same form as Σ_{n-1}.

6. By Bochner's theorem, the spectral density reads, for $w \in \mathbb{R}$,

$$f(w) = \frac{1}{2\pi} \int_{-\infty}^{\infty} \frac{1}{2\beta} e^{-\beta|t|} e^{-iwt} dt.$$

Split $f(w)$ in integrals over $\mathbb{R}^+$ and $\mathbb{R}^-$. Then, noting that the function $t \to e^t$ is a primitive of itself,

$$\int_0^{\infty} e^{-\beta|t|} e^{-iwt} dt = \frac{1}{\beta + iw} = \frac{1}{\beta + iw} \frac{\beta - iw}{\beta - iw} = \frac{\beta - iw}{\beta^2 + w^2}.$$

Similarly,

$$\int_{-\infty}^{0} e^{-\beta|t|} e^{-iwt} dt = \frac{1}{\beta - iw} = \frac{\beta + iw}{\beta^2 + w^2}.$$

Hence

$$f(w) = \frac{1}{4\pi\beta} \frac{1}{\beta^2 + w^2} (\beta - iw + \beta + iw) = \frac{1}{2\pi} \frac{1}{\beta^2 + w^2}, \qquad w \in \mathbb{R}.$$

To verify the existence of a continuous version, note that the integral

$$\int_{-\infty}^{\infty} |w|^{\epsilon} f(w) dw = \frac{1}{2\pi} \int_{-\infty}^{\infty} \frac{|w|^{\epsilon}}{\beta^2 + w^2} dw$$

is finite for $\epsilon < 1$.

7. First, let us calculate the Fourier transform of the box function ϕ. Now,

$$\int_{\mathbb{R}} \phi(s) e^{-i\xi s} ds = \int_{-1/2}^{1/2} e^{-i\xi s} ds = \frac{e^{-i\xi/2} - e^{i\xi/2}}{-i\xi} = \frac{\sin(\xi/2)}{\xi/2}.$$

The convolution of ϕ with itself is, for $t \in \mathbb{R}$, given by

$$\phi * \phi(t) = \int_{-\infty}^{\infty} \phi(s)\phi(t-s) ds = \int_{-1/2}^{1/2} 1\left\{t - \frac{1}{2} \le s \le t + \frac{1}{2}\right\} ds,$$

the length of the intersection

$$\left[-\frac{1}{2}, \frac{1}{2}\right] \cap \left[t - \frac{1}{2}, t + \frac{1}{2}\right].$$

The intersection length is equal to $\min(1/2, t+1/2) - \max(-1/2, t-1/2)$ provided that the intersection is not empty. Hence, for $|t| \le 1$, $\phi * \phi(t) = \theta(t)$. Recalling that the Fourier transform of a convolution is the product of the Fourier transforms, one obtains the desired result for the function θ.

8. Note that

$$\rho(\theta) = \sum_{j=0}^{\infty} \sigma_j^2 \left[\frac{e^{ij\theta} + e^{-ij\theta}}{2}\right]$$

is in the spectral form of Bochner's theorem with $\mu(j) = \sigma_j^2/2$ for $j \in \mathbb{Z}$. Clearly μ is non-negative and symmetric. It takes finite values whenever

$$\sum_{j=0}^{\infty} \sigma_j^2 < \infty.$$

The cosine is uniformly continuous on its compact domain, so ρ is continuous as a limit of uniformly continuous functions.

Continuous versions exist if

$$\sum_{j=0}^{\infty} j^{\epsilon} \sigma_j^2 < \infty$$

for some $\epsilon \in (0, 1)$. Plug in $\sigma_j^2 = (\alpha+\beta j^{2p})^{-1}$. Then for $2p - \epsilon > 1$, that is, for $p > 1/2$, ρ is well-defined and the corresponding Gaussian field admits a continuous version.

9. The sill is

$$\lim_{|t|\to\infty} \gamma(t) = \alpha + \beta,$$

the nugget

$$\lim_{|t|\to 0} \gamma(t) = \alpha.$$

The partial sill is the difference between the two limits, β.

10. By Theorem 2.2, the general expression is

$$\begin{aligned}
\hat{X}_{t_0} &= \frac{1}{\sigma^2} \begin{bmatrix} \rho(t_0,t_1) & \rho(t_0,t_2) \end{bmatrix} \begin{bmatrix} 1 & \rho \\ \rho & 1 \end{bmatrix}^{-1} \begin{bmatrix} X_{t_1} \\ X_{t_2} \end{bmatrix} \\
&= \frac{1}{\sigma^2} \frac{1}{1-\rho^2} \begin{bmatrix} \rho(t_0,t_1) & \rho(t_0,t_2) \end{bmatrix} \begin{bmatrix} 1 & -\rho \\ -\rho & 1 \end{bmatrix} \begin{bmatrix} X_{t_1} \\ X_{t_2} \end{bmatrix} \\
&= \frac{1}{\sigma^2} \frac{1}{1-\rho^2} \{(\rho(t_0,t_1) - \rho\rho(t_0,t_2))X_{t_1} + (\rho(t_0,t_2) - \rho\rho(t_0,t_1))X_{t_2}\}.
\end{aligned}$$

For the special cases one obtains the following expressions:

- $\frac{1}{\sigma^2}\frac{1}{1-\rho^2}\{\rho(t_0,t_1)X_{t_1} - \rho\rho(t_0,t_1)X_{t_2}\}$, which does depend on X_{t_2};

- 0 as X_{t_1} and X_{t_2} do not provide any information;
- $\frac{1}{\sigma^2}\left\{\rho(t_0,t_1)X_{t_1}+\rho(t_0,t_2)X_{t_2}\right\}$.

The mean squared prediction error is

$$\rho(t_0,t_0)-\frac{1}{\sigma^2}\frac{1}{1-\rho^2}\begin{bmatrix}\rho(t_0,t_1) & \rho(t_0,t_2)\end{bmatrix}\begin{bmatrix}1 & -\rho\\ -\rho & 1\end{bmatrix}\begin{bmatrix}\rho(t_0,t_1)\\ \rho(t_0,t_2)\end{bmatrix}$$
$$=\rho(t_0,t_0)-\frac{1}{\sigma^2}\frac{1}{1-\rho^2}\left\{\rho(t_0,t_1)^2+\rho(t_0,t_2)^2-2\rho\rho(t_0,t_1)\rho(t_0,t_2)\right\}.$$

For the special cases one gets the following:

- $\rho(t_0,t_0)-\frac{1}{\sigma^2}\frac{\rho(t_0,t_1)^2}{1-\rho^2}$;
- $\rho(t_0,t_0)$;
- $\rho(t_0,t_0)-\frac{1}{\sigma^2}\left\{\rho(t_0,t_1)^2+\rho(t_0,t_2)^2\right\}$.

11. Assume that the covariance structure of $(E_t)_{t\in\mathbb{R}^d}$ is known as well as β and m. Write Σ for the covariance matrix of E_{t_i}, $i=1,\ldots,n$, and K for the $n\times 1$ vector with entries $\mathrm{Cov}(E_{t_0},E_{t_i})$. Then

$$\hat{X}_{t_0}=m(t_0)'\beta+K'\Sigma^{-1}(X_{t_i}-m(t_i)'\beta)_{n\times 1}$$

according to Theorem 2.2.

If β were unknown one might try to estimate it, for instance by the maximum likelihood method. The log likelihood of the observations is proportional to

$$-(X_{t_i}-m(t_i)'\beta)_{1\times n}\Sigma^{-1}(X_{t_i}-m(t_i)'\beta)_{n\times 1},$$

so the score equations are

$$2M'\Sigma^{-1}(X_{t_i}-m(t_i)'\beta)_{n\times 1}=0,$$

where M is the $n\times p$ matrix whose rows are the $m(t_i)'$. Hence, provided that the matrix $M'\Sigma^{-1}M$ is invertible,

$$\hat{\beta}=(M'\Sigma^{-1}M)^{-1}M'\Sigma^{-1}Z,$$

writing Z for the $n\times 1$ vector of observations X_{t_i}. Finally, plug $\hat{\beta}$ into the expression for the kriging estimator.

12. First compute

$$\hat{m} = \frac{\frac{1}{\sigma^2(1-\rho^2)}\begin{bmatrix} 1 & 1 \end{bmatrix}\begin{bmatrix} 1 & -\rho \\ -\rho & 1 \end{bmatrix}\begin{bmatrix} X_{t_1} \\ X_{t_2} \end{bmatrix}}{\frac{1}{\sigma^2(1-\rho^2)}\begin{bmatrix} 1 & 1 \end{bmatrix}\begin{bmatrix} 1 & -\rho \\ -\rho & 1 \end{bmatrix}\begin{bmatrix} 1 \\ 1 \end{bmatrix}} = \frac{X_{t_1} + X_{t_2}}{2},$$

the mean. Then plug $\hat{m}$ into the simple kriging estimator (cf. Exercise 10) to obtain

$$\begin{aligned}
\hat{X}_{t_0} &= \hat{m} + \frac{1}{\sigma^2}\frac{1}{1-\rho^2}(\rho(t_0,t_1) - \rho\rho(t_0,t_2))(X_{t_1} - \hat{m}) \\
&+ \frac{1}{\sigma^2}\frac{1}{1-\rho^2}(\rho(t_0,t_2) - \rho\rho(t_0,t_1))(X_{t_2} - \hat{m}) \\
&= \frac{X_{t_1} + X_{t_2}}{2} + \frac{1}{2\sigma^2}\frac{1}{1-\rho^2}(\rho(t_0,t_1) - \rho\rho(t_0,t_2))(X_{t_1} - X_{t_2}) \\
&+ \frac{1}{2\sigma^2}\frac{1}{1-\rho^2}(\rho(t_0,t_2) - \rho\rho(t_0,t_1))(X_{t_2} - X_{t_1}) \\
&= \frac{X_{t_1} + X_{t_2}}{2} + \frac{(\rho(t_0,t_1) - \rho(t_0,t_2))(X_{t_1} - X_{t_2})}{2\sigma^2(1-\rho)}.
\end{aligned}$$

When $\rho(t_0, t_2) = 0$, $\hat{X}_{t_0}$ is given by

$$\frac{X_{t_1} + X_{t_2}}{2} + \frac{\rho(t_0,t_1)(X_{t_1} - X_{t_2})}{2\sigma^2(1-\rho)}.$$

If additionally $\rho(t_0, t_1) = 0$ then

$$\hat{X}_{t_0} = \frac{X_{t_1} + X_{t_2}}{2},$$

the mean of X_{t_1} and X_{t_2}. In both cases the expression for $\hat{X}_{t_0}$ involves both X_{t_1} and X_{t_2}.

If $\rho = 0$,

$$\hat{X}_{t_0} = \frac{X_{t_1} + X_{t_2}}{2} + \frac{(\rho(t_0,t_1) - \rho(t_0,t_2))(X_{t_1} - X_{t_2})}{2\sigma^2}.$$

The mean squared prediction error exceeds that of simple kriging by a term

$$\frac{(1 - \mathbf{1}'\Sigma^{-1}K)^2}{\mathbf{1}'\Sigma^{-1}\mathbf{1}} = \frac{\left(\sigma^2(1+\rho) - \rho(t_0,t_1) - \rho(t_0,t_2)\right)^2}{2\sigma^2(1+\rho)}$$

according to Theorem 2.4.

13. Since the null-space is non-trivial, one can find an n-vector a such that $\Sigma a = 0$ and $\text{Var}(a'Z) = a'\Sigma a = 0$. Then $\text{Cov}(c'Z, a'Z) = c'\Sigma a = 0$ for all vectors c. Also $0 = \text{Cov}(X_{t_0}, a'Z) = K'a$. We have shown that K is orthogonal to the null space of Σ. Therefore, by the symmetry of Σ, K lies in its column space.

14. Write

$$\left(\sum_{i=1}^n c_i X_{t_i} - X_{t_0}\right)^2 = \left(\sum_{i=1}^n c_i (X_{t_i} - m(t_i)'\beta) - (X_{t_0} - m(t_0)'\beta) + \left\{\sum_{i=1}^n c_i m(t_i)' - m(t_0)'\right\}\beta\right)^2.$$

The last term is zero under the constraint and may be omitted. Consequently the mean squared error is equal to

$$\mathbb{E}E_{t_0}^2 + \mathbb{E}\left(\sum_{i=1}^n c_i E_{t_i}\right)^2 - 2\mathbb{E}\left(E_{t_0}\sum_{i=1}^n c_i E_{t_i}\right) = \rho(t_0, t_0) + c'\Sigma c - 2c'K.$$

The p-dimensional Euler–Lagrange multiplier $\lambda \in \mathbb{R}^p$ adds a term

$$\lambda'\left(\sum_{i=1}^n c_i m(t_i) - m(t_0)\right) = \lambda'(M'c - m(t_0)).$$

Hence, the score equations are

$$2\Sigma c - 2K + M\lambda = 0$$

and

$$M'c = m(t_0).$$

Pre-multiplication of the first score equation by $M'\Sigma^{-1}$ and the fact that $M'c = m(t_0)$ yield $\lambda = 2(M'\Sigma^{-1}M)^{-1}(M'\Sigma^{-1}K - m(t_0))$ and consequently

$$\Sigma c = K - M(M'\Sigma^{-1}M)^{-1}(M'\Sigma^{-1}K - m(t_0)),$$

from which the desired result follows.

EXERCISES IN CHAPTER 3

1. Suppose that $(x_j)_{j \neq i}$ is feasible in the sense that $x_j x_k = 0$ whenever $j \sim k$. Then

$$\frac{\pi_i(1 \mid x_j, j \neq i)}{\pi_i(0 \mid x_j, j \neq i)} = \begin{cases} a & \text{if } x_j = 0 \text{ for } j \sim i \\ 0 & \text{otherwise} \end{cases}$$

depends on the neighbours of i only, so X is Markov with respect to $\sim$. Furthermore, if $x_j = 0$ for all $j \sim i$ then $\pi_i(1 \mid x_j, j \neq i) = 1 - \pi_i(0 \mid x_j, j \neq i) = a/(1+a)$. If $x_j = 1$ for some $j \sim i$ then $\pi_i(0 \mid x_j, j \neq i) = 1$.

Consider a lattice that consists of two adjacent sites labelled 1 and 2 and take $y = (0,1)$, $x = (1,0)$. Then both x and y have positive probability of occurring, but $\pi_2(y_2 \mid x_1) = \pi_2(1 \mid 1) = 0$.

2. Without loss of generality, consider the first two elements of X. If the joint covariance matrix is $\Sigma = (I - B)^{-1}K$, we know that the conditional covariance matrix of the first block consisting of X_1 and X_2 is $\Sigma_{11} - \Sigma_{12}\Sigma_{22}^{-1}\Sigma_{21}$. To find an explicit expression, use the hint applied to $I - B$. Thus, $A_{12} = -B_{12}$, $A_{21} = -B_{21}$ and $A_{22} = I - B_{22}$. Partition the matrix K in four blocks too, say K_1, K_2 on the diagonal, 0 off the diagonal.

Now,

$$\begin{aligned} (A^{-1})_{11} &= I + B_{12}(I - B_{22} - B_{21}B_{12})^{-1}B_{21}, \\ (A^{-1})_{12} &= B_{12}(I - B_{22} - B_{21}B_{12})^{-1}, \\ (A^{-1})_{21} &= (I - B_{22} - B_{21}B_{12})^{-1}B_{21}, \\ (A^{-1})_{22} &= (I - B_{22} - B_{21}B_{12})^{-1}. \end{aligned}$$

Hence the conditional covariance matrix $\Sigma_{11} - \Sigma_{12}\Sigma_{22}^{-1}\Sigma_{21}$ reads

$$(A^{-1})_{11}K_1 - (A^{-1})_{12}K_2(K_2)^{-1}((A^{-1})_{22})^{-1}(A^{-1})_{21}K_1$$

$$= K_1 + B_{12}(I - B_{22} - B_{21}B_{12})^{-1}B_{21}K_1 - B_{12}(I - B_{22} - B_{21}B_{12})^{-1}B_{21}K_1 = K_1.$$

Since K_1 is diagonal, X_1 and X_2 are uncorrelated and therefore, being normally distributed, independent.

Unconditionally, the covariance between X_1 and X_2 is $\Sigma_{11} = (A^{-1})_{11}K_1$, that is,

$$(I - B_{12}(I - B_{22})^{-1}B_{21})^{-1} \begin{bmatrix} \kappa_1 & 0 \\ 0 & \kappa_2 \end{bmatrix}.$$

Here we use the simplification $(A^{-1})_{11} = (I - B_{12}(I - B_{22})^{-1} B_{21})^{-1}$. As this matrix is not necessarily diagonal, X_1 and X_2 may be dependent.

3. The local characteristics are well-defined normal densities. Using Besag's factorisation theorem, the joint density would be proportional to

$$\frac{\pi_1(x \mid 0)\pi_2(y \mid x)}{\pi_1(0 \mid 0)\pi_2(0 \mid x)} = \exp\left[-\frac{1}{2}(y - x)^2\right], \quad (x, y) \in \mathbb{R}^2.$$

However, this function is not integrable.

4. Since $\pi_i(0 \mid y_{T\setminus i}) = e^{-\mu_i}$, respectively $\pi_i(l \mid y_{T\setminus i}) = e^{-\mu_i}\mu_i^l/l!$ for $l \in \mathbb{N}$, by the factorisation theorem,

$$\frac{\pi_Y(y)}{\pi_Y(0)} = \exp\left[\theta \sum_{i\sim j;i<j} y_i y_j - \sum_{i\in T} \log y_i!\right].$$

Now $\theta \sum_{i\sim j;i<j} y_i y_j \leq 0$ for $\theta \leq 0$ and therefore

$$\sum_{y\in(\mathbb{N}_0)^T} \frac{\pi_Y(y)}{\pi_Y(0)} \leq \sum_{y\in(\mathbb{N}_0)^T} \exp\left[-\sum_{i\in T} \log y_i!\right] = \left(\sum_{l=0}^{\infty} \frac{1}{l!}\right)^{|T|} < \infty.$$

For $\theta > 0$, without loss of generality consider the first two sites and suppose that $1 \sim 2$. Then

$$\frac{\pi_Y(y_1, y_2, 0, \ldots, 0)}{\pi_Y(0)} = \frac{e^{\theta y_1 y_2}}{y_1! y_2!}$$

should be summable. However, the series

$$\sum_{y_1=0}^{\infty} \sum_{y_2=0}^{\infty} \frac{e^{\theta y_1 y_2}}{y_1! y_2!}$$

diverges as the general term does not go to zero.

5. The first task is to find the maximum likelihood estimator for μ. Assume that B is a symmetric matrix with zeroes on the diagonal such that $I - B$ is positive definite. Then the log likelihood $L(\mu; X)$ is

$$-\frac{1}{2}(X - \mu\mathbf{1})'(I - B)(X - \mu\mathbf{1}).$$

The score equations is given by

$$0 = \mathbf{1}'(I - B)(X - \mu\mathbf{1}).$$

Therefore

$$\hat{\mu} = \frac{\mathbf{1}'(I - B)X}{\mathbf{1}'(I - B)\mathbf{1}} = \frac{\sum_{t\in T} X_t(1 - \sum_{s\in T} b_{st})}{|T| - \sum_{s\in T}\sum_{t\in T} b_{st}}$$

is a linear function of X, hence normally distributed with mean μ and variance $(\mathbf{1}'(I - B)\mathbf{1})^{-1}$, that is, $1/(|T| - \sum_{s\in T}\sum_{t\in T} b_{st})$. The variance does not depend on μ. A two-sided test rejects if

$$|\hat{\mu}| > \frac{\xi_{1-\alpha/2}}{(|T| - \sum_{s\in T}\sum_{t\in T} b_{st})^{1/2}}$$

or, equivalently, if

$$\left|\sum_{t\in T} X_t(1 - \sum_{s\in T} b_{st})\right| > \left(|T| - \sum_{s\in T}\sum_{t\in T} b_{st}\right)^{1/2} \xi_{1-\alpha/2}.$$

Here $\xi_{1-\alpha/2}$ is the $1 - \alpha/2$ quantile of the standard normal distribution and $\alpha \in (0, 1)$ the desired level of the test.

An alternative would be to use the likelihood ratio test statistic

$$\Lambda(X) = \exp\left[L(0; X) - L(\hat{\mu}; X)\right] = \exp\left[\frac{1}{2}\hat{\mu}^2\mathbf{1}'(I - B)\mathbf{1} - \hat{\mu}\mathbf{1}'(I - B)X\right]$$
$$= \exp\left[-\frac{(\mathbf{1}'(I - B)X)^2}{2(\mathbf{1}'(I - B)\mathbf{1}}\right].$$

The likelihood ratio test rejects the null hypothesis for large values of

$$-2\log\Lambda(X) = \frac{(\mathbf{1}'(I - B)X)^2}{\mathbf{1}'(I - B)\mathbf{1}} = \frac{(\hat{\mu})^2}{\mathrm{Var}(\hat{\mu})}.$$

Under the null hypothesis, $-2\log\Lambda(X)$, as the square of a standard normally distributed random variable, is χ^2-distributed with one degree of freedom. It is interesting to observe that the two approaches lead to the same test!

6. A potential V is normalised with respect to 0 if $V_A(x) = 0$ whenever $x_i = 0$ for some $i \in A$. This is clearly the case for sets A of cardinality one or two. For larger A, $V_A(x) = 0$ too.

7. By definition, $V_\emptyset = 0$. For $A = \{i\}$, by Theorem 3.2,

$$V_{\{i\}}(y) = -\log \pi_i(0 \mid 0, \dots, 0) + \log \pi_i(y_i \mid 0, \dots, 0) = -\log y_i!$$

and for $A = \{i, j\}$, again by Theorem 3.2, $V_{\{i,j\}}(y)$ is equal to

$$\log \pi_i(0 \mid 0, \dots, 0) - \log \pi_i(y_i \mid 0, \dots, 0)$$
$$- \log \pi_i(0 \mid y_j, 0, \dots, 0) + \log \pi_i(y_i \mid y_j, 0, \dots, 0),$$

so

$$V_{\{i,j\}}(y) = -y_i y_j 1\{i \sim j\}.$$

Since the joint distribution is proportional to

$$\exp\left[- \sum_{i \sim j; i<j} y_i y_j - \sum_{i \in T} \log y_i! \right]$$

(cf. Exercise 4), all other potentials vanish.

8. Write x for the realisation on the set A of crossed sites, y for that on dotted sites. Then, reasoning as in the proof of the spatial Markov property,

$$\pi_A(x \mid y) \propto \prod_{A \cap C \neq \emptyset} \varphi_C(x_{A \cap C}, y_{C \setminus A}),$$

where C runs through the family of cliques with respect to $\sim$. Now, the cliques with respect to $\sim$ are the empty set, singletons and pairs of horizontally or vertically adjacent sites. The latter always combine a crossed and dotted site. Hence the factorisation does not contain terms with two different x_is and the proof is complete.

9. As mentioned in Example 3.4, the local characteristics at $i \in T$ are normally distributed with variance κ_i and mean

$$\sum_{j \neq i} b_{ij} x_j = \sum_{j \sim i} b_{ij} x_j.$$

Therefore, the local characteristic at i depends on $x_{T \setminus i}$ only through x_j at sites j that are neighbours of i. Hence the CAR model is a Markov random field. Its joint probability density function satisfies

$$\log \pi(x) \propto -\frac{1}{2} x' K^{-1}(I - B)x = -\frac{1}{2} \sum_{i \in T} \frac{x_i^2}{\kappa_i} + \frac{1}{2} \sum_{i \in T} \sum_{j \in T} \frac{b_{ij} x_i x_j}{\kappa_i}.$$

Hence $\varphi(x_i) = \exp(-x_i^2/(2\kappa_i))$ and

$$\varphi(\{x_i, x_j\}) = \exp(b_{ij} x_i x_j/(2\kappa_i)) = \exp(b_{ji} x_i x_j/(2\kappa_j)),$$

recalling that $K^{-1}(I - B)$ is symmetric by definition. If $i \not\sim j$, then $b_{ij} = 0$ and consequently $\varphi(\{x_i, x_j\}) = 1$.

10. The proposal mechanism in a Metropolis–Hastings sampler could be to select a site uniformly at random. If site i is selected, a new label could be chosen according to $\pi_i(\cdot \mid x_j, j \neq i)$.

    To prove convergence, observe that the chain restricted to feasible states is aperiodic due to self-transitions. It is also irreducible, since to get from feasible state x to feasible state y, one may change all 1s in x to 0 first, then change those sites with label 1 in y to 1. By Proposition 3.2, π_X defines an invariant probability measure. An appeal to the fundamental convergence theorem completes the proof.

    To find a Monte Carlo maximum likelihood estimator for a, consider the ratio $\pi_X(x; a)/\pi_X(x; a_0)$, for example with respect to the reference parameter $a_0 = 1$, and note that the ratio of normalising constants can be written as an expectation. Finally, approximate the expectation by an average over a sample from $\pi_X(\cdot; a_0)$ obtained by the method just described.

11. The maximum likelihood estimators that optimise

$$L(\beta, \sigma^2; Y) = -\frac{1}{2\sigma^2}(Y - X\beta)'(I - B)(Y - X\beta) - n \log \sigma$$

are

$$\begin{aligned} \hat{\beta} &= (X'(I - B)X)^{-1} X'(I - B)Y \\ \hat{\sigma}^2 &= \frac{1}{n}(Y - X\hat{\beta})'(I - B)(Y - X\hat{\beta}). \end{aligned}$$

To see this, proceed as in Section 3.5 for the SAR model with $(I - B')(I - B)$ replaced by $I - B$.

Regarding maximum pseudo-likelihood estimation, the local characteristics are Gaussians with mean

$$\mathbb{E}(Y_i|Y_{T\setminus i}) = (X\beta)_i + \sum_{j\neq i} b_{ij}(Y_j - (X\beta)_j), \quad i \in T,$$

and variance σ^2. Therefore

$$\begin{aligned} PL(\beta, \sigma^2; Y) &= -\sum_{i\in T} \frac{1}{2\sigma^2}\left(Y_i - (X\beta)_i - \sum_{j\neq i} b_{ij}(Y_j - (X\beta)_j)\right)^2 \\ &\quad - n\log\sigma \\ &= -\frac{1}{2\sigma^2}(Y - X\beta)'(I - B)^2(Y - X\beta) - n\log\sigma. \end{aligned}$$

Note that $PL(\beta, \sigma^2; Y)$ is equal to the log likelihood of the SAR model. Hence the maximum pseudo-likelihood estimators $\tilde{\beta}$ and $\tilde{\sigma}^2$ are given by

$$\begin{aligned} \tilde{\beta} &= (X'(I-B)^2X)^{-1}X'(I-B)^2Y \\ \tilde{\sigma}^2 &= \frac{1}{n}(Y - X\hat{\beta})'(I-B)^2(Y - X\hat{\beta}). \end{aligned}$$

12. Write $S_l^i(x)$ for S evaluated at the configuration y that takes the value l at site i and is equal to x at all other sites. Then the local characteristics can be written as

$$\pi_i(x_i \mid x_{T\setminus i}) = \frac{\exp(\theta S(x))}{\sum_{l\in\{0,1\}} \exp\left(\theta S_l^i(x)\right)}, \quad i \in T, x \in \{0,1\}^T.$$

Therefore,

$$\log \pi_i(x_i \mid x_{T\setminus i}) = \theta S(x) - \log\left(\sum_{l\in\{0,1\}} \exp(\theta S_l^i(x))\right).$$

Take the derivative with respect to the parameter θ to obtain

$$S(x) - \frac{1}{\sum_{l\in\{0,1\}} \exp(\theta S_l^i(x))} \sum_{l\in\{0,1\}} S_l^i(x) \exp(\theta S_l^i(x)).$$

The second term is equal to $\mathbb{E}_\theta\left[S(X) \mid X_{T\setminus i} = x_{T\setminus i}\right]$. To complete the proof, sum over all sites and equate the pseudo-likelihood score equation thus obtained to zero.

13. We claim that

$$\pi_X(x)q(x,y) = \pi_X(y)q(y,x)$$

for all $x, y \in L^T$. To see this, note that $q(x,y) = 0 = q(y,x)$ if x and y differ in two or more sites. For such x and y the claim obviously holds as it does for $y = x$.

Thus, assume that x and y differ in exactly one site, say $i \in T$. Then,

$$\begin{aligned}
\pi_X(x)q(x,y) &= \pi_X(x)\frac{1}{|T|}\pi_i(y_i \mid x_{T\setminus i}) \\
&= \pi_i(x_i \mid x_{T\setminus i})\mathbb{P}(X_{T\setminus i} = x_{T\setminus i})\frac{1}{|T|}\pi_i(y_i \mid x_{T\setminus i}) \\
&= \pi_i(x_i \mid x_{T\setminus i})\frac{1}{|T|}\pi_X(y) = q(y,x)\pi_X(y).
\end{aligned}$$

It follows that $A(x,y) = 1$ and the detailed balance equations coincide with the claim.

14. The greedy algorithm optimises, iteratively over $i \in T$,

$$\frac{-1}{2\sigma^2}(y_i - l)^2 + \theta \sum_{j \sim i} 1\{x_j = l\}$$

as a function of $l \in L$. For $\theta = 0$, the optimal l is that label in L that is closest to y_i. For $\theta \to \infty$, l is chosen by a majority vote under the labels of sites that are neighbours of i.

EXERCISES IN CHAPTER 4

1. For $k = 0, 1, \ldots$,

$$\begin{aligned}\mathbb{P}(N_X((0,t]) = k) &= \mathbb{P}(X_1 + \cdots + X_k \leq t; X_1 + \cdots + X_{k+1} > t) \\ &= \int_0^t \frac{\lambda^k r^{k-1}}{(k-1)!} e^{-\lambda r} e^{-\lambda(t-r)} dr = e^{-\lambda t} \frac{(\lambda t)^k}{k!}\end{aligned}$$

using the fact that the sum $X_1 + \cdots + X_k$ is Erlang distributed. Therefore $N_X((0,t])$ is Poisson distributed with parameter λt. Plug in $k = 0$ to see that the void probability of $(0, t]$ is equal to $\exp(-\lambda t)$.

2. The cumulative distribution function of the squared distance $d(0, X)^2$ of X to the origin can be written in terms of a void probability. Indeed,

$$\mathbb{P}(d(0,X)^2 \leq r) = 1 - \mathbb{P}(d(0,X)^2 > r) = 1 - \mathbb{P}(X \cap B(0, \sqrt{r}) = \emptyset),$$

where $B(0, \sqrt{r})$ is the closed ball centred at 0 with radius $\sqrt{r}$. Since $1 - v(B(0, \sqrt{r})) = 1 - \exp(-\lambda \pi r)$, $d(0, X)^2$ is exponentially distributed.

3. Observe that for any bounded Borel set $A \subset \mathbb{R}^d$,

$$\begin{aligned}&\mathbb{P}((X \cup Y) \cap A = \emptyset) = \mathbb{P}(X \cap A = \emptyset; Y \cap A = \emptyset) \\ &= \mathbb{P}(X \cap A = \emptyset)\mathbb{P}(Y \cap A = \emptyset)\end{aligned}$$

by the independence of X and Y. Since X and Y are Poisson processes, the product of the two void probabilities is

$$\begin{aligned}&\exp\left[-\int_A \lambda_X(z)dz\right] \exp\left[-\int_A \lambda_Y(z)dz\right] \\ &= \exp\left[-\int_A (\lambda_X(z) + \lambda_Y(z))dz\right],\end{aligned}$$

the void probability $v(A)$ of a Poisson process with intensity function $\lambda_X + \lambda_Y$. An appeal to Theorem 4.1 completes the proof.

4. For a Borel set $A \subseteq [0, 1]^2$,

$$\alpha^{(1)}(A) = n\mathbb{P}(X_1 \in A) = n|A|$$

is absolutely continuous with product density $\rho^{(1)}(x) = n$ for all $x \in [0,1]^2$. Similarly, for two Borel sets $A, B \subseteq [0,1]^2$,

$$\begin{aligned} \alpha^{(2)}(A \times B) &= \mathbb{E}\left[\sum_{i=1}^{n}\sum_{j\neq i} 1\{X_i \in A; X_j \in B\}\right] \\ &= n(n-1)|A||B| \end{aligned}$$

since X_i and X_j are independent when $i \neq j$. Moreover, $\alpha^{(2)}$ is absolutely continuous with second order product density $\rho^{(2)}(x,y) = n(n-1)$ on $[0,1]^2$. Turning to derived statistics, the second order moment measure is

$$\mu^{(2)}(A\times B) = \alpha^{(2)}(A\times B)+\alpha^{(1)}(A\cap B) = n(n-1)|A||B|+n|A\cap B|,$$

the covariance reads

$$\mu^{(2)}(A \times B) - \alpha^{(1)}(A)\alpha^{(1)}(B) = n|A \cap B| - n|A||B|$$

and the pair correlation function is

$$g(x,y) = \frac{\rho^{(2)}(x,y)}{\rho^{(1)}(x)\rho^{(1)}(y)} = 1 - \frac{1}{n}, \quad x, y \in [0,1]^2.$$

Since the point process is defined on the unit square only, it cannot be stationary. The pair correlation function and first order product density are constant. The latter is also strictly positive, so X is second order intensity-reweighted moment stationary.

5. First consider the one-dimensional case. For $x > 0$,

$$[a,b] \cap [a+x, b+x] = [a+x, b]$$

if $x \leq b - a$ and empty otherwise. Similarly for $x < 0$,

$$[a,b] \cap [a+x, b+x] = [a, b+x]$$

provided $-x \leq b - a$. In both cases, the length is $b - a - |x|$ if $|x| < b - a$ and zero otherwise. Repeating these arguments for all components in d dimensions, one obtains

$$|W \cap W_x| = \prod_{i=1}^{d}(b_i - a_i - |x_i|)^+.$$

6. By (4.2), the first two moments are given by

$$\mathbb{E}\left[\widehat{\lambda(x_0)}\right] = \int_{B(x_0,\epsilon)\cap W} \frac{\lambda(x)}{|B(x,\epsilon)\cap W|} dx$$

and

$$\begin{aligned}
\mathbb{E}\left[\left(\widehat{\lambda(x_0)}\right)^2\right] &= \mathbb{E}\left[\sum_{(x,y)\in(X\cap W)^2}^{\neq} \frac{1\{x\in B(x_0,\epsilon)\}}{|B(x,\epsilon)\cap W|}\frac{1\{y\in B(x_0,\epsilon)\}}{|B(y,\epsilon)\cap W|}\right] \\
&\quad + \mathbb{E}\left[\sum_{x\in X\cap W} \frac{1\{x\in B(x_0,\epsilon)\}}{|B(x,\epsilon)\cap W|^2}\right] \\
&= \int_{B(x_0,\epsilon)\cap W}\int_{B(x_0,\epsilon)\cap W} \frac{\rho^{(2)}(x,y)}{|B(x,\epsilon)\cap W||B(y,\epsilon)\cap W|} dxdy \\
&\quad + \int_{B(x_0,\epsilon)\cap W} \frac{\lambda(x)}{|B(x,\epsilon)\cap W|^2} dx.
\end{aligned}$$

Provided $\lambda(\cdot) > 0$, the variance is

$$\int_{B(x_0,\epsilon)\cap W}\int_{B(x_0,\epsilon)\cap W} \frac{(g(x,y)-1)\lambda(x)\lambda(y)}{|B(x,\epsilon)\cap W||B(y,\epsilon)\cap W|} dxdy$$

$$+ \int_{B(x_0,\epsilon)\cap W} \frac{\lambda(x)}{|B(x,\epsilon)\cap W|^2} dx.$$

If there is replication, write $T_i(X_i)$ for the estimator $\widehat{\lambda(x_0)}$ applied to X_i. The combined estimator is then the average $\sum_{i=1}^n T_i(X_i)/n$. The expectation is not altered by replication. The variance however is much reduced, by a factor $1/n$. (Also the problem of distinguishing between inhomogeneity and clustering disappears).

7. The log likelihood function based on $\mathbf{x} = \{(x_1,y_1),\ldots,(x_n,y_n)\}$ is given by

$$n\log\beta + \alpha\sum_{i=1}^n y_i - \beta\int_0^1 e^{\alpha y} dy.$$

The score equations read

$$\begin{aligned}
0 &= \frac{n}{\beta} - \int_0^1 e^{\alpha y} dy = \frac{10}{\beta} - \int_0^1 e^{\alpha y} dy; \\
0 &= \sum_{i=1}^n y_i - \beta\int_0^1 y e^{\alpha y} dy = 5.82 - \beta\int_0^1 y e^{\alpha y} dy.
\end{aligned}$$

Numerical optimisation yields $\hat{\alpha} = 1.00$, $\hat{\beta} = 5.82$. The determinant

$$\frac{n}{\hat{\beta}} \int_0^1 y^2 e^{\hat{\alpha} y} dy - \left(\int_0^1 y e^{\hat{\alpha} y} dy \right)^2$$

of the Hessian matrix $H(\hat{\alpha}, \hat{\beta})$ is positive. Since the principal minor $-n/(\hat{\beta}^2)$ is negative, $(\hat{\alpha}, \hat{\beta})$ maximises the log likelihood function.

To test the null hypothesis that $\alpha = 0$, use the likelihood ratio test. Under the null hypothesis, the maximum likelihood estimator is $\hat{\beta}_0 = 10$. Therefore, the likelihood ratio test statistic is

$$\begin{aligned} \Lambda(\mathbf{x}) &= \frac{f(\mathbf{x}; 0, \hat{\beta}_0)}{f(\mathbf{x}; \hat{\alpha}, \hat{\beta})} = \frac{(\hat{\beta}_0)^n \exp\left[-\hat{\beta}_0\right]}{(\hat{\beta})^n \exp\left[\hat{\alpha} \sum_{i=1}^n y_i - \hat{\beta} \int_0^1 e^{\hat{\alpha} y} dy\right]} \\ &\approx \exp(-0.41) \end{aligned}$$

and $-2 \log \Lambda(X) \approx 0.81$ should be compared to an appropriate quantile of a χ^2 distribution with one degree of freedom.

8. The interaction function is strictly positive and hence hereditary. It is not locally stable. To see this, note that $\gamma(u, v)$ is strictly larger than one if $||u - v|| > (\beta/\alpha)^{1/6}$ and has an asymptote at one for $||u - v|| \to \infty$. The continuity of the interaction function implies that there exists a constant $\gamma > 1$ such that $\gamma(u, v) > \gamma$ if $||u - v||$ lies in an appropriately chosen interval $[r_1, r_2]$, $(\beta/\alpha)^{1/6} < r_1 < r_2 < \infty$. Consequently the conditional intensity $\lambda(u|\mathbf{x})$ is larger than γ^n for point patterns $\mathbf{x}$ containing n points $x_i \in \mathbf{x}$ such that $||u - x_i|| \in [r_1, r_2]$. Since $\gamma^n \to \infty$ as $n \to \infty$, the conditional intensity cannot be bounded.

9. A sufficient condition for integrability is that there exists some $\beta > 0$ such that

$$|V(n)| \leq \beta n \text{ for all } n \in \mathbb{N}_0.$$

Use induction with respect to the number of points as in the proof of the Hammersley–Clifford theorem to show that for $\mathbf{x} \neq \emptyset$ the interaction functions satisfy

$$\varphi(\mathbf{x}) = \exp\left[- \int_W \sum_{\mathbf{y} \subseteq \mathbf{x}} (-1)^{n(\mathbf{x} \setminus \mathbf{y})} V(C_{\mathbf{y}}(w)) dw \right]$$

$$= \exp\left[-|\bigcap_{x\in\mathbf{x}} B(x,R)| \sum_{i=1}^{n(\mathbf{x})} \binom{n(\mathbf{x})}{i} (-1)^{n(\mathbf{x})-i} V(i)\right],$$

using the notation $n(\mathbf{x})$ for the cardinality of $\mathbf{x}$.

The first equation in the claim clearly holds when $\mathbf{x}$ is a singleton. Assume that φ has this form for configurations with up to $n \geq 1$ points and let $\mathbf{x}$ be such that $n(\mathbf{x}) = n$. Then, for $u \notin \mathbf{x}$,

$$\varphi(\mathbf{x} \cup \{u\}) = \frac{f(\mathbf{x} \cup \{u\})}{\prod_{\mathbf{x}\cup\{u\} \neq \mathbf{y} \subset \mathbf{x}\cup\{u\}} \varphi(\mathbf{y})}$$

$$= \exp\left[-\int_W \left\{V(C_{\mathbf{x}\cup\{u\}}(w)) - \sum_{\mathbf{x}\cup\{u\}\neq\mathbf{y}\subset\mathbf{x}\cup\{u\}} \sum_{\mathbf{z}\subseteq\mathbf{y}} (-1)^{n(\mathbf{y}\setminus\mathbf{z})} V(C_{\mathbf{z}}(w))\right\} dw\right].$$

Change the order of integration in the double sum in the integrand above and note that

$$\sum_{k=0}^{n((\mathbf{x}\cup\{u\})\setminus\mathbf{z})-1} \binom{n((\mathbf{x}\cup\{u\})\setminus\mathbf{z})}{k} (-1)^k = -(-1)^{n((\mathbf{x}\cup\{u\})\setminus\mathbf{z})}$$

to see that the first equation in the claim holds for configurations with $n+1$ points too.

The expression can be simplified by considering the Venn diagram of the balls $B(x_i, R)$, $x_i \in \mathbf{x}$, $i = 1, \dots, n = n(\mathbf{x})$. A point $w \in W$ that is covered by $B(x_i, R)$, $i = 1, \dots, k$, but not by $B(x_i, R)$ for $i = k+1, \dots, n$ contributes

$$-\sum_{i=1}^{k} V(i) \binom{k}{i} (-1)^{k-i} \sum_{j=0}^{n-k} (-1)^{n-k-j} \binom{n-k}{j}$$

to $\log \varphi(\mathbf{x})$. The second sum is zero except when $n = k$. Hence only points that are covered by all $B(x_i, R)$, $i = 1, \dots, n$, contribute, and their contribution is equal to

$$-\sum_{i=1}^{n} V(i) \binom{n}{i} (-1)^{n-i}.$$

To show Markovianity, suppose that the point pattern $\mathbf{x}$ contains two points x, y such that $||x-y|| > 2R$. Then $B(x,R) \cap B(y,R) = \emptyset$ and a fortiori $\cap_{z \in \mathbf{x}} B(z,R) = \emptyset$. Therefore $\varphi(\mathbf{x}) = 1$ if $\mathbf{x}$ is no $\sim$-clique. By the Hammersley–Clifford theorem, the point process is Markov with respect to $\sim$.

10. Fix β and consider estimation of R. Note that, for $\mathbf{x} = \{x_1, \ldots, x_n\}$,

$$f(\mathbf{x}) = \beta^{n(\mathbf{x})} \frac{1\{||x_i - x_j|| \geq R, x_i, x_j \in \mathbf{x}, i \neq j\}}{Z(\beta, R)}$$

with

$$Z(\beta, R) = \sum_{m=0}^{\infty} \frac{e^{-|W|}}{m!} \beta^m \int_W \cdots \int_W 1\{||u_i - u_j|| \geq R, i \neq j\} du_1 \cdots du_m.$$

In particular, $f(\mathbf{x}) = 0$ for $R > \min_{i \neq j} ||x_i - x_j||$. Moreover, $Z(\beta, R)$ is the probability that a Poisson process on W with intensity β does not place points closer than R together. Hence $Z(\beta, R)$ is decreasing in R and $f(\mathbf{x})$ increases in R on $[0, \min_{i \neq j} ||x_i - x_j||]$. Thus, the maximum likelihood estimator

$$\hat{R} = \min_{i \neq j} ||x_i - x_j||$$

is the smallest inter-point distance and does not depend on the unknown β.

Having estimated R, optimise the Monte Carlo log likelihood ratio for the parameter β, which is given by

$$n \log \left(\frac{\beta}{\beta_0} \right) - \log \left[\frac{1}{N} \sum_{j=1}^{N} \left(\frac{\beta}{\beta_0} \right)^{n(X_j)} \right]$$

with respect to the reference parameter $\beta_0 > 0$. Here $X_1, \ldots, X_N$ is a sample from the hard core model on W with parameter β_0 and $n(X_j)$ denotes the cardinality of X_j, $j = 1, \ldots, N$. The alternative maximum pseudo-likelihood estimation method was discussed in Section 4.9 for the more general Strauss model.

11. Since $f(z) = 1\{z \in B(0,R)\}/(\pi R^2)$, by Theorem 4.6,

$$\begin{aligned} g(x,y) &= 1 + \frac{1}{\lambda_p}\int f(x-z)f(y-z)dz \\ &= 1 + \frac{1}{\lambda_p}\left(\frac{1}{\pi R^2}\right)^2 \int 1\{z \in B(x,R) \cap B(y,R)\}dz \\ &= 1 + \frac{1}{\lambda_p}\left(\frac{1}{\pi R^2}\right)^2 A(||x-y||, R). \end{aligned}$$

Finally, use the hint.

12. Write ω_d for the volume of the unit ball in $\mathbb{R}^d$. Then, for $r \geq 0$,

$$\begin{aligned} \mathbb{P}(X \cap B(0,r) = \emptyset) &= \mathbb{E}_\Lambda \exp[-\Lambda\omega_d r^d] = \int_0^\infty m e^{-m\lambda} e^{-\lambda\omega_d r^d} d\lambda \\ &= \frac{m}{m + \omega_d r^d}. \end{aligned}$$

Hence $F_m(r) = \omega_d r^d/(m + \omega_d r^d)$. To estimate m, suppose that X is observed in a compact set $W \subset \mathbb{R}^d$ and use the minimum contrast method that compares the function F_m to the empirical empty space function

$$\hat{F}(r) = \frac{1}{|L \cap W_{\ominus r}|} \sum_{l_i \in L \cap W_{\ominus r}} 1\{X \cap B(l_i, r) \neq \emptyset\}, \quad r \in [0, r_0],$$

over a finite set $L \subset W$ of points. The average is restricted to the set $W_{\ominus r}$ of points in W that are further than r away from the boundary ∂W to compensate for edge effects and r_0 should be set smaller than the diameter of W.

13. Let $B \subseteq A$ be a bounded Borel set. The conditional void probability is given by

$$\mathbb{P}(N_X(B) = 0 \mid N_X(A) = n) = \frac{\mathbb{P}(N_X(B) = 0; N_X(A \setminus B) = n)}{\mathbb{P}(N_X(A) = n)}.$$

Since $N_X(B)$ and $N_X(A \setminus B)$ are independent and Poisson distributed, the right hand side reduces to

$$\frac{e^{-\Lambda(B)} e^{-\Lambda(A \setminus B)} \Lambda(A \setminus B)^n/n!}{e^{-\Lambda(A)} \Lambda(A)^n/n!} = \frac{\Lambda(A \setminus B)^n}{\Lambda(A)^n},$$

using the notation $\Lambda(A) = \int_A \lambda(a)da$.

Next, consider the point process Y that consists of n independent and identically distributed random points scattered on A according to the probability density $\lambda(\cdot)/\Lambda(A)$. Then

$$\mathbb{P}(N_Y(B) = 0) = \frac{\Lambda(A \setminus B)^n}{\Lambda(A)^n}.$$

An appeal to Theorem 4.1 concludes the proof.

Theorem 4.2 is the special case that $\lambda(\cdot) \equiv \lambda$. For the Neyman–Scott model (4.11), one obtains the mixture model

$$\frac{\lambda(a)}{\Lambda(A)} = \frac{\epsilon + \lambda_c \sum_{x \in \mathbf{x}} f(a-x)}{\epsilon|A| + \lambda_c \sum_{x \in \mathbf{x}} \int_A f(a-x)da}.$$

14. The posterior distribution given $\mathbf{y}$ with $n(\mathbf{y}) = n$ is

$$c(\mathbf{y})\mathbb{E}\left[e^{-\Lambda|W|}\prod_{j=1}^{n}\Lambda \mid \Lambda = \lambda\right] f(\lambda) = c(\mathbf{y})e^{-\lambda|W|}\lambda^n m e^{-m\lambda}$$
$$\propto \lambda^n e^{-\lambda(|W|+m)},$$

an Erlang distribution with parameters $n+1$ and $|W|+m$. Its mean is

$$\mathbb{E}\left[\Lambda \mid \mathbf{y}\right] = \frac{n+1}{|W|+m}.$$

Index

◎

编辑手记

曾经看到过一段网文是这么说的：

> 在终极的分析中，一切知识都是历史；在抽象的意义下，一切科学都是数学；在理性的世界里，所有的判断都是统计学.

世界著名数学家 W. C. 莱茵博尔特(W. C. Rheinboldt)也曾指出：

> 不太严格地讲，大多数物理应用中所采用的决定性的数学模型都基于这样的观察，即一旦一个物理系统各成分之间的局部相互作用决定了之后，它的总体行为也就被决定了. 对于非物理过程，总体行为往往不能通过对局部行为的观察得到满意的预测，因此统计方法以及像自动机理论、形式语言理论、图论和组合数学这样的数学分支就成为有用的了，它们都处理总体结构.

本书就是一部统计学方面的英文专著，中文书名或可译为《空间统计学理论：概述》.

本书的作者为 M. N. M. 范·利舒特(M. N. M. van Lieshout),荷兰人,荷兰阿姆斯特丹数学与计算机科学中心(CWI)的高级研究员,并在特温特大学担任空间随机学教授.

正如本书前言中所述:

> 今天,我们以图片形式接收了很多信息. 从数学的角度来说,这样的数据可以被分成各种类别,每一个都拥有它们自己的突出特点. 比如,在经典的地质统计学中,在给定数量的固定位置观察到一些空间可变量,人们对它在未观察到的位置的值感兴趣. 人们可能会想到根据一些方便放置的钻孔的测量值来预测土壤中的矿石含量,或者根据测量数据构建空气污染地图. 在其他的情况下,由于技术限制或私人原因,数据以聚合形式被收集为区域数或离散图像. 典型的例子包括卫星图像、断层扫描、疾病图或农业田间试验中的产量. 在这种情况下,目标通常是空间平滑或锐化,而不是预测. 最后,数据可能由一组与随机空间位置相关的对象或现象组成,人们的主要兴趣在于该组合的几何排列,例如研究地震或显微镜下观察到的细胞样式.
>
> 空间数据的统计分析值得作为一个单独的主题处理,因为它在许多方面不同于"经典的"统计数据. 通常只有一个观察值可用,因此需要以适当的平稳性假设的形式进行人工复制. 图像的大小或空间模式中的对象数量通常很大,此外,可能存在各种规模的交互作用. 因此,一个交互的或者层次的说明是有用的,通常需要结合蒙特卡罗(Monte Carlo)方法.
>
> 本书将会描述上面提到的每一个数据类别的数学基础,展示一些模型,并讨论统计推断. 每章首先介绍理论,然后使用资源 R 包将其应用于说明性示例中,列出一些练习,最后以参考文献结尾. 阅读本书的先决条件是对概率和统计学的熟悉程度需要达到数学、工程学或统计学研究生的预期水平. 事实上,这些内容源于荷兰研究生院"Mastermath"的讲座,适合作为一个学期的介绍内容. 想要了解更多信息的人可以参考克雷西(Cressie)(Wiley, 2015 年)、班纳吉(Banerjee)、卡林(Carlin)和盖尔范德(Gelfand)(CRC, 2004 年)以及加埃德(Gaetan)和盖永(Guyon)(Springer, 2010 年)的优秀专著或详尽的《空间统计手册》(*Handbook of Spatial*

Statistics)(CRC,2010 年).

本书的目录为:

3.10 参考文献

第4章 空间点过程

4.1 欧几里得(Euclid)空间上的点过程

4.2 泊松(Poisson)过程

4.3 矩度量

4.4 平稳性概念与积密度

4.5 有限点过程

4.6 帕潘格洛(Papangelou)条件强度

4.7 马尔可夫点过程

4.8 泊松过程的似然推理

4.9 有限点过程的推理

4.10 考克斯(Cox)过程

4.11 分层建模

4.12 使用R的示例

4.13 练习

4.14 参考文献

现在的图书市场中,好书不多,烂书大卖.魏晋时期有个阮籍“落拓江湖载酒行”,走到楚汉战场的时候,开了一句很得罪人的地图炮,他说“时无英雄,使竖子成名”.

这话在图书市场大概率为真!

刘培杰

2023年12月2日

于哈工大

刘培杰数学工作室
已出版(即将出版)图书目录——原版影印

书　　名	出版时间	定　价	编号
数学物理大百科全书.第1卷(英文)	2016－01	418.00	508
数学物理大百科全书.第2卷(英文)	2016－01	408.00	509
数学物理大百科全书.第3卷(英文)	2016－01	396.00	510
数学物理大百科全书.第4卷(英文)	2016－01	408.00	511
数学物理大百科全书.第5卷(英文)	2016－01	368.00	512
zeta函数,q-zeta函数,相伴级数与积分(英文)	2015－08	88.00	513
微分形式:理论与练习(英文)	2015－08	58.00	514
离散与微分包含的逼近和优化(英文)	2015－08	58.00	515
艾伦・图灵:他的工作与影响(英文)	2016－01	98.00	560
测度理论概率导论,第2版(英文)	2016－01	88.00	561
带有潜在故障恢复系统的半马尔柯夫模型控制(英文)	2016－01	98.00	562
数学分析原理(英文)	2016－01	88.00	563
随机偏微分方程的有效动力学(英文)	2016－01	88.00	564
图的谱半径(英文)	2016－01	58.00	565
量子机器学习中数据挖掘的量子计算方法(英文)	2016－01	98.00	566
量子物理的非常规方法(英文)	2016－01	118.00	567
运输过程的统一非局部理论:广义波尔兹曼物理动力学,第2版(英文)	2016－01	198.00	568
量子力学与经典力学之间的联系在原子、分子及电动力学系统建模中的应用(英文)	2016－01	58.00	569
算术域(英文)	2018－01	158.00	821
高等数学竞赛:1962—1991年的米洛克斯・史怀哲竞赛(英文)	2018－01	128.00	822
用数学奥林匹克精神解决数论问题(英文)	2018－01	108.00	823
代数几何(德文)	2018－04	68.00	824
丢番图逼近论(英文)	2018－01	78.00	825
代数几何学基础教程(英文)	2018－01	98.00	826
解析数论入门课程(英文)	2018－01	78.00	827
数论中的丢番图问题(英文)	2018－01	78.00	829
数论(梦幻之旅):第五届中日数论研讨会演讲集(英文)	2018－01	68.00	830
数论新应用(英文)	2018－01	68.00	831
数论(英文)	2018－01	78.00	832

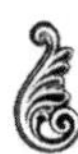

刘培杰数学工作室
已出版(即将出版)图书目录——原版影印

书 名	出版时间	定 价	编号
湍流十讲(英文)	2018—04	108.00	886
无穷维李代数:第3版(英文)	2018—04	98.00	887
等值、不变量和对称性(英文)	2018—04	78.00	888
解析数论(英文)	2018—09	78.00	889
《数学原理》的演化:伯特兰·罗素撰写第二版时的手稿与笔记(英文)	2018—04	108.00	890
哈密尔顿数学论文集(第4卷):几何学、分析学、天文学、概率和有限差分等(英文)	2019—05	108.00	891
偏微分方程全局吸引子的特性(英文)	2018—09	108.00	979
整函数与下调和函数(英文)	2018—09	118.00	980
幂等分析(英文)	2018—09	118.00	981
李群,离散子群与不变量理论(英文)	2018—09	108.00	982
动力系统与统计力学(英文)	2018—09	118.00	983
表示论与动力系统(英文)	2018—09	118.00	984
分析学练习.第1部分(英文)	2021—01	88.00	1247
分析学练习.第2部分,非线性分析(英文)	2021—01	88.00	1248
初级统计学:循序渐进的方法:第10版(英文)	2019—05	68.00	1067
工程师与科学家微分方程用书:第4版(英文)	2019—07	58.00	1068
大学代数与三角学(英文)	2019—06	78.00	1069
培养数学能力的途径(英文)	2019—07	38.00	1070
工程师与科学家统计学:第4版(英文)	2019—06	58.00	1071
贸易与经济中的应用统计学:第6版(英文)	2019—06	58.00	1072
傅立叶级数和边值问题:第8版(英文)	2019—05	48.00	1073
通往天文学的途径:第5版(英文)	2019—05	58.00	1074
拉马努金笔记.第1卷(英文)	2019—06	165.00	1078
拉马努金笔记.第2卷(英文)	2019—06	165.00	1079
拉马努金笔记.第3卷(英文)	2019—06	165.00	1080
拉马努金笔记.第4卷(英文)	2019—06	165.00	1081
拉马努金笔记.第5卷(英文)	2019—06	165.00	1082
拉马努金遗失笔记.第1卷(英文)	2019—06	109.00	1083
拉马努金遗失笔记.第2卷(英文)	2019—06	109.00	1084
拉马努金遗失笔记.第3卷(英文)	2019—06	109.00	1085
拉马努金遗失笔记.第4卷(英文)	2019—06	109.00	1086
数论:1976年纽约洛克菲勒大学数论会议记录(英文)	2020—06	68.00	1145
数论:卡本代尔1979:1979年在南伊利诺伊卡本代尔大学举行的数论会议记录(英文)	2020—06	78.00	1146
数论:诺德韦克豪特1983:1983年在诺德韦克豪特举行的Journees Arithmetiques数论大会会议记录(英文)	2020—06	68.00	1147
数论:1985—1988年在纽约城市大学研究生院和大学中心举办的研讨会(英文)	2020—06	68.00	1148

刘培杰数学工作室
已出版(即将出版)图书目录——原版影印

书　　名	出版时间	定　价	编号
数论:1987 年在乌尔姆举行的 Journees Arithmetiques 数论大会会议记录(英文)	2020－06	68.00	1149
数论:马德拉斯 1987:1987 年在马德拉斯安娜大学举行的国际拉马努金百年纪念大会会议记录(英文)	2020－06	68.00	1150
解析数论:1988 年在东京举行的日法研讨会会议记录(英文)	2020－06	68.00	1151
解析数论:2002 年在意大利切特拉罗举行的 C. I. M. E. 暑期班演讲集(英文)	2020－06	68.00	1152
量子世界中的蝴蝶:最迷人的量子分形故事(英文)	2020－06	118.00	1157
走进量子力学(英文)	2020－06	118.00	1158
计算物理学概论(英文)	2020－06	48.00	1159
物质,空间和时间的理论:量子理论(英文)	2020－10	48.00	1160
物质,空间和时间的理论:经典理论(英文)	2020－10	48.00	1161
量子场理论:解释世界的神秘背景(英文)	2020－07	38.00	1162
计算物理学概论(英文)	2020－06	48.00	1163
行星状星云(英文)	2020－10	38.00	1164
基本宇宙学:从亚里士多德的宇宙到大爆炸(英文)	2020－08	58.00	1165
数学磁流体力学(英文)	2020－07	58.00	1166
计算科学:第 1 卷,计算的科学(日文)	2020－07	88.00	1167
计算科学:第 2 卷,计算与宇宙(日文)	2020－07	88.00	1168
计算科学:第 3 卷,计算与物质(日文)	2020－07	88.00	1169
计算科学:第 4 卷,计算与生命(日文)	2020－07	88.00	1170
计算科学:第 5 卷,计算与地球环境(日文)	2020－07	88.00	1171
计算科学:第 6 卷,计算与社会(日文)	2020－07	88.00	1172
计算科学. 别卷,超级计算机(日文)	2020－07	88.00	1173
多复变函数论(日文)	2022－06	78.00	1518
复变函数入门(日文)	2022－06	78.00	1523
代数与数论:综合方法(英文)	2020－10	78.00	1185
复分析:现代函数理论第一课(英文)	2020－07	58.00	1186
斐波那契数列和卡特兰数:导论(英文)	2020－10	68.00	1187
组合推理:计数艺术介绍(英文)	2020－07	88.00	1188
二次互反律的傅里叶分析证明(英文)	2020－07	48.00	1189
旋瓦兹分布的希尔伯特变换与应用(英文)	2020－07	58.00	1190
泛函分析:巴拿赫空间理论入门(英文)	2020－07	48.00	1191
卡塔兰数入门(英文)	2019－05	68.00	1060
测度与积分(英文)	2019－04	68.00	1059
组合学手册. 第一卷(英文)	2020－06	128.00	1153
*一代数、局部紧群和巴拿赫*一代数丛的表示. 第一卷,群和代数的基本表示理论(英文)	2020－05	148.00	1154
电磁理论(英文)	2020－08	48.00	1193
连续介质力学中的非线性问题(英文)	2020－09	78.00	1195
多变量数学入门(英文)	2021－05	68.00	1317
偏微分方程入门(英文)	2021－05	88.00	1318
若尔当典范性:理论与实践(英文)	2021－07	68.00	1366
伽罗瓦理论. 第 4 版(英文)	2021－08	88.00	1408
R 统计学概论	2023－03	88.00	1614
基于不确定静态和动态问题解的仿射算术(英文)	2023－03	38.00	1618

刘培杰数学工作室
已出版(即将出版)图书目录——原版影印

书　　名	出版时间	定　价	编号
典型群,错排与素数(英文)	2020－11	58.00	1204
李代数的表示:通过 gln 进行介绍(英文)	2020－10	38.00	1205
实分析演讲集(英文)	2020－10	38.00	1206
现代分析及其应用的课程(英文)	2020－10	58.00	1207
运动中的抛射物数学(英文)	2020－10	38.00	1208
2－纽结与它们的群(英文)	2020－10	38.00	1209
概率,策略和选择:博弈与选举中的数学(英文)	2020－11	58.00	1210
分析学引论(英文)	2020－11	58.00	1211
量子群:通往流代数的路径(英文)	2020－11	38.00	1212
集合论入门(英文)	2020－10	48.00	1213
酉反射群(英文)	2020－11	58.00	1214
探索数学:吸引人的证明方式(英文)	2020－11	58.00	1215
微分拓扑短期课程(英文)	2020－10	48.00	1216
抽象凸分析(英文)	2020－11	68.00	1222
费马大定理笔记(英文)	2021－03	48.00	1223
高斯与雅可比和(英文)	2021－03	78.00	1224
π 与算术几何平均:关于解析数论和计算复杂性的研究(英文)	2021－01	58.00	1225
复分析入门(英文)	2021－03	48.00	1226
爱德华·卢卡斯与素性测定(英文)	2021－03	78.00	1227
通往凸分析及其应用的简单路径(英文)	2021－01	68.00	1229
微分几何的各个方面.第一卷(英文)	2021－01	58.00	1230
微分几何的各个方面.第二卷(英文)	2020－12	58.00	1231
微分几何的各个方面.第三卷(英文)	2020－12	58.00	1232
沃克流形几何学(英文)	2020－11	58.00	1233
彷射和韦尔几何应用(英文)	2020－12	58.00	1234
双曲几何学的旋转向量空间方法(英文)	2021－02	58.00	1235
积分:分析学的关键(英文)	2020－12	48.00	1236
为有天分的新生准备的分析学基础教材(英文)	2020－11	48.00	1237
数学不等式.第一卷.对称多项式不等式(英文)	2021－03	108.00	1273
数学不等式.第二卷.对称有理不等式与对称无理不等式(英文)	2021－03	108.00	1274
数学不等式.第三卷.循环不等式与非循环不等式(英文)	2021－03	108.00	1275
数学不等式.第四卷.Jensen 不等式的扩展与加细(英文)	2021－03	108.00	1276
数学不等式.第五卷.创建不等式与解不等式的其他方法(英文)	2021－04	108.00	1277

刘培杰数学工作室
已出版(即将出版)图书目录——原版影印

书　　名	出版时间	定　价	编号
冯・诺依曼代数中的谱位移函数:半有限冯・诺依曼代数中的谱位移函数与谱流(英文)	2021－06	98.00	1308
链接结构:关于嵌入完全图的直线中链接单形的组合结构(英文)	2021－05	58.00	1309
代数几何方法.第1卷(英文)	2021－06	68.00	1310
代数几何方法.第2卷(英文)	2021－06	68.00	1311
代数几何方法.第3卷(英文)	2021－06	58.00	1312

书　　名	出版时间	定　价	编号
代数、生物信息和机器人技术的算法问题.第四卷,独立恒等式系统(俄文)	2020－08	118.00	1199
代数、生物信息和机器人技术的算法问题.第五卷,相对覆盖性和独立可拆分恒等式系统(俄文)	2020－08	118.00	1200
代数、生物信息和机器人技术的算法问题.第六卷,恒等式和准恒等式的相等 问题、可推导性和可实现性(俄文)	2020－08	128.00	1201
分数阶微积分的应用:非局部动态过程,分数阶导热系数(俄文)	2021－01	68.00	1241
泛函分析问题与练习:第2版(俄文)	2021－01	98.00	1242
集合论、数学逻辑和算法论问题:第5版(俄文)	2021－01	98.00	1243
微分几何和拓扑短期课程(俄文)	2021－01	98.00	1244
素数规律(俄文)	2021－01	88.00	1245
无穷边值问题解的递减:无界域中的拟线性椭圆和抛物方程(俄文)	2021－01	48.00	1246
微分几何讲义(俄文)	2020－12	98.00	1253
二次型和矩阵(俄文)	2021－01	98.00	1255
积分和级数.第2卷,特殊函数(俄文)	2021－01	168.00	1258
积分和级数.第3卷,特殊函数补充:第2版(俄文)	2021－01	178.00	1264
几何图上的微分方程(俄文)	2021－01	138.00	1259
数论教程:第2版(俄文)	2021－01	98.00	1260
非阿基米德分析及其应用(俄文)	2021－03	98.00	1261
古典群和量子群的压缩(俄文)	2021－03	98.00	1263
数学分析习题集.第3卷,多元函数:第3版(俄文)	2021－03	98.00	1266
数学习题:乌拉尔国立大学数学力学系大学生奥林匹克(俄文)	2021－03	98.00	1267
柯西定理和微分方程的特解(俄文)	2021－03	98.00	1268
组合极值问题及其应用:第3版(俄文)	2021－03	98.00	1269
数学词典(俄文)	2021－01	98.00	1271
确定性混沌分析模型(俄文)	2021－06	168.00	1307
精选初等数学习题和定理.立体几何.第3版(俄文)	2021－03	68.00	1316
微分几何习题:第3版(俄文)	2021－05	98.00	1336
精选初等数学习题和定理.平面几何.第4版(俄文)	2021－05	68.00	1335
曲面理论在欧氏空间 En 中的直接表示(俄文)	2022－01	68.00	1444
维纳—霍普夫离散算子和托普利兹算子:某些可数赋范空间中的诺特性和可逆性(俄文)	2022－03	108.00	1496
Maple 中的数论:数论中的计算机计算(俄文)	2022－03	88.00	1497
贝尔曼和克努特问题及其概括:加法运算的复杂性(俄文)	2022－03	138.00	1498

刘培杰数学工作室
已出版(即将出版)图书目录——原版影印

书　　名	出版时间	定　价	编号
复分析:共形映射(俄文)	2022—07	48.00	1542
微积分代数样条和多项式及其在数值方法中的应用(俄文)	2022—08	128.00	1543
蒙特卡罗方法中的随机过程和场模型:算法和应用(俄文)	2022—08	88.00	1544
线性椭圆型方程组:论二阶椭圆型方程的迪利克雷问题(俄文)	2022—08	98.00	1561
动态系统解的增长特性:估值、稳定性、应用(俄文)	2022—08	118.00	1565
群的自由积分解:建立和应用(俄文)	2022—08	78.00	1570
混合方程和偏差自变数方程问题:解的存在和唯一性(俄文)	2023—01	78.00	1582
拟度量空间分析:存在和逼近定理(俄文)	2023—01	108.00	1583
二维和三维流形上函数的拓扑性质:函数的拓扑分类(俄文)	2023—03	68.00	1584
齐次马尔科夫过程建模的矩阵方法:此类方法能够用于不同目上的的复杂系统研究、设计和完善(俄文)	2023—03	68.00	1594
周期函数的近似方法和特性:特殊课程(俄文)	2023—04	158.00	1622
扩散方程解的矩函数:变分法(俄文)	2023—03	58.00	1623
多赋范空间和广义函数:理论及应用(俄文)	2023—03	98.00	1632
分析中的多值映射:部分应用(俄文)	2023—06	98.00	1634
数学物理问题(俄文)	2023—03	78.00	1636
函数的幂级数与三角级数分解(俄文)	2024—01	58.00	1695
星体理论的数学基础:原子三元组(俄文)	2024—01	98.00	1696
素数规律:专著(俄文)	2024—01	118.00	1697

书　　名	出版时间	定　价	编号
狭义相对论与广义相对论:时空与引力导论(英文)	2021—07	88.00	1319
束流物理学和粒子加速器的实践介绍:第2版(英文)	2021—07	88.00	1320
凝聚态物理中的拓扑和微分几何简介(英文)	2021—05	88.00	1321
混沌映射:动力学、分形学和快速涨落(英文)	2021—05	128.00	1322
广义相对论:黑洞、引力波和宇宙学介绍(英文)	2021—06	68.00	1323
现代分析电磁均质化(英文)	2021—06	68.00	1324
为科学家提供的基本流体动力学(英文)	2021—06	88.00	1325
视觉天文学:理解夜空的指南(英文)	2021—06	68.00	1326
物理学中的计算方法(英文)	2021—06	68.00	1327
单星的结构与演化:导论(英文)	2021—06	108.00	1328
超越居里:1903年至1963年物理界四位女性及其著名发现(英文)	2021—06	68.00	1329
范德瓦尔斯流体热力学的进展(英文)	2021—06	68.00	1330
先进的托卡马克稳定性理论(英文)	2021—06	88.00	1331
经典场论导论:基本相互作用的过程(英文)	2021—07	88.00	1332
光致电离量子动力学方法原理(英文)	2021—07	108.00	1333
经典域论和应力:能量张量(英文)	2021—05	88.00	1334
非线性太赫兹光谱的概念与应用(英文)	2021—06	68.00	1337
电磁学中的无穷空间并矢格林函数(英文)	2021—06	88.00	1338
物理科学基础数学.第1卷,齐次边值问题、傅里叶方法和特殊函数(英文)	2021—07	108.00	1339
离散量子力学(英文)	2021—07	68.00	1340
核磁共振的物理学和数学(英文)	2021—07	108.00	1341
分子水平的静电学(英文)	2021—08	68.00	1342
非线性波:理论、计算机模拟、实验(英文)	2021—06	108.00	1343
石墨烯光学:经典问题的电解解决方案(英文)	2021—06	68.00	1344
超材料多元宇宙(英文)	2021—07	68.00	1345
银河系外的天体物理学(英文)	2021—07	68.00	1346
原子物理学(英文)	2021—07	68.00	1347
将光打结:将拓扑学应用于光学(英文)	2021—07	68.00	1348
电磁学:问题与解法(英文)	2021—07	88.00	1364
海浪的原理:介绍量子力学的技巧与应用(英文)	2021—07	108.00	1365

刘培杰数学工作室
已出版(即将出版)图书目录——原版影印

书　名	出版时间	定　价	编号
多孔介质中的流体:输运与相变(英文)	2021—07	68.00	1372
洛伦兹群的物理学(英文)	2021—08	68.00	1373
物理导论的数学方法和解决方法手册(英文)	2021—08	68.00	1374
非线性波数学物理学入门(英文)	2021—08	88.00	1376
波:基本原理和动力学(英文)	2021—07	68.00	1377
光电子量子计量学.第1卷,基础(英文)	2021—07	88.00	1383
光电子量子计量学.第2卷,应用与进展(英文)	2021—07	68.00	1384
复杂流的格子玻尔兹曼建模的工程应用(英文)	2021—08	68.00	1393
电偶极矩挑战(英文)	2021—08	108.00	1394
电动力学:问题与解法(英文)	2021—09	68.00	1395
自由电子激光的经典理论(英文)	2021—08	68.00	1397
曼哈顿计划——核武器物理学简介(英文)	2021—09	68.00	1401
粒子物理学(英文)	2021—09	68.00	1402
引力场中的量子信息(英文)	2021—09	128.00	1403
器件物理学的基本经典力学(英文)	2021—09	68.00	1404
等离子体物理及其空间应用导论.第1卷,基本原理和初步过程(英文)	2021—09	68.00	1405
磁约束聚变等离子体物理:理想MHD理论(英文)	2023—03	68.00	1613
相对论量子场论.第1卷,典范形式体系(英文)	2023—03	38.00	1615
相对论量子场论.第2卷,路径积分形式(英文)	2023—06	38.00	1616
相对论量子场论.第3卷,量子场论的应用(英文)	2023—06	38.00	1617
涌现的物理学(英文)	2023—05	58.00	1619
量子化旋涡:一本拓扑激发手册(英文)	2023—04	68.00	1620
非线性动力学:实践的介绍性调查(英文)	2023—05	68.00	1621
静电加速器:一个多功能工具(英文)	2023—06	58.00	1625
相对论多体理论与统计力学(英文)	2023—06	58.00	1626
经典力学.第1卷,工具与向量(英文)	2023—04	38.00	1627
经典力学.第2卷,运动学和匀加速运动(英文)	2023—04	58.00	1628
经典力学.第3卷,牛顿定律和匀速圆周运动(英文)	2023—04	58.00	1629
经典力学.第4卷,万有引力定律(英文)	2023—04	38.00	1630
经典力学.第5卷,守恒定律与旋转运动(英文)	2023—04	38.00	1631
对称问题:纳维尔—斯托克斯问题(英文)	2023—04	38.00	1638
摄影的物理和艺术.第1卷,几何与光的本质(英文)	2023—04	78.00	1639
摄影的物理和艺术.第2卷,能量与色彩(英文)	2023—04	78.00	1640
摄影的物理和艺术.第3卷,探测器与数码的意义(英文)	2023—04	78.00	1641
拓扑与超弦理论焦点问题(英文)	2021—07	58.00	1349
应用数学:理论、方法与实践(英文)	2021—07	78.00	1350
非线性特征值问题:牛顿型方法与非线性瑞利函数(英文)	2021—07	58.00	1351
广义膨胀和齐性:利用齐性构造齐次系统的李雅普诺夫函数和控制律(英文)	2021—06	48.00	1352
解析数论焦点问题(英文)	2021—07	58.00	1353
随机微分方程:动态系统方法(英文)	2021—07	58.00	1354
经典力学与微分几何(英文)	2021—07	58.00	1355
负定相交形式流形上的瞬子模空间几何(英文)	2021—07	68.00	1356
广义卡塔兰轨道分析:广义卡塔兰轨道计算数字的方法(英文)	2021—07	48.00	1367
洛伦兹方法的变分:二维与三维洛伦兹方法(英文)	2021—08	38.00	1378
几何、分析和数论精编(英文)	2021—08	68.00	1380
从一个新角度看数论:通过遗传方法引入现实的概念(英文)	2021—07	58.00	1387
动力系统:短期课程(英文)	2021—08	68.00	1382
几何路径:理论与实践(英文)	2021—08	48.00	1385

刘培杰数学工作室

已出版(即将出版)图书目录——原版影印

书　　名	出版时间	定　价	编号
论天体力学中某些问题的不可积性(英文)	2021—07	88.00	1396
广义斐波那契数列及其性质(英文)	2021—08	38.00	1386
对称函数和麦克唐纳多项式:余代数结构与 Kawanaka 恒等式(英文)	2021—09	38.00	1400
杰弗里·英格拉姆·泰勒科学论文集:第 1 卷.固体力学(英文)	2021—05	78.00	1360
杰弗里·英格拉姆·泰勒科学论文集:第 2 卷.气象学、海洋学和湍流(英文)	2021—05	68.00	1361
杰弗里·英格拉姆·泰勒科学论文集:第 3 卷.空气动力学以及落弹数和爆炸的力学(英文)	2021—05	68.00	1362
杰弗里·英格拉姆·泰勒科学论文集:第 4 卷.有关流体力学(英文)	2021—05	58.00	1363
非局域泛函演化方程:积分与分数阶(英文)	2021—08	48.00	1390
理论工作者的高等微分几何:纤维丛、射流流形和拉格朗日理论(英文)	2021—08	68.00	1391
半线性退化椭圆微分方程:局部定理与整体定理(英文)	2021—07	48.00	1392
非交换几何、规范理论和重整化:一般简介与非交换量子场论的重整化(英文)	2021—09	78.00	1406
数论论文集:拉普拉斯变换和带有数论系数的幂级数(俄文)	2021—09	48.00	1407
挠理论专题:相对极大值,单射与扩充模(英文)	2021—09	88.00	1410
强正则图与欧几里得若尔当代数:非通常关系中的启示(英文)	2021—10	48.00	1411
拉格朗日几何和哈密顿几何:力学的应用(英文)	2021—10	48.00	1412
时滞微分方程与差分方程的振动理论:二阶与三阶(英文)	2021—10	98.00	1417
卷积结构与几何函数理论:用以研究特定几何函数理论方向的分数阶微积分算子与卷积结构(英文)	2021—10	48.00	1418
经典数学物理的历史发展(英文)	2021—10	78.00	1419
扩展线性丢番图问题(英文)	2021—10	38.00	1420
一类混沌动力系统的分歧分析与控制:分歧分析与控制(英文)	2021—11	38.00	1421
伽利略空间和伪伽利略空间中一些特殊曲线的几何性质(英文)	2022—01	68.00	1422
一阶偏微分方程:哈密尔顿—雅可比理论(英文)	2021—11	48.00	1424
各向异性黎曼多面体的反问题:分段光滑的各向异性黎曼多面体反边界谱问题:唯一性(英文)	2021—11	38.00	1425
项目反应理论手册.第一卷,模型(英文)	2021—11	138.00	1431
项目反应理论手册.第二卷,统计工具(英文)	2021—11	118.00	1432
项目反应理论手册.第三卷,应用(英文)	2021—11	138.00	1433
二次无理数:经典数论入门(英文)	2022—05	138.00	1434

刘培杰数学工作室

已出版(即将出版)图书目录——原版影印

书　　名	出版时间	定　价	编号
数,形与对称性:数论,几何和群论导论(英文)	2022－05	128.00	1435
有限域手册(英文)	2021－11	178.00	1436
计算数论(英文)	2021－11	148.00	1437
拟群与其表示简介(英文)	2021－11	88.00	1438
数论与密码学导论:第二版(英文)	2022－01	148.00	1423
几何分析中的柯西变换与黎兹变换:解析调和容量和李普希兹调和容量、变化和振荡以及一致可求长性(英文)	2021－12	38.00	1465
近似不动点定理及其应用(英文)	2022－05	28.00	1466
局部域的相关内容解析:对局部域的扩展及其伽罗瓦群的研究(英文)	2022－01	38.00	1467
反问题的二进制恢复方法(英文)	2022－03	28.00	1468
对几何函数中某些类的各个方面的研究:复变量理论(英文)	2022－01	38.00	1469
覆盖、对应和非交换几何(英文)	2022－01	28.00	1470
最优控制理论中的随机线性调节器问题:随机最优线性调节器问题(英文)	2022－01	38.00	1473
正交分解法:涡流流体动力学应用的正交分解法(英文)	2022－01	38.00	1475
芬斯勒几何的某些问题(英文)	2022－03	38.00	1476
受限三体问题(英文)	2022－05	38.00	1477
利用马利亚万微积分进行 Greeks 的计算:连续过程、跳跃过程中的马利亚万微积分和金融领域中的 Greeks(英文)	2022－05	48.00	1478
经典分析和泛函分析的应用:分析学的应用(英文)	2022－03	38.00	1479
特殊芬斯勒空间的探究(英文)	2022－03	48.00	1480
某些图形的施泰纳距离的细谷多项式:细谷多项式与图的维纳指数(英文)	2022－05	38.00	1481
图论问题的遗传算法:在新鲜与模糊的环境中(英文)	2022－05	48.00	1482
多项式映射的渐近簇(英文)	2022－05	38.00	1483
一维系统中的混沌:符号动力学,映射序列,一致收敛和沙可夫斯基定理(英文)	2022－05	38.00	1509
多维边界层流动与传热分析:粘性流体流动的数学建模与分析(英文)	2022－05	38.00	1510
演绎理论物理学的原理:一种基于量子力学波函数的逐次置信估计的一般理论的提议(英文)	2022－05	38.00	1511
R^2 和 R^3 中的仿射弹性曲线:概念和方法(英文)	2022－08	38.00	1512
算术数列中除数函数的分布:基本内容、调查、方法、第二矩、新结果(英文)	2022－05	28.00	1513
抛物型狄拉克算子和薛定谔方程:不定常薛定谔方程的抛物型狄拉克算子及其应用(英文)	2022－07	28.00	1514
黎曼-希尔伯特问题与量子场论:可积重正化、戴森-施温格方程(英文)	2022－08	38.00	1515
代数结构和几何结构的形变理论(英文)	2022－08	48.00	1516
概率结构和模糊结构上的不动点:概率结构和直觉模糊度量空间的不动点定理(英文)	2022－08	38.00	1517

刘培杰数学工作室
已出版(即将出版)图书目录——原版影印

书　名	出版时间	定　价	编号
反若尔当对:简单反若尔当对的自同构(英文)	2022-07	28.00	1533
对某些黎曼-芬斯勒空间变换的研究:芬斯勒几何中的某些变换(英文)	2022-07	38.00	1534
内诣零流形映射的尼尔森数的阿诺索夫关系(英文)	2023-01	38.00	1535
与广义积分变换有关的分数次演算:对分数次演算的研究(英文)	2023-01	48.00	1536
强子的芬斯勒几何和吕拉几何(宇宙学方面):强子结构的芬斯勒几何和吕拉几何(拓扑缺陷)(英文)	2022-08	38.00	1537
一种基于混沌的非线性最优化问题:作业调度问题(英文)	2023-03	38.00	1538
广义概率论发展前景:关于趣味数学与置信函数实际应用的一些原创观点(英文)	2023-03	48.00	1539
纽结与物理学:第二版(英文)	2022-09	118.00	1547
正交多项式和q-级数的前沿(英文)	2022-09	98.00	1548
算子理论问题集(英文)	2022-09	108.00	1549
抽象代数:群、环与域的应用导论:第二版(英文)	2023-01	98.00	1550
菲尔兹奖得主演讲集:第三版(英文)	2023-01	138.00	1551
多元实函数教程(英文)	2022-09	118.00	1552
球面空间形式群的几何学:第二版(英文)	2022-09	98.00	1566
对称群的表示论(英文)	2023-01	98.00	1585
纽结理论:第二版(英文)	2023-01	88.00	1586
拟群理论的基础与应用(英文)	2023-01	88.00	1587
组合学:第二版(英文)	2023-01	98.00	1588
加性组合学:研究问题手册(英文)	2023-01	68.00	1589
扭曲、平铺与镶嵌:几何折纸中的数学方法(英文)	2023-01	98.00	1590
离散与计算几何手册:第三版(英文)	2023-01	248.00	1591
离散与组合数学手册:第二版(英文)	2023-01	248.00	1592
分析学教程.第1卷,一元实变量函数的微积分分析学介绍(英文)	2023-01	118.00	1595
分析学教程.第2卷,多元函数的微分和积分,向量微积分(英文)	2023-01	118.00	1596
分析学教程.第3卷,测度与积分理论,复变量的复值函数(英文)	2023-01	118.00	1597
分析学教程.第4卷,傅里叶分析,常微分方程,变分法(英文)	2023-01	118.00	1598